CW01176622

FAYTE & BLOOD

Gen Velzian

Draven Publishing

Copyright © 2025 Gen Velzian

All rights reserved

The characters and events portrayed in this book are fictitious. Any similarity to real persons, living or dead, is coincidental and not intended by the author.

No part of this book may be reproduced, or stored in a retrieval system, or transmitted in any form or by any means, electronic, mechanical, photocopying, recording, or otherwise, without express written permission of the publisher.

*For Lorna: Beautiful, Brave, Born
under the Divinity of Power.*

GEN VELZIAN

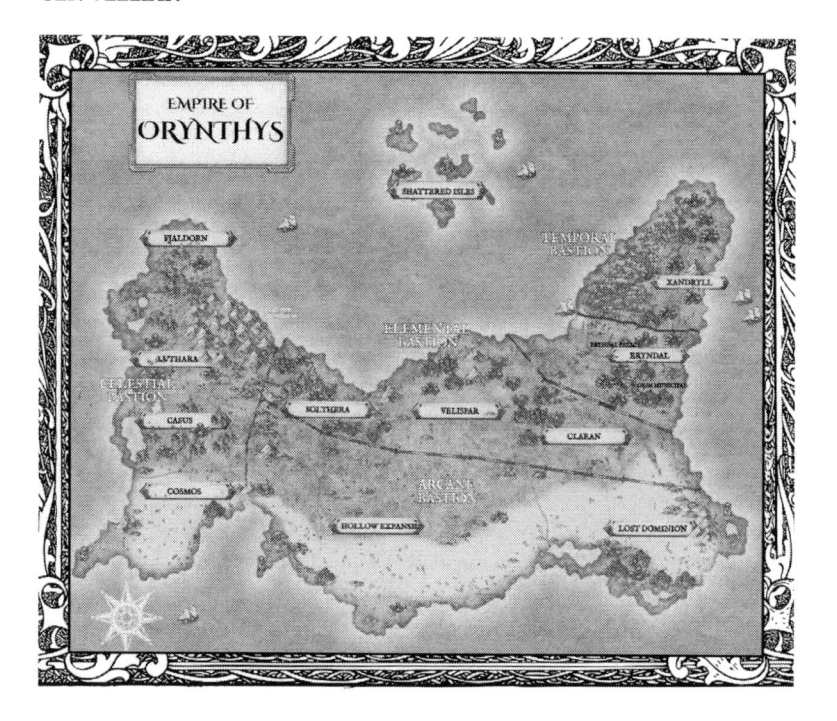

FAYTE & BLOOD

SEVEN MOONS
AND THEIR DIVINITIES

- **SOMER** — FORGIVENESS
- **SCHTTY** — EARTH
- **AFLUENTA** — WAR
- **MOIR** — WRATH
- **LIPE** — WATER
- **LORNEA** — POWER
- **PINYA** — SUN

Moon diagram: lent by the Hall of Solthera within the Elemental Bastion in return for the use of one Foresight Seer under two moon cycles.

2

CHAPTER ONE

"It is the duty of a postal worker to maintain impartiality in all matters, honouring both the written word and the trust placed in them by all citizens, be they of mortal or aemortal descent."

Orynthys Postal Manual, Volume 2, Section 5.1

"I didn't mean to *run* from you."

It's a bare-faced lie, but half of what's said in Grim Municipal is exactly that – bare-faced lies. To lie is to survive, and I'm not ready for certain death just yet. Not death by aemortal, and death by the Sable Legion aemortal is the worst kind of all.

As the Sable Legion guard's eyes bore into mine, sending all sorts of *fuck-me* vibes, I swipe a bead of sweat off my forehead. He reaches out for my shoulder, and I jolt back into a wall, algae-crusted and foul-smelling, cursing the dirt that's already marring my work tunic. My uncle was killed by the Legion, *by accident*. They reached out to grab his shoulder and crushed his skull in the process. His funeral sounds bleak; Mother couldn't afford much, so she served bison knuckle and read crap poetry.

I'm not about to have my skull *accidentally* crushed, not today, not when half the poetry books related to Archons and the powers-that-be have been banned anyway.

"Are you from the Heartlands?" the guard asks, his coryns—brown horns shot through with silver—catching the midday sun. Winter still lingers, the moon cycles harsh, but right now, it's a beautiful, fresh afternoon. An afternoon worth staying alive for.

"Affirmative," I reply, glancing through the smoke towards Old King Alley. Just a few more steps, and I would've made it to work. The Courier's Keep beckons, the mortal postal service that's kept me employed for sixteen long moon cycles now.

He clicks his tongue impatiently, his eyebrow ring shifting as it casts a shadow that splits his eye in half. "Care to explain why you're out here when there's a green smoke warning underway?"

Oh, that. I'd been ignoring the mossy smoke billowing through the air, a warning from a fallen battalion, spelled to spread across Eryndal, our kindom that is one of twelve in Orynthys. The aemortal soldiers must've sent this smoke right before a battalion fell—one of the posts along our border with Claran or Xandryll suffering an attack that's wiped out the entire outpost. When a battalion falls, it's likely something has crossed our border—something as innocent as a newborn durlem lemur with too much accidental power, or as sinister as a necromancer or silicrite.

I rub at my neck, sticky above my tunic. I'd know if there was a serious threat. I receive the postal news first, before anyone in Eryndal. We haven't received any hints of enemy activity. Getting to work is more important, especially with the Sable Legion flooding the streets and conducting random building checks.

"I need to get to work," I say, shrugging. "The postal elves are still coming tonight, whether there's an attack or not."

His gaze sharpens. Perhaps if I worked in the bank, or even the sex district, I might've earned some sympathy. But couriers aren't exactly high priority in the municipal. Rarely has anyone complained to King or Queen about a late parcel.

"It's against regulations to be out during a smoke warning," he growls. "I might've had no choice but to slay you where you stand, woman." He looks around but finds no one else in the smoky, foggy alleyway. His shoulders twitch down slightly. "What's your name?"

"Elira Corvannis." At least I can be honest about that. I'm well-known around these alleyways, the postmistress with the tight opal-coloured bun, the neatly-tied tunic, the quill behind one ear. The one who gets up early to comb her hair back neatly, packs her lunch with care, shines her sandals. I might have a reputation for having a stick up my arse, but I *can* let loose. "Thank you for not... slaying me."

I don't mean to undermine his phrasing, though his eyes flash as if I've challenged him. I am genuinely grateful. Enough mortals have been slain at the hands of aemortals that I know their usual approach: slay first, ask questions later. The way he looks down at my bare legs might hint at why I'm still alive. Most people are still wearing woollen gaiters, but I always run hot.

During warnings—when the border has been breached, or a battalion has fallen—we're supposed to stay indoors, preferably at our family homes. Homes that are preferably not damp shacks in the slums, but semi-structural dwellings. My mother's house is a proper walled shack in the Heartlands, deemed a safe place to lock up.

"Listen, Elira Corvannis," the guard mutters, looking around again, his gaze darkening even as he adopts the tone of someone trying to earn my trust. "I should arrest you where you stand. You're breaking the rules, and my orders are clear." The top of my head prickles. I know what's coming next. He continues, "Of course, if you make it worth my time, I could consider letting you off without a word to the royals."

Make it worth his time. He really is a dirty bastard.

"I'm married," I lie. "And besides, I don't have any of the aemortal contraceptive elixir. I would hate to get pregnant with a half-blood, and have both of us slain for our sins."

My eyes blaze as I look at him, daring him to disagree. In Eryndal kingdom, and in our empire of Orynthys, half-aemortals are strictly banned, their existence punishable by death for all parties involved. Infants have been slain the moment their barely developed horns started to form, their parents executed in humiliating and imaginative ways. While the rule stems from an expected arrogance spat out by the aemortal courts, who would consider sex with a mortal akin to sex with a diseased goat, it's encouraged because of the level of uncertainty. Could a half-aemortal live forever, or would they lead a strange half-life?

The Legion guard just rubs his chin with one skin-cracked hand, then leans in. "I've got the elixir. Always carry it when I'm passing Muriel's."

Pig, my mind hisses. Muriel's is at the centre of the sex district, home to hookers with legs up to my short-ass chin, who call out sweet nothings to passing guards and apple-cart pushing salesmen.

"I'm married," I say again, more sweetly this time, hoping my shaking voice doesn't give me away. I doubt this guard, his ethics clearly rattling around the overspilled sewage drains that fill the city with pungencies, cares much for my marital status. "I'm surprised you would stoop so low as to bed a mortal woman. Do the aemortal beauties at The Howling Cask not respond to your... charm?"

Again, he looks at me as if unsure whether I'm being impudent or naïve, the latter born from the fact that if I take the piss out of him, he really will have me slain. I've never been to The Howling Cask, a tavern in the first aemortal town after the palace, but I've heard rumours of beautiful women, helmet-donning men, and a sparkling post-slay crowd.

"I could have you sent to Eryndal gaol for the night." His eyes shine. "Some of the prisoners there haven't seen a woman in many, many moons. They would have a fine time with you."

I swallow down the hot bile that fills my throat, feeling like I'm being drowned by toxic bilge water.

"And don't think one of the royals will come save

you." His dark eyes break apart my soul. "The princes are far too busy to risk their necks for some mortal postwoman."

I don't doubt it. While the King and Queen are never seen around Grim Municipal or Eryndal at large – presumably too busy drinking fine wines and twirling around their palace – the two princes can often be found sauntering around the lands on their mares. They are devilishly handsome, but utter arseholes, as handsome men are wont to be.

The aemortals are bad enough as a whole, without this one needing to remind me of the royals. The only clean water that is pumped from deep under Eryndal is redirected to the aemortal town; we are left with fountains of cloudy, brown liquid from which to sup. The only grain grown in Eryndal is purchased by the aemortal town, leaving us with dirty roots and dregs to purchase. And everyone in Grim Municipal – even slum-dwellers and brothel-workers – pay a city tax to the Mayor, which goes directly to improving the aemortal infrastructure. We are an afterthought, bled dry by aemortals who wish, no doubt, that there was a quick way to kill us and build over our wasteland.

But there are five times as many mortals as aemortals in Eryndal, and even if they are lean fighting machines, they couldn't be certain of winning.

The Legion guard looks around, his eyes shining, another check that's intended to make me feel safe while reassuring himself that no one can see us.

And then he grabs me.

He pushes me against the wall of the damp

alleyway, his hands strong on my shoulders, his leering face so close that I can smell his putrid breath, and he reaches down for the bottom of my tunic. I move with a speed he isn't expecting and get there first. Underneath my tunic, I wear a makeshift bandolier – an offcut of one of Mother's old pillowcases – into which I've stuck one of my silver letter openers. A heavy, precious thing, and about the only item in this empire that excites my little postmistress heart. It'll be a shame to waste it, but needs must, I think, as I snatch it out of the bind around my waist, pulling it from the underside of my tunic so quickly that the silver is merely a bright streak of light in the damp alleyway.

    I lunge forward, silver outstretched, a billow of wispy green smoke briefly overtaking my hand, and as I attack, it finds its mark. The fleshy area where armour meets, but no joins tug. The letter opener sinks into flesh and sinew, and I shudder as he gasps, the silver finally hitting bone. The moment is drawn out by a bird overhead, a harsh black thing with an even harsher sound, the caw cutting apart my scalp. The guard's eyeballs loosen, roll back. I yank the weapon out of his body, his hand still mobile enough to reach my leg. His fingers grasp at my thigh, confusion rolling like a pendulum between his mind and his body, the latter catching on only as blood starts to jet from his midriff. Hot, crimson blood, which immediately attacks my battered postmistress tunic, as he reaches out for my face, his fingers curling inwards as if grasping for something – anything – to destroy.

    I dart backwards, my body lithe, volatile, as he sinks to his knees, the thudding sound marred by a relentless wind, which causes the sign of the nearby tavern – my favourite tavern, The Dwarven Bombard – to creak under rusty chainmail. My silver letter opener, one of only four I own, is still coated in his blood, but I jam it back into its makeshift bandolier, covering it over with my regulation-issue tunic, the one I've had for ten moon cycles. I can feel his wet blood against my hip.

I am not a fighter nor a murderer, and my lungs ache as I pant, and watch him bleed out on the shined cobblestones, a background of sewer-stained inlets and smoke-stained clay walls reigning down on both of us. The Sable Legion are a foreboding, ruthless aemortal army. They've sat under the instruction of the royals ever since the summation of the Thousand Cycle War, a war that still stains much of our infrastructure, and the faces of anyone older than me. My mother says it was a time of beasts roaming the municipal streets, having easily broken through our land borders like a fist through wet tissue.

Though the war had various battles, the topics of which are discussed at length on ugly tapestries pinned to tavern walls, the general consensus was that royalty would take over from the Archons—elected beings who once sat at the top of each Bastion. While the Archons were often the most skilled with fayte, the aemortal magic, and demonstrably better at fending off enemies than our mostly-absent royal family, they also took autonomy away from each kingdom. And now we have aemortals like him guarding us.

The Sable Legion guard gurgles, blood dripping from his lips. Then he goes silent, his back stiffening. He might be fine; the healers at the palace gallipot surely patch up aemortals all the time. But it depends on how badly damaged he is. I've heard stories of them burning hopeless cases with blue fayte, sending the soul of the aemortal (if they have one) to Thekla and beyond, as told by the palace necromancer.

I hope they choose to burn this one. I hope I never have to see him again when I dash through Grim Municipal's alleyways, just trying to make it to work. I need the sigils to buy scraps of meat for Mother and me, or to afford Seren's next round of rehab. I whisper a prayer to the Divinities as I rush toward my job, wondering at my own nerve, praying after potentially *murdering* a man, and whether the Divinities will enjoy or abhor my heresies.

CHAPTER TWO

"If we *are* under attack, why'd I get stuck with the most obsessive postmistress in Orynthys?" Nerissa mutters darkly from the doorway. Maybe she's talking to me. Hard to say. Her gaze is fixed on the shopfront, on the shutters—her customer-facing domain. *Not my jurisdiction, sweetheart.* I'm strictly the sorting room postmistress; I sell stamps and wares now and then, but mostly I sort post into bags, ensuring every item is correctly stamped.

By the time I've darted into The Courier's Keep, the blood has vanished from my tunic, wiped clean from my bare legs. For some strange reason, it's as though the fayte in the green smoke had cleansed me, perhaps the guard's magic working to wipe my guilt away before Nerissa sees me. Perhaps Sable Legion blood is spelled to tidy itself up.

I don't mention the assault to Nerissa. Not when she's clutching her tunic, her face bone-white, her nose ring catching the light with each shift of her head.

I reach under my tunic and pull out the silver makeshift knife, slamming it down onto my desk with an anger I've never felt before. The guard would have forced himself on me, then carted me off to the city gaol. That's how they work. That's what they do. It's why our teachers used to whisper, "Never trust an aemortal, kids." Even now, as my body shakes, as guilt and fear finally crash through me, I know I could have been in a much worse situation—used and arrested for risking my life during a battalion warning.

The letter opener catches my attention, its absurd cleanliness making it hard to comprehend. There's no blood, no crimson staining its blade, no sticky substance clinging to the hilt. As I stare at it, something hums in the air, an ancient, cruel voice whispering to me:

It's gone. It's been cleaned. I did it for you.

I snatch the letter opener back up, shoving it into a drawer. My heart hammers in my throat. I feel like I'm losing my mind as much as I am my innocence. I've never stabbed anyone before, never used my makeshift weapon before. There's a desperate part of me that wants to know if he'll survive, or if he'll be deemed irreparably damaged by the gallipot. If he lives, I know he'll be waiting outside the next time I go through Grim Municipal. And next time, I doubt he'll hesitate before driving his own knife into my chest, filled with anger and thirst for retaliation.

"Just get the posters and let's go," Nerissa snaps from the front room. She's annoyed because I've paused to tidy up, to ensure the postal sacks *are* ready for the elves, nocturnal creatures who slip in through the trapdoor into the sorting room. I've just stabbed a guard, possibly killed a man, but I still have my duty.

That's who I am.

My obsessive need to do things properly has caused many arguments between Nerissa and me. She's both my boss—technically—and my best friend.

Everywhere I look, there are words. Smudged ink, solemn curves, spelling *killer*—killer, killer, killer— alongside the sluggish beat of my heart. A cursed, shitty envelope lies in front of me, releasing foul scents into the usually solemn air of my sorting room. The room that should bring peace, not the stink of what I've done. I had opened it, rewritten the invitation in the same hand, redrawn the address, cleaning the blood from my inkwell and my quill.

Because I can rewrite post with blood. It's a strange skill—one I'm not proud of. It's something I haven't told Nerissa, or Mother, or Seren. Shame silences me, or perhaps a nagging voice at the back of my mind that says: *Mortals shouldn't be able to do that.*

I am mortal. I am one-hundred-percent mortal. And yet, I know what they would say: I can deal in the devil's magic.

Mother and Seren aren't hugely accepting of anything involving aemortals, which is to be expected since my uncle was slain by them. Nerissa is strongly against anything that might involve magic. If any of them thought me to be more than mortal—or if the Sable Legion found out that this little mortal can employ a tiny amount of fayte—it could easily lead to my execution.

And so, I keep quiet, even though I continue to do it. It's a release for me. It was my obsessive sense of duty that enabled me to discover this small gift a few moon cycles ago. I used to rewrite envelopes using fresh ink, but it was obvious—and highly illegal. To tamper with post, anyway, is a crime, but to actually rewrite it, just so that someone's auntie might get her prescription from a healer, or a baby announcement might reach distant relatives, or a funeral invitation might be sent across lands, is madness. But a voice had been insistent in the front of my skull, my own voice turned strange, and kept hounding me to use my own blood to rewrite an envelope set for the chute. I eventually caved in, pricking my finger and dipping the quill in the resulting drop.

And when I rewrote the address that time, the blood turned to ink on the envelope, the exact shade and handwriting of the original. I was so scared, so confused, that I vomited all over the envelope immediately. By the time I pulled myself together enough to try again, I was ready to accept it: I can utilise a small amount of fayte—something that only abounds in the aemortals—to achieve this useful tinkering of post.

It must be a helpful offering from a Divinity. Of the seven main Divinities, Orynthys' core gods, which align with the moons, one of them surely took pity enough to help a mortal get post out on time. Perhaps they knew I was a sucker for duty—an obsessive worker who'll do anything not to lose my job. Breaking the rules meant delivering the post correctly, and if this were a kingdom of right and wrong, I like to think I dance under the former. Even if the last letter I rewrote seemed a little too much like a threat, the smudged, curled cursive detailing only: *Reconsider before it is too late to be forgiven.*

The address on the envelope had been: *The New Mate, Crown of the Elements, Fjaldorn.*

And I had burned it immediately after writing it. Fjaldorn is a distant kingdom so far removed that we rarely receive letters or post bound for there. While our citizens' dalliances sometimes extend to neighbouring kingdoms—when duty calls—they never stretch as far as Fjaldorn, the dusky land in the Celestial Bastion. *Reconsider before it is too late to be forgiven* hadn't sat right with me; I'd burned the letter, removing the threat. Oops.

"We need to go, Elira. You got the posters?" Nerissa's lunar-pale face stares at me, nose ring glinting under the oil lamp's glow. Her tunic pulls against her hourglass figure, her long fingernails clicking against the doorframe, causing her silver earrings to swing. She wears them—silver—to repel beasts. Ear-attacking beasts, I wonder, on days when I'm feeling sardonic.

"Yeah, grabbing them now." I rub my eyes with a knuckled fist. I must collate the anti-royalty posters.

I look around. The sorting room I know like the hallways of Seren's rehab clinic. Piles of paper, bobbled bottles of rich-coloured ink, an ornate hearth with the faint scent of soot. I don't tell Nerissa what I'm thinking —that I'd rather face an attack here, surrounded by these trinkets, quills, and bottles, than return to my family dwelling. I push aside the latest Eryndal news report, delivered by Feldrin this morning. Yesterday, when the air was normal and the battalion were a distant thought, I'd been sifting through the report, looking for something useful to pin to the outside shutters. There's news of a herb for acne discovered on the Shattered Isles, the Map of the Monarchy being stolen from Solthera.

I tap the desk, stomach clenching. We've never had green smoke, as much as the war classes at school prepped us for it: *"Run. Fucking run, and don't stop 'til you get home and bolt the door shut."* And that was just Major General Drystan, brought in to give a 'Show n Tell' talk, and asked to leave after the fifteenth 'fuck'. Our school didn't allow us to shy away from danger, knowing that as mortals in an empire run by aemortals, our fates were already taunting hellions of fire and ash.

There's a noise from outside, from Old King Alley, where the bank and the small butcher's shop stand in proud clay formations, where the oddities of the other districts—sex workers, fortune tellers, clay-pipe purveyors—are discouraged. The noise is something akin to footsteps, an officious ringing in the damp, smoke-filled air that sets my teeth instantly on edge. Nerissa's by my side in an instant, forcing the oil lamp to hiss out with two freshly-licked fingers.

She whispers, "The Sable Legion must be patrolling, trying to capture whatever's broken through our borders. We need to burn the posters, now."

"But they'll see the smoke," I hiss back. The chute is linked still to a chimney, and the type of smoke that will billow is not likely to be confused with the trail of weedsmoke from clay pipes, the likes of which are common around certain areas of the municipal.

Annoyance rolls from my best friend's shoulders as she places a hand on her abdomen, as if the situation has birthed some sort of stress demon in her stomach. "You wanted to sort the mail."

"We still have a job to do," I snap, knowing that the Sable Legion might very well sense our presence here. Even though fayte is finite and not handled by all aemortals equally—some barely able to summon a flame from their fingertips, and others able to shapeshift enough to sprout gills and breathe underwater—there are those with Gifts.

And while I can't be sure that any of these Gifts will help them find us, where we huddle in the backroom surrounded by anti-royalist, and by extension, anti-Legionist, propaganda, I can barely swallow as pounding boots stomp toward our shopfront. Nerissa dares to grab the nearest poster, the slogan a messy smear, thought up by her as I rolled my eyes, and spools it up tightly, the tube easier to hide than the incriminating artwork.

A knock pounds against The Courier's Keep door. The thud seems to transform into a maddened wolf as it bounds around the shopfront, leaping into the sorting room and taking up place in my throat. And so I blurt, "I stabbed a guard."

Nerissa's eyes flash white as they swivel towards me, her mouth agape in the darkened light of my favourite room, which seems suddenly to be filled with doomsayer wolves, howling my own personal funeral march. Dusk has given way to bleached moonlight, rendering our pitiless shopfront in bone and ivory, something I can't appreciate as the knock sounds again.

My heart thuds: *Badoom, badoom, badoom.*

"You stabbed a guard," she squeaks. There's no time for debate. If we don't answer, then the guards might ram the door down. We cannot risk that; they are more likely to find our propaganda by force, than if we welcome them in the doorway. Perhaps they have tracked me down; perhaps the guard I stabbed was able to gasp out my name or description—there can't be many opal-haired women wearing a Keep tabard—and his cronies have sought me out for punishment.

"Coming," I shout, buying us time to breathe.

Nerissa grabs my arm and sounds appalled as she manages to choke out, "We're not *going*. They must be here to arrest you. For stabbing a guard." Her eyes can't handle it, her hand still clenched to her stomach, and I mentally map out every possible escape route. But there's only the trapdoor, and there's a chance that the guards *aren't* here because of my violence, in which case we might seal our fate if we attempt to escape now. Answering the door means possible death, but escaping from the Sable Legion and failing means certain execution.

As my arms prickle, I mutter one word to Nerissa: "Hide."

CHAPTER THREE

I take a sharp breath in, toss as many posters as I can into the chute, and then stride to the front door, the quills hanging from the ceiling like poltergeists as I pass through the shopfront. This is it. Time to face my punishment, to face the crime I committed earlier, and to stop them from breaking the door down and finding both of us.

The door swings outward, and a small amount of delight leaps into my chest as the guards are forced back, until the door meets the window-shutter with a boom that fills Old King Alley. Their boots clack on the cobblestones as they steady themselves, their helmets rising and falling, making them look, for a brief moment, like pointed deities. The Legion helmets are designed to accommodate their coryns, and the polished steel winds around, emphasising their horns. Their headwear stills, and their faces seem to shrink as they tuck their chins back. They are no more than ten Sable Legion guards, with two cloaked figures on horses further back.

I refuse to quake in my regulation-issue sandals

and my faded, once-burgundy tunic, with *The Courier's Keep* logo embroidered in gold across one breast. I have never forgiven the army for their treatment of my uncle, and even though I never met him, his death occurring before I was born, it's stained Mother enough that we breathe hate. And so it is with much derision and clearly forced politeness that I say stiffly, "Can I help you?"

One guard has the good sense to snort, turning me into nothing more than an impudent mortal, which is less likely to get me killed than being an anti-Legion activist. I silently thank him for making me seem harmless, even if the swiftly shrinking and harmless mortal that the guards are now looking at is, in its own way, insulting. I'd rather be insulted than dead, especially when I have Mother and Seren to look after.

"There's been an attack on one of our comrades," the closest guard grunts.

"I'm sorry to hear it," I say breathlessly, ignoring the thrum of my heart, which can be a coward at times. "I do hope you all seek the therapy you need."

There is a hum of silence, and I imagine Seren – my loud, forthright sister – letting out a guffaw before telling me that one day my bluntness will sign my own death certificate. The guards do not laugh, but I swear I see one of the cloaked figures shake slightly, as if I have at least given that stranger cause for amusement.

"He's been wisped to the palace gallipot for recovery," the guard grunts, and my thrumming heart pauses and sinks. *Recovery.* "But we must ask you, maiden. Have you seen anything that might explain his injury? Our battalion has fallen, and we wish to understand the nature of the attacking beasts."

I invert my lips and rub them together as if I'm thinking hard. At least I'm not in trouble. Not yet. The guard I stabbed was clearly in no state to pass along my name, nor describe me to his cronies. Which gives me the advantage of a head start, if I am to try and prevent him finding me again. I want rid of these guards and their strange cloaked friends before they find Nerissa or our anti-royalist propaganda, but I'm not sure how much they will believe.

"Yes, I saw something," I say, developing an ethereal tone – something the fortune-teller near the dance hall would approve of. I have their attention now. Each of the guards stares at me, while green smoke billows down the alleyway, briefly causing the nearby bank sign to flash before it is swallowed whole. "It was a beast. A creature from another realm. From the Cecedit Mountains."

"The *Cecedit Mountains*," one of the guards stammers. They all shift, tiny steps that speak volumes, even as we are all in relative safety, and they are only facing a mortal postmistress with three good letter openers.

"Yes," I say, looking up at the skies. "It was... half invisible, and it had great glowing eyes of—"

"What a crock of bullshit," a loud voice interrupts, followed by a burst of laughter. The sound comes from the two cloaked figures. As I stare, one laughs so hard that he almost falls off his white mare, and instead chooses to dismount rather than accidentally face-plant onto the cobbles. As if they are connected, the other figure dismounts as well, and they throw their hoods back. One continues to laugh while the other raises an impatient eyebrow. Two sets of silver coryns shine under the moonlight, horns that are allowed the full force of impact without helmets to mar their hair.

It's the princes. The two aemortal princes from the palace; Prince Kaelion, who is looking at the cobblestones while he chuckles, and Prince Disryn, who rubs a skinny, dark eyebrow as he gives his guards looks of admonishment. And shit. I've never seen them up close before, never dared to breathe near them, and even though I generally disagree with every part of their ruling strategy, aren't they just the two most magnificent men I've ever seen.

Well, Kaelion is *magnificent.* The most beautiful man in Orynthys, surely. Maybe it is guilt and pain addling my mind, but now I understand why many of the horny adolescents in Grim Municipal have Kaelion posters on their bedroom walls, why they write him love letters that I hand to the royal couriers with rolling eyes, why – despite a hatred for aemortals that runs deep – I hear his name giggled all the time in sensible company.

"If I *did* have to sleep with an aemortal," people trill to one another, "then it would have to be the older prince. Have you seen his arms?"

Well, now I have. And even though I'm sure they can do things to a woman, I'm too old to start pinning up posters. Besides, their beauty is how aemortals capture you. Nerissa went on a date with an aemortal man once. His father was the head of the Sable Legion, still our sinister Major General, and his son was visiting *The Courier's Keep* on urgent army business when he got talking to Nerissa. Their flirtatious chat swelled and filled the entire shopfront, and before I could point out that army aemortals are hardly better than royal aemortals, they arranged to meet at The Dwarven Bombard that evening.

The date had gone well. Too well. They ended up tangled in Nerissa's bedsheets, a night she only admits after several elvin wines was the best sex of her life thus far. After the deed was done, Nerissa closed her eyes and fell asleep.

When she woke up, he was gone, and the bodies of her parents were spread across their ramshackle kitchen. Their mouths were filled with soil, their gullets clogged with earth. They must have suffocated to death.

It was the first time, during my lifetime anyway, that the aemortals had needlessly slaughtered mortals, without a proper reason. Nerissa slept with an aemortal boy, and then her parents were killed. Retaliation for something the aemortals consider unnatural, despicable.

My best friend has spent her life knowing that her choice of lover is the reason her parents were murdered. There are no excuses in this world, only reasons, and this was a gut-wrenching reason that rippled outwards from Nerissa's house, inflicting rage into every municipal household. Her suitor was punished for courting a mortal, and Nerissa was punished by aemortals, because sex between an aemortal and mortal is banned. I can only be grateful that they let

Nerissa live, but my gratitude is a short-lived emotion when it sits under an iron tonne of anger.

The annoyed prince – Disryn, whom we in the municipal secretly call *Dismal* – strides up to me, his hunting leathers glinting menacingly under his cloak. They're both wearing the leathers of hunters, rather than robes or traditional princely attire, and I must admit, the look suits them, even though it should be banned for aemortals to be both handsome and wearing badass hides.

Dismal peers into the shopfront behind me, the gloom seeming to reflect itself on his flawless skin. "Search the shop," he barks.

I can feel my face pale as I brush hair out of my eyes, a rare occurrence given it's usually pulled back in a neat bun with no strands escaping. I swallow. "There's really no need. We're not harbouring any beasts or creatures, and we're only here to ensure postal services continue during this turbulent time."

"Why do I feel like everything out of your mouth is bullshit, woman?" Dismal snaps. And to be fair, he's absolutely spot on in his summation, even if it causes anger to dart through me like fast-acting poison.

"Why do I feel like everything out of *your* mouth is bullshit too, Your Highness?" I snap, as shined boots fill our little courier shop, each guard ducking to get his audacious helmet through the doorway.

Everyone seems to pause as my words ring around the small space. I look up to the sky, hoping to see Somer, the moon under the Divinity of Forgiveness, but instead see Lipe, the moon of the Divinity of Water, high tonight. Which will be no use to me, unless I start to drown in my own tears and beg her to spare my lungs. I'd sooner risk drowning than the punishment I'm about to receive, for both my words and the incriminating posters that fill the sorting room. If the guards find those...

"How dare you—" Dismal does not stride forward, even as his hand twitches. "What's your name, wench?"

I lift my chin but don't reply, even as the other prince – Kaelion – continues to chuckle, a vague sense of admiration breaking through his tone, though he doesn't move or progress any further. I wonder why. Perhaps he wants to distance himself from this random raid on two mortal women, or perhaps my blazing anger has already scared him off. The guards are far too keen to destroy everything beautiful and normal in my life. I hear a small squeak and briefly close my eyes. They've found Nerissa. Which means they might also have found...

"What's this then?" I hear one of the guards growl.

My stomach bottoms out as heavy footfalls eat the space between me and the sorting room. Then, helmets glint under Lipe's moon as the guards reappear. One has Nerissa by the scruff of her postal tabard, and the other holds a poster. A screwed-up, half-legible, badly rendered, dripping blue paint poster—one that was meant to aid the protest being planned for the Elven Summer Fayre. An opportunity to gather as many municipal folk as we can and stand at the feet of the royals with our pleas.

At least they seem to have only found one of our protesting artefacts. Nerissa must've made quick work of hiding the others.

I recognise the poster the guard clutches. Oh, faytes. It could've been any of the posters, the many pleas to reallocate funding in the municipal, to bring more autonomy back to the people, to banish monarchy rule. But no. It had to be this poster that the Sable Legion guard must have yanked from between Nerissa's paint-stained fingers, because clearly the Divinity of Humour – who doesn't exist, but might as well – is running rampant tonight.

"What does it say?" Dismal asks, stepping forward as the guard holds the scroll up to the moonlight and they all squint, reading words that we thought were funny when we painted them.

It is the other prince that reads it. Prince Kaelion, the huge, magnificent being that I might like to stop and stare at on any other occasion. His amused voice growls the words in a low tone that prickles at the nape of my neck. "'It's not O-KAE to have such DISMAL rule!'"

Fuck, fuck, and again, FUCK.

I don't wait around to be slaughtered. All attention is on the poster, as Dismal rereads it, his voice confused. I take a sharp breath in. Lunging forward so quickly that no one registers what's about to happen, I yank Nerissa away from the guard. Her tunic pulls, but I have a firm hold on her arm, and as the guard stumbles and lets her go, I shriek, "RUN!" at the top of my voice.

And she does.

CHAPTER FOUR

There's a reason Nerissa is running the entire courier service for Eryndal, despite being only three moon cycles older than me. She's quick, and despite the mass of billowing hair that makes working unbelievably impractical, she manages to dart away from the guard's outstretched hands, as Dismal shrieks something about catching us, and my lungs gasp out a desperate rhythm. Our sandals slap against the cobbles of Old King Alley as we run, emerald snakes of smoke from the fallen battalion overtaking us on either side. My legs burn with acid as we sprint. This alleyway ends in a ramshackle wall, the vestige of something once grand, now crumbled. I know we can climb it.

When we were children, Seren and I used to do this, knowing it was the quickest way to reach the concourse that leads to the centre of Grim, without having to double back to Quiet Street.

Nerissa's sandals are the first to stop slapping the stones as we halt in front of the wall, which rises at about double my height. It's worn down, with grooves and missing bricks that offer ample foot- and handholds. I don't wait to see the expression on Nerissa's face; I launch myself at it, my fingers finding purchase in the first divots, my fitted sandals quickly finding their footholds. My arms aren't the strongest, but I haul myself halfway up before I realise that not only is Nerissa not following, but I can hear the heavy footsteps of the guards catching up to us.

"Climb over," I shout, my voice frantic as I glance back at Nerissa, who looks shrunken under Lipe's moonlight. She's silent, opening and closing her mouth, eyes flicking between the heavens and the grimy, sewage-stained floor below her.

This isn't the time to be careful or delicate. But Nerissa seems frozen, her usual boldness gone. I've never seen her like this before, like she genuinely cares if she lives or dies, and it unnerves me. This city isn't a place for valuing life too highly; risks are expected, and if you survive one, you live to face the next. Sure, we could tumble over the wall and land on an apple cart, or an unfortunate fortune-teller, or even another patrol. But that risk is better than the certain arrest and execution we'll face if the guards catch us.

"You have to," I start to say, but it's too late. The glint of their helmets flashes under Lipe's moon, as they half-run, half-march, clearly mindful of appearing controlled in front of the royals.

I could escape. Only two more handholds, and I'd be over. A quick fall to the other side, and I'd be in the centre of Grim, where I could make my way to the Heartlands, to my mother's house. Or maybe to Seren's place in the centre. She and her girlfriend Isolde run a flower business, and their shack opens onto a busy square. It's a haven of colour and life, and I know they'd hide me, no questions asked. Seren's loyalty is like a bison's, unshakable and steadfast.

But still, something pulls at me. I'm not sure if I could leave Nerissa behind, and I'm not sure if she could ever forgive me for it.

"Go," Nerissa suddenly shouts, and my heart stops. The guards have reached her. One grabs her shoulder, and another raises his hands, summoning a weak amount of fayte in his palms. All aemortals can wield fayte, but it varies in power. Only those with Gifts are truly dangerous, but even this weaker fayte could stun me, or force me to fall from the wall.

I can't leave her. I won't. And somehow, the Sable Legion knows this. I hear one of the guards crumpling the poster in his fist, and as I glance behind them, my breath catches. The princes are here. They arrive atop their mares once again, their cloaks pulled back so the full glory of their silver coryns are revealed. The sight is blinding, their horns catching the moonlight and casting eerie shadows over the cobblestones.

Prince Kaelion and Prince Disryn. Two of the most dangerous men in Orynthys.

And now, I'm trapped between the wall and the guards, with nowhere to run. Fuck, Kaelion looks good on a horse. His entire face smoulders, even though he's too far away for me to properly examine – thank the faytes for that. My feet make the decision before I've fully registered that I'm about to walk to my death, and the sole of my right sandal pulls out of its groove and starts to descend. My left foot follows, and then my hands leave behind the safety of the wall as I jump to the ground, wiping stone dust off my tunic, resisting the urge to curse.

The guards are on me in an instant. Two of them dart forward and grab my arms with more force than necessary. Stale breath slaps against my face, as a billow of green smoke washes in from a distant outpost, briefly hiding us all in its metallic-tasting grasp. As it lets go and moves on, it drifts up and over the wall, and my jealousy is so acute that I can taste bile on my tongue. One of the guards who holds me hisses "bitch" under his breath, and the satisfaction is immediate. But I don't smile, I don't react at all as the two princes dismount again, Dismal staggering forward, as if he's finally understood the poster, and the fact that 'DISMAL' refers to him.

"I'll see you both thrown into the gaol," he snarls, his pale skin and dark hair standing in direct contrast with the delicate flush that has crept from his hairline. "Is anyone else in on your little scheme? Give us names, and we might not execute you."

"Don't waste time, brother," Prince Kaelion sighs, looking up at the sky, clearly bored by his brother's theatrics. "We have greater enemies right now. The stealing of the map has led to an enemy breach, it seems, and we still have no idea what has been sent."

"We'll find the monsters later." Dismal eyes me with a shining, black gaze. "If there is to be a coup in this city, we need to know."

"What do you care, brother? You'll soon be studying seaweed on the Shattered Isles. A coup is no business of yours." Prince Kaelion sounds far too calm, given the poster that's just been revealed. I wonder if he considers us so small a threat that he can't be bothered to expend energy on actually looking at us.

"While I'm studying the healing effects of *plantweeds*, I would like to be reassured that my entire family aren't about to be slain by mortal hags."

"Mortal WHAT?" I roar, as Nerissa stamps on her captor's foot. It does precisely nothing, the Legion guard not even flickering an eyebrow. My arms are starting to go numb from being grasped by vice-like aemortal hands, and yet if there is another enemy on the horizon, presumably the reason the green smoke warning has been sent, then we are all equally in danger.

Eryndal is one of the few kingdoms where the majority of residents are mortal. The palace may be filled with aemortals—beautiful, horned beings who descend from lores and nightmares—but for mortals in Grim Municipal, seventy moon cycles is as long as we can hope to live. Supposedly, the aemortals are descended from fay, the original genus destroyed during a vast natural disaster, and they reappeared many moon cycles later, alongside fayte, their magic. Unlike fay, who were truly immortal, the aemortals emerged somewhat softer, more easily ruined. Some teachings suggest they ascended above mere mortals through the completion of tasks set by the Divinities, but such lore is only debated in hushed voices late at night in candlelit taverns.

"We should all get inside," I mutter, looking around. "It's most likely that silicrites have been sent if they took down a battalion."

"What?" Dismal asks. I look at him, and his annoying face momentarily makes my tongue freeze. Why *should* I tell them? Give them information that will help them take down whatever beast has been sent into our territory? The Courier's Keep is the front-facing news outlet in the city, receiving daily reports from Orynthys elves. We decide what to share with our citizens and what we keep behind. I've read enough about silicrites—the vast, spider-like, winged beings formed in the Cecedit Mountains—to have nightmares, and yet information that Dismal seems to want. "Take them to the gaol," he suddenly snaps, clearly unable to process the fact that this small city postmistress knows more than he does. "We can better question them in the playrooms."

The word jolts a shock through my body. The terminology is used for the torture chambers, the interrogation rooms—more suited to flotillas of Culu pyrates encroaching on our coastland than two women who know nothing of the oncoming enemy. I cannot be tortured for information that I do not have, and Nerissa seems to be thinking along the same lines as she croaks out, "We don't know anything about this attack. We've heard only of silicrites in news reports. Please, leave us be."

"Your begging is a nice glimpse into what's ahead." Dismal turns and strides back to his mare. Both horses seem to sense what's going on, their heads lowered, as if reacting to our imprisonment. The guards on either side of Nerissa and me start to drag us back the way we came, toward the city centre and the underground network that leads to the gaol—a place I've never been, but heard enough about to fill an entire moon cycle's worth of nightmares.

As I pass Prince Kaelion, his position shifts so that he's forced to look at me. Really look. Two guards splay my arms outwards, my shoulder sockets forced apart like repelling magnets, and as pain shoots down my biceps and into my hands, and my feet stumble, my stomach flips. My breath catches somewhere high in my throat.

It's his eyes—the prince's eyes. They've caught me. Amber shot through with tiny shards of blue and green, vivid in a world where everything else seems made of greying bone.

And the way he's looking at me. As if I've suddenly become fascinating.

CHAPTER FIVE

Even in his annoyance, Prince Kaelion is brutally attractive. Tall, with broad shoulders, he seems around thirty, though with an aemortal, you never really know. His lion-like hair, a blend of gold, bronze, and deep mahogany brown, sweeps back from his broad forehead and nests around his coryns. Only a few strands fall forward, and I fight the urge to pull my arms free and tuck them back—or to stare too long at his horns, which mark him as aemortal. His neck stands thick above his leathers, his face framed by chiselled cheekbones and strong lines. Stubble darkens his chin, casting shadows that seem to move as the thick muscles in his jaw shift to control his temper. His broad shoulders are warrior-like, his arms nearly as thick as my waist. His hands are huge, tanned, and—glancing down, I notice—clenched.

I shudder. It doesn't matter that he's beautiful. A silver blade is beautiful. Not so much when it's killing you.

"Leave her be," Kaelion says, his voice strange. Tangled. Tight. I look back up at his eyes, and they catch me again. Damn lust wars with sense in my chest, the two wolves fighting, sending all sorts of feelings up the back of my neck and around my body. I lock my gaze with his, succumbing to the lustful whirling around my midriff, a place that really ought to know better than to stare into the eyes of the most handsome and dangerous aemortal in all of Eryndal.

The guards don't seem to hear him, and I continue to stumble on, though our gazes are locked now. I twist my head – fayte knows why – even as pain streaks through my right arm, sending tiny spots into my vision. I shouldn't be succumbing to my base urges, attracted in a raw and painful way to the man who is sentencing me to torture and, potentially, death. I struggle against my binds, even as Kaelion's eyes burn into mine. He looks like he wants to fuck or kill. To succumb to his own urges, which flicker darkly behind those frustrated eyes. Why is he looking at me like that? Like he's reading my face and can't understand it.

"LEAVE HER BE," he suddenly roars. The sound is so loud and unexpected that even Nerissa's guards drop her, their helmets spiking into the air as they all jump in shock. My arms are free again, and still Kaelion looks at me, his chest panting now, his eyes roving up to my hairline and back to my face. "Who are you?" he demands.

"Elira Corvannis." I stumble over my own name, my tongue suddenly too swollen to speak. Nerissa rubs her arms.

"What are you doing, brother?" Dismal looks between Kaelion and me, as if he's missing something. As if I have just brandished a weapon or revealed myself to be something more than a simple mortal postmistress. And now all of these soldiers know my name, the same name that is likely to be uttered by the aemortal I stabbed earlier as soon as the gallipot healers recover his senses. "She mentioned silicrites, brother. We cannot let that go without further investigation. I mean, we can only hope it's silicrites, and not the Bonenor Flesh-Wielder sent to strip another one of our army patrols of their skin, but we need to find out what she knows."

"Let her go," Prince Kaelion instructs, firmer now. I can't bear the way he's looking at me, as if I'm an ancient text that he's trying to decipher, but I'll take the free pass, snatch it up before he changes his mind, before he decides that whatever he's seeing when he looks into my eyes is something he wants to capture after all. At his words, the guards take a slight step backwards, demonstrating that they have, indeed, left me alone, even though the one who called me a bitch earlier looks like he's pulling himself free from sticky toffee.

"We would've escaped the gaol anyway," I say, my voice weirdly breathless, as I grab Nerissa. I'm not going to wait around any longer; we all heard the prince. Even though the guards shuffle and twitch, clearly struggling between their primal urge to attack and suppress us mortals, and a clear instruction from a powerful royal, they all watch as we first stumble, then trip, then find our feet and outright fucking run. I cast one glance over my shoulder, the prince's eyes capturing me again, and something I can't decipher flickers through his features. But I can't stay to ponder. The guards, standing rooted under their elaborate helmets, suddenly look like shined nails in a stone sarcophagus, the alleyway bearing down on all of them as we run.

"Yeah, we would've escaped the gaol anyway," Nerissa shouts, and suddenly we're both cackling as we run, our howls breaking through the empty streets, bouncing against the closed shutters, filling the thick green air.

CHAPTER SIX

Nerissa was sixteen when her parents were killed. A kindly couple, the Zephyrs, friends of Nerissa's parents and two people sent straight from the Divinities, took her in and insisted that she live with them as long as she wanted. While Nerissa could scrape by on her courier earnings, the real value in her new adoptive parents was their love and company. They welcomed her home from long days in the shopfront with steaming stew and a comfortable futon to sleep on. While we encouraged Nerissa to stay at our house whenever she was able, I was still sharing the second bedroom with Seren back then, and the sleeping options available were fairly bleak. Our living room futons were spitting out straw faster than we could stuff it back in, and our few rugs were thin and biting to sleep on. Mother had only recently stopped working in the sex district, now that I was bringing in courier earnings, and the dwelling was slowly being pieced together after many years of not being able to afford both grain and candles.

  I see Nerissa off, bidding her goodbye when the lane up to her house becomes visible. I continue into the Heartlands, the greener area on the outskirts of Grim

Municipal, where our dwelling sits atop a ramshackle hill alongside various other shacks and outbuildings. Mother's house is made from boards and clay, the roof tin, the doors properly fitted. Many of the other dwellings aren't so lucky, and Woodpecker Rinzer, Mother's cantankerous neighbour, lost the entire left side of his house under the Divinity of War's moon.

I knock twice on the door and wait for Mother to open it. But instead, it's Seren who tugs the door inward, sticking her pale face into the gap, her vivid red hair tumbling around her shoulders. A purple scarf wraps tightly around her neck—a superstition among the city dwellers. Purple became the official colour of peace in some long-forgotten decree, one I'm sure flesh-eating beasts don't bother to read. My sister doesn't look particularly happy to see me, but then she rarely looks particularly happy, so I take it upon myself to be glad to see her. I'm glad that Seren has managed to escape the city centre, if only to roll her eyes at me and duck back inside the house.

"Glad you're alive," she calls in a bored voice, her russet hair curling above her waist.

I step into the world of my family home and slam the door closed behind me, hearing the series of locks that Mother's friend Oswin installed as they click into place. Oswin is a fisherman who spends vast stretches of time at sea, returning every few moon cycles. When I was young, he tried to teach me to hunt animals and build fire, but I was too busy making sure that Seren had food, that Mother didn't go through any more episodes, to appreciate the raw, bleeding mass of doe that he left out for me to skin. Now, I would gladly scale multiple walls for another doe, a chance to eat fresh meat and don fur.

The thought of blood swings through my mind and rests atop the image of the guard I stabbed earlier. He's in recovery. He'll no doubt try and track me down just as soon as his thick, aemortal skin is stitched back together. I swallow, my throat burning.

"Elira," Mother's voice travels through the small dwelling, mingling with the rattling of the tin roof. I inhale, attempting to expel everything that has happened, replacing it with the soothing scent of incense. I need to be strong—for them.

Striding into the belly of our dwelling, I find Mother propped on a futon in the main living space, her feet tugging at rugs depicting stormy seas. She looks troubled, as I would expect—since the final days of war, I'm not sure she has dealt with such a warning.

"Creatures must have attacked Eryndal," I say by way of greeting, not bothering to look around at the draped fabrics, as if we live in a tent. Seren resumes stitching flower stalks into a crown using eryndaisies—a flower grown only in our kingdom. "I just met the princes in Grim," I continue. "Their guards came to our office thinking we might know something."

That gets their attention. My sister wrinkles her brow and says, "Tell us from the beginning."

And so I do. Sort of. I omit that I stabbed the guard who tried to blackmail me, and I tone down the impact of Kaelion's devastating looks—likely to earn a disgusted grunt from my sister—and instead focus on the main element. They let us go. By the time I finish,

Seren has disappeared into a world of her own thought, most likely a world driven by her favoured conspiracy theories, some of which extend to musing that the King and Queen were slain many years ago and no one is telling us. Given their lack of appearance in the municipal, she might be right.

"He saw something when he looked at you," Mother whispers. She looks beleaguered—no, more than beleaguered, she looks *devastated*. It is not a usual look on my mother, who flits between steely and exhausted. She works with Seren now, picking the required stalks for Serenity Flowers to exhibit in their city-centre shack, possibly the happiest place in the entirety of Grim Municipal. Mother no longer has to offer her body to miscellaneous men to afford us a life. When she worked in a brothel, she would buy herself a small wooden carving after each man was done with her; now, the folksy figurines line a shelf in our privy: wolves, bears, a silver-birch cat.

"Yes," my tone is grim. There's a bowl of stewed peaches on the low table by the pantry door, and I stride over and pluck one out.

"They want all mortals dead," Seren declares as I take bites of steaming peach, trying not to burn myself. "They let in the beasts."

I suppose she might be right. After a millennium of learning to use their fayte, and another millennium of aemortals and mortals becoming comfortable living side-by-side, the Thousand Cycle War hit. And when it did, every tenuous relationship was held under a microscope. Perhaps they were scared of forming friendships that could not last. An aemortal befriending a mortal can only end painfully for the former. So their smugness was projected internally as well, and royalty, alongside their kingdom's royalists, began to abhor the power of the Archons—the powerful beings who ran each Bastion. The war occurred, royalists won, and mortals were allowed to live as an afterthought.

That's what the aemortals have done. Emerged from the Thousand Cycle War victorious, and allowed a handful of mortals to survive and procreate.

"I spose they've opened the battalion on purpose, to make it look like an accident," my sister continues, rubbing her chin. Despite her love of conspiracy theories, there are a few similarities between Seren and me. Our height, for one; we are both short-asses, hovering around the shoulders of Grim Municipal when everyone's queuing for water. Our attitudes are another; while Seren speaks before she thinks, I think in anger and end up at the same destination. We both live for offcut day at the butchers, dream of owning a cart from which we might sell wares on sunny days, and care enough about cleanliness that we used to steal soap shards from the gallipot chutes.

But that is where the similarities end. She is russet to my fair, strong-jawed to my oval-faced, dark-eyed to my green. Seren is chaotic and loud to my neat-obsessed and anxious. She is twenty-seven cycles to my thirty, and while her father is Never-Around Oswin, mine walked out when I was a baby and didn't look back.

I am too busy trying not to burn myself on the delicious, tart peach juice that spills across my tongue to notice Mother climb up from the futon and join me, until I hear her hesitant breaths by my ear. "I need to talk to you," she murmurs, just as Seren exclaims, "Or it's the Vale of Eternity attacking us!"

"It can't be Claran," I mutter. Seren used the kingdom's Archon-given name, but since the end of the war, we have reverted to the pre-war land names: Claran instead of the Vale of Eternity. "They've invited our citizens to the fire party next month."

"You think the news broadcasts at The Courier's Keep are the answer to everything," Seren retorts, her tone dripping with disdain. "It's like a cult. You need to get a life. When are you and some bloke from the Dwarven going to make babies?"

"Seren," Mother admonishes, her tone half-hearted.

My ears burn. Seren knows I haven't bled. I might not be able to procreate, even if I wanted to. And if I did want to, some random man from the shadowed corners of my favourite tavern is not who I would choose to share that miracle with. I do get asked; all too often, some drunk suitor will sway over to me and declare his love. He's *seen me around*. Thinks we should *get together sometime*.

They don't actually like me; they're into the version of me they choose to see. The neat, orderly courier manager, with my faded tunic and my blonde bun. The one who never misses a day of work, even when I'm sick as hell from one of Nerissa's birthday parties, who might bake a cake for a special occasion. They see *that* girl—the one who's put together—but they don't see the mess underneath. The anxiety, the constant need for order, the fear of abandonment. And if they don't see that side of me—or, to be fair, if I've never shown anyone the ugly parts—then how can anyone *like* me? Surely love requires truth. And I've never been truthful enough to give any man the full picture.

"I don't need a sperm donor," I reply stiffly, wishing I were at The Dwarven Bombard with Nerissa. She knows the truth—that I've slept with a few of the men in the tavern, and none have really been *it.* I dream of deeper connections, two people endlessly fascinated with each other, the kind of hunger that consumes you whole and leaves you shaking, gasping for more. With the tavern lads, it was the kind of lacklustre hunger you feel when you can't be bothered to go food shopping.

"And that's not the answer to everything," I continue. "Having someone to sleep with doesn't solve every problem."

"Boning is the answer to everything," Seren says sagely, tapping the iron fire poker against the floor with an air of mock authority. "Boning and love."

"*Love*," I echo, the word heavy with derision. "Love won't protect us from further harm."

Seren rolls her eyes. She glances at Mother, a subtle flick of her gaze. The heat in my ears flares, and my mind scrambles. Have they been talking about me? Mother mutters again, "I need to speak with you." She touches my arm, her hands clammy against my skin. "Come to the outhouse. It's important."

CHAPTER SEVEN

"A postal worker shall observe the Code of Silence, never speaking of their tasks to those not involved in the postal system, preserving the privacy of each individual's communication, whether it be of mundane or momentous nature."

Orynthys Postal Manual, Volume 2, Section 7.7

I don't want to be wading through air that's thick as treacle. A branch flies past me, carried by a rip-roaring gust. I duck just in time, but it nicks my face, leaving a sharp sting and a trail of tears that whip away in the wind. Mother's white tunic, smudged with soil and stains, whirls as the gale catches her. Her frizzy opal hair, pulled back into a loose, tumbling bun, is seized under the moonlight.

"Mother!" I shriek, my voice torn from my tongue. I stumble forward, hands out in front as I stagger across the irksome ground of the chicken yard, my eyes squinting against the onslaught of debris and smoke. "Come back inside!"

"Hurry!" she shouts, her voice barely audible through the howling wind. She holds the outhouse door open, her tunic whipping wildly around her legs, as if she is a ship struggling to maintain sail in a storm. The wind is fayte-imbued, created by the fallen battalion to spread the smoke further.

Where in the name of all seven moons are our royal overlords? The aemortal King and Queen are probably too busy twirling under the hypnotism of sweet violin music to bother joining their sons in the dirty streets of Grim Municipal. And while I am – obviously – ecstatic that they weren't in attendance during my possible arrest and subsequent release, they might have shed light on the prince's strange attitude, the way he looked at me.

Mother's hand clamps onto my arm, her nails shoving into my skin. With a panicked yank and a twist that sends my ribs aching, she steals me inside and slams the door. I wipe tears from my cheeks, the only sound the faint, nagging creak of the roof as wind tests the nails. I take a deep breath. It stinks like a mischief of canyon rats have made this their home.

"Well?" I prompt. Without a word, Mother turns and crosses to a stack of bales. Her hands rise to her hair, tugging free the red ribbon, which she winds absently around a piece of hay. The roof rattles under the fists of humourless gods.

"Lies are a virus," she mutters, her voice low. The roof clatters. The wind howls.

"What?" I ask, my forehead aching.

Lies are a virus.

I rub my smoke-clammed hands together and look at her. My mother's parents died young, her brother killed by the Sable Legion after he stole gallipot herbs to treat a child dying in the slums. His skull was crushed, and the child died anyway. Mother has known death like her only friend in this bleak city, and she's given up, perhaps never had anything *to* give up. I see it in her fallen shoulders, her carved cheeks, her empty eyes. My usual denial has fled right now, the part of me that convinces myself that she's fine. She has never been the person that I've always pretended she is.

But still, she's never kept secrets before.

"To... to win, you have to have knowledge." Her voice is fragile, like smoke might carry it away. Her hands wind the ribbon round and round the piece of hay. Every bone in her fingers presses white. "To become a true version of yourself, you have to know yourself intimately."

"Right." I glance to the door. She's clearly having an episode. Her brother was killed in such a brutal way that it must've broken her beyond repair. Without his skilled labour funding her, she had no choice but to join the brothels, the only hope for a woman without education nor contacts. Going through all that will do something to a person.

"I need to tell you something."

"I know, and I want to hear it," I urge. This feels like dealing with difficult customers at The Courier's Keep. I take a deep breath, steadying myself, and glance again at the shaking roof. The wind has managed to tug one of the rattling sheets loose. A sliver of outside is visible through the gap – a thin, jagged shape, like the blade of a knife. If there are silicrites out there, winged beasts made from the stuff of nightmares, then we don't stand a chance.

Mother seems oblivious to this, as she whispers, "It's bad, Elira. It's really bad."

Ice hits my body, snuffing out my impatience in an instant. Is she ill? Dying? "What is it?" I whisper, mouth dry.

"When you were an infant, and I was... breastfeeding," she begins, taking a deep, shuddering breath. The exhale rings around the tiny space, a shaky, hollow sound. "I drank wolfsbane each morning."

"Wolfsbane?" I ask, my mind catching up.

"Yes." A tear spills down her cheek. She looks guilty. "A healer friend sourced it for your... for me."

My mind trips over itself, trying to catch up. Relief laps through me, a warm and giddy wolf. She's not sick. "That's a tincture for change," I murmur, trying to recall everything I've read about herbs.

"It is." Her voice is steely now, sharp and cold. She sounds less like my scattered mother and more like a witch delivering a prophecy.

"What are you saying?"

"I limited your growth." She rubs her forehead, kneading the skin. "I didn't want you to... I was healing you. Ultimately. But you need to know."

My mouth opens. Closes. My sense of self wavers and fluctuates. I don't know what she's talking about. And yet, I should, our school choosing to dedicate entire moon cycles to healing herbs and tinctures. But after sixteen full moons in the courier industry, I can sooner weigh a parcel in my hand than remember the five types of bane. "Did you drink... wolfsbane with Seren?"

Her lips purse slightly. "No. I didn't. But this can't be a surprise to you, Elira. You've always known."

"No, I haven't," I immediately state, annoyance zipping through me. "I had no idea."

"Don't be naïve, girl," Mother suddenly hisses, eyes flashing. "You must have known. Of course you knew."

"I... I really didn't." I feel entirely wrongfooted. Mother's looking at me as if accusing me of keeping this secret. She does this sometimes; gets irritated when she is supposed to feel guilty.

I breathe in, trying to find my inner calm, as I try again. "Why did you drug me as a baby?"

"You don't need to say it like that," she snaps. She breathes in through her mouth, and looks at the ground, the skin around her ears colouring. "I would never drug a baby."

I open my mouth again. Close it. My breath tastes stale, sour with unspoken questions. I feel queasy. Why? Why did I need to change? Mother is impossible to deal with sometimes. She's already clammed up, resolutely not meeting my eyes. It took a lot for her to admit to doing something wrong, and now she blames me for not knowing.

I'll go to the library. I'll read everything I can about wolfsbane. Maybe then, I'll be able to think clearly. Maybe then, I'll have the strength to demand the truth. Silence stretches between us. Mother's attention flits between the trembling roof, the rattling door, and the worn straps of my sandals.

"When I met your father," she says at last, her voice softer, almost wistful, "he was in Eryndal on business."

"I know," I say, though the truth is, I've never been told the full story. She's dropped hints here and there, but cycles stretch between these rare admissions. Everything inside me feels as if it's burning. I think the feeling is shame.

"He took me dancing," she continues, reaching for her ribbon. Her hands tremble. "We had a wild time. But I didn't want that lifestyle. His lifestyle. Always travelling. Always… And then I met Oswin."

"Once Father had already left," I say. "You were alone, and then you met Oswin, and had Seren."

"Something like that," she replies, but she keeps her attention fixed on the hay. "We had a wild time," she repeats softly, her words heavy with longing, or regret, or something in between.

I swallow, wrong footedness and shame washing through me. I feel dirty, drugged, and yet I have done nothing wrong. Betrayal wars with shame in my chest, and I find that I can't look at her any longer.

CHAPTER EIGHT

"Your father must have been a client," Seren suggests, her eyes glittering black in the single flickering candle. Mother hums to herself in her bedroom, the sound tedious, onerous, or perhaps just inciting annoyance because my insides are on fire.

"He said goodbye," I mutter, remembering the feel of his shirt. How he'd cried. "He had feelings for her, I know it. He can't have paid her."

"Even monsters can have manners, Lira," Seren purrs, kneading the soft head of the candle between finger and thumb. It bothers me, her ruining the candle. Soon, it'll go out, and I might not be able to relight it. And Mother drank wolfsbane. She changed me at birth. I had no choice, control was taken away from me.

"I wish I was back in the sorting room," I murmur. It's not that I don't enjoy spending time with Seren, it's just that she makes me even more anxious. She fights fire with fists.

"You know what, Lira?"

"What?"

"You're here with your family, there's danger outside, and yet you're saying you wish you were back at that damned courier's office..." Something flashes across Seren's face—hurt, maybe, though I choose to ignore it. I just want normality. I just want to know my fifty silver sigils are safely buried by the outhouse, the result of many moon cycles of saving. I want to know why I was so awful that I had to be changed at birth, and yet Seren didn't.

"I get that you're like, Lady Organised. A control freak, someone who needs to pretend to have their shit together..." Seren takes a sharp breath, holding it for a beat, then releases it in a rush: "But you've let your need for an organised life suck away your entire personality."

Her tone cuts like a blade. Before I can reply, she pushes up from her futon. Stomps off to the kitchen. She disappears, the door swinging shut behind her with a finality that makes the room feel colder. And then I'm alone. Her words ring in my head, reverberating in the quiet like a curse. *You've let your need for an organised life suck away your entire personality.*

They echo and echo, carving themselves into my skull, tracing cold fingers down my bones. Is that why Mother drugged me at birth? Why Prince Kaelion chose to release me, rather than bothering to take me to the gaol? Because both saw something odd, something not right, something that wasn't even worth killing me for?

CHAPTER NINE

The next morning, I have to go to The Courier's Keep, my place of work in the centre of the city. I have to. Mother *drugged me* as a baby. Seren thinks I have no personality. I can't stay here, I just can't. I don't deal well with anger; I need time to think about things, scared that I might lash out and later regret it.

I unbolt the shutters enough to peer outside. The smoke has mostly dissipated, leaving the air clear but heavy, as though the world itself is holding its breath. There's no noise, no life bustling on the dirt track outside. Grim Municipal feels shellshocked—quiet, uneasy, but no longer a place of immediate danger.

Still, it's unusual that it's so quiet outside. Everyone else must be paying heed to the smoke that continues to linger in the sky.

I dip out the side door and escape around the back of Mother's shack, heading for the outhouse. The lingering traces of green smoke still cling to the air, choking at my throat like the taut string of a kite. A high-pitched whistling fills my ears, and then I realise it's coming from me—my throat, screaming into the oblivion that is the smoke's warning. I wrench the chicken feed trough toward me, pulling until it topples, spilling corn across the earth. The wind grabs at it instantly, spiralling the feed away as I drop to my knees, my hands scrabbling frantically through the soil.

I don't have time to search for the spade in the outhouse. Not if the smoke is still here, not if the warning is still maintained. My fingernails scrape against the dirt, tearing it away in frantic handfuls. Tears splatter across the backs of my hands, ripped from my eyeballs by a sour wind, smearing soil as I fight to keep myself together. Finally, my fingers hit metal. The ornate carvings of the silver box scrape against my fingertips, the swirling patterns a blessed relief. I tear away more earth, yanking clumps aside until my box of sigils is exposed.

The fifty silver sigils that I've managed to save for my own house. I first buried it when Seren started stealing from Mother to buy substances. My hands fumble desperately for the two hilts embedded in its lid, and I wrench them free. My silver letter openers.

I loop them into my makeshift bandolier and head back through the house, unlocking the front door and throwing it to meet the wind.

"You're crazy!" my mother shouts as my sandals hit the gritty terrain of outside. I'm wearing a regulation-issue postmistress tunic, this one less worn than yesterday's, just in case I bump into anyone. It is always worth looking one's best, I tell myself, trying not to think about amber eyes digging into my soul.

I ignore Mother, but her voice follows me into

the street. "Elira, don't you understand? The battalion's warning—there's creatures outside! There's smoke in the air. This isn't a game!" I stop in my tracks, but I don't turn. "Please," she continues, her voice quieter now, trembling. "I can't lose you." The weight of her words presses down on me, but I don't look back. I can't. I have to go. I have to. Otherwise, I might tear them both apart, such is the feeling that swells, unchecked in my chest. And so I stride on, and Mother is forced to slam the door closed behind me, her final huff grating across the back of my skull.

I need to know what wolfsbane does. The postal elves will know, if I can summon Feldrin, the cleverest of the lot, with the correct whistle. Sometimes, they ignore me, but sometimes they humour my elvin-whistles, learned during extra classes at school.

A sharp, stinging drizzle slaps against my face as I walk. Clouds overhead billow into shapeless sheets, shifting in the wind, tugged along like hung laundry. Along the first alleyways, the houses turn blank faces toward me, wooden shutters tightly bolted. Mossy froth gathers in doorways.

My own mother drugged me because she wanted me to be different. I swipe away an angry tear with the back of my hand. Above me, birds have tumbled back into the sky, circling ominously, soaring on taut wings, their caws harsh and grating. Everything feels designed to test my endurance. Considering Grim Municipal is never a particularly prepossessing sight, today it is utterly otherworldly. Any lingering charm has been leeched away, replaced by grey winds and demon birds. Stained walls have been licked from the bottom by sewage, and blown from the top by fire smoke. I entertain, for a fleeting moment, the possibility that I might be insane. There is danger here—real, tangible danger. Every other family has shuttered their windows.

Will the Sable Legion patrols still be on the streets? Will they have discovered the other posters, the remaining contraband that could have both Nerissa and me slaughtered for our dissent? My whole body simmers with rage at the injustice of punishments doled out for our inability to speak freely, even as I am only imagining the ramifications. In reality, we were nearly dragged to gaol, but were freed by Kaelion and his indecipherable eyes.

Much as his charity irks me, if we had been forced into the underground cells, we would have escaped. I reassure myself of that, even if it's false confidence from someone with very few skills in the areas of jailbreaking and subterfuge.

I'm fully in the mouth of the alleyway now, the wind subsided but still noisy behind me, tossing store signs back and forth where they hang on rusty arms. I dampen my hair back as I look around. All I see is smoke and ugly buildings, neither vouching for the rumour that there are creatures loose in the city. Rowdy birds the colour of onyx dip and soar in the sky, always visible in my outer peripheral, my façade of false confidence flailing as the shuttered windows stare at me.

While there always seems to be something alive inside me that I can scarcely control – an anxiety, a fury, a pulse that seems connected to something far away from our rotten city – they both crave gentle comfort like anything else means succumbing to ego. It's not that I want *more,* I think grimly as I press against the unthinkable wind, but it's that sometimes I feel like a wild animal pressed among mortals.

A figure brings me up short. It's outside The Courier's Keep. And it's seen me.

CHAPTER TEN

A mortal face on a vast, bug-like body. Long, spindly legs click against the cobblestones. Grey, snake-like skin overlaps in loose, wrinkled folds, cascading down the central body like a rotting cloak. Around its neck, the skin gathers in tangled heathers and amethysts, grotesque and glistening, underneath wings that can render this monster airborne. He's a silicrite. A beast from another kingdom.

His razor-sharp pincers tap rhythmically against the ground, and then he stretches a wide, red smile in my direction, his wings twitching. I've never seen a silicrite before. Only read about them in the very worst of children's storybooks. Without realising it, I am holding my hands out, my fingers splayed, as if to surrender.

"Now, what to do," the silicrite muses, his many legs beginning to shift, carrying him closer. I can't move. Either side of me, clay buildings loom, their shutters stained with fire smoke and froth. They tower endlessly, offering no escape.

"What to do, indeed," the bastard purrs, cocking

his head, his legs clicking forward like a death march. He licks his bottom lip with a long, black tongue, moving towards me at a leisurely pace, though I don't miss the hungry glint in his black eyes, as if supper has just arrived. I can't breathe. My heartbeat feels detached from my body, as if it's thumping somewhere outside my chest, out of sync with my breathing. My entire being is flooded with something colder, whiter, and hotter than fear. I have never, in my life, been this terrified.

"Kill you, or steal you," the beast muses aloud. "Enjoy you, or slay you?" My scalp burns with icy fire, a sting so sharp it feels like it's peeling the skin from my skull. He's talking to himself, rather than a fellow silicrite. That, at least, is some small relief. I daren't pull my gaze from his grotesque face, but I cast around a peripheral net and don't latch upon any other shadows moving up the alleyways. He operates alone.

A silicrite. An honest-to-fayte *silicrite*. Where the fuck has he come from?

"Where have you... why are you here?" I demand, my voice thin and dry, the words sticking to my parched tongue. I wrack my brain for any scrap of knowledge, any hint I might have caught from The Courier's Keep broadcasts, but nothing about silicrites breaks through the fog of my racing thoughts. The back of my neck tingles, wave after wave of clammy fear creeping up my spine like frozen fingers clawing at the nape of my neck.

I feel out of control, and I feel helpless, and I hate both of those fucking things.

"Oh, she speaks!" The silicrite lets out a harsh,

barking laugh. "Maybe I will enjoy you, after all. Do you scream?"

"Never," I lie, the word brittle and hollow in the air. His spindled arachnid legs click and clack across the cobblestones, like knives against stone, each sound sharper than the last.

This is it.

This is where I'm going to die.

The centre of my forehead pings faintly, a weak pang that feels like a whisper, as if someone's trying to send me a message. As if I've just been kissed by an angel. And then I remember. The two silver letter openers slung across my hips. Silver is lethal to most curse-created beasts. Through my friendship with a courier from the Lost Dominion, I've managed to get hold of four rare openers. Even though one was used to slay the Sable Legion soldier just yesterday – or to put him in the palace gallipot at any rate – I still have two at my disposal, pressed against my jutting hipbones.

"I'm going to enjoy you for a long time, girl," he says, taking another slow step forward. He's only three yards away now. Close enough that I can smell him—the sickening stench of rot rolling off his body. Expired flesh left to fester, mixed with the acrid smoke of burning funeral pyres.

Bile loosens my dry tongue. "Stay away from me," I manage, voice raw with the effort of pushing the words past the knot in my throat. I glance around, but all I see are clouded alleyways and closed shutters. My hand flies to the bandolier slung across my hips, worn since the green smoke first appeared, and I yank free one of the silver weapons. The makeshift bandolier is just a strip of fabric—a ripped pillowcase.

Mother's pillowcase. A faint floral scent rises as I unsheathe the silver, and for a brief, unbearable moment, it stings my heart. My mother and sister are safe at home.

"Oh, you have a knife. How quaint," the beast jeers, his smile stretching wider, though it never reaches his cold, calculating eyes. "But you know, child, silver doesn't work on me." He pauses, voice dripping with mockery. "I am land and stars. Surely your parents taught you that you can't use silver on a star?" My grip falters. My hand drops slightly. Is he telling the truth? Can this monstrosity—this grotesque, unnatural thing—really be born of the stars?

"You're lying," I force out. With my free hand, I unhook the second letter opener. "I'm going to slice through you, and you're... and you're..." My words trail off as he moves closer, sweeping right up to me.

The stench of his rotting flesh hits like a physical blow. I can see the fine black hairs sprouting from his grey, spindly legs, like parasites feeding off wet leather. His pincers gleam like precious gems—wet, sharp—and the bile surges again, threatening to choke me as putrid air presses in. I shrink back, my mind racing. Where do I stab him? The silver's all I have. But is it enough? The joints of his legs—they look thinner, more vulnerable than the rest of him. But would that kill him? I've never killed a beast before, and yet I have stabbed something – someone – before, any vestiges of innocence I might have held swiftly judging me and coming up short.

"I'm bored of you now, girl," he says suddenly, his voice cold as ice, his face leaning closer to mine. I feel my breath hitch as his foul body looms over me, every fibre of my being screaming for escape. It was my recklessness that got me into this mess. My obsession with order, my need for the safety of the sorting room. I am going to die because of my own compulsions. *I'm so sorry, Mother. Seren.*

I brace myself for impact, even as my arm flies forward, lacking impact, lacking conviction. I'm not holding the silver hard enough; as it reaches the creature's leathered skin, the tip refuses to break through. My fingers have no purchase. The knife slides *backwards,* my grip too loose, and pain shoots through me as I slice open my own hand.

Fuck.

I slide my palm forward, regain purchase, but I've already served to injure myself. The beast hasn't even noticed. He's paused, his nose just inches from my hair.

His movements slow, and for a fleeting moment, I wonder if I'm seeing a crack in his monstrous façade. His head tilts, his many legs shifting, his wings flexing. He inhales deeply, drawing my scent into his wet, flaring nostrils.

"Well," he says, his voice soft, almost excited. "That's interesting."

CHAPTER ELEVEN

"What is?" I gasp, raising my makeshift dagger into the air. My hand trembles violently, as the wind howls through the alleyway, rattling the nearest window shutters, filling the air with a trembling, haunted whine.

"Your scent," the beast murmurs, leaning closer, his voice dark and unnervingly soft. "You almost smell as if... no, you can't..." He's so close now I could reach him. My fingers could scrape the thin, grey skin of his neck. "You smell like the heir, but you have no coryns. Can it be?"

"I am mortal," I spit, tasting metal on my tongue as he advances, his skin thick and rolling like a living, repulsive mass. "I have no coryns." But it makes me think. This is a beast from another land, one who likely knows more about herbs and tinctures than I ever will. "Tell me, beast," I say, my voice trembling, but growing stronger despite myself. "What do you know of wolfsbane?"

He pauses, his spindly legs grinding to a halt. Around us, dust has been kicked up from the dirt of the alleyway, and it seems to linger in the air, settling like ash on my skin. "You've taken wolfsbane," he murmurs, lowering his head to peer into my eyes. "Is this what you are telling me? You've taken wolfsbane to remove your coryns?"

I clench my teeth, swallowing the bitterness rising in my throat. My stomach drops as the truth tries to cloak me, heavier than the smoke in the air. I do not need this beast confusing me with an aemortal. I do not need—

"Tell me, woman. Who is your father?"

"He was a lowly brothel visitor," I snap, my fist clenching the silver so tightly that any normal person would have bled by now. Fayte bless my dried-up body and my inability to bleed from anywhere.

"Even kings need their fun, woman," the beast purrs, lifting its head slightly to give me a look of pure condescension. This might be the only chance I get. I draw back, pulling the letter opener near my ear—and—

I strike.

The beast turns as I lunge. I miss its neck. The momentum throws me off balance, and I fall forward. But my weapon finds another target—it plunges deep into the side of the creature's eye socket. A violent jolt shudders through my arm, shooting up into my shoulder as the letter opener drives further in, piercing through soft tissue until it hits something harder. Brain matter. I taste magic—thick, metallic—clenching my eyes shut as the sensation surges through my body.

And then I feel it. Swollen, hot blood erupts from the eye socket, as though it had been waiting for permission. It hits me in sticky, boiling splatters. I open my eyes, clamping my lips together as the searing liquid coats my scalp, dripping down my neck. Both the beast and I collapse to the ground. Its final sound is a wicked, bone-chilling screech, a howl so sharp it claws down my spine and splinters through my legs.

And then—silence. Window shutters rattle faintly in the distance. Blood burns against my skin. I let go of the letter opener still embedded in the beast's skull, rolling onto my side. The cobblestones are cold and unforgiving against my ribs. My shins ache, but I can barely feel them anymore. I lift the hem of my tunic, wipe the creature's blood from my face, the fabric soaking through almost immediately.

I'm alive; that's what matters. A foot away from my trembling fingers, the silicrite's legs curl tightly into its body. Thick black liquid pools between cobblestones, a sharp stench hitting the air. It's not blood, not really. I remember a story about silicrites and golems—that neither bleeds, but instead is filled with toxic poisons, sludgy substances. Perhaps neither me nor the dead silicrite were ever meant to bleed.

My own obsessiveness – the monster in my chest – nearly got me killed. I stagger to my feet, legs trembling. I'm still not safe. My hand is sliced open, and even though it's not bleeding, I'm pretty sure I saw the fleshy inners of a tendon last time I looked properly.

Even The Courier's Keep might not be safe, now that I know there truly *are* silicrites attacking our kingdom. I can't lock myself away. I don't even have food in there. And if the people of Grim Municipal are too scared to come outside, too terrified to speak or band together, then what can I even do? What can anyone do?

CHAPTER TWELVE

I stagger forward. The narrow alley next to the bank looms, shadowed and cramped, hiding a fountain alcove. I push forward until I reach both, and then press the stone dial. Tan-coloured water bursts forth, and I plunge my hands in, scrubbing away the poison and grime, the liquid biting at my skin.

Once the basin drains, I lean down, scooping dirty water into my mouth, hoping to wash away the burning in my throat. I swallow. But it doesn't settle. Thick, hot acid surges upward, filling my nostrils, pricking my eyeballs. My stomach churns, and I lean forward, forehead resting against the stone gargoyle above the fountain.

I don't know what to do.

I am a postmistress, a duty-bound worker who only breaks the rules on very rare occasion, most notably when I rewrite post. And even that is done with good intention. Annoyance at my own idiocy slices through my forehead, searing pain at the exact centre of my skull. Even in my wildest reed-smoking days—lounging on Bluebell Bridge with Nerissa—I've never experienced such out-of-body despair. I can't think. All I want is to go back to my normal life—my daytimes with Nerissa at The Courier's Keep, weekends spent down The Dwarven Bombard or picking flowers with Seren.

My nice, normal life. I exhale sharply, and scan the dim alley. "I'm stuck down an alleyway," I mutter aloud, knowing full well that talking to myself won't speed my way to sanity. "And my last letter opener's on the stones." My words hang in the air, bitter and sharp. These streets smell of smoke from those who wander with clay pipes, sucking their much-needed vice as they puff and hock up black phlegm. No doubt my letter opener will be found by one such crone.

Now is not the time to lament stationery.

"So basically," I mutter with a bitter snort, "I'm fucked."

"I wouldn't say that," a voice muses. My heart leaps into my chest as I whirl around, hands instinctively lifting in front of me.

The heat in my forehead flares as his marred gaze checks me.

A man leans against the wall further down Quiet Street, half-hidden in shadow. He's dressed in fighting furs—black boar skins and bristled animal hide. Across his forehead, a black band rests, adorned with long silver feathers that obscure most of his face and fall to his collarbone, the band sitting beneath his dark silver coryns.

"Who– who are you?" I press my back against the cold alleyway stone. The moisture soaks through my tunic, and the crunch of grit stabs into my skull. Is he from the Sable Legion? He doesn't look the type—too fancy, too... clean.

"Just a messenger from the palace," he mutters, his eyes flicking to my feet. I follow his gaze and catch sight of my leather sandals—practical, a little battered, but still holding together. His lip curls. Is he judging my shoes? At a time like this?

"Regulation sandals," I gasp, the words tumbling out before I can stop them.

"I see." His face twists, like he's suppressing a smile. "And are they cheap to purchase, these... regulation sandals?" As he speaks, I catch the glint of his teeth—gilded in metal, gleaming faintly even in the dim light of the alley. They distract me from a retort, even as my mind scrabbles to remember how much I paid for these shoes, many moon cycles ago.

"And who might you be?" he asks, his tone polite, almost deliberately so. He reaches up to part the long silver feathers obscuring his eyes, making an effort to look me over properly. I study him in return, trying to decipher the strange mixture of hauteur and curiosity in his gaze. I can't sense any immediate danger from him. He doesn't look like he's about to dismember me or rip my throat out. If anything, he seems... bored.

But it's the bored ones you have to watch out for. The worst predators are the ones who hurt you just to amuse themselves.

"Elira Corvannis." I can't think of a good reason not to tell him my name.

"No," he replies softly, tilting his head. His grey eyes lock into mine. The fountain beside me gurgles as the basin empties itself. I glance toward Old King Alley, where my silver letter opener lies on the cobblestones. Could I make a run for it and grab it? Could I kill a palace messenger if it came to that? "Elira... not Corvannis," he continues, his eyes narrowing slightly. He squints at me as though reading this information directly from my mind. Except he can't be. Because he's wrong.

"I'm a Corvannis, just like my mother and sister." The words come out forcefully, but my stomach churns as I speak. My mother and sister. I hope they're safe.

"Your... sister." He screws up his face, brow furrowing deeply. Then he shakes his head, the feathers on his headpiece ruffling as if stirred by an invisible breeze. "No."

"No what?" I snap, my voice rising. "She is Seren Corvannis. We have both taken our mother's surname. As is our choice." I glare at him, daring him to contradict me.

"I don't dispute that," he replies, his voice low and measured. I inhale sharply through my nostrils, fighting to calm the fire licking at my nerves. I just killed a *silicrite.*

"Then what," I snap, "do you dispute?" And why in the Divinities' names are we still standing here, in this dank alleyway, when a creature from another realm could swoop down any moment?

"But half," he says slowly, each word carefully measured. "That's why I was confused... because I can't feel her."

"*Feel* her?" I repeat, horrified and confused. The words hang in the air like daggers, pricking at my spine, making my skin crawl.

He looks around the open alley, his gaze becoming alert. We're exposed here, and neither of us looks remotely equipped for another attack. "I need your help, Elira. Otherwise, you might die."

"I'm not going to help you," I mutter derisively, not stopping to think what he might want. Aemortals are famously cunning. The only threat to me has been eradicated. I eradicated it. I glance down at my hand, and immediately look away. The skin across my palm flaps open, pink and white underneath. My forehead swoops, woozy.

"A girl has been killed at the palace. She was a mortal girl, adopted by the royals when she was found wandering as an orphan child. The queen likes to have girls around, you see."

I shudder, guilt gnawing at me again, even though it makes no sense. I couldn't have been there to save this girl, if she was indeed mortal. If she was a strictly banned half-aemortal, then the palace might have had her purposely killed; it's forbidden for an aemortal to have a child with a mortal.

"Right." I swallow. I am duty-bound. I need to show that I respect our queen, while also being afraid of her, while also disliking how this kingdom is run.

"Your laceration needs tending to," the messenger continues, glancing at my hand. I will myself not to look at it again. The pain is, in turns, making me giddy and faint. "And I daresay you could do with a glass of peach juice."

I smile. What a silly thing to say. This aemortal

doesn't care about me. He doesn't want to fix my hand and feed me peach juice.

"I suppose you'll insist on wearing those sandals." His eyes fix on my shoes. "A fine picture we'll make when we arrive at the palace. It is safe there now, only a lone silicrite who has fled. There might be more in this city. If you laugh at the idea of being healed or recovering with fruit sugar, you might at least entertain this trip by knowing that another attack on you could be imminent."

"More silicrites," I say, accidentally wiping my injured palm against my tunic, sending blinding pain juddering through me. "What do you mean, 'when we arrive at the palace'?"

He doesn't answer right away, just looks at me. As if I'm a fox, and he's the mouse—watching, studying, calculating my every movement. He wants us to go to the palace. I think of amber eyes, of magnificent shoulders and unexpected charity. I feel like an addict excited to be taken to my next hit, but that's ridiculous.

As I swallow down everything that shouldn't be, I lift my chin, maintain my waxy demeanour, and ask the question that I should have started with. "How did you find me?"

"The more prudent question," he muses, his eyes narrowing as he sizes me up, "is how did the silicrites find you?"

"They didn't find me," I reply, meeting his ash-coloured gaze. "It was not me they sought. There was talk of an heir. He said I smelled like an heir, and asked me about… about some other stuff." Like my paternity.

I am not about to court such random words on my tongue, not when smoke still rages around us.

The messenger nods, a sharp motion. Sludge from a nearby wall splashes onto the cobblestones. "The King of another land is seeking his heir," the man mutters, his eyes lifting to the sky as if it holds some secret. "Or else, someone is. Someone who thinks such a conquest is worth going to war over."

"No one's going to war," I say, voice flat, almost mechanical. I swallow hard, trying to steady my breath. "I would know about it. I... I get all the news before anyone else in Eryndal. There are things the aemortals don't even—"

"Don't be dense, Elira," he interrupts, his voice cutting through my words like a blade. "That might get you into a lot of trouble, given everything that's coming." I feel the sting of his words before I can hide it. *It's like a cult*, Seren had said. And now, *Don't be dense*. I'm being stripped of any illusions that the world I've built for myself still makes sense. I swallow again, hating the lump in my throat.

I am brave. I am duty-bound. I protect our citizens' post every day. I miss the comfort of stamping envelopes, the wax-crusted stamp pounding down onto crisp paper. I miss the smell of ink, the rhythm of routine.

"Silicrites are stone creatures—creatures without blood, bone, or flesh," he continues, his tone indifferent, as though reciting a fact rather than explaining something urgent. "They're generally enslaved, instructed. But the creature you encountered was a silicrite of moving stone. They can transmute themselves into their arachnid form, but they remain bloodless—apart from their eyeballs, of course."

He smirks, a cold flicker of amusement in his gaze. I feel my stomach tighten as I recall the horror of that encounter, the remnants of the squashed eyeball still clinging to my postmistress tunic. I grind my teeth, my patience snapping.

"As lovely as your little biology lesson is," I say, voice laced with frustration, "care to explain why this means war is coming?"

"I have a feeling they know something we do not. It's unusual to send silicrites when negotiations could be done face-to-face. Why send creatures like that to do an aemortal's bidding? Why attack you—a pathetic, unarmed woman—when they could have come across more tolerable?"

"Pathetic?" I growl, my chest tightening. "I might ask why they didn't attack you, given your irritating—"

"If you find me irritating," he interrupts, his voice laced with warning, "I dare say you might want to control your temper before meeting the royal family. Prince Kaelion has a temper of his own. I cannot see that he would take kindly—"

"I have no intention of seeing that arrogant—"

"Be careful what you say, Elira." The messenger sighs deeply. His fingers move gracefully through the air, tracing invisible lines in the space around him. Transformist symbols, the shapes flickering into life. I taste the sharp, metallic flavour of fayte in the air, but it's the movement that catches my attention. The way the magic twists and bends, alive in ways that seem almost unnatural, as the symbols become fayte.

"I have not wisped with another before," the messenger explains under his breath. Without warning, the air itself seems to snap. A rush of wind bursts around the messenger and me, strong enough to whip my hair around my face, and the feathers on his headpiece flutter violently as if caught in a storm. The world around us bends—folds in on itself—like the pages of a book collapsing inwards. He strides forward, reaches out, and clutches my arm, his fingers backed in thick leather plates that curl over his knuckles.

We are wisping. This is how some stronger aemortals travel, pushing through a giant metaphysical hoop, leaving one place to appear in another. I have seen them both wisp away from where they are standing, and wisp to appear, but I have—of course—never wisped before. And it is terrifying. My ribs feel like they're being crushed, as if air is attempting to suffocate me from all sides. I stumble forward, my hands shooting out instinctively to grasp the nearest thing for support—the messenger's other leather-clad arm.

And yes, I don't want to wisp, to leave the solidity of Grim Municipal and its dank and dreary cobblestones. But my hand is flapping open, and I don't want to be left alone, not if there are more silicrites.

Besides, amber eyes kept interrupting my dreams last night. Call me curious.

The messenger's presence remains just a shadow at the edge of my fading consciousness, as we wisp into the palace grounds.

CHAPTER THIRTEEN

The sandstone palace has been stretched by the hands of gods, its apple-crumble exterior extending further than my eyes can see, ivy consuming its vast, semi-eroded body. A domed roof stretches between towering spires, a riot of pearl tiles reflecting the sky, puddling in aquamarines. Iron railings curl tightly around the perimeter of the fortress, twisted and cold, forming a thick boundary between us and the looming stronghold. When I'd imagined the palace, I had pictured something grand—light, with expansive halls, gilded plinths, wild bacchanalian parties filled with music, candles, laughter. But this? It's bohemian. Heavy.

The grounds teem with aemortals, members of the Sable Legion striding past in their grand helmets, healers running with heavy bags and wooden cases, stretchers being pulled from a gate on the opposite side of the castle, weighed down with injured bodies. There is blood on the ground nearby, and a huge streak of black liquid, the exact shade of the silicrite poison, across a turret. Apart from one shattered area of the wall nearest us, there is no other evidence of an attack. The messenger said that the silicrite had *fled*.

The noise of people shouting is immense, but they are all headed for the other side of the palace, a distant doorway sucking them in like mudflies to a honeypot.

The palace is several hours on foot from the centre of Grim Municipal, despite seeming to dominate from above, mostly hidden by a wall that no one I know has ever dared pass, apart from the few mortals hired for cleaning when the aemortal cleaning staff are called to battles. It's generally accepted that mortals are better at scrubbing toilets than maintaining themselves against torture.

"I can't believe I'm at the royal palace," I whisper. I've never seen anything so grand. I try to ignore the faint, cloying tang of fayte in the air, seeping into my skin as we progress and the gates groan shut behind us, metal scraping metal. I can't tell if it's the palace that smells of magic or if it's me, power pressing in from every side.

I don't even know my companion's name. I'm following a stranger, a man who seems far too comfortable with our situation. I glance at him, and at the same moment, his eyes flick to mine.

"You'll be back in no time," he says, his voice smooth. "I'm Elrind."

"Stop doing that."

"Stop what?" His voice is an exaggerated mockery of innocence. His pace quickens as he strides toward the castle steps, his feathers ruffling, as if they're part of the wind. I glare after him, my stomach twisting. I can't say it—I can't say "stop reading my mind." Because no one can do that, can they? That's not possible. If he can, it's not something I want to acknowledge. The fear of confirming it makes me clamp my jaw shut.

We approach the vast palace doors, their opulence faded with age and the Divinity-sent winds we receive under certain moons. Gold arches and emerald studs, once dazzling, are now dull and scuffed, worn by time, the details almost indecipherable. I barely make out the shape of a bird and an arrow, the gemstone-created symbol nearly lost to cycles of neglect, before the doors groan open with a hollow sound, far too loud for their grandeur.

Aemortals start to emerge from the doorway. I stop walking instinctively, and Elrind halts beside me. Should I run? The thought bursts through my head, frantic, but I hesitate. Where would I go? Past the gates and down the hill, I can see the high wall that separates this land from Grim Municipal, a cold, impassable barrier. There's no escape that way.

I look back up at the aemortals emerging before me.

Palace workers, clad in ornate feathers and layers of fabric. Some are entirely cloaked, their faces concealed behind intricate headbands and woven patterns of feathers, while others—kitchen staff in crisp white overalls, butlers in rich burgundy velvets—wear their attire with the same quiet dignity. They form a perfect, silent line, their gazes fixed ahead, their postures straight.

Wordlessly, they split into two rows, leading up to the grand entrance of the palace in front of us. My feet feel frozen in place, my lungs struggling for breath as I stand motionless, the indent of their V-shape.

The workers turn, all eyes on me, and I feel a sudden, inexplicable weight in my chest. Two lines of staff—in kitchen whites, velvet coats, and ceremonial blue robes—gaze at me with unsettling focus. The chirp of a bird echoes in the air above, a single, lingering note that seems to stretch out in the tense silence. The wind stirs around my ankles, brushing the hem of my poison-soaked tunic against my skin. My arms prick with the cold, and I swallow hard, struggling to control the rising panic.

And then—

The butlers closest to the door bow first. Their deep burgundy coats ripple slightly as they lower their heads. The kitchen staff follow, one by one, their heads dipping as their chef hats flutter with the motion. The sound of their quiet, synchronised gestures fills the space between us, as if the air itself holds its breath in reverence.

The robed figures follow suit, their faces hidden beneath layers of fabric, their eyes concealed by the folds of feathers. They lower their heads in perfect unison, the motion smooth and deliberate.

And then Elrind. He turns to face me, his expression unreadable. The briefest flicker of something passes through his eyes—an emotion I can't quite place—and with a fluid, practiced movement, he joins the others in a deep bow.

Every single person in the courtyard. Every single one of them, from the butlers to the kitchen staff to the robed figures, is bowing.

To me.

A postmistress from Grim Municipal.

"Why?" I whisper, trembling in my tunic.

CHAPTER FOURTEEN

"Why did everyone bow?" I hiss, struggling to keep up with Elrind's strides as we move through countless majestic hallways. I had no choice but to follow the messenger into the arteries of the castle. We pass suits of armour, impossibly beautiful paintings, dripping candelabras, every hallway lined with worn tapestries, depicting Divinity lore and bloody battles.

"It is a great honour to have you here, Elira." Elrind's voice is strained. "And it is a great honour for you to be invited to the palace. Will you please try to—"

"I'd hardly say I was invited," I interrupt. "I need to fix my hand, yes—"

"I must encourage you to control your temper, no matter if the servants have deemed you something worthy—"

"Why should I change who I am? What are the royals going to do, slaughter me before I have a chance to get back to my family?" Even as I rage, his words have piqued a curiosity in me. Perhaps the servants don't usually bow. Perhaps they have deemed me *worthy* somehow, as if my postal tunic has bought me respect.

"If the royals choose to devour you, then I can't stop them," he says in a low breath.

"You're seriously saying that?" I bite out, incredulous. "What are you, a palace lapdog?"

Elrind doesn't flinch. His posture is stiff, controlled. But beneath the surface, I can see the flicker of annoyance, the barely contained exhale of frustration that leaves his lips as he speaks again. "You may not understand the magnitude of the situation, Elira," he says, voice clipped. "But this palace and its inhabitants are not to be trifled with. It's not just an invitation—it's an honour that you don't seem to appreciate. The royals are—" He pauses, as if carefully considering his words. "They have their reasons for what they do. And you should respect that."

I scoff at him. "Respect? For what? For hiding away in a gilded cage while the rest of us starve? I'm not here for a royal tour, Elrind." I can hardly explain why I've really joined him on this impromptu trip, without explaining that I'm curious to see the prince again, to ask him why he let me go.

"Oh, don't play with her, Elrind."

I whip my head toward the low, sly voice that interrupts so suddenly. But there's no one in the hallway. Just a small, silver cat sitting in the centre of a battered emerald rug, staring directly at us. "I must say, she's a lot prettier than I imagined," the cat croons.

The cat *crooned*. The cat is speaking.

I look at Elrind, wondering if he can hear it too, or if it's just another voice in my head, like the ancient one that told me to write with blood.

But Elrind just rolls his eyes. "This is Tryx. You can basically ignore everything he says."

"Well, that's a nice way to greet a Divinity, isn't it?" the cat muses.

I freeze. Is it really... can it really be...? This cat is a *god?* I feel my face pale. Imaginary flames lick over my skin. I am before one of the Divinities, one of the ruling...

Both the cat and Elrind burst into laughter.

"See what I mean, Elira? Ignore everything he says. Idiot." Elrind strides off without looking back, and I have no choice but to hurry past the talking cat, who clearly *isn't* a Divinity, following in the messenger's wake.

CHAPTER FIFTEEN

Elrind seats me in some sort of antechamber, while a kind aemortal healer drops pipettes of a dark liquid onto my wound. It hisses as it meets bone and sinew, but my pain is overtaken by curiosity as I see a glimpse into the royal throne room at the far end of the antechamber. Their voices ring out across dark-marble flooring.

"If this is Fjaldorn declaring war, then we need to act immediately! I want us to assemble—"

"No one's assembling anything. They got what they—"

"Mother, you can't honestly say we're going to look the other way in the middle of this hostile attack! The creature has fled, and I didn't see either of you joining me in attempting to kill—"

"No one said anything about looking the other way, darling, but we barely have the troops readied," the Queen interrupts. It sounds like her husband and son are at loggerheads—the King and Prince Kaelion. The latter, momentarily, slams the breath from my chest as he sweeps into view. He's just so darned nice to look at.

He's wearing his hunting leathers sans-cloak now, and overlapping tongues of leather fall from his shoulders, lined in veins of stark silver to match his coryns. His bronzed hair is more tousled than it had been last night, as if he's spent all night running his hands through it.

Or *someone else* has spent their night running their hands through it, a part of my mind mutters. It seems likely; he just *reeks* of lothario.

I pull my hand away from the healer, and stand up. I need to get closer. I'm usually the first port of call for the Eryndal mortals to understand kingdom news. If we are under attack by Fjaldorn – a kingdom on the other side of Orynthys – then I need to know.

Elrind has disappeared somewhere, and the healer objects, but accidentally drops her bottle to the floor and has to dive down to retrieve it. My feet move as if possessed, my sandals light on the marble, wolflike, a wave of excitement rolling over me as I get closer to the prince. I conceal myself in the doorway, and swallow down the guilt of eavesdropping as the shadows give me a full view of the room.

It's the grandest place I've ever seen in my life. Black marble flooring, dazzling gold furniture, two huge, ornate thrones. Above it all, a gilt candelabra hangs from a ceiling painted to resemble the night sky, and against one wall, a vast bookcase displays hundreds of leather-bound tomes. And while it's beautiful, I can't ignore the disfigurement of the King and Queen's faces, which capture my attention and don't release it. Each bears a half-face of thick tattoos: winding shapes that twist into forms too intricate to fully comprehend.

What has happened to their faces? I've seen them in pictures, renderings on the walls of various municipal dwellings. But the paintings never showed this. I stand frozen in the doorway, my nerves prickling across every inch of my body. The royals are flustered, their eldest son battle-worn, covered in blood and dust. The Queen raises a trembling hand, rubbing her eyebrows as though trying to knead away a headache. Her tattooed eyebrows, on her tattooed face. Shock has stilled me.

Mother has told me the Queen's story, and it's a brutal one.

Born a Foresight Seer, a specific type of future-seeing Seer, her life was shaped by a cruel fate. Her father, struggling with deprivation, saw her and her Gift as nothing more than a commodity. Even aemortals, with their enhanced abilities, can fall victim to poverty's crushing grip. He believed powers could be inherited—a rumour that spread empire-wide when a Heartseer birthed another Heartseer. It was the first time a Gift had seemingly been passed down through blood, rather than granted by a Divinity during conception.

Seizing on this belief, her father realised her earning potential. A Foresight Seer might birth one of her kind. After her first bleed, he rented the future queen to greedy families, treating her as nothing more than a dam cow, a breeding vessel. Forced into situations she did not consent to, the Queen bore children for nameless fathers, the babies whisked away before her blood and pain could be wiped from the gallipot bed.

When the first child was old enough to show his Gift, nothing happened. The father, having paid a substantial amount of sigils, was furious. There would be no inheritance, no magic. One by one, the fathers demanded their money back from the Queen's father, whose rage consumed him. The non-gifted children—useless to their paying fathers—were killed.

Exhausted from cycles of suffering, the Queen was too far gone to See what was coming. Her Gift flourished only in times of strength. She didn't foresee the beatings from her father until it was too late. Afterwards, she could barely walk. He threw her limp body into the forest, abandoned to the mercy of cruel beasts and darkness.

It was there that the young King found her. His Majesty was thrust into power at fifteen, when his parents decided to attend a small skirmish on the outskirts of Claran, thinking it would be a simple affair. A dispute over mountain coal, of all things, ignited the conflict. But the situation spiralled when a rogue coal trader revealed a newly-born terrian, kept caged since birth. The terrian, a small, violent creature descended from dragons, killed everyone on the battlefield, and in one catastrophic event, the gawky teenage boy back at the palace became King.

Grief swallowed him whole. Trauma froze him. And then, in the midst of his despair, he found the future Queen in the forest. As my mother tells the story, it was love at first sight.

After she had recovered and told him of the men who had paid her father, he ensured that every one of them was slain in the most humiliating way. Public executions. Ripped apart by force. Towed behind horse-drawn carts along the streets. One was hung above the Thealean Sea, left for water creatures to drag him under. Each met a painstakingly slow death. At the Queen's request, the King spared her father. She couldn't bear to see him meet such a fate, even after all he had done. Instead, the man was exiled to the Cecedit Mountains—a place filled with undead creatures and shadows.

I do not make the mistake of thinking the Queen frail or delicate as I study her thin wrists and wispy hair. This woman is a fucking survivor.

"I don't want to be dragged into battle again, brother," Disryn mutters, brushing dust from his front. I hadn't noticed him lounging in a deep chair. "I'm supposed to be revising." Oh, fayte. Here we go. This is why we call Disryn 'Dismal'; he is one of the most arrogant, selfish men alive (or not *alive,* depending on how aemortals view themselves). At least Kaelion gives some semblance of a shit about the fact that creatures are reining murder down upon our city.

"No one's getting in the way of your application, Dis," the Queen sighs.

"We have more important matters than your studies, Disryn," the King chastises.

I struggle to focus on the words of either the Queen or King, given how their faces seem stamped by a malevolent Divinity. While we are afraid of the Sable Legion, and the Legion are afraid of the King and Queen, perhaps our royal overlords answer to the Divinities more than they like us to think.

"Indeed we do," Kaelion thunders, throwing his

hands in the air. "I am alone in my bid to secure this kingdom, it seems. What do Fjaldorn want? Does anyone know, or are we to let them murder every being in Eryndal?"

The king's face reddens, a vein standing out on his forehead. He snarls, "I did not want you to fight alone."

"You did not have to sign the treaty!" Prince Kaelion roars, his face reddening. "We could have found another way. You've exiled yourselves, rendered your position in this kingdom useless—"

"That's quite enough, Kae," his mother snaps. Perhaps it's the use of his nickname, or perhaps it's the sight of her, looking as though she might faint, but he bites his tongue, his thick neck moving as he swallows. I try not to notice the way his mouth moves. This is not the time to admire pretty mouths.

"Believe me when I tell you that you have not asked a single question that we don't torment ourselves with every night," the Queen murmurs, her voice steely. "We stand in our kingdom to protect our people, and yet we cannot step outside these walls without fearing certain death. Often, it feels as if we are already dead."

The Prince exhales, his body shuddering as he forces himself to calm. His thick arms flex as he puts his hands behind his head, fanning out his elbows as if forcing himself to breathe. I notice something tucked into his pocket, the exact shape of a hipflask, and I wonder whether he's been drinking this morning. He has that whole tortured-poet vibe going on.

Elrind coughs, and I jump out of my skin. He'd

been standing right next to me, and I hadn't noticed. The speed with which the immortals' heads snap in our direction in response to his cough is almost comical. Prince Kaelion drops his arms. Dismal sits up fully.

I swallow, my pulse quickening as four sets of penetrating aemortal eyes appraise us. Each of them looks me up and down, glancing first at my tunic, splattered with black blood, then infuriatingly, at my sandals. My regulation-issue postmistress leather sandals—worn for nearly ten cycles. Dismal gasps.

Oh, for fayte's sake.

"Something wrong with my shoes?" I ask.

A stunned silence follows, and into the stillness, Elrind lets out a tiny, barely audible whine—like, *Why'd I bring her here?*

"Yeah, there's something wrong with them, apart from the fact they're hideous." Dismal stands from his chair, tall and slender like a beanpole peacock, his pointed face framed by coryns curled angrily into his dark curls. Multiple necklaces—cords and silver—drape around his neck, and his black hair flops over part of his forehead, tucking behind his ear. His coryns are the darkest of all four, thick, curled black appendages, with only a hint of the silver our land is known for.

"Disryn," the Queen chastises, grabbing her husband's arm. The King places his hand over hers, his gaze fixed on me, his marred face twisting into strange, unreadable expressions.

Kaelion still hasn't said anything. From here, I notice the tanned sheen of his skin, as though the sun itself shimmers in his veins. Thick eyebrows cast shadows over his eyes, arching above his prominent, straight nose, and fluttering down to his chin, which holds a tiny cleft.

Yes, the princes are nice enough to look at, but handsome or not, they are both—famously—arseholes. Arseholes and aemortals, which is reason enough to want them dead.

CHAPTER SIXTEEN

"What's wrong with my sandals?" I growl, dragging my gaze away from the mysteriously fuming Kaelion to focus on his irritating brother. "They're approved sandals, from The Courier's Keep." Once again, my hot-headedness has overtaken my sense. I shouldn't let one annoying man ruin my unexpected conference with the royals.

"They've cut your foot." Dismal raises an eyebrow in that irritatingly superior way. He doesn't recognise me from last night, which says everything about how far his head is up his own arse. "Clearly, you have strange black blood, woman. Are you a begging hag?"

"Am I WHAT?" I explode.

There's a pitcher of water on a dainty table near Disryn. I want to grab it and throw it over him, so badly. Only, water is precious, and the palace gets the real stuff, the clean stuff, and while I might consider attacking a prince, I would never waste a precious resource.

"That black blood," Elrind hastily says, shifting ever so slightly closer to me, his stance almost protective, "is the blood of the silicrite Elira killed."

The Queen shrieks. The King fumbles, dropping her hand. Kaelion's face tightens, muscles rippling under his hunting leathers. There's a glint of interest hidden deep within that amber. I get the impression he hasn't told his family nor the palace security about last night, about our posters and our attempts to flee. Why did he let us go?

"You shouldn't take on a silicrite, girl. Not a mortal, and especially not a little one like you," the King blusters. "We've spent our whole lives training, girl."

Am I imagining it, or do I hear Prince Kaelion let out a low snarl of anger? I must be imagining it.

The King sounds dubious as he continues, "They used silicrites at the end of the war, but they were always shrewd things. Too clever. Too single-minded. Certainly not something for a little mortal like you to attack."

Kaelion's back tightens as he turns to look out through the charmed window, showing a full panorama of the sky and gardens, the city wall beyond. There are no golems nor silicrites soaring through the piercing winter sky. But still, Kaelion doesn't relax.

"I have brought her here in case the silicrite attacked her on purpose," Elrind advises. "Perhaps Elira is what they were seeking. We know why Fjaldorn is attacking—"

"We do not!" booms the King. His tone startles even me, and I move back slightly. "If the King of Fjaldorn thinks a few flying spiders are going to scare us, he's not in his right mind! What does he want then?

What does this king want, apart from our attendance at his nuptials?"

He stares aggressively at Elrind, until the messenger purses his lips, speaking no more. I get the impression that Kaelion and Elrind have discussed Fjaldorn at some point, as the eldest prince does not look surprised by Elrind's motive for bringing me.

"Elira, my darling," the Queen says, stepping forward, her wispy hair ruffling as she moves.

"It is normal to bow to the Queen," Elrind mutters.

I catch a movement in the corner of my eye. Kaelion, the older brother, turns with a whisper of a smirk, and it sends a sharp pang of annoyance through my chest. Still, I know what my mother would say if she heard I'd been granted a private audience with the King and Queen. She'd be horrified if I let my hot-headedness get in the way of my manners.

"Apologies, your majesties," I mutter, bowing for the first time in my life. I straighten up as quickly as I can, aware that my face is burning. Just a mortal bowing to aemortals. Just a fox bowing to hunters.

"Who are your parents, girl?" the King asks, squinting as he looks at me.

"My mother is Liora Corvannis. She and my sister work in my sister's flower shop in the municipal."

"And your father?"

I swallow down the pain at my father being brought up *again*. When I think of him, I think only of betrayal; he left me and never looked back. "A simple merchant. Mother refuses to tell me his name." I don't look at Kaelion. I'm covered in otherworldly blood, my tunic ragged and torn, my hair matted.

"I assume Elrind has really brought you here to ensure your safety after what must have been a harrowing attack," the Queen says politely. "You have your kingdom's thanks for your service."

I stare at her, deciding what to say. Amber eyes prick the corner of my vision, and so I dare to mutter, "I am grateful to your eldest son, for ensuring my safety in the city last night."

Kaelion freezes. I see his jaw grind, the muscle bulging, as if he's deciding how to respond. He finally murmurs, "I was just doing my duty."

The Queen smiles vaguely, as the King lets out a hollow laugh, one that borders on hysteria. "We don't even know who this woman is," he says, to no one in particular. "We need to know if she was targeted, or unlucky. And why does she reek of healing tinctures?"

Kaelion steps away from the window and takes a few strides closer to me, closing the distance somewhat, his eyes fixed on mine again. It's the same look he gave me before, as if he's confused. I feel that same tug in my soul, telling me that he's sorting through the fragments, his amber eyes eating me alive. He towers over me, even as he stops a few metres away, barely visible with the sun behind him.

Is he a Seer?

CHAPTER SEVENTEEN

I glance down at Kaelion's clothes, at the hunting leathers he wears, and notice a rip across his knee that I hadn't seen before. His skin is gashed open.

"You're cut," I say, my mind blank.

"I heal faster than you," he replies quietly. "Is your foot hurt? You shouldn't have gone after a silicrite."

I look back up, distracted by the lines of his jaw, the thickness of his hair, the way the light catches him from behind. A warrior, yes, but also beautiful. I wonder if he thinks himself superior to mortals. Even though the battle that killed the King's parents was over something as trivial as mountain coal, there has never been a war over mortals. We are, as always, side notes in a long history of aemortal greed.

"No," Prince Kaelion suddenly whispers, eyes still hooked on me as I look back at him. "It can't…"

The words still every single person in the room.

"What is it?" the Queen snaps, moving swiftly to

stand in front of her son. "What do you see? What is she?"

Kaelion blinks, stepping back, as if waking from a dream. He doesn't look at me again, but his forehead has gone pale, and I feel a weight settle between us. He sucks in a sharp breath and mutters, "It was nothing to do with the mortal woman."

Liar, my mind screams.

"Then what scares you so?" the Queen asks.

"It was just a daydream." He turns towards the window. Nearby, Elrind has frozen completely. If he's reading my mind, he must be having a raucous time. The man who let me avoid arrest last night keeps staring at me. I am too tired to feel embarrassed about the fact that I've been finding Kaelion seriously hot, and Elrind might be reading that.

"We were attacked, as well," the Queen tells me, her voice taking on a dramatic turn. "They came here, too. It wasn't just Grim—the mortal lands." She licks her lip, a nervous tic. "A child was killed on our own soil."

I breathe in through my nose, trying to steady my nerves. Both Kaelion and Elrind react to her words, their postures tightening. "We should organise a pyre," Elrind mutters.

"I've already requested the Pathseer and the Mancer." Kaelion's voice is thick with emotion. "The girl will have a proper send-off."

"There's been such a lot of tension lately between us and Fjaldorn." The Queen smiles sadly at me, the movement pulling her tattoos into strange shapes.

"They think we have something of theirs, it seems. They are not telling us what, only sending beasts to try and find whatever they feel has been taken."

"How do you... know? That they are searching for something," I croak. My throat aches. I need to go home.

"The king's mate has requested clemency to visit. But she would like to visit alone, and we know nothing of her. We cannot let a stranger into our palace, and she has refused our requests to visit her, with guards. She has said she needs to come here, and upon our last letter, admitted she was planning on finding something in Eryndal."

I blink. I haven't heard about any of this in the news reports I receive at The Courier's Keep. Is it possible that we don't receive everything?

"Utter nonsense," the King huffs. "To attack us without warning, to insinuate we have stolen something. We need to know whether this girl was attacked on purpose," the King demands, of no one in particular, as he gestures towards me. Misery thuds into my stomach, cold and heavy. Of course I wasn't attacked on purpose, and yet both the queen and Dismal are nodding blithely – as if silicrites only attack with reason – while Kaelion remains silent. I open my mouth to protest the king's words, readying myself for another Elrind eye-roll extravaganza, when a blinding flash of light appears.

The entire fayte-imbued window illuminates. The two thrones, pushed against one wall, along with the gold trinkets, lavish paintings, and the beautiful faces of the royal immortals, all gasp in a sudden glow.

A beam of sunlight pricks through the crimson, landing on an ornate table.

"A message from the Divinities," the King whispers, letting go of his wife, who staggers as if she hasn't learned to stand alone.

"But which Divinity?" Kaelion asks. "It is Moir tonight, the Divinity of Wrath."

"Divinities do not need their moon active to provide us with messages, Kae," the Queen murmurs. "It might help, but we are not to question a Divinity's actions. It cannot be Wrath, surely, although the colour…" She takes a step towards the table, where sunlight collects in a ball. I glance towards Elrind, but beyond his feathers, he looks just as stupefied.

The ball of sunlight vanishes, leaving behind…

A quill. It's my turn to step forward. The King makes to stop me, but I move too quickly. I pass Kaelion as I walk, and I can't help but notice his body move as I do, as if we're in a miniature dance.

A blink ago, there was only a table, and now a quill sits atop the wood. A message from beyond. It's the most beautiful thing. Two feathers, one a treacle-like amber, the other a pale cream, form the vane. The shaft gleams in solid, reflective precious metal, flashing in the opulent royal colours of the throne room. I whisper, "It's beautiful."

"When were you born?" someone demands from the belly of the room. I ignore them, unable to tear my gaze away from the perfection of the nib—unused, unstained. The feathers…

"The Divinities gift according to your birthright. SOMEONE TELL ME WHEN THIS WOMAN WAS BORN!" The King's voice ricochets around the walls.

I reach forward, and the whole room seems to hold its breath. My trembling, pale fingers touch the length of the top feather. The colour stirs something deep in my stomach.

It's the colour of thick, liquid amber, shot through with the faintest specks. The exact colour of...

I pull my fingers back quickly, before I'm forced to look at Kaelion's eyes.

"This must be for you," I say, voice hoarse. I don't turn to face him, but I can feel his presence beside me. The scent of cedarwood bonfires washes over me. That's him. Crackling cedar and wild countryside. Passionate nights lying on fragrant gorse, under intense starlight. I turn my head away, shaking off the visions that his smell invokes.

"When were you born, Elira?" he murmurs, voice tight.

"Midnight between two moons." My eyes roam over the second feather. A pale silver, but within the strokes, darker flecks shimmer. "The Divinities of Sun and Power. I change my choice depending upon my mood."

It's a silly thing. There are seven moon cycles, each corresponding to a specific Divinity. There are Divinities of War and Water, Sun, Power, Wrath, Forgiveness, and Earth. There are Lesser Divinities, gods who haven't bestowed much of their power upon our empire of Orynthis. One such Lesser Divinity is the

Divinity of Body, from whom the Flesh-Wielder that Dismal mentioned came.

Barely anyone aligns themselves with Lesser Divinities, given that there are only a few people born between moons, on the rare night that a moon does not grace the night's sky. Only aemortals can be gifted by the Divinity that aligns with the moon they were born beneath; the Flesh-Wielder was born when the Divinity of Body's lesser moon was prominent in the gaps between the seven major moons, and the Queen was granted her Seer Gift when she was born under Somer, the Divinity of Forgiveness owning Seeing.

Despite my doubts, other superstitious mortals align their birth moon with the corresponding Divinity. There are crackpot psychics who create forecasts, and some mortals live their lives by these predictions. I refuse to accept postal matter containing such prophecies. I'm given articles that say things like, "Those born under the God of War should watch out for dirty laundry this moon phase," and I'm expected to nail them to the window shutters.

It's a firm no from both Nerissa and me, even though, as someone born under the Divinity of Forgiveness, she secretly hoards such information. On nights when Somer shines, Nerissa lays out crystals in formation, asking for absolution for her greatest sin. If I'm pushed to engage in one of those prescribed predictions, like at Nerissa's tenth birthday when her parents brought in a haggard psychic, I tend to choose the Divinity of Power, the moon of Lornea present just breaths after my birth.

"You were born between moons," Kaelion

mutters.

I look up at him, and I swear his amber eyes send a genuine thunderbolt straight through me. My forehead tingles with pleasure, an uncontrollable reaction that causes my breath to catch. My stomach stirs, warmth flooding my chest. His eyes are just so deep. I could get lost in them. My breath gasps from my chest, but I look away and it swiftly returns to normal. *Don't be weird, body.*

I take a step backward, trying to regain control.

"So, you don't have a Divinity," Dismal muses. "Guess you might have a different god entirely. Is there a God of Pens? Stationery?" He snorts at his own words. "Maybe the Divinity of Feathers sent us a message to say we should get this mortal girl back to her mud shack."

"Fuck you," I retort instantly.

Elrind groans. The King coughs. And then Kaelion opens his mouth, tilts his head back, and lets out the loudest laugh I've ever heard. His guffaw soon turns into a throaty chuckle as he brings his head back down and looks at me. Really looks at me.

His stupid amber eyes hook me again. I catch myself watching him longer than I should, lingering on the line of his jaw and the strength of the muscles there. I force myself to look away, irritated with my own thoughts, even as I enjoy him laughing. I would enjoy making anyone laugh.

"You heard her, Disryn," Kaelion says, mirthful. "Be silent, for once."

"Got a crush on the girl already, Kae?" Dismal's

tone turns nasty, and I snap my attention back to the quill, my chest becoming ice and fire. "Ready for another exploit? I heard you took two wenches to your bed just last night, brother. Were they not enough for you, that you now seek dirty mortal nectar?"

I can't listen to it. I just can't. I glance towards Kaelion, but for some reason, there's a fucking smirk on his face. His arrogant, exquisite face. My mind reels, but I mask myself in calm and antipathy. Two looks of which I am a master.

"Don't be idiotic," Kaelion says, his tone light. "I was merely enjoying some time at The Howling Cask."

"That tavern is a place for damaged alcoholics," the King spits, suddenly furious. Kaelion only smirks, a look I can see out of my damned peripheral vision. His three-way activities are no concern of mine. My hand already feels better, my palm numb under the power of the healing tincture. I am splattered in black blood and wearing my ugly sandals, and I need to get home.

"Someone, arrest the mortal," the King huffs.

Oh, fayte.

"I'll take her home," Kaelion growls, stepping closer so that I can feel his body heat and smell his delicious, woody scent.

Two wenches? When does a man have time to please two aemortal beauties at once?

"Send the quill to the healers," the Queen instructs. "They might be able to pick apart any fayte imbued into it. If it was a message for Elira, then they will tell us its meaning. Kae, make sure you take note of where she lives, so you can wisp there if they find something."

"We cannot let her *go*! We must lock her in the gaol until we've established whether she holds whatever the silicrites were looking for!" The King is talking to his wife, and I look towards Kaelion, as if challenging him to keep me here. Or lock me in the gaol. I'm still shaking. I'm getting the impression that no one really listens to the king.

The eldest prince rolls his eyes at his own father's theatrics. It seems we are going to ignore the highest power in our land. Rebellion streaks through me like delicious lightning. I feel giddy.

"Come with me," Kaelion instructs before he strides off. He flicks a bracelet out of his sleeve, a simple circle with a few silver coins on, and fiddles with it in one hand as he walks. That familiar scent—cedarwood, bonfires, crackling stars—fills the air, causing me to close my eyes briefly. I snap them back open. Pull yourself together, Elira. One handsome aemortal prince, and you're forgetting everything you believe in.

"Funnily enough," I snap, as I'm forced to hurry to follow him, "I'm not actually a palace dog."

Kaelion drawls over his shoulder: "And here I was, about to tell you to stay off the furniture."

Oh, Divinities.

CHAPTER EIGHTEEN

"Shouldn't you be fighting at the borders?" I ask Kaelion. His hunting leathers stretch across his broad back as he stalks ahead, his every movement radiating warrior strength.

"The attackers are dead. The other borders didn't fall, and we're recuperating the Crow Battalion immediately. I've wisped to the Raven Battalion and rearranged their holding. For now, we are safe. How's your hand?"

"Oh." I hadn't realised he'd noticed my injury. I lift my palm and examine the pink scar, which looks days old already. "Fine, actually." My footsteps scrape lighter as we walk along endless corridors. "I need to get back to The Courier's Keep." It's the best place to check the latest news reports, to make sure that there are no further silicrites on the horizon, unknown to our arrogant royals. After that, I can go home.

"What's your thing with this courier place?" Prince Kaelion screws up his nose as I catch up with him. It makes him look, for a brief moment, almost mortal. And then I see the coryns, silver with a muted glow. "Is it code for something? Are you running some sort of hedonistic fayte-imbued drug ring, calling it 'The Courier's Keep'?"

He looks hopeful. Don't we both. A drugs baroness with inter-realm peddlers and a supply of the Lost Dominion's best exports would suit someone who runs around a palace with a handsome prince.

"No, I mean the actual courier office. Where I work. Sorting post." I let him digest that for a moment, before the question bursts from my lips: "What's happened to their faces?!"

He slows in his walking, and I wonder if I've overstepped the mark. And then he says, his voice laced through with pain, "They made an agreement with the Divinity of War. That's why they have godsburns."

I stare at his bracelet, confused. He flips a linked coin back and forth, his fingers strong, adept. "They have godsburns?"

"The marks on their faces. When an aemortal makes a deal with a Divinity, a god, the Divinity can choose to show that deal however they wish. With the Divinity of War, mine and my father's god, she can be a little... elaborate. Showy." He adds bitterly, "But having a godsburn so prominent on a face is definitely an Orynthys first."

"So they made a deal with a god," I murmur, trying to catch up. "The Divinity of War."

"Right. They... after the war, they were given a choice. Stay inside, and the Divinity of War would let the mortal city survive. Many aemortals wanted rid of mortals, and the goddess knew that. Or, they could continue parading and representing the palace, and watch Grim Municipal burn to the ground."

I blink at him. His parents made a deal to spare the mortals of Eryndal, but as a result, they have to stay inside. Forever. My neck prickles. "They... why would the Divinity make such a deal? What benefit does she have, your parents staying inside?"

"Oh, I think it was the most impossible but reasonable thing the Divinity could think of." He lets out a quiet laugh and looks at the bracelet on his wrist. "Highlight the power of the Divinity, weaken the reputation of the royals, lest we mistake ourselves as the highest power." We've reached a darker hallway, where only a few candles burn.

He moves so quickly that I don't have time to think, nor stop him. One moment, we are striding along, my feet tugging at worn rugs while my mind tries to ignore the fact that I'm in close proximity with one of the most powerful men in Orynthys, and the next–

He has me pinned against the wall. He moves so quickly that he's grabbed my wrists and whirled me backwards before my mind's had a chance to catch up, his fingers strong as they slide up and press against my palms, his eyes travelling down my body and back to my face, his forehead creased. His breath hits my lips. There are barely inches between us, and my heart slams into my throat, as my hands hanker to reach down under my tunic and grab for the letter opener. But I can't fight the prince, can't stab him. And not only because of this stupid *feeling* that seems thick in the air between us, but also because he could probably crush my skull if he wanted to, with no ramifications.

I'm gripped by an overwhelming desire to tilt my chin up and part my lips slightly, to make myself available for him to swoop down and shove his tongue into my mouth, but with a monumental force of effort, I refrain. It doesn't stop him from seeming to read this straight from my mind as his amber eyes bore into mine, his eyes hungry, his face twisted in confusion, his hands effortless against me, even though they hold my entire weight against the wall.

And so I lift my leg, and knee him in the balls. Not hard, not using my entire strength, but enough that he lets go – more's the pity – and falls backwards. Even aemortals have balls, and it was the first thing we were taught in war classes at school: *Gut 'em the easy way first, kids: eyes, face, throat, balls.* I fall from the wall and rock on the spot for a moment, the shadowed corridor pitching up and down as my breathing catches up.

He gasps: "Why d'you do that?"

"Why'd you pin me against the wall?" I hiss, shuddering. I've just hurt an aemortal prince. I *will* be carted to gaol. Ice trembles down my spine.

His eyes sharpen as he mutters, "I was trying to check that my first instinct was right. If there was something possessing you, I was hoping to see it, or at least scare it enough to come forward."

Possessing me. Lightning tears a pathway through my mind, hot, insistent anger that wants me to destroy the prince where he stands, but I swallow it down, just as I always swallow down my hurt, my anger, my anxious brain. I really am courting my own arrest.

"Fool," I hiss, the anger inside me bucking and hissing. It's the way he looks at me as if I'm a beast, a monster, a silicrite, not a decent mortal woman with opal hair and green eyes, with a solid job and a loving family, a woman who – oh, I don't know – is actually a woman and not some fucking possessed *demon*.

We're both panting, and the moment thickens and twists around us, even as I *am* forced to tilt my chin so that I can have a proper look at his face, and he straightens up, not allowing the full emotion of whatever he's thinking to pass into his tight jaw. Want and pain flicker across his eyes as he glances down at my tilted chin, my lips, the expression something that I've *never* seen across the tavern lads' faces when they've looked at me.

"Let's try again, Little Flame." He pulls back, slightly breathless, looking briefly up at the ornate ceiling as if trying to pull himself back together. *Little Flame*; where did that nickname come from? "Get to know each other."

I balk. Clearly, he has a Gift, something beyond just the standard fayte that aemortals are able to use. Gifts are rare, but perhaps it makes sense that a prince holds one, is able to Wield one, whatever it is. While fayte – the aemortal magic – descends from fay and can be used depending upon how much an aemortal holds, if any, this is quite different from having a Gift. From Wielding.

Typical aemortals can create a flame, can

somewhat transfigure objects, can create heat and energy, can mould transformist symbols in the air to do their bidding, but a Gift is a specific, often terrible magic that Gift-holders are able to Wield. This involves something more powerful than typical fayte, something channelled straight from a Divinity, and as such, Gift-holders are far more feared than a typical aemortal.

And the prince might have a Gift.

"Okay, well first question, then. What are you?" I demand, my voice thick in the corridor, tension cutting through everything, so thick it practically chokes me.

"What are *you*?" he counters.

"I-" My forthcoming tirade is broken by heavy footfall, which marches towards us from the way we arrived. Something in my chest pokes at me, annoyed at being interrupted.

"Tell me," the prince suddenly urges, reaching out a hand, a damned huge tanned hand, and almost touching my face, before thinking better of it and letting his arm fall. A strange, rippling feeling dances through my stomach, my midriff, as I lock onto his gaze again, wishing that I had more to tell him than the truth: I am Elira, a postmistress, a woman who has saved fifty sigils for a new house, a woman with a small circle of friends and a few former lovers who lurk in the shady tavern in town.

But I say none of this, because he is looking at me as if I'm someone.

"Prince Kaelion, Your Highness," a rough voice drawls as the first figure appears beside us. Kaelion and I drag our eyes away from each other, adrenaline sparking through my whole body. What the hell is with this prince? It feels as if I'm dancing with the devil, courting something so dangerous it might just get me killed.

Oh, faytes. The man who's so rudely interrupted us is Major General Drystan, widely known to be the biggest arsehole in Orynthys, the head of the Sable Legion, and the father of the aemortal boy that Nerissa had sex with. His oily skin and thin moustache sit beneath a protruding nose and a small forehead, his coryns a dirty, slicked silver that reflects the light from the candle sconces on the walls. He doesn't wear a helmet, even though his cronies who are coming up behind him all wear theirs. This man has more than his fair share of fayte, and I've heard that he can break a backbone in less than a minute, can burn a body by summoning fire straight from the air, can change a soldier into a canyon rat and back again. Rumours that I have never had any intention of exploring, given that I have, thus far in my life, managed to avoid the head of our army, and the man now glowering at me as if he's been sent for my head.

I stabbed one of his soldiers. Divinities, save me now.

"What is it?" Kaelion asks, his voice swelling and resuming the same tone that he used with his father. Powerful, all-encompassing, taking no shit.

"We've been instructed to take the mortal woman home by foot," the Major General barks, other guards now flanking him. "It's deemed risky to wisp the mortal."

"I wisped here," I mutter, but my voice is so low that only Kaelion hears. He flashes his eyes towards me, as if taking the situation in again, and I try to ignore the tiny divot that forms between his eyebrows. Always so confused when it comes to me.

"You should not wisp with her, Your Highness," the Major General advises, as if he can read the prince's protests right from his mind. "It is safer to have our squad escort her."

"Is it really necessary to have an *entire squad* escort me?" I ask, but once again my voice is annoyingly quiet. I can barely hear anyway, over the pounding of my own heart, my palms still fizzing as blood returns to my fingers. *Please, body, don't tell me that you have a crush on a prince*. You and every other bloody woman in Orynthys. Not to mention the fact that he bedded two women just nights ago, his conquests at the aemortal tavern likely known to everyone in the palace.

No, I need a sensible, normal man, perhaps one who sells apples in the centre of Grim Municipal, who likes to read news reports with me, who grows turnips or–

"If anyone touches a single hair on her fucking head," the prince snarls, "then I'll personally tear them limb from limb, and ensure the pieces are burned so far apart from one another that your soul has no hope of passing through Thekla and beyond, and people dare not utter your name in even the most filthy taverns in Orynthys."

Okay, he's thrown me off my daydreams of a handsome turnip grower.

"You are to escort her straight home," the prince snaps, adjusting his leathers. The shape of his hipflask presses against the inner seams, and the bracelet peeks out from under his sleeve. "I need to check the Crow Battalion, and if it is deemed unsafe," he all but rolls his eyes, "to wisp Elira, then I shall heed your advice. Please ensure her family is secure in their dwelling before you return."

"Yes, Your Highness," the Major General barks, stepping forward and reaching for me. I yank my arm away before he can grab it. I'm not going to let any member of the Sable Legion touch me, even if he is ranked more highly than most. There's a moment, just a tiny breath, when I see something dark flash across the Major General's face, but it is soon masked under duty, a feeling I know well. My entire life is duty. "Come now, girl."

The prince starts to stride off, in the direction we were headed, but he glances back at me. Just a fleeting glance—a millisecond that stretches into eternity. As if he wants to remember my face. I stare back, my eyes wide, my body trembling. Something shifts in his expression, and then, without another word, he's gone.

CHAPTER NINETEEN

The air tastes like freedom as we leave the palace doors, the strange green smoke still winding amongst the clouds, a faint fug of fayte-tanged rain clinging to the wind. I breathe out the breath I had been holding as we descend the stone staircase: the Major General, five soldiers, and me.

What a difference a single night has made. Yesterday, I was being chased, perhaps by these very soldiers, threatened with torture in the playrooms at the gaol. Yesterday, I stabbed one of their comrades, leaving him to bleed out on the cobblestones. And yet right now, I am buoyed by a strange sense of power, an infallible feeling that has been bolstered, no doubt, by the way the prince looked at me.

We take a sharp left, stepping along a path that has been hacked through the wildflowers. I suppose the soldiers might know a shortcut of which I am unaware; I would have exited the vast iron gates first and progressed down the hill. My route would have left me open to any kind of airborne attack, and so it's without much trepidation that I allow myself to be led, thinking mostly of those amber eyes, and the strangely marred faces of the King and Queen.

Why did the prince pin me against the wall? Was he hoping to provoke some sort of reaction from a potential... *what* inside me? What on earth is his Gift, that he thinks me to be something more? True, I stabbed a silicrite. And true, I can rewrite post with blood, about the strangest thing that occurs in my neatly organised life. It is not normal for a mortal to be able to use fayte, and yet that is what I smell whenever I dip my quill into an inkwell of blood, pumped from my own body and stored for such an occasion. My obsessive need to do my job correctly—getting out birth announcements, funeral invites, healer instructions— without delay, mixed with a strange smugness that I can do something unusual. We all want to be special, overseen by the Divinities in a way that picks us out from the crowds of other hopeless cases.

Is that what the prince saw? That I am a mortal using aemortal Gifts to my benefit?

"Where are we going?" I think to ask, as the smell of fresh earth rises to meet me. Literally *rises*. As we approach a side door, the earth around us moves, lifting and twisting into shapes in the air. A breath later, it has spun into a vast creature that stands outside the door, gripping the handle. Its body is made entirely of earth, branches protruding from its head, its mouth gaping, tiny shells and stones glinting like piercings. It is a creature made of soil...

A Gift-created monster.

I'm prevented from taking a step back by the guard behind me, who pushes me forward, as the leering creature sways and gurns, reeking of deep soil and decaying rodent. I look around wildly, panic exploding in my chest. The Major General is sweating profusely, grinning through the sweat, fayte crackling from his hands. His eyes glint as I look at him.

"Meet Terragast," the head of the Sable Legion croons, his forehead beading. My brain is struggling to catch up. The Major General has a Gift. He is a Wielder. An Earth-Wielder, born under Shiiy, gifted by the Divinity of Earth.

"Come," the soil-man booms, his voice a deep bellow as he yanks the door open, its iron hinges heavily rusted, its depths the open mouth of a crooked-toothed creature. Stale, dank air hits my face.

"You don't want to know how quickly he can suffocate you if you don't comply, Elira," the Major General snorts. And then he grabs me and shoves me inside the doorway. And that's when my little postmistress brain finally goes: FUCKING RUN. Run, RUN, and don't look back.

FUCK.

FUCK.

FUCK.

Why have I allowed myself to be trapped in this cellar, guards hissing and guffawing in the doorway? It's too late to escape. Two guards stride in with me, and the door slams. I hear the sound of soil splattering as Terragast falls. The guardian of the torture cells, it seems.

It takes a breath for a guard to summon a flame from his fingertip, and the tower room we've entered flickers to life. A staircase winds upwards, and another gapes from the stone floor, slick with a shine. Not blood, please, Divinities, don't be fucking blood. It smells stale, and yet I can hear sounds: metal against metal, a distant scream, the sounds of carts being pushed, muffled instructions barked. We are below the palace gallipot.

"Go," one of the guards urges, pushing me onward, towards the gaping hole that leads to a set of stairs descending into blackness.

Only the stone floor is slippery, my feet struggling to find purchase, and his shove forces my body into a momentum that my footing can't sustain. My sandal slips, and I arc forward. My heart leaps into my throat. I close my eyes. As I fall down the stone staircase into unknown darkness, I curse my own naivety. I have allowed myself to be thrown down here by aemortal guards who have never indicated themselves to be anything but sinister. The prince trusted them. Perhaps he is in on this— the plan to eradicate this rebel protester once and for all.

My body bends, as time slows. Stale, dank air takes its time to wind fingers around my face, pulling me further into its sinister belly. As my head cracks against the stone at the bottom of the staircase, I barely have time to swallow down my own self-hatred before a figure steps in front of me, his boots newly-shined.

CHAPTER TWENTY

"I went to pay your family a visit," he rasps, his voice barely recognisable from the soldier in the alleyway yesterday. There are always ramifications. Always. "But they'd already been taken. Canyon rats will always breed with canyon rats. No doubt your family exhibit the same filthy manner that you do."

"What?" My head is still spinning as if I've consumed too much elven wine, and the two sconces that he's lit on the walls of this underground cellar are forcing moving shapes to dance in menacing patterns through my already blurred vision. I can see his eyebrow ring glinting in the dim light, casting that spliced shadow down one eye. I rasp, "What do you mean, taken?"

It can't be true. Cold shards of ice dance through my chest as I struggle to push myself up, my skull aching where it hit the floor. The other two guards have disappeared outside, their voices fading entirely.

And I am here. Thirty cycles of living the exact

same way, undertaking the exact same moon cycle over and over again, only to have my neat life obliterated in the space of two days. Sweat drips from my forehead. My body is afraid, even if my mind is spiraling through a vortex, probing both sides of my brain for answers. I open my mouth to protest, to ask further questions, to remain in my naivety for a while longer, but I don't get the chance.

Crack.

The underside of his boot meets my cheekbone as he kicks me, slamming his foot into my face, forcing me to fall backwards as stars obliterate my vision. Pain —white-hot pain—jolts through my skull as I scrabble backwards, my spine hitting the cold wall, raw panic clutching at me.

Is my nose broken? Is my cheekbone? Has he shattered my *skull*? I can't see, spots of pain overtaking my vision, clawing at the front of my eyeballs.

"You know," the guard gasps for breath. Is he still recovering from yesterday? He places a hand across his midriff, where his armour gapes apart. "I wondered why a little postmistress was carrying around dangerous weapons."

"In case beasts attack," I gasp, reaching up to touch my wet face. Tears mix with snot, with the bile that dribbles from my split lips. My whole body aches, even as it pounds with the message – *stupid, stupid Elira* – and my tongue is swollen as I say, "Silver works on beasts." I can't have him suspecting me of treasonous plans, carrying knives to slay the royals.

Not that it matters what he thinks, given I'm

clearly about to die. In this dank cellar, underneath the very palace that is supposed to protect the people of Eryndal. The irony hits hard, tastes rank, blinds me. I've only lived for thirty cycles. Even my uncle, murdered by this corrupt Legion, lived longer.

"No beasts have attacked in many moon cycles." He cocks his head to one side, his form a huge shadow in the candlelight. I could try to make a run for it, escape up the stairs, but the Major General is on the other side of the door. He will only send me back down, or slay me, perhaps hike my body up on a spike to warn other rebel protesters, as has been done before. I can't let my mother and Seren find me like that.

I swipe again at my wet cheeks, as he saunters forward, his thick boots almost silent on the stone floor. He lifts his hands, and a glowing ball appears between his palms, a roiling circle of energy. I choke on my own mucus as I scurry back, pure animal instinct taking over, horror pulsing through me, even as something else in my body reacts to the Wielding, something that hums and sings in equal measure, that takes hold of my jaw and eases the pain in my cheekbones, that thrums along my ribcage and grasps at my heart.

"What are you going to do to me?" I hiss, my fingernails scrambling for purchase on the stone floor, as I move like a cornered cat into the depths of the cell, a hot tear trickling down my cheek. "Burn me? Set me alight?"

"I might." He drops one arm and lets the fayte hang, illuminating his wretched, wicked face. As he leans forward, and I catch a glimpse of his eyes, something seems to come loose inside him, his eyes becoming unfocused, deranged. "Or I might force you to ingest it, watch as it burns you from the inside. Your eyeballs will be the last things to flame." He leers over me. He is no longer interested in me as a sexual plaything, a maiden to debase so that he can feel powerful. No, that galley has passed. Now, I am nothing more than an animal to be wounded, a prick against his pride.

He throws.

I pounce out of the way, but his wretched ball of magic still finds me, burning my skin instantly, as if he's thrown a pot of boiling stew across my body. I scream as it blisters, heating and rolling through me, sending white-hot shards through my brain, my skull, down my spine. I gasp for breath and taste it on my tongue: metallic, thick, fierce. I reach out to try and cling to the stone, to find something, anything, to hold onto, but still pain roils through me, agony and a strange, twisted voice—a voice that can only be that of a Divinity—as it laughs and laughs, a sound that beats into my ears and gnaws at my neck.

Only, my throat is aching, pulsing, burning. The laughter is coming from me. That cruel, ancient cackling is coming from my gullet, leaving my lips as if my lungs are being squeezed, and as I open my eyes, I see brilliant shards of gold beaming from my body, hitting the walls and the guard so brightly that I can barely see. A streak of silver light, like a cat running for freedom, darts at the corner of my vision, as the guard screams in a different way.

He has fallen onto his back, grasping at the gold beams, which seem to be scratching and clawing at his flesh. As I watch, a gold curl, a coiled finger, ekes out a gouge in his cheek, peeling it back until fresh, crimson blood flows down his face and pools in the stubbled groove of his neck. The glowing coil lifts the blood, siphoning it from his body as if the very air is being controlled, multiple golden arms travelling of their own accord, swords of sunlight that highlight every algae-covered stone, every telling bloodstain on the floor from former murders down here in the depths of hell.

Two things happen in quick succession:

One, I hear a raging snarl from the doorway above, a sound so raw and animalistic that it stabs every hair on my body until they stand on end, and

Two, the golden fayte disappears from the air, leaving me panting and gasping, and the guard sobbing and swearing.

The prince makes quick work of throwing himself down the stairs, and then Kaelion fills the gap between the cell and the path to freedom, his face murderous, his own chest gasping as he takes in the scene. He can no longer see the golden fayte that broke from my body, no longer hear that terrible laughter that clutched at my throat. He can only see me, face sodden, nose almost definitely broken, clinging to the shadows of the cell, as the guard pushes himself up to seated, his eyebrow ring dripping blood.

Kaelion lets out another snarl as he whips one hand into the air, sketching transformist symbols so quickly that I don't have time to even try and decipher one from another. And then he rains them down on the guard, the fayte hurtling from his hand into a net around the soldier, a brilliant, blinding net.

"I didn't need saving," I gasp, ungratefully, as I clutch at my own throat, fucking freaked out from the laughter that had burst from it. Is the prince right? Have I been possessed? Was that a Divinity, or worse, gasping from my throat? If they were, were they saving me? It seems that I'm unharmed, my body now rippling with adrenaline but not weighed down by pain. Was the golden light that filled the air my own fayte, bursting from something inside me? And if so, am I right in thinking that I could've saved my own arse anyway, without Prince Fucking Kaelion saving me a second time?

"That may be the case," Kaelion growls, not ripping his eyes from the guard, who seems to be dissolving under the net of pure fayte. "I would rather the Sable Legion don't harm a single fucking opal-coloured hair on your head. Not in any land that I live in, and not under any single Divinity that I plan to align with."

I pant into the silence. Regroup my thoughts. My heart beats thickly, sluggishly in my chest as I stagger to my feet, his words making me feel strange, digging holes in the walls I've formed to keep everyone out. My face prickles, the muscles in my jaw seeming to come alive again, my chest lighting up from within.

"What does that…" I'm not quite sure what to say. And so I say, as the guard's skin starts to blister and boil, "Are they still outside?"

"Who?" He breaks his focus away from the guard for a single half-breath, and it's long enough for the fayte to collapse away from the soldier's body. The guard starts gasping for air again, even as his skin is wretched and marked, boiled and burned. Kaelion looks, suddenly, furious. "Who was upstairs?"

"The Major General," I gasp. "And his squad. The ones who were supposed to take me home."

"The Major General was in on your *torture*," the prince snarls, eyes wild, face slick with sweat. Fayte is finite, and it can use up an aemortal's energy. To even have enough to render the guard the way he is says everything about Kaelion's prowess as a magic Wielder, but the way his chest rises and falls as he pants says everything, in my opinion, about him as a ruler. If the aemortals and royalty look down on mortals, force us to live in such conditions, then it seems that Kaelion disagrees.

"He said my mother and sister had been taken," I choke, the words slapping against the inside of my skull as they come back to me. It can't be true. It was a lie to throw me off, to distract me while the guard planned all of the terrible things that he was going to do. "I need to get home. I need to check they're okay." I stagger forward, even as I remember what the prince was supposed to be doing instead of coming to save my pathetic mortal arse. "Is the Crow Battalion okay? You were supposed to be checking it, right? Are we secure?"

The guard groans and gasps, reaching out one hand as if he's trying to clutch an apparition in the air, while the prince *looks* at me. Properly looks, at my matted hair, my broken face, my shaking body.

"I'll go to your house," he says, sounding, for

the first time, unnerved. His shoulders fall as he steps forward, closing the distance between us. A wave of cedarwood washes over me as he reaches forward and straightens my tunic, his hands hot against the fabric, my neck. I can only imagine what I look like. He swallows, and I try to ignore the way his throat swells and declines, the way he's struggling to align his own thoughts. "I'm sure they haven't been taken, but I'll check. Rotten guards will lie, cheat, steal. He was probably just trying to unnerve you."

The same way I'm unnerved as I look up at his face, his amber eyes shining in the glow from the sconces. Why does he even care that I've been taken down here? I deserve punishment; I stabbed a guard, I helped create anti-royalty posters. Why is he offering such mercy, such forgiveness, to a random woman that he's only met again because I had the misfortune of stumbling across a silicrite?

"I'm coming," I say, without hesitation. "I need to go home."

"I don't know if it's safe. I don't know that there aren't more silicrites in the city, Elira. It would be irresponsible to take you with me."

There's something in that word, something that causes a flicker of energy to stroke itself against my ribcage, that sends a similar look through his eyes. *Irresponsible.*

Like an aemortal and a mortal.

"I'm coming," I repeat, voice firm. A shadow of respect flashes across his face, and he nods, his eyes dark in the flames from the sconces. I glance down at the guard on the floor as he lets out yet another whine, the pleading note of a broken instrument, grating across my presence. No doubt the palace gallipot will stitch him up for a second time.

Actually.

Fuck that.

"Do you have a knife?" I demand, looking about the prince's person. How I manage to continue skimming my eyes without latching onto a single impressive part of him is testament only to the urgency of the situation.

"Sure." His eyes are hard as granite as he lifts his hand, drawing fayte into the air, until a silver blade shines from his palm. Wordlessly, he hands me the dagger, the solid black hilt cold against my new scar.

"You're not going to try and stop me?" I ask, glancing down at the guard. He's realised what's coming and started moving backward and whimpering. Just like I was doing before, a cornered cat in a locked cell, at the mercy of the bully with the weapons.

"You're a strong woman, Elira." Kaelion almost shrugs, but there's a tension beneath his leather armour. "I'll support whatever you need to do."

I wipe my face again, all too aware that I'm still wearing my filthy tunic, and now I have bile matted in my hair. The next time I see the prince, I *will* be wearing something that doesn't scream *I just spent a year living in the forest and eating swamp bugs*.

I look down at the Sable Legion guard, his helmet rolled off in a shadow somewhere. He snarls at me and spits at my feet as I step forward. It's one thing knowing that he will try to find me again and again until I'm dead. It's a whole other thing knowing that he went to my family dwelling. The point where he made my family his target is the point he really fucking pissed me off. He's sealed his own fate.

After I've covered myself in the guard's hot, red blood, after the prince has set fire to the body and performed the ritual to send the dead guard's soul through Thekla, Kaelion holds out his hand. Wordlessly, I grab onto it, my blood-covered fingers sliding between his warm, calloused digits.

And we wisp.

CHAPTER TWENTY-ONE

We're in my domain. The central alleyway of Grim Municipal, Old King Alley, near The Dwarven Bombard, the bank, the butchers, Quiet Street. And there is life! People have started to re-emerge from their homes, window shutters thrown open, the sizzling smell of fresh oilcake wafting from a bakery, chatter filling the air. I see one of the bank workers that I often talk to on our lunch breaks, and I wave at him, but his eyes widen as he stumbles backward and disappears into a doorway.

Well, that's one way to be told that I look like shit.

An apple cart pusher sees us in the middle of the alleyway, the prince and I, and immediately turns his cart in another direction, fear flitting through his eyes. An older woman, who I recognize as the city gossip, sticks her head out of the nearby hair salon window, and her face sparks with delight. This will be something to talk about at the next dancehall meet-up.

"Everyone's back outside," I croak, my throat

suddenly dry. It is discombobulating, standing here with the prince, being stared at by my friends and city denizens. I wonder if anyone has heard about the silicrite, or if the Sable Legion managed to clean up that mess before everyone started re-emerging. This city is a place of not asking questions, of moving on or drowning, of not questioning why their local postmistress is covered in her own snot, standing dishevelled beside the next in line to the throne.

I feel hot and sticky and wish the damned wind from the green smoke might make a reappearance. A cool breeze sounds heavenly right now, given I can feel the guard's blood on my wrists. I won't feel guilty for defending my family.

"Time moves quickly," the prince murmurs. "The warning is over; people will get on with their lives."

"You mean, time moves quickly for mortals," I mutter, as I start to walk. The prince deftly strides to catch up, his footsteps heavy on the cobbles. He's stuck his hands in his pockets, as if he feels awkward. "Our lifetimes are nothing to someone like you." It's a bizarre thing to be angry about. He can't control mortal lifetimes, can't begin to take responsibility for the split between mortals and aemortals. If it seems unfair that I'll be dead long before the prince has even started to age properly, it's really not his fault. And yet, it seems like an easy way to deal with all this emotion tearing through me: turn it into anger.

"Why'd you wisp us here?" I rasp, swallowing as his step falls alongside mine.

"I don't know where you live."

The city chugs on around us. People hurry to work, while others scrub the cobbles outside their stores, light their ovens, and send spirals of fire smoke into the smoggy air. If my mother and sister had been taken, the clockwork of this city would not have started ticking again. It was just the guard, messing with my mind.

"The Map of the Monarchy has been stolen," the prince mutters. We continue to walk, and I continue to ignore the stares and outwardly gaping mouths that surround us. As we pass a tavern, I smell frothy mead and peanuts. I can only imagine what'll be said in the Bombard tonight: Elira Corvannis has been dallying with the Crown Prince!

"Isn't that strange?" Kaelion continues, as I prickle, a multitude of feelings working their way through me. "It's almost impossible to break into the Solthera vaults. I know the King of Solthera, he's one of the cleverest men in Orynthys. Those vaults would have been spelled beyond anything we can even imagine here, impossible to crack. I don't get it."

He sounds as if he's discussing the weather, and yet there's a steeliness, a challenge beneath his words. And, I suppose, he has come to the right woman, because I have read and remembered every single news report I've ever received. We are lucky enough to get encyclopaedic knowledge of key Orynthys artifacts at The Courier's Keep, just in case stolen goods ever get shipped through our networks, and so it is with a gratifying sense of distraction that I humour him. And show off, just a little bit.

"It's unusual to have stolen the map," I agree,

as we leave the last alleyway. The Heartlands rise ahead, greener and fresher than the dire network of smoggy arteries we've left behind. "The libraries and vaults of Solthera house far more interesting artifacts. The original elven tapestries, an ancient Guide to the Divinities, some heretic anti-monarchy emblems."

I try to keep my voice normal. Never mind the fact that Nerissa and I have studied images of the emblems created during the war to protest monarchy rule, carved by Archon supporters with a hatred of blood-based rule. My mother has a banned copy of *The History of Archons*, which she keeps under a loose board in the outhouse. As a child, I would read the well-worn pages, spurring me to question everything. Equally, the detail the book gives about our own questionable Archon, a ruler who oversaw the Temporal Bastion with a slightly psychopathic ruling style, makes the argument *for* monarchy rule as well. There are songs written about him, which are also banned, and so they are known word-for-word by every child in Eryndal.

"The very fact that thieves have chosen to steal the map, rather than anything else..." the prince starts.

"Means that someone, somewhere, is probably trying to contest the monarchy," I add, as we arrive at the first Heartland houses, shacks with tin roofs and colourful gardens, laundry lines rehung after the smoke warning, rock-battered washing hung by wooden pegs. Long grasses whisper either side of the golden-brown dirt track we progress along. "Why are you mentioning it? Do you think it has something to do with the attack?"

I glance at him, and that is my first mistake. Because I can see it. Beneath the gritted jaw, the shadow of stubble, the innocence in his amber eyes, is something darker. Something worried. I stop walking, and he's forced to do the same. I wait until he's turned fully to me, before asking, "What is it?"

"It's not for me to bother you with." He smiles, but it doesn't reach his eyes. And I wonder... is there a chance that Kaelion has been as lonely as I? Perhaps, as a prince, it's hard to find people to open up to. Everyone expects him to be brave, to hold his shit together. He might be even lonelier than I was. Am. Whatever.

"Bother me," I demand, closing the distance between us and looking up at him. I give him my sternest postmistress look, the look I'm forced to give when someone's trying to post firearms to their irresponsible friend.

"I can't... do you know what the Map of the Monarchy is?" He looks around, but everyone is either in their houses or working in the city. The golden dirt track is empty.

"Yes." I scan my memory, tattered scroll after tattered scroll leaping into my mind's eye. "It's the only artefact in Orynthys that's been blessed by all seven major Divinities, right? It shows the monarchy of each land, who's in charge and the rightful heirs. It's always changing, or at least it changes when someone dies."

"Right," he agrees. And then he sighs, clenching his jaw. "The thing is... See, the thing is... I really shouldn't be telling you this."

I don't ask him why he is. My guess is that I'm a mortal; I'll probably be dead, my natural lifetime expired, by the time the map is found. I am an easy confidante for him, and I don't make the mistake of thinking that it is anything more. And so I encourage, "I hear top-secret news reports every morning, Kae. Just tell me what's on your mind."

His eyes find mine, and start to burn into my soul, as they are wont to do. Something inside me has calmed, my instant response to someone in need, and I wait, as various feelings rise and travel across his troubled face.

"My father... he struggled with his virility," Kae whispers, his gaze locked on mine. I swallow. "And so they brought in someone else. Someone who was able to... help. The king is not my biological father."

Holy shit.

I don't move a single muscle on my face.

"They didn't tell anyone." He looks around again, then brings his focus back to me. He lowers his voice even further. "No one knows apart from our family, Elrind and Tryx. That's it. And the King of Solthera, but he's a decent guy. Wouldn't have told anyone. Anyway, after that my parents were happy; they had their heir. And then Disryn arrived, naturally, with no struggles at all, and the true heir was born."

Holy fucking shit.

I do not move a single damn muscle.

"They couldn't say anything. Not when it's widely known that I'm heir. And that's the way it's always been, I've been trained from childhood, they've created an heir that everyone expects to run Eryndal if my parents are destroyed. But the Map of the Monarchy..."

"Shows Disryn as the heir to this kingdom," I whisper. Our didactic laws mean that Disryn would overtake Kaelion to the throne, given his parents are the natural king and queen, rather than just the queen.

"Yes," he says, his voice low and husky. He slips his hand into the inside of his jacket, and my mind struggles to catch up as he pulls a hip flask out, flicks the lid off, and takes a swig. "Gah," he breathes. He proffers it to me. The dangerous scent of araq, the dodgy local spirit, burns my nostrils as I shake my head, confused. This is not the time to fall apart and get drunk.

"What happened to your, umm, birth father?" I ask, trying to ignore the way he slips the hip flask back into his inside jacket, all so quickly that I question whether it happened. His lower lip shines, and I suppress an urge to lean forward and bite it.

"The king ordered his execution, as soon as I was born." Kaelion's face doesn't betray a single emotion, and yet I swear the glimmer dies from his eyes. "He is no longer here."

"I'm so sorry." I reach out and touch a finger to the front of his leathers, right in the centre of his chest. My hand is shaking, my nail dirty, and yet he lets out a relieved sigh, as if I've given him permission to let go of the tension. "I can't imagine what it must be like to know your father had your biological father killed. And to know that if the map is found..."

"If the map is found, Disryn will be king. Something he does not want to happen, nor I. My parents will be furious, my– my father had forgotten the map, until he learned of a deal made to keep it under lock and spell in Solthera's vaults, only accessible by the King of Solthera."

"And you think that's why silicrites have attacked? Because someone's seen the map?"

"I don't know," he admits, still looking down at my finger on his chest. "But it seems like interesting timing."

"I have to check on my family," I murmur, knowing that I'm breaking the moment. If anyone is looking out of their windows right now, they must be throwing a gossip party. Their postmistress with her hand on the eldest prince.

Kaelion immediately snaps out of his vulnerability and steps away, yanking his shoulders back and looking around, as if checking for enemy danger. "Yes, let's go," he says, all business again. He starts to stride up the hill, and I follow, my mind whirring.

"I warn you, my house is nothing special. It's not like... it's not a palace." Something hot is humming through me. I refuse to recognise it as shame.

"The palace is a community building, Elira. Nothing more. It's not my house, it's a place for anyone in Eryndal to visit, stay, heal, whatever they need." His voice is calm and controlled. "Don't get me wrong, it's a nice place to live. You'd... anyone would like living there. There's lots of privacy."

Wait, what?

"I'm just going to level with you," the prince says, taking a deep breath in as we walk. We pass more houses, and people's faces appear in open windows and doorways, watching. Someone smiles and waves at me, and I can't stop a sheepish grin from coiling upon my lips. "I want to be honest with you. I feel like... I don't know, there's just this thing here."

What thing? Is he referring to the strange feeling that prickles up my spine whenever I catch a scent of that damned delicious cedarwood? As he looks at me, the magnificent prince striding along the Heartlands dirt track, my chest flips a beat.

"I do have a Gift, Elira. A strange Gift, one that allows me to see Gifts."

"You're a Giftseer," I whisper. He can see Gifts in other people, can see where a Divinity has granted power. Which means...

"You saw something when you looked at me?" I demand, my neck prickling. "Did you see a Gift?"

"I did," he murmurs, his voice low, his eyes helpless. "But it can't be. It must be a mistake. Mortals aren't gifted. Unless..."

"I'm not mortal," I finish, my lips turning numb. My heart thuds along in my strange chest. Mother fed me wolfsbane at birth, and Kaelion thinks I've a Gift. "The Divinity of Forgiveness births Seers," I say, my brain catching up. "And you were famously born under the Divinity of War. You shouldn't be a Giftseer, you should be a Destroyer, someone who can tear down bridges, blow up cliffs, or else another one of War's whimsies."

He screws up his face. "I don't have time to..." His voice trails off.

"Have time to what?" I prompt, my heart starting to thud in my chest. I knew it, I fucking knew it. I'm weird. Strange. I have a Gift. And it can't be merely a parlour trick, not if he's reacting this badly to having to tell me. He wants to be honest with me. Open. Why—

"FUCK," he suddenly snarls, as he continues to squint. As if he can see something over my shoulder. Something that I haven't noticed yet, something that my mortal eyes, not as strong as his aemortal vision, didn't see as we lumbered up here. He lunges forward and grabs my hand, and we wisp the remaining fifty paces to my family's front door.

The one hanging loose on its hinges.

CHAPTER TWENTY-TWO

I exhaust myself searching.

Every day, after a quick breakfast with Nerissa, I tackle another section of Grim Municipal. I find Seren's house empty and head to Isolde's family home instead. Isolde knows nothing, and she's too frightened to open her window shutters. From behind the wood, she shouts that she and Seren had a row about the Crow Battalions' warning, and she believes Seren has fled in a fit of rage. Perhaps Mother followed her. Perhaps that's why they are both missing, their house covered in blood.

Blood. It was everywhere, across every surface. When I stumbled into my mother's house, I opened my mouth, and the low, guttural scream that echoed from my body, tearing into every fibre of my being, causing the scarves that dangled from the ceiling to waver and tremble, scared even me.

I visit the fields where Seren and Mother flower-picked. The workers, framed by vibrant pinks and heady purples, have no news. I visit the early morning flower market, swirling pollen in the first light of day, but there's nothing.

I trudge through sewage-slicked slums, checking under boards, searching the pale, frightened faces for a flash of red hair or a heavily pierced lip. Everywhere in the slums, there are mortals with missing limbs, appendages lopped off as punishment for stealing, smuggling, attempting to break into another land. I check areas where repeated ordinances have forbidden the construction of new dwellings, where fields merge into farms, and tenements give way to a hive of industry — thick with tanneries, slaughterhouses, breweries, foundries.

I scour the banking district, a cacophony of gambling brokers rolling dice, aristocrats counting sigils, dubious signs promising life-changing savings accounts. I pass by oyster carts, hatters, silk-weavers, and a fortune-teller, the last of whom declares, in a voice dripping with doom, that my death is near.

I interrupt lawn bowling tournaments, dancehalls filled with twirling ladies in elaborate dresses, rowdy taverns filled with drinkers and singers, and the sex district, where workers call out illicit offers. I remember the Sable Legion guard, the one we killed, who always carried the contraceptive elixir when passing Muriel's. I remember Kae, and I push the thoughts of him far, far away, where guilt can't tear them into dirty rags.

I break into a card game at an underground saloon my sister used to frequent, only to be swiftly thrown out. I pay to enter a playhouse during an evening comedy performance, standing on stage and shouting Seren's name to the crowd. I steal a dinghy and sail down the bleak, murky Rotgut River, scanning the mudlark-filled banks for a glimpse of her vivid hair. Children play, screeching loudly near sewers that overflow and steam. And yet, I find nothing.

Vallorn, a Sable Legion guard, is stationed outside of Nerissa's house, where I'm staying, but he has no news. Eventually, after a week, he tells me to stop searching. I've already angered the underground saloon and been physically thrown from the playhouse. I've flirted with arrest by stealing a boat. I'm lucky to still have both hands.

When Kaelion tries to visit, I don't invite him in. I can't; I'm too engulfed by guilt. I should have been there.

And then he sends a message via Vallorn that shatters any semblance I had of holding myself together. It invokes such fury that I almost tear Nerissa's futon apart.

"He wants you to know he might be able to find out where they are, but first he needs you to do something for him," Vallorn says, from the doorway, as Nerissa and I huddle under her blanket.

"What?" my best friend and I ask in unison.

"He said... he needs you to steal something. For him. And then he'll, umm, maybe say where your family are." Vallorn trembles. As well he ought.

It is Nerissa that replies, my tongue too stilled by shock to pay heed to such ridiculous blackmail. She snarls, "You can tell *the prince* that any information he has on Liora or Seren's whereabouts should be shared immediately, and should not come with blackmail. If I find out that your lot have anything to do with them being missing, I will slice your testicles from your body without mercy."

Vallorn stands in the doorway until I sigh and force myself off the futon. It is all very well being hot-headed, but not if it risks losing much-needed information. I stumble into the main room in Nerissa's shack, where a fire smoulders and crackles from a grate in the midst of the Zephyrs' clutter, baubles and trinkets on every available surface.

And holy Divinities, if the sight of the prince leaning casually against the outer doorway doesn't send a dart straight through my chest. It should be illegal to look like that, all thunderous eyes, tanned skin, glowing coryns. He scans my body, and then looks relieved, even as I purse my lips. I wish I'd thought to throw something over the nightgown I've borrowed from Nerissa.

But no matter. It seems he's ready to blackmail me, no matter what I wear.

CHAPTER TWENTY-THREE

"Yes?" I ask, my eyes already a challenge. I ignore the way he looks me up and down, the slight lift in his eyebrow, the new gleam in his eyes. I ignore it all. "Tell me, then. You have information about my mother and sister?"

"I didn't say that."

"You did," I mutter. My throat aches as I speak, but I force myself to focus. I inhale deeply through my nostrils, trying to steady my breath, my pulse, even as the ache in my side pokes at me—reminding me of my own mortal fragility. I miss the sorting room. I miss the smell of fresh wax and paper. I miss the simplicity of gossiping with Nerissa over lunch, laughing about customers, or the strange things that find their way into the post.

"What are you thinking?" Kaelion asks, his voice dropping to a low, dangerous pitch.

I *can't* tell him I'm thinking about post. He

already thinks I'm running some kind of saucy criminal operation, because no one could possibly love couriering this much. My heart hammers in my throat, my body humming with adrenaline. The temptation to blur my thoughts, to focus on anything but him, is overwhelming.

"How best to kill you."

He laughs. Actually laughs. What kind of messed-up relationship is this? "If you're agreeing to help me—" He trails off, clearly waiting for something.

"I'm not agreeing to anything."

He looks at me, his eyes catching the flicker of firelight, his expression unreadable. "So, it's a no?"

"I'm not going to steal just to get information." My words are steady despite the trembling in my chest. I don't need him to spin me some half-hearted story about my family. I don't need to risk my life just to be misled by some charming, conniving aemortal.

"Fine, well if you—" He starts again, but I cut him off:

"What did you want me to steal?" Curiosity pushes through despite myself. I don't intend to risk execution, but the question burns. I need to know what the price is for my family's lives.

He studies me carefully, and mutters, "I want you to cross the wall—"

"To the palace?" I interrupt.

"No," he breathes, raising an eyebrow. "The other wall."

I freeze, my breath catching in my throat. "The one behind the aemortal towns?" I ask, dread twisting in my gut. I already know where this is going.

"The one that leads to—"

"Xandryll," I finish, voice tight. My pulse quickens. Mortals have had their hands cut off for trying to break into Xandryll, planning to forage the forests for herbs. The land that neighbours us is a place of pure wilderness, cabins and weaponry, locals with strong opinions—the first ones to suggest that mortals should be shipped to one contained island—and their own terrifying army.

"Xandryll," he confirms, leaning forward, that same intensity in his gaze. The air between us crackles, tension thickening as his words hang in the room like smoke.

"Why would you want me to break into Xandryll?" I ask, humouring his ridiculous request, but the reality of it burns into me. I know the borders well —no mortal can cross them easily, and Xandryll? It's not just a town; it's a heavily warded land that only the privileged or the insane dare try and enter. Not to mention the dangerous creatures lurking within the forests that clutch its borders.

"To forage something for me, from the Ancient Forest," he answers simply, as if it's the most casual request in the world.

"Oh, wonderful. So after presumably surviving the dangers of your aemortal town and the menacing patrols of the Sable Legions at the borders, I'm to venture into the famously dangerous forest of nightmares?" I force out the words, every syllable thick with sarcasm.

Kaelion doesn't even flinch. His eyes are steady, intense, as if he's calculating the weight of my words against his own secret plans.

"And what exactly is it you are so desperate to forage, that you would risk killing me, when you went to all the bother of saving me before?" I ask, making my tone as sharp as possible, trying to push him, to get him to crack—anything, to gain some control in this ridiculous mess.

His response catches me off guard. "I would like you to forage me some wolfsbane."

"Wolfsbane." Cold shudders through me. Kaelion doesn't look away, doesn't waver, his gaze calm, patient. He looks at me as if we're equals. He looks at me as if he knows something I don't. The look frightens me more than I want to admit.

"Wolfsbane," I repeat, the word rattling from my lips.

CHAPTER TWENTY-FOUR

The prince left quickly after I turned him down. I pointed out that he should give me any information he has regardless, that I shouldn't have to steal to be handed what he knows. Information is not a privilege, it's a *need* in my situation. And I might have told him to go fuck himself, as well.

Oops.

The great clock in the sky continues gasping on as my sister and mother remain missing. Under powerful moons, the nightmares come. Seven-foot-high creatures with spindly, clicking legs. Kings with ruined faces. Queens with trembling hands. Royalty seething with rage, their fury palpable, and the messenger who can taste it in the air. Blinkered servants with shadowed eyes. Talking cats who lurk in dark hallways. And a blackmailing prince with a tanned jaw and amber eyes, vast shoulders, a gaze that doesn't relent.

I wake, and feel like an empty vessel, drained and

rendered useless.

The beasts must have taken Mother and Seren.

Nerissa stops waking me after three nights of screaming. She moves into the kitchen, sleeping on a straw futon beside the wood-fired oven. She boils coffee on the stove and cooks elaborate treats: candied pumpkin sorbet with pecan brittle, smoked mushrooms with celeriac butter, fired ribs with grilled apple peel. I eat each offering with gratitude, my aching body remembering all the ways that I need to repay her, when life is back to normal.

One morning, she lights the oven for breakfast, and I catch the scent of burning cedarwood.

It makes me feel lighter.

The Dwarven Bombard is packed. The tables are full, spilling over with groups of locals laughing over mugs of frothy ale, others with solitary figures hunched over their drinks, lost in thought. The fire crackles merrily in the corner, and a group of musicians strums a lively tune near the bar, lutes held aloft behind fuggy trails from clay pipes. Dwarves sit at the bar discussing deep matters over pints of brambleale, their thick beards brushing the nut-covered flagstone floor. Above, vast tusks of creatures too ancient to name line the walls, flanked by medallions and leather necklaces. Tobacciana is displayed beneath these beasts, carved pipes and ceramic ashtrays, dug up from pre-war Orynthys, borrowed during the occasional lock-in.

I recognise a handful of the faces here—locals, some of whom have frequented The Courier's Keep.

A few wave at me with familiar smiles, but there's something about their greetings now. Sympathy weighs down their mouths, heavy as stone. Death is a regular visitor in Grim Municipal, but potential-death-by-silicrite is not, and so I earn additional concern from the useless gazes that are offered my way without me requesting them. Sympathy is nothing more than passive-aggressive gratitude that they are not in the same position.

And I refuse to believe that my family are dead.

I catch sight of a shady group gathered at a corner table. They're unmistakable—anti-royalists, a group of disgruntled workers who despise the aemortals and the royals as much as they love to hate. They gather here, plotting and colluding in their corner, their stance more aggressive than our friendly protests at summer fayres.

A large group makes way, pushing aside a small table for us. I turn to thank them, but they've already resumed their conversation, our presence forgotten. My fingers twitch with the desire to hold something in my hands, something that might help ground me. A sword, perhaps.

"So, I got some Claran syrup yesterday," Nerissa sighs, waving towards Chuck, the dwarven barman, who knows our order. "It was vile."

"Of course it was," I agree, leaning back in my seat. "That's why they feed it to our infants. Fatten them up. You need Cecedit Mountain honey, that's the real stuff."

Chuck sets our drinks down, and my brambleale sloshes over the sides of the tankard.

My week at Nerissa's has changed me. My innocent, organised personality has been ripped away, just like my mother and sister. I've been lied to about the wolfsbane. I've been blackmailed, asked to steal from another land in exchange for information that should be rightfully mine. My soul feels gritty from deception and extortion. I sweep up my tankard and take a long slug of ale.

"Maybe when I've saved up enough," Nerissa muses, as I breathe out and set my tankard onto the stained wood.

I grin at her, and at my smile, pride flashes in Nerissa's eyes. She's lost both her parents, so she understands the disorienting nature of grief. And grief when you don't even know if they're dead hits different.

I queue at the bar for our second round, the fire crackling and warming the backs of my legs. The world outside is frightening, and I need to find Oswin and decide how we'll reach out to Fjaldorn. Did they target Mother's house specifically, or was it random?

"A sigil for your thoughts?" Rhett, one of the tavern's regulars and a guy I've slept with twice, sweeps up behind me and puts his arm around my neck, pulling me into him.

"Hi," I say, twisting and noticing the glazed look in his eyes. Rhett is a devilish flirt, and perhaps the best-looking man in Grim Municipal. Tall with sandy blonde hair and a lip ring, his body is almost entirely tattooed from the neck down.

"Hey, Lira." He tilts his head to one side. Looks at

my mouth. "Missed you."

"Ha." Where's Chuck? Why is the queue so slow? I'm not in the mood for Rhett. Not right now. "Can't say the same, I'm afraid."

"Oh, you wound me." As he grins, a dimple appears in his cheek.

No, no, and no. I don't have time to flirt with Rhett. Not when there are so many other things going on.

"In case you hadn't realised, my family are missing. I don't have time to fool around with you."

"But you're so damn good at fooling around. I miss your tits."

Oh, faytes. He went there. He leans forward and makes to try and kiss me, but his eyes are glazed and I manage to take a step back.

"My family are missing," I repeat firmly, as someone shouts their order to Chuck.

"You're so beautiful when you're sad," Rhett whispers, his breath heavy and sluggish, lingering far too close. He leans in, pressing his lips to the side of mine—wet, hot, and uninvited.

"Get off!" I cry, slapping him away. "I don't want to kiss you. Get off me!" I shove his face, but his lips linger on my hand, still warm and unwanted. I screech and scramble backwards, knocking into someone, my heart racing as heat floods my face. Irritation burns through me, as my body almost gags, anger flaring, the emotion arriving as quick as lightning.

And then, like a dark cloud settling over the

room, a voice cuts through the chaos—low, controlled, and dangerously calm.

"Well then. What are you doing with the postmistress?"

My heart stutters, stalls, scoops itself into my throat.

CHAPTER TWENTY-FIVE

Both Rhett and I have frozen, mid-step. The room cascades into silence, the air thick with tension. Even the music halts, the notes hanging unfinished in the stillness as I turn.

Kaelion stands at the door, his eyes scanning me slowly from my boots to my hair. His body seems to rock inside his leathers, keeping his rhythm, which is, as always, calmer than mine. I've backcombed my hair into a mane, and when his gaze settles on my face, he winks at me. The fucker *winks* at me, his eyes sparkling, lips twitching.

I'm wearing Nerissa's leather jumpsuit. The last few times he's seen me, I've been covered in blood, covered in my own spit, and wearing either a stained work tunic or Nerissa's grey nightgown. He hasn't seen me dressed up, my hair out of its usual bun, tumbled around my shoulders, my lips slicked with belladonna root.

His gaze bores into me like a heavy weight,

making my chest tighten. I can't stop myself from reacting—my breath catches, my heart thumping. But I can't let him see that. Not when his mere presence rattles me like this. Not when he's basically blackmailing me. And please tell me he hasn't come to try and save me, a-fucking-gain. He looks as if he's hungry for Rhett's murder. Chuck calls out a welcome in the background, excited to have royalty in his little tavern.

I inhale deeply, trying to steady myself, and say as calmly as I can, "What are you doing here, Your Highness?"

Everyone listens. Kaelion's eyes narrow, just slightly. He doesn't respond immediately. Instead, he offers something that could be a smile, but it's too sharp, too dangerous—slick with ill intent. His expression suggests he's enjoying this, enjoying watching me squirm.

And then he looks at Rhett.

"I heard something untoward was occurring," he says smoothly, his voice as slick as the smile he's barely holding back. Then, he breathes in deeply, letting his chest expand. He doesn't look like he prepared much for this visit—his leathers are untidy and hastily wrenched on, the sleeves rolled up to his elbows, revealing forearms corded with muscle. His gaze flickers back to me, just for a moment, and he takes a slow breath. His expression softens, as if he wants to say something else. After all, this man has told me his biggest secret, something so huge that it could change our entire monarchy.

The sharpness returns to Kaelion's stare as he looks back at Rhett. He glares at him as if he's some sort of trespasser, as if my former lover has dared to cross some invisible royal line, stepping into a space that only Kaelion is supposed to occupy. It doesn't make sense. If he's going to go to such lengths to protect me, then why not tell me everything he knows? Why risk my life, sending me into Xandryll?

This man is not my friend.

I smile dangerously, forcing the words out: "I am perfectly fine with my boyfriend here. But thank you for coming."

Kaelion barely controls his expression. Surprise flickers. Surprise and something else. Something I must be imagining. "Boyfriend?" His voice softens. It catches me off guard, a small pang in my chest before I can lock it away. Rhett lets out a tiny squeal, but otherwise says nothing, his eyes flicking between us. He seems smaller, somehow.

"This man is your boyfriend?" Kaelion's gaze slides back to Rhett, his tone demanding. My stomach flutters in a way I can't explain. I grit my teeth, forcing myself to ignore the way his voice wraps around me. No. I will not be distracted. Not when he needs to be punished for his coercion. He should tell me everything he might know about my family's whereabouts, and not send me to dangerous forests on a death mission.

"Yes, and we are terribly happy together. I love kissing him!"

"Really?" Rhett asks excitedly.

"I think it's time you left," interrupts a loud,

grating voice. It's one of the anti-royalists from the corner. The man is a foot shorter than Kaelion, but his wide frame and ruddy face make him imposing as he strides forward. His friends murmur from behind him, soft crooning noises that drip with malice. Every patron in the tavern has stopped to watch.

"Oh, I recognise that bracelet," the mortal sneers, looking at Kaelion's wrist. The smile on his face is ugly, twisted by some dark history. "I've seen that before."

"You've seen it before." Kaelion's voice is tight.

"Aye, that I have." His grin widens. "That was a good day."

Kaelion clenches his fists, and I taste the metallic tang that always lingers when I re-write people's post. Fayte. Kaelion wants to rip this man limb from limb, something that would be no trouble for a powerful aemortal like him. The man wouldn't stand a chance. But Kaelion's reputation is at stake.

I'm distracted by Rhett, who's muttering a rhyme under his breath: "Never to an aemortal side bring, a glare nor weapon nor silver thing." I shudder. The verse flashes through my mind; we were taught it in mortal primary school. It warned us not to look an aemortal in the eye. Just stay still, and they were more likely to pass without attacking. Like a common beast. Like a wolf.

And then I catch something glinting in the corner of my vision, something that makes my blood run cold. I turn to see the silver knife pushed through the knuckles of the ruddy-faced mortal. His weapon is small, but liable to destroy an aemortal if he strikes in the right spot.

He's going to stab Kaelion. And Kaelion hasn't seen.

"Stop!" I scream, my voice rising in terror as the mortal lunges forward. His fist shoots out, aimed at Kaelion's chest—the power in his grip designed to puncture organs that are irreversibly damaged, even for aemortals.

I fucking *lunge*.

Something happens to time as I leap. Fayte coats my tongue, iron hissing in my nostrils, as my hand slams into Kaelion, pushing him out of the way. My other fist connects with the mortal man's skull, the knife slipping from his hand as his head cracks into my knuckles. Fayte engulfs me, something different than before, something ancient.

Blood—thick and hot. Screaming. I hear Nerissa curse, Rhett shriek, someone else cry out. A candle falls, splattering hot wax across the floor. Drinks are thrown at the fire, the hiss as they're extinguished reverberating in my bones. I let out a cry, my knuckles in pain, my forehead bursting. Air rushes from my lungs as something solid presses around me.

Not presses. *Grabs* me.

I grip Kaelion's arm, my fingers tightening into the warmth of his skin as he starts to wisp us away, cedarwood mingling with fayte, overtaking every ounce of sense in my body.

Our limbs start to disintegrate in front of my best friend, who stands frozen, mouth agape. Nerissa is staring at Kaelion's arm, at the bracelet pressed against my front. Her face has turned deathly white, her lips parted in a way that chills me. I want to ask her what's going on, but it's too late. We're already entering the space between time and place, an unnerving nothingness where reality blurs into fragments. The world that was, suddenly gone.

Kaelion's grip on my leather jumpsuit tightens, pulling me closer to him. I can feel the heat of his body radiating against mine, his breath close to my ear. And then, as if he's speaking to himself, I swear I hear the words growled into my ear: "Nice leathers, postmistress."

CHAPTER TWENTY-SIX

"I killed him," I gasp, collapsing onto the dewy grass. I heave, bile rising in my throat. I close my eyes, willing my breath to slow and my heartbeat to steady. I felt his skull shatter in my hand. But it can't have. I'm a mortal woman; I barely have enough strength to bruise a cheekbone.

"Yes, you probably did," Kae agrees, his tone controlled. "I wonder where that fayte came from. Strange." He's forcing himself to sound light, trying to calm me. He can't thunder at me, not now—not when I've just killed a man and dragged the royal family into it. If the corner table in The Dwarven Bombard already hated the royals, now they've witnessed a mortal's death and a prince whisking away their local postmistress.

"Fayte," I gasp. That's what I felt. That's what I tasted when my fingers met the mortal's skull. I crushed his skull, just as the Sable Legion crushed my uncle's. And I'm only a mortal. I can't do such things. Even

Nerissa was horrified. I've isolated my best friend, I've sealed my fate. I can't go back to the Bombard. I can never show my face there again.

A tentative hand brushes my back, just for a second. It feels like fire, and then it's gone, as if he's been burned. But it was there—his vast, warm palm heating the very core of my spine. I swallow hard, trying to anchor myself to something real. I drop back onto my heels, blinking against the rush of emotions swirling through me.

"I need to tell you something," the prince murmurs, looking up at the sky. "And oh, how I wish I didn't have to. But, it might help you to know, sometime."

I bite my lip. Breathe. "Okay…"

"Silver does not slay aemortals," he murmurs.

"Silver does not slay aemortals," I repeat, the words prickling my scalp. I know that. I know that he might not have died, that the silver key the man held —which many mortals mistakenly believe can destroy aemortals as well as some beasts—might not have killed Kaelion. Oh, but what if it *had?*

"It can kill beasts, silicrites, anything formed from a curse, but it does not harm aemortals in the way mortals believe. But thank you." He sounds odd. "It's not… I'm not used to people trying to save me, to save my life. And he very well might have succeeded in his bid to destroy me beyond repair."

I take a deep breath in, trying to remember how I feel about Kaelion. He's not telling me everything; he might know where my family are. A shard of ice flicks through my heart as I try and collect the pieces of my soul back together.

"I thought you were being attacked." Kae's voice is quieter now, tinged with something I can't quite place. That's what Vallorn would have heard. Me screeching for someone not to kiss me, to get off me. I don't ask Kaelion why he even cares.

My hands leave long, dark stains on the grass, but this time, it's real blood I carry with me—not the silicrite's. Mortal blood. Shadowed crimson under the moonlight. The colour of a normal human man, who lived in Grim, who spent his evenings in the tavern. I close my eyes, force my breath to slow.

I've gone from a life of predictability, of routine, to this—becoming a murderer. Cold-blooded, irredeemable. And with my family still missing, and my best friend looking at me like she doesn't know me anymore... How can I ever return to the way things were? True, I wasn't really living before. I'm starting to realise that now. I was *surviving*. I want to do more than just survive. I want my life to be more than work; I want to live. I want passion, excitement, and...

Two huge hands slip under my armpits and lift me to standing with effortless strength.

"Everyone will see if you stay down there," he mutters, his hand firm in the small of my back, guiding us toward some kind of ornate hedgerow. I blink, the heat of his touch searing through my leathers. Where are we?

Moonlight dances on fronds of swaying jasmine and neat borders of wildflowers, their petals curled into impossible spirals, long stalks dangling over seas of white. Snowdrops, magnolias, white tulips, night phlox—obedient rolls of ivory spread across the vista, while the winter flowers of clematis cluster around the foot of the nearest turret wall. We're in the castle gardens. Nearby, the thick iron gate, now gleaming with a light sheen of fayte, stands solidly under the moonlight. Serene birds sail through the inky skies above. It's beautiful.

"Seen by who?" I ask, inhaling magnolias. To one side, there's that undulating sea of white flowers, releasing the sweet, nostalgic scent of garden summers. And to the other, there is him.

We've never stood in such close proximity before. I look up, slowly.

"They're having a ball at the palace," he murmurs. "Since my parents can't leave, they throw events here. Before, they could visit townspeople, attend schools, maintain military events, but ever since..." He swallows, his throat rippling. "They've had to rely on people coming to them."

"Has it been hard for you?" I ask, really looking at him. Yes, there's the handsome face, the wide shoulders, the deep amber eyes. But there's something else. A pain, raw and hidden. Not only are his parents trapped indoors thanks to the cruelty of a Divinity, but his father had his birth father killed. So much has happened *to* him, and he hasn't been able to do a damn thing about any of it.

But still, he's keeping secrets. My mind is becoming muddled.

Kae runs a hand through his hair. "I just wish they hadn't made the deal. More than anything. Never negotiate with a Divinity. Never—" He cuts himself off with a hiss, his horns flaring as his hand pushes against them, their sudden intensity visible in the moonlight. "Sorry, Divinity," he mutters, rolling his eyes at me.

"Can she *hear* you?" I ask, horrified, my eyes darting to his coryns. The shimmering silver tips ripple softly under the moon, no longer just glowing, but now molten and alive with energy, their undulations subtle but undeniably powerful. Coryns have always been a topic of fascination in Grim Municipal; horns that distinguish the aemortals as something separate from mortals, but also the source of their fayte, it seems. Cruel kings have had coryns extracted from the heads of rebel aemortals, severing their abilities.

"Sometimes," Kaelion sighs, "she chooses to listen in. I was born under the Divinity of War. She gets bored." His coryns settle back into their usual state. The shine was beautiful, molten silver running along ornate rivulets. Other lands have coryns in different colours, but it's hard to believe that any could be as beautiful as the patterned silver network that runs across his horns, like a vast net of river tributaries all joining and spiralling off.

He takes a breath in, and jokes, "The most important rule of my world here is: Never piss off a Divinity."

"Funny, the most important rule of my world is: Never fuck an aemortal." Oh, faytes. It darted into my mind and onto my tongue before I could stop myself —born from the many times that Nerissa and I have repeated this simple rule—but I shouldn't have *said it out loud*. He has the good grace to let out a breathy laugh, while not making any sort of eye contact.

"So, you can't speak ill of her," I dare to say. He should be allowed free speech, should be allowed to open up to me. Or to anyone. I don't care if it's me. "You're all prisoners."

"We are all connected to a Divinity, us aemortals," Kaelion says ruefully, his gaze dropping to me. "I know the mortal city clings to moons, to the reassurance of a known fate, but for us, it's somewhat true. The Divinities aren't cruel gods doling out punishment. For those of us born with a drop of Divinity, they're part of us. Sometimes, it's not the goddess speaking, but my own guilt for speaking ill. It feels like chastising myself. I try not to employ too much self-hatred, even though I couldn't stop my parents from becoming bound to the shadows."

"That's not your fault," I say instantly, "They saved Grim Municipal. They saved… me."

His eyes flash darkly, a look I can't quite decipher. "My mother hasn't been able to See much these last few cycles," he murmurs, lifting his gaze to the full moon. It is Somer tonight. The Divinity of Forgiveness will be running rife, planting dreams and nurturing crops. "She can go cycles without a vision, which is expected at her age. But still, she's been having night episodes. I– I found her in the back kitchen a few nights ago, writing the same words over and over in tree sap upon every surface."

"That's scary," I admit, imagining Mother writing

all over the kitchen implements. "What was she scribing?"

"*Two powers, one fate.*"

CHAPTER TWENTY-SEVEN

"Two powers, one fate," I repeat, the words tugging at something distant in my mind. I can't think. Not with him towering over me like this, smelling like cedarwood, his thick jaw clenched with muscle. As if he's about to lean down and kiss me.

But he's keeping secrets. My chest hurts so much I can barely breathe.

"Why won't you tell me where my family is?" My voice trembles, the words barely more than a whisper, the accusation burning my eyeballs.

"Your family..." His voice softens, and he steps back, rubs his eyes with one massive hand, his fingers flexing with muscle. "I... I can't tell you anything. Not yet. But please, trust me, this is the only way we might have a chance at the truth." His eyes trail from mine up to my forehead, and I notice the shift in his gaze—something uncomfortable. "It is not usual for a mortal to have something that I cannot... see."

"So, you think I'm something more? Like an aemortal or a beast?" My lips feel numb as I speak, as if they're being pelted by iced raindrops.

Instead of a proper reply, he just mutters, his eyes burning into my soul, "I wish to create a reveal from wolfsbane." The wind picks up around the nearest turret, almost as if it, too, can feel the weight of his words.

"To uncover what I really am?"

"Yes." He can't reassure me this time, not when everything about me is uncertain, not when I might have been changed by my mother at birth. Not when I might have been born a—

"Monster," I whisper, my eyeballs burning with unshed tears.

"You? Never," Kaelion mutters, his voice rough with conviction. He takes a sharp breath in, and then turns away slightly, as if he's already said too much. His shoulders tense, and I'm left with a sense that there's more he's not telling me. "I think your change can be used as leverage," he continues, his voice softer now, guarded. "I hope to use the promise of it to glean information from one who has too much time on her hands."

"So you don't even know where they are?" I gasp, my head swirling with emotions.

"I do not," he admits, and it slices through my chest. "But I have deployed two hundred Sable Legion members to search. They are cutting through the lands as we speak, gathering what information they can. I have it on authority that they are alive, but it's a matter of finding out where they've been—"

"What did you just say?"

He looks at me, his eyes reflecting the starlight, steady but sombre. "I didn't want to tell you," he sighs. "Until I knew it was true. I didn't want to burden you with false hope. But trust me, I'm doing everything I can. You think that Vallorn stands outside a mortal house every week, when someone goes missing? I have them under the highest royal instruction to do everything they can for... the situation."

"Because I'm something different?" I whisper, my throat tight as I struggle to process his words. Why would he go to such lengths for someone like me? Two hundred of the fiercest aemortal soldiers are out there, hunting for my family. Who might be alive. Dare I dream? "Have you ordered this because you see something when you look at me? Because you're using your Gift?" I demand, my face flushed.

"Among other reasons." He lets out a harsh, bitter laugh, as if annoyed at his own feelings, and I instinctively take a step back. The soft call of a nightbird forces the faux-smile to drop from Kaelion's face. "I visited your home again," he murmurs.

My knees nearly buckle. Somehow, I find my voice. And of all the things to say, I blurt, "Did you like it?"

He doesn't look at me as he says, "A bald man was crying on the floor, and half a brood of chickens were running around the living space. It smelled like lavender." His lip almost twitches. Shame floods through me. A royal, from the palace, in my mother's shack. Our draped scarf walls, our mismatched collection of wooden ornaments, and the chickens—for fayte's sake, the *chickens*.

"That was Oswin," I say, my lips numb. "Seren's father."

"He cares for you all," the prince murmurs. "After he invited me in, I saw how much effort he'd put into cleaning up the chicken blood. The silicrites consumed half your brood, I'm afraid."

Chicken blood. My body jolts, as if struck by cold lightning. It's more than I've dared to hope for. I look at him, stunned, too shocked to speak for a long moment. Kaelion shifts, moving fully into my line of sight. His face is lined with something close to care, something that tastes like moonlight and jasmine, that hits like fire and thunder.

"Chicken blood," I repeat, barely a whisper. Relief floods me, making me giddy. They might not be dead. But they are missing. Which might be worse than death. I can't relax. Not yet. I still feel carnage ahead, but there's a flicker of something that wasn't there before —hope. "Thank you." My voice is so croaky I can barely speak. "For going there. For seeing Oswin."

"He showed me your systems. Your food system, your scrolls for meals, your laundry plans. He said you like to have everything ordered. That sometimes you can't sleep unless you've made a timetable for the next week." His voice is gentle, but I can't stand the way he's exposing me. He would have seen everything—my sad little timetables. Breakfast of bread and oil, work all day, a dinner of mutton liver or whatever offal we could afford. All inked on scrolls and pinned around the dwelling. The prince has seen it all.

"Many people are organised," I mutter, cursing Oswin for his indiscretions. The thought of inviting a prince into the house to see my laundry rota is too absurd to bear.

"I liked seeing it," Kaelion says softly. "I liked knowing you better." His voice is unbearably tender, like he's reaching into something deep inside me, and I'm not sure I want him to. The same word rings constantly around my head: *Why?*

CHAPTER TWENTY-EIGHT

I wonder if I can borrow some Sable Legion soldiers, send them to Oswin with a note: *Don't show this handsome warrior prince my laundry schedule.* For fayte's sake.

"Sometimes, I can't sleep." His voice drops again. "I curse my mother and father for their deal with the Divinities. Guilt consumes my mind. I go undercover to The Howling Cask. Drink my sorrows away, until I can't think anymore, until I forget how lonely I've been. I haven't learned how to deal with guilt and loneliness—only how to drown them, as if they're enemies that vanish with daylight."

My chest tightens. Lonely. But he was with two women the night before we met; he can't surely be lonely.

I have been lonely. While I've spent evenings writing rotas, putting charcoal to scrolls, I've never bared myself to anyone. Not truly. I haven't talked about Father leaving, or the guilt that comes from knowing what Mother had to do to feed me when I was young. The burdens I've swallowed down, shoved deep, so I could appear a functional member of society.

But what if anger is necessary? What if it's about facing emotions head-on, instead of pretending they don't exist? What if we need all of those feelings—the sadness, the rage—to truly experience the highs, too? The joy. The freedom. The love.

Prince Kaelion stands just inches away. I look up, and in his stormy amber gaze, I see everything. Confusion. Pain. Loneliness. His warm breath brushes against my forehead. Loneliness is an ailment that spares no one, mortal nor aemortal.

I murmur, "What are you thinking?", feeling the heat of my blood pounding through my body. I'm too hot in Nerissa's leathers, too constrained.

And yet... I should run. I'm with an aemortal. A hunter. Someone who could've crushed that anti-royalist without a second thought. I'm just a mortal, staring at a beast. His coryns curl upward from his thick hair, gleaming in the moonlight, as if to demonstrate my point. He doesn't break eye contact, not for one single fucking breath.

"I'm thinking," he mutters, looking down at me, his eyes almost black, "about your boyfriend, and how he shook when he saw me."

My gut twists. I murmur, "Right."

"And I'm also thinking," he mutters, raising an eyebrow ever-so-slightly, as if he's seen through my boyfriend lie, "how dangerous this is."

I gasp for breath, my entire body igniting. *Two wenches.* That's who he took to his bed the night before the attack. Two wenches. I hate this man. I hate him for the blackmail, not the two wenches, I remind myself. I don't care about that.

"Why is it dangerous?" I breathe. The sound of string music, distant violins, drifts from somewhere nearby, as if the palace doors have been thrown open to let the sound escape.

"Well, Elira Corvannis," he breathes my name, low and measured, "for many reasons. Not least because you've now killed a silicrite, an aemortal, and a mortal. I'm not sure my father would approve of me being out here with you alone. You're starting to get a reputation."

I inhale, tasting his sweet breath on my tongue. Dangerous. Everything about this is dangerous. "You're a prince," I mutter, barely able to get the words out. "And I'm a postmistress. You fit in, and I don't, I never have. But also, I'm organised, I like structure, order. And you're..."

I think about the hipflask that presses out of his leathers.

"Ha." He lets out a soft laugh, a sound that causes my pulse to stutter. "Sometimes, it's those that stand out, that don't fit the mould, that are easier to love. Because you are what you are; you don't try to hide."

Easier to love. I can't hear this. Can't drink the poison he's feeding me. This aemortal is trying to blackmail me. He's not telling me everything. He's trying to seduce me so that I'll steal his stupid herb, so that I'll find the wolfsbane for him. He's not—he's not—

He lifts a hand, slow and deliberate, his fingers brushing my jawline. It's a touch I could stop at any moment. But I don't. My body reacts before I even have time to think, tingling, alive. His fingers trace my bone with agonising slowness, setting off fireworks that rush through my skin, burning my skull, sending shivers down my spine.

"I thought you were being attacked," he mutters softly, as if to himself. His words carry more than just concern. He sounds genuinely surprised, and more than a little unnerved. "And my whole body *bruised*. I'm not sure why."

I've never been so aware of my physique, every single part from my feet, almost numb and fizzing, to the hairs on the nape of my neck, standing on end. My body is taut, aching with need and frustration, but I can't let this happen. He's an aemortal prince. He's coercing me.

I can't trust him.

But my face is angled towards his. My treacherous, lusting face.

"I lied," I admit, his eyes already flashing, as if he knows what I'm going to say. "Rhett isn't really my boyfriend."

The moonlight traces every line, every shadow. The curl of hair across his forehead, the humour and lust in his eyes, as he just looks at me. He knew I was lying. Damn it. I part my lips slightly, and he notices. He lets out an audible half-sigh, a groan of wanting. His fingers find the delicate nape of my neck, then wind through my hair, cradling my skull as he looks into my eyes.

"Beautiful," he whispers, bringing his other hand up to stroke the hair back from my forehead. "Eyes the colour of emeralds and moss. Where did you come from?"

"Apparently a mud hut, if your brother's to be believed," I quip breathlessly. My body aches for him. I want to tell him how much it means to me – him opening up about his loneliness earlier – but the words don't come. And now's not the time, not when he's flipped from vulnerable to sexual deviant in the space of a few violin notes.

He lets out a soft chuckle.

"Or perhaps the space between two moons," he murmurs, that familiar confusion flitting across his face again. "Certainly, I've never met anyone like you."

"And do you meet a lot of women, down at The Howling Cask?" I murmur. I need to know. If he's sleeping with a different woman under every moon...

"Why, are you jealous?" He cocks his head to one side. It's irritating.

"Of course not," I retort. I could also sleep with a different man under every moon, should I choose to saunter into the murky corners of The Dwarven Bombard and risk various venereal diseases. "You're nothing to write home about, Kae."

Lies. It's all lies, and he smirks as he looks down at me.

"Look, I drink too much, I smoke, I gamble," he mutters, not dropping my gaze. "I have issues that need sorting, yes. But I don't tend to frolic around castle gardens with beautiful women. That's not on my typical agenda."

I blink. That was a lot of information to digest. He drinks, smokes, gambles.

"Why do you do all of that?" I whisper.

His expression becomes serious as he says, in a soft, tender voice, "Often I run from my own mind. When I stick around, I destroy things. Do you want me to kiss you?"

CHAPTER TWENTY-NINE

"What?" The question is so abrupt that I step backwards, even as my body hums: FUCK YES. I want to utter: *Maybe we should stay and examine the mental bombshell you just dropped: when you stick around, you destroy things.* It breaks apart my shrivelled, black heart.

"Just wondering." He gives me a sweet, boyish grin, which instantly demotes him from scary royal to cute, silly boy. "I can't read your mind."

He's giving me a headrush with this change in direction, and yet, it makes sense. Seren functions by turning her vulnerability into anger. Perhaps the prince turns his into seduction. And two can play. I deserve some fun.

"Do you *want* to kiss me?" I ask, sweet as Claran syrup. I delight in the way his eyes suddenly flash. His hand drops from my hair, and a wicked smile crashes across his face. Just as he opens his mouth to reply, there's a cough from nearby.

A cough. From a messenger who should really know better.

"Elrind." Prince Kaelion takes another step back and blinks through the moonlight, his gaze shifting towards the castle, as if he's suddenly remembered where we are. "Is everything okay?"

The messenger steps forward into my line of sight, his feathers obscuring his face. Whether he's blushing or just finds me an impudent flirt who's lured the precious prince away from his palace, I can't tell. "You are late getting ready, Your Highness." Elrind's voice is as polite as ever. If he's judging either of us for being in the gardens, my arm covered in blood, he says nothing. "And the maids have set out Elira's dress in the West Wing."

"My dress?" I ask at the same time as Kaelion says, "Elira's dress?"

"Yes. I assume you are inviting your guest to the ball?" Elrind asks, his voice taking on a steely tone—like, *if you're going to fraternise around hedgerows with this woman, then you damn well better invite her to the ball.*

The *ball*.

I've never, in my life, been to a ball. Sure, we've thrown a little courier soirée during the Eryndal Sword Festival or Midsummer Celebration. I once served Luthara-moon-baked bison knuckle. It went down well.

"I can take you home," Kaelion mutters. "If you don't... want to come."

His hesitance tears at my chest. I think he *wants* me there. At the ball. Oh, fayte. I think about going home. Walking into Mother's abandoned house, Oswin crying on the futon. Or going to Nerissa's, and feeling like an imposition. The prospect of home doesn't seem as appealing as it used to.

Besides, if I stay then I can press the prince for information. Surely things have escalated between us now, and he can start to trust me more. Scrap his idiotic wolfsbane request.

"I would *love* to attend the ball," I say. Neither the prince nor Elrind looks convinced.

CHAPTER THIRTY

The King's voice thunders as a maid leads me toward the West Wing. A door nearby is cracked open, releasing the voice of the senior royal: "WHAT HAVE YOU DONE?"

I freeze mid-step. The Queen murmurs an indistinguishable response, her voice thick with tears. I shouldn't be eavesdropping.

"We can't keep her," the King bellows, as the Queen's cries intensify. Are they talking about me? About *keeping* me? "I don't want her here. Not in my castle, not here. Banish her to the Cecedit Mountains, among her own kind!"

My stomach turns. The maid continues ahead, cornflower blue robes billowing. I don't know whether to stay and listen, or demand to be taken home. I can't stay if the King's furious about my presence. If he's going to banish me to the Cecedit Mountains...

"I'm sorry," the Queen's voice breaks through. "I had no other choice. I couldn't face it again. The heartbreak, the pain... you—you don't know what it's been like for me."

"I do," the King says, his voice dipping in volume. "I do, darling. But I still want rid of her."

I scurry away from the doorway, my heart hammering in my chest.

It's heavy. They strip it from me and scrub, pluck, and clean my naked body, as if I have somehow marred the beauty of the silks. And then they readorn me, only to strip it away again.

By the time the dress is taken for the fifth time, I sit shivering in my chamber, despite the fire roaring in the grate and the fayte-imbued windows. I stare at my body in the long mirror, noticing how my ribs have hollowed, the sharp cut of my collarbones. Other maids have disappeared to find undergarments, but there is nothing petite enough, it seems. I cross my arms and shiver. I am a mortal at an aemortal ball.

The prince had wanted to kiss me. What does that mean? Is it just the convenience, the fact that we were both exhausted from butchering a man in the palace cellar and then crushing a skull in the tavern, or are things like that part and parcel of the prince's usual routine? Have I entered his own version of a humdrum universe, where it's perfectly acceptable to waltz into the palace with blood down your arm, after a proposition by the hedges?

And can anything even happen, when his father seems to want to exile me to a place of nightmares?

I stare at my reflection, wondering what I am. Clearly, my father wasn't a normal mortal—or, if he was, then I've inherited fayte in some unexpected way.

There's the blood, the way I can mimic ink. There was the feathered quill that appeared upon my arrival at the palace. The prince said he sees a Gift.

But I don't have coryns. Unless...

Unless wolfsbane – a tincture for change – can get rid of them as a newborn, a small voice whispers.

Which might make me...

A half-blood. A banned semi-breed. A result of a forbidden tryst.

If I am found out to be a half-aemortal, I'll be executed. Or banished to the Cecedit Mountains... Exactly where the King wants to put the mysterious 'her'.

Absolutely not. I'll refuse. I'd sooner end my own life than be outcast to the most evil place in Orynthys.

"Sigil for your thoughts?"

The voice makes me jump. It's the sly voice of a silver cat. I twist in my chair, instinctively wrapping my arms around myself to shield my body. The cat, Tryx, lies on the bed, his body forming a divot in the thick bedspread.

"Hello," I say flatly. He—if it is a 'he'—doesn't seem phased by my attempt to keep my modesty intact. And I suppose he wouldn't. He probably slinks through all kinds of castle situations. Which makes me wonder about what I've overheard. Perhaps this cat might tell me something. "Have the King and Queen stopped, uh, arguing?" I ask, trying to keep my expression innocent, devoid of emotion.

I need to know if I'm likely to be banished before I

have a chance to see Prince Kaelion again. Or, you know, save my family from their unknown fate. Have they been kidnapped as punishment for harbouring a half-breed?

The cat yawns, stretching its mouth so wide that I can see a fleshy pink tongue and a row of razor-sharp teeth. It snaps its jaw shut and then gives me what could almost be called a smile. "Yes, they have," he says, following his words with a half yawn. "The Queen has done something terrible."

I swallow. "Inviting me to the ball?"

"My, my. We are self-obsessed, aren't we?" He sounds amused. I cough, feeling a blush creep up the sides of my face, along my jaw—the same place where the prince's hand stroked earlier. I open my mouth to reply, but I have nothing to say.

"It's not about you," the cat says flatly. "They weren't arguing over you. As much as you might like to wish your name upon such powerful tongues."

"I don't," I say quickly, trying not to imagine Prince Kae's powerful tongue. "I don't wish for anything, apart from finding my family."

"Ah, yes. Liora and Seren. A tragedy, most certainly." The cat extends one paw and licks the length of it.

"You know their names?" My voice vibrates.

The cat stops licking. Stares at me. "Of course I know their names, Elira. Everyone in the palace is concerned for them. I cannot—"

I'm on the bed in an instant, underwear be

damned. I pin the cat down, my face inches from his. Pet or not, I'll tear him limb from limb if he lies to me. "Where is my family?" I spit, grabbing whatever furry part of him I can. He doesn't squirm or try to escape, simply stares at me as if I'm boring him.

"I don't know," he says, almost too calmly. "I truly don't. I could take an educated guess, of course. We all could. Does your prince not have any information that he could share with you?"

"He won't tell me unless I steal this damned herb," I growl. I feel a bit ridiculous, keeping a talking cat pinned down while I'm as bare as the day I was born. I hope the maids are prepared for what they might walk in on.

"Then I suggest you steal the damn herb," Tryx responds slyly. "It's your only hope. The princes are the most clever aemortals you'll find around here. The King and Queen are limited, poor souls, trapped for eternity. But your little prince? He's on the ground. You should talk to him, steal his herb."

"But I don't understand why he won't tell me exactly why he needs it." I glower at Tryx, as if it's his fault.

"It might amuse her. I daresay that Kaelion has a few reasons for wanting to earn the Goddess's favour," Tryx hums. "Perhaps he is deciding which is most important to him."

I sit back on my heels and release Tryx. I glance towards the window, where the full moon—Somer—glimmers over the palace grounds. Is Tryx right? Should I steal the wolfsbane, just to find out what Kaelion knows? But that feels like supporting his goddess's behaviour.

"She is rather fine," Tryx purrs, his voice low and mocking. "We talk often. She finds me comical, I daresay, the Divinity of War. She loves the prince very much." His eyes continue to glitter, and I feel something hot stir in my chest. I swallow hard, irritation seeping through me. "Disryn was quite shocked when I told him you were here," Tryx continues, his eyes glinting.

A pitted section of rock drops into my stomach. "Why tell him? You know he's just going to make it hard for Kae!" I fling my hands up in frustration.

"Oh, I'm sorry. I didn't realise that you and I are *Best Friends Forever*. Might we have a pillow fight next?"

A bark of laughter rips out of him, as I glare, and snap: "And I didn't realise that you were a fucking comedian."

It only serves to make him laugh harder.

CHAPTER THIRTY-ONE

My heart drums as I descend the vast staircase.

The dress is lighter than before, swishing around my ankles with every step. Layers of silver sparkle like a cloudy night sky, billowing in every direction. My hair is pinned high atop my head, soft curls cascading around my ears. Beneath the dress, I have a slip, the silk cool and smooth against my skin. I don't think I've ever been this clean, and I know for certain I've never been so well-dressed. From the grand ballroom to my right, violins and flutes sing, but the atrium I'm descending into is empty. Suits of armour stand at attention, swords raised beneath slick portraits—stern men with beady eyes that seem to follow my every movement.

I take a deep breath, the weight of the dress aching my shoulders. My spindly shoes feel like they're struggling to maintain purchase on each step. What am I doing? Do I really intend to enjoy a ball, while my family might be out there, alive, somewhere?

What am I doing?

I stop on the next stair down, my stomach churning. I must have lost my mind agreeing to come here. The proximity to the prince, it addled my brain. I haven't been thinking clearly. I haven't been myself. I am Elira of The Courier's Keep. I like certainty. I love my family. And they are missing. I need to find them.

Tryx was right; I need to get the damn wolfsbane. It's the only way. Talking it out with that annoying cat has given me clarity. I'll amuse the Prince's goddess and buy her information. If anyone knows where my family is, it's the Divinity of War.

I see a guard hovering, barely visible, and snap, "I need to talk to Prince Kaelion." He merely nods and filters from the room, leaving me with the impression of many more guards hidden in the shadows.

I take a deep breath in. Solidify my plan.

The prince brings ballroom sounds when he finally strides in, as if lutes have been laid under his feet as he walks. I can hear voices too—laughter and the swish of dresses against marble floors. He looks at me. Just looks. He takes in the gown, the glow of my skin, my hair piled high. And okay, it feels good. The wonder on his face, the dirty, dark light in his eyes, the way he examines every inch of me, hungry and searching. He wants me. I suppose the palace staff have done their job.

For his part, the prince looks astonishingly beautiful. A velvet navy suit with tails, broad across his shoulders. His white shirt, a few buttons undone, reveals a glint of perfume resting just below his collarbones. His skin looks tanned and delicious.

Dismal strides in, overtaking Kaelion, who is still

rooted to the spot, his mouth slightly open in surprise.

"So, it's true. My brother has invited a mortal girl to the palace." Dismal glances between me and Kae, eyebrows raised. There's no malice in his voice—just surprise. "Is this to be a relationship? Are you courting this girl?" He pauses. "Because I don't like surprises, brother. If the cat hadn't told me—"

"That damned cat," Kaelion growls, ripping his eyes from me and looking toward the top of the staircase as if he could murder Tryx with his gaze alone.

"If Tryx hadn't told me," Dismal continues, voice firm, "then I might have only seen her on the dancefloor and had no rhyme nor reason to expect her there. I might have even thought to slay her."

Slay. The portraited eyes of powerful men seem to watch me, the weight of their judgement suffocating. I am in enemy territory now, and I keep letting myself forget that rather prudent fact.

"As it is," Dismal calls, to no one in particular, "I told my dear brother to gut the mortal. It does not benefit to have a prince in love with a pauper. Even the children's rhymes tell us so."

"You know she has every right to be here," Kaelion growls, as my mind reels and replays Dismal's words. "Watch your temper, brother, she's stabbed our guards for less."

I suppress an urge to laugh. I don't like being reminded of my violence, even as I appreciate him suggesting to Dismal that I'll have no problem shanking a bastard prince. Perhaps I would feel the same as Dismal if Seren were to bring an aemortal home. I'd want to protect her, even if it meant fighting against what she wanted.

"Her rights are not being discussed here, brother," Dismal claims. "It is her mortal body that we are discussing."

I shudder. *Mortal body.* What an awful term.

"Should someone ask me why we have brought this mortal woman in—"

"Then we tell them the truth," Kaelion exclaims, throwing his hands in the air.

"Which is what?" I ask. My voice betrays me, wobbling. Above us all, a gilt gold chandelier drips candlelight onto our finery. What is the truth? Is he hoping to kill me by setting an impossible mission, the same way the Divinities commanded the King and Queen to stay indoors forever?

Dismal answers, but he looks to Kaelion to do so. "You have told her nothing, have you?"

"What is there to tell me?" I demand, unable to keep the edge from my voice.

"I think you should probably kill her." Dismal ruffles his hair.

"I think you should probably go fuck yourself," I say, with an attitude I wouldn't have dared summon just weeks ago.

Dismal lifts an eyebrow, as Kaelion snorts out a laugh. And then the eldest prince says, "I have nothing to tell, because I don't know, brother." His tone rises in frustration. "We must... there must be a..." He looks around hopelessly, his words trailing off. "She must break into Xandryll. She must source wolfsbane. We have none here; I've asked every healer in the land."

My stomach twists violently.

"Wolfsbane is prohibited in the Temporal Bastion," Dismal hums. "Are you hoping for her instant execution when she's caught carrying it?"

Instant execution. My throat tightens. But... my mother had it when I was born. How had she managed to get hold of it if it's banned?

"And this wolfsbane will give me answers, will it?" My voice steadies. If wolfsbane can help find my family, then I'll risk it. A potential death for those I love seems like a reasonable trade-off. If I have to satisfy an unreasonable Divinity in the process, then so be it. "Or am I risking my life for your amusement?"

"What is this plan of yours, Kae?" Dismal sighs, crossing his arms. "Because I don't think the Divinities will be able to remove my name—"

"You cannot answer for the Divinities," Kaelion growls, his voice echoing from the baroque ceiling.

What does Kaelion want to ask of the Divinities?

"Oh, Elira," a voice interrupts, and I turn to see Elrind stepping in from the ballroom. He bows. "You look ravishing. That gown was made for you."

"It was made for someone much more powerful," I mutter.

"It is perfect on you," Prince Kae instantly murmurs.

I blink.

Before I can respond, the queen sweeps in, instantly overwhelming the room. A vast golden tiara sweeps back from her hairline, spiralling around her coryns, accentuating the otherworldly horns, and flowing into a golden plumage that spills gracefully over her shoulders. Her gown, a rich blend of gold and vivid purple, glimmers in the light, her silken gloves stretching beyond her forearms. It's easy, for a moment, to forget the tattoo that consumes half of her face, as she looks up at me and clutches her chest.

"Oh, my darling Elira," she gasps dramatically. Our queen has a flair for the theatrical. "You are the most beautiful denizen I have ever seen in this palace—mortal or aemortal."

Mortal or aemortal. I get the impression the queen has no idea about my potential status as a half-breed, nor the request the prince is making of me.

"Your beastly son is dating a mortal, it seems," Dismal drawls. "Will he never fall into line? I can't imagine the kingdom they'd create." He breaks into a devious grin that his mother can't see, and then, with an air of mockery, strides past the white-faced queen, disappearing into the ballroom.

"We're not," I say. "Dating, I mean."

I'm trying to spare her worry, that her son might be involved with a poor mortal girl. But she doesn't listen to me, she's only heard Disryn, and what I don't expect is the expression that floods her face. Her eyes widen, and she staggers backwards. Kae releases me, moving quickly to support her. Violins screech in the background. Elrind is quick to step in, catching her before she falls. I stagger, grabbing the banister for support.

"Is it true?" the queen gasps, her voice thin with shock. Kae helps her to stand again, his hands on her shoulders. My stomach churns. I clutch the banister.

"It is none of your concern what happens in my personal life," Kae murmurs, his voice barely above a whisper, yet it carries around the grand room. "And this is not the place to have this…"

I want to say I'm sorry. I want to reassure her, tell her that we're not even dating, for fayte's sake. But I can't. The look on Kae's mother's face—the way she stares at me, the horror in her eyes—is all too much. I can't speak. Why is Kaelion not sticking up for me? Has he been trying to keep me hidden?

Kae's hands remain on his mother, steadying her, trying to instruct her to pull her dramatic arse together. Because there truly is nothing going on, and the queen had thought me to be invited because of my mother and sister being missing. Perhaps they bring in charity cases all the time, to give us a taste of the finest elven wine, payment for our pain.

They must feel sorry for me. And Kaelion has been *hiding* me.

My head spins. My body aches. Is Kae ashamed of having invited me? Why is it so terrible for Her Majesty? And then, in the midst of it all, a voice—my voice—breaks through.

Get the wolfsbane, find out what they know, and get the fuck out of here.

I take a deep breath, trying to steady myself.

Before the decadent smells of the ball's feast can stop me, before anyone can say anything more, I start running.

CHAPTER THIRTY-TWO

"Did Kae send you?" I hiss, stomping further through the long grasses that sweep the hillside beyond the palace. I've left the iron gates behind, alongside my heavy, multi-layered dress and deadly shoes. Now, I wear only the silk slip beneath the night sky, and yet I'm burning with the heat of a thousand suns as Tryx hustles alongside me.

"No one *sends me* anywhere," the cat sizzles, stalking past. "I am not a servant nor a messenger. I am a creation born of the earth and the stars, the sun and the moon. I am a fayte-made being, and you ought to respect such rarity."

"My, my. We are self-obsessed, aren't we?" I mutter. It's the same thing the cat said to me earlier, but I'm not expecting a reply. "Do you know the quickest way to the border?"

"I know the quickest way to an armoire filled with protective clothing."

"You're not going to try and drag me back to the palace?" I thought that was his purpose—after all, he's appeared out of nowhere, a splash of silver in the ghostly grasses.

"Fayte, no. I would pay to watch a scrawny thing like you try to cross the border and break into Xandryll. I've come along for the entertainment. Parties are dreadfully dull."

I glance over my shoulder. Kae isn't following me. Neither is Elrind. The royal family is hopeless. Idiotic, aemortal royalty. They care only for themselves. They'd sooner send me to possible death than miss a single dance opportunity at their glamorous ball. They keep secrets, extort women, and throw mixed signals everywhere.

I can barely breathe, the lump in my throat becoming so painful. I feel betrayed, I feel ashamed. I blink to clear my vision, and then more damned tears gather and burn my eyeballs. A cold, sharp sensation lances through me, as if my heart has cracked down the middle, setting my skin alight. And he's not even here to see it. To see what he's done to me. I guess I'm nothing more than a passing distraction to him – to the prince who bedded two women in one night – his fleeting curiosity already lost its allure.

"Why'd he even send me on this mission?" I choke out, my voice so thin I almost don't recognise it. It trembles in the air, full of a vulnerability I can't hide. I hate it. I hate how exposed I feel, how raw. I never felt like this in my old life, never.

Why have I agreed to risk my life getting him

a herb, just so he can use it to amuse a Divinity and potentially get me information? Have I been blinded? Am I a fool? I wish I could tear my heart from my chest and throw it into the Xandryll forest, just to stop feeling everything. But it's already too late. It's in me now, the bitter ache of feeling like I'm not enough for him. Not enough for his family.

Tryx doesn't reply, and when he suddenly turns toward a stone outhouse, I follow, wiping the tears from my face. Thick hunting leathers don't sound like such a bad idea, after all, and I need to focus on moving forward. On getting the damned herb, and getting Mother and Seren back. After that, the prince can go to Thekla for all I care.

"You know," Tryx muses, as we find ourselves in a damp-smelling antechamber packed with coats, boots, and hunting rifles, "you can't blame the prince for not telling his mother. It's quite a big deal, inviting a woman to a ball at the palace."

"A mortal, you mean," I say, voice flat.

"Hmm. What size do you wear? I daresay these will fit best." Tryx nudges his head against a series of leather hems.

"I'm not upset that he didn't tell his mother. We're not children," I say, grabbing the top set of leathers from the hook. The weight is immense. It looks like boar skin. "We're *strangers*, for fayte's sake. Of course, he doesn't want to burden her with something like this." I stick one bare foot into the depths of the leather trousers, and am met with a softness I wasn't expecting. "I'm upset because instead of asking his goddess to find them—like any decent mortal would—he's making me do this stupid task."

I yank the leathers round my hip bones. They sit a little loose, but at least they're warm.

"That's a good reason to be annoyed," Tryx agrees, flexing against the doorframe. "I like your pluck." I breathe out. The dim moonlight picks up my breath in the air. "You really have no idea, do you?"

I turn to look at the cat, winding a thick jacket around me. I have an idea that I might be half-aemortal, yes. It's a fucking millstone around my neck, one that might wind up getting me killed. So I'm not about to voice it out loud. Not about to read my own death sentence.

"What?" I adjust the jacket's lapel, which hugs my neck the same way the prince's leathers had that first time I saw him. I push the memory away, trying to forget the garden, that moment when he asked if I wanted him to kiss me. My midriff aches, but I force the thought aside. He hasn't even come after me.

Except, I was upset when he tried to save me in the tavern. I don't need saving – I don't – but my dichotomy of a brain would like him to at least seem *interested* in supporting my treacherous journey. Am I the problem? I confuse even myself.

"Prince Kae is not a monster. He's a lonely man." Tryx yawns. "He has the weight of the kingdom upon him, and the deal his parents made has only piled on his royal duties. We can all see the toll it's taken. He used to smile, you know."

"He still smiles," I argue, thinking of his face

under the moonlight.

"Not for many." Tryx's voice is tinged with sadness. The window rattles as the evening wind picks up from the grounds outside.

"Let me tell you a story, Elira," Tryx starts, as I lift various pieces of leather to start assembling my gear. "Across the furious Thealean ocean and past the Shattered Isles, there is a kingdom that's up to no good."

"Fjaldorn," I mutter, the name like a weight on my tongue.

"It is ruled," Tryx continues, "by a gullible king. An aemortal king, but still, a foolish one. His court is in turmoil, his heart has been stolen – the kingdom is lawless. They have weapons. An army double the size of the Sable Legion, including a full brigade of silicrites and golems."

"Silicrites and… golems." I swallow hard.

"Indeed," Tryx affirms, a flicker of amusement in his eyes. "The Bone-and-Flesh-Wielders can't touch the silicrites and golems. They're made of stone. No flesh, no bone, no blood. They're the perfect weapons against the most powerful foes this empire faces."

"The most powerful Wielders aren't from the Divinity of Body," I reply immediately. "The Divinity of War—"

"Can impact the outer world. The bridges, the sabres, the castle walls. But what use is that if mortals and aemortals alike still have the ability to protect themselves? If their minds are strong enough, their bones resilient enough, their flesh tough enough to withstand torture?"

I pause, absorbing his words.

"It's not always the flashy Divinities that hold the most power, Elira," Tryx adds, his tone oddly contemplative. "Sometimes even I am surprised. And I've lived for eleven thousand cycles."

I open my mouth to respond, but find no words.

"Silly kings make terrible leaders," Tryx hums, rolling his shoulders. "The true power of the Celestial Bastion has been dissolved since the abolition of the Archons."

I furrow my brow, trying to place the Celestial Bastion's history. Since each royal family within the twelve lands of Orynthys has taken control after the abolishment of the Archons, they've had to quickly adapt. And for our dear royals, that means relying on the Sable Legion to patrol, to rule, and a land ruled by an army is nothing more than a microcosm of fear and trauma. The Sable Legion are trained to be ruthless, new recruits dropped into the famously evil Cecedit Mountain range and told to survive for a moon. Under the Divinity of Forgiveness's moon, this might be an easy task – murderous beasts and shadowy magic aside – but under the Divinity of Wrath's moon, the elements can destroy a guard within heartbeats.

And while aemortals can't be killed in the traditional sense, they can be destroyed, devastated, their organs irreversibly damaged, their minds taken. They are not able to heal themselves, only those with healer Gifts or medical studies able to help. And immortality tied to insanity is surely worse than a death sentence.

Celestial are isolated from the remaining bastions by the vast Cecedit mountain range, but it's still possible they could journey here, especially with silicrites and golems. They wouldn't need to stop for hunger or toilet breaks; they're an impenetrable, relentless army.

"But they have no reason to attack another land," I say. Just because they can, doesn't mean they would.

"Oh, silly lady." Tryx sighs. "To return to my earlier point: you don't understand that Kae's done much better in this match than you. You just wait, dear Elira. He may not be upset about who you are, but rather afraid that he can't equal your stature."

"He's a full foot taller than me," I reply flatly. I've got the leathers on, and now I slip my feet into thick, fur-lined boots. They're snug and warm, perfect.

"Stature in position, you dense woman," Tryx mutters, rolling his eyes. "Just stick with Prince Kae, Elira. Fayte knows, it's about time the both of you had something to smile about. He's a good man. He'll keep you safe."

"I don't need a man to keep me safe," I growl, the words tumbling out before I can stop them.

"If you say so." Tryx flexes his claws on the floor, amused. "But needing people isn't such a bad thing, you know. Two lonely souls, joining in a blazing flame of imperial glory, or something."

I don't have the energy for his philosophy. I pull stray hair behind my ear, frustrated. Everyone else seems to think they know what's best for me.

"Right, shall we go and get you killed, then?" Tryx asks cheerfully, already turning toward the outside. His tail flicks into the air as he strides out, leaving the door wide open—an invitation to change my mind, if I want.

I stomp my feet and march forward.

Stupid little cat.

CHAPTER THIRTY-THREE

Somer's moon lifts in the sky as we trek through the aemortal towns, the time not aided by Tryx, who talks loudly and insistently about utter nonsense. Every time we pass someone, I duck behind bushes, carts, and alleyways to keep out of sight, my heart beating in my throat, that damned cat calling out greetings as if he's taken an evening promenade.

The aemortal towns are not so different from Grim Municipal. There's less smoke here, a sense of cleanliness and openness that the dark, damp alleys of the municipal could never boast. Pruned trees line the streets, the roads glittering with specks of silver as if made of moon and star. We pass a ramshackle tavern, set in shadows at the entrance to an alleyway, and my heart leaps into my throat. The Howling Cask.

The place the prince goes to drown his sorrows, to feel less lonely. The windows are dirty and stained, the walls fit for Grim Municipal's very worst slums. A smell of canyon rat droppings rolls from the entrance, as two aemortal crones groan loudly to one another from the steaming doorway. I recoil.

Can he really be so lonely that this is his sanctuary? Beneath the veneer, I sense damage: damage about what people might do to him, and the damage that people might find if they really get to know him.

I swallow down my own hypocrisy.

My insides lurch when we pass an aemortal courier service. I recognise the name; this company passes on anything meant for the mortals. The storefront is drenched in gilt-gold, the courier's name sparkling with fayte so that it practically gleams in the night. As we pass, the shop sends a sweet, melodic note into the air, and I can't help but roll my eyes. With all the fayte these aemortals can conjure, they use it for advertising gimmicks.

By the time we reach the imposing outer wall of the border, I'm sweating in my thick leathers, and I still have no idea how I'm going to get past. We touched vaguely on the borders during war class at school. Two walls form the perimeter, and between them patrols the Sable Legion. There aren't enough soldiers to station groups, so the regular battalion-to-battalion patrols are complemented by fayte-triggered alerts.

During the war, when the Sable Legion was split between royalists and Archon supporters, the borders became a battlefield. Many parts of the walls were obliterated, and some soldiers refused to control migration checks, or ward off unwanted visitors. Cross-border crime became rampant. Mother used to tell us stories of Xandryll beasts and Claran predators roaming through Grim Municipal and the aemortal towns, creating havoc. After the Archons were killed and the royal family gained power, the borders were rebuilt. Non-sanctioned immigrants—beast or otherwise—were destroyed.

I creep up to the wall and place both hands on the stone. It seems to hum beneath my palms. I can taste fayte on my tongue—sharp, metallic, like Kae when he's angry, when he wants to crush a mortal skull in a tavern.

Was that only earlier this evening? It feels like eons ago now. Midnight creeps above us, the moon anchoring itself in a violet sky. We're lucky to be undertaking this raid under a full moon—and the fact it is Somer, the moon that sits under the Divinity of Forgiveness, might only be a good omen—but the weather can shift between lands, and there's no guarantee we'll have the same fortune in Xandryll.

This wall is imbued with fayte. Which means the patrols aren't the only danger. If I try to scale it, there's a chance the wall will do some strange magic and throw me off, or even kill me. Compared to the smaller wall between Grim Municipal and the aemortal lands—a non-magical separation rather than a fierce division—this wall towers, dominating the night sky.

Above, birds circle, black silhouettes free to roam between lands. One lets out a sharp caw, likely alerting someone to our presence.

"You can feel it, can't you?" Tryx stretches lazily against the wall. "I can see it on your face. You look like a greedy child in a sweetshop."

I pull my hands away from the wall and glare at him. "Remind me again why you came?"

"Do you want to know how to bring it down, or not?"

I glance around, hoping there's not a regiment of Sable Legion on the other side of the wall, eavesdropping. Climbing over the wall is one thing, but destroying part of it? That's a death sentence by Legion squad. "*Bring it down*? Are you insane?"

"You need to learn sooner or later, woman." Tryx saunters toward me and lifts one paw. I look down just as his claws sink into the leather of my boar-skin trousers.

"Oww! Brat!" I rub my leg, my eyes instantly watering.

"I need an entry point for your body if I'm to help you the first time," Tryx says, moving toward the punctured leather. "We just need to stir it. It's been dormant for a long time. You're the most repressed person I've ever met, in every way possible."

"I'm not repressed," I snap, shaking my leg to dislodge the sting.

"Oh, but you are, dear. You've let your overwhelming self-control iron out any semblance of freedom your fayte might desire." His words land too close to Seren's accusation, and my throat tightens. I swallow against the lump of emotion.

"If I... if I steal the wolfsbane," I start, my voice quieter than I intend, as vulnerability gets its raven-like claws into me, "will people try and make me... change?

To become aemortal?"

It's a pretty big fucking question. But Tryx, as ever, is unfazed.

"Yes," he answers immediately. "But you'll only become what you were supposed to be, before Liora interfered. Your father is aemortal, Elira."

My heart slams into my ribcage. I take a step back, my mind stumbling. I knew it. Of course, I knew it. He had to be, but to hear Tryx say it so suddenly, so confidently. When I think of my father, I think betrayal. And the betrayer was aemortal. *Aemortal.*

"Why didn't you tell me before?" I demand, my throat choking, aching, raw. "Who is he?" My mother slept with an aemortal. It's true. It's all true. She took wolfsbane to stop me developing coryns, to keep me mortal. Tryx's words echo around my skull. Prick at my eyes. The cat lets out a hum, a strange and strangled laugh. He won't tell me. He won't explain how he knows that I'm a…

"I can't become half-aemortal," I whisper, my whole body prickling.

"Not even to save your family?" the damned cat presses. His words hit like a brick. I falter, unable to respond. Of course, if I knew for sure that it would guarantee their safety, I would sacrifice my mortality without hesitation. But to do so just for information… to become a monster…

My mind whispers: *I was always supposed to be a monster.*

And Prince Kaelion isn't a monster. Neither is

Dismal, as insufferable as he is. The King and Queen aren't monsters. There's a possibility mortals have been wrong all along. I swallow, trying to stop the tears in my eyes from falling. The man who left us, who didn't look back, was aemortal. How nice for him. He still means nothing to me.

And then there's Mother. Not telling me. Keeping it secret all this time. That betrayal stings a hell of a lot more. It feels as if my heart has been attacked by honeybees.

"I suppose there's the risk that the prince will slay you, as he is obliged to do for all half-aemortals," Tryx says, continuing a conversation I am not enjoying. "Even more so than the village dwellers. Perhaps you'll sprout just one coryn, and they'll lop you in half."

"Delightful," I say, trying to control my breathing. Would the prince really *kill* me? It seems that all routes end in my death. But this foraging is all I can do to gain information about Mother and Seren. I fucking hate this kingdom.

"All magic requires sacrifice," Tryx hums, almost absentmindedly. "Be thankful it's not a proper blood sacrifice. You merely give up being a helpless little lamb and become a lion."

"I don't want to become a lion," I snap, chest tight.

"You do, Elira," he replies. "You really do. You're just scared."

The wind picks up, carrying the scent of fayte with it, the rustle of leaves from the nearby orchard brushing against the air.

"Let's just get across," I say, my voice rougher than before. Everything that Tryx has said is not new news. The last few days have been culminating in this, hinting towards it. But to bring the father I never knew into such close focus, to know that he's aemortal... I can't handle it.

"What do I need to do?"

"Just... stay... still," the cat murmurs, his claws flicking as he rips a larger hole in my leathers. With fluid movement, he uses the same quarter-moon-shaped nail to slice his other paw, the one resting on the ground.

"What are you—"

"Quiet," he hisses, lifting his paw into the bone-coloured moonlight. There's no blood there—just a shimmer of molten gold. It glimmers in a kaleidoscope of colours, similar to the windows at the palace.

"What are you?" I whisper, staring at him, as my chest constricts, confusion overwhelming me. Tryx presses his golden-clad paw against my cut leg, and I watch, frozen, as the flowing gold seems to rise out of him, curling and weaving its way toward the blood that's clotting around the scratch. I can't breathe. It's as though the world has slowed, every sound becoming muffled as my skin tingles, alive with energy, and then —

It bursts inside my chest.

The force is so violent, I feel it in my bones. A roar erupts, not just in my ears but inside me, flooding my veins with a searing heat. That voice, that power, vibrates through every inch of my body. It reverberates deep inside me, shaking my very core as though I'm made of glass, ready to shatter. I gasp for air, but it feels like I'm drowning. My heart pounds, thudding against my ribs like a war drum, each beat too loud, too strong. I feel the blood rushing through my veins, hot and heavy, as though it's too much for my body to contain.

My chest constricts, the weight of the magic building inside me, pushing against my lungs.

There it is. There it is. There it is.

The thirst. It latches onto me, pulling me, consuming me as my throat burns, as my eyes sting. The beast within me rages. It claws at my insides, desperate to break free.

The suppressed animal inside me ROARS.

I am here. I am here—and I am free.

CHAPTER THIRTY-FOUR

"I thought you hated dramatics," Tryx muses. He licks my face, and the cold, wet trail of his tongue sends a shiver down my spine. "You know, when you first arrived at the palace in that disgusting tunic, I thought you'd realised."

"Realised what?" I croak, my throat sore and raspy. I open my eyes, blinking at the moon above, which seems to flicker in time with my pulse.

"It was winter, dear. Every other mortal in Grim Municipal was bundled up in hideous purple shawls and fur boots. And you? You were sauntering around with bare legs and a scrap of dirty fabric."

I blink, my vision swimming in pinpricks and shooting stars. "It was only dirty because of the silicrite blood," I mutter, my breath shallow, the stars above wobbling with my unsteady heartbeat. "My laundry schedule was on time." My body aches, but it's different this time. It feels wild, electric, delicious.

"Besides the point," Tryx snaps. He licks my face again, and the revolting wetness forces me to sit up. I don't want to be entirely covered in cat spit. "Up you get. I thought that would revive you."

I steady myself, pushing my thoughts into focus. But then Tryx's words hit me: "No, it seems strange to me that you didn't realise you don't feel the cold."

"I feel the cold," I argue, but even as the words leave my lips, I'm scrambling to piece my thoughts together. There's dust on my leathers.

"No, you don't. Not really." Tryx's voice sharpens, irritation flickering beneath the surface. "I'm surprised no one pointed that out to you, back in your little mortal village."

"It's a city," I say automatically, my mouth moving before my brain fully processes the dust on my clothes. "And people did. They used to say I was hardy. Nerissa said it all the time. Everyone thought I just preferred the way the tunic looked with bare legs, but the truth is, I was always perfectly fine in the regulation tunic. I guess they must've made it from a strong material."

Tryx hisses, frustration thick in his voice. "*Dense* woman." His words are suddenly laced with a deeper, sharper edge. "Stop being dense, Elira. Don't tell me I'm wasting my time here."

I look at him, alarmed, and then glance beyond him—toward the wall. Toward where the wall stood. A vast chunk of it has been obliterated. Rock and stone are scattered everywhere, shards of rubble and lichen strewn in a chaotic heap all around us. The wall is in pieces. And we are on the other side, in Xandryll.

"Did I do that?" I whisper, my spine prickling. I stagger to my feet, the adrenaline coursing through me making it easier than before. My insides are humming, alive with energy. What did the cat inject into me?

"Now you're getting it. Yes, you did that. You can do a whole lot more if you stop acting like a dense, pompous mortal."

"I *am* a dense, pompous mortal," I mutter, my voice trailing off as I turn to look in the other direction. A forest, black as night, stretches endlessly before me. There are no lights here—no candles, no bonfires. The moonlight, still and silent, colours everything in bone and pearl.

"Wrong," Tryx mutters as he carefully climbs over a pile of rubble and starts heading toward the forest. "Are you coming? There's a Sable Legion patrol on its way. They'll be here in precisely... oh, let me see... zero seconds."

"What?"

"HALT," a voice commands, sharp and demanding. Multiple voices echo back.

I turn, my heart freezing in my chest. Ten of them. All wearing the Sable Legion uniform—massive, aemortal, and radiating power. Their pale skin gleams, their ornate silver helmets spiralling around their coryns, patterns lost in the darkness.

The Sable Legion. The most elite of the aemortal forces. They are trained for cycles in brutal combat, subjected to pain and torture to forge them into the ultimate warriors. They are dropped into the Cecedit Mountains in their first week, forced to survive alone. They are trained not to feel, not to react.

They are trained to kill.

"GET HER!" one of the Legion screams, and before I can react, a bright, hissing flame shoots in my direction—a blazing mix of blue and shocking orange. The fire slices through the darkness, shattering the rubble and stardust.

"You might like to run one of these days," Tryx calls from somewhere far behind me, but I'm too focused on the advancing death fire.

It moves faster, crackling, blasting straight for me. My feet are glued to the ground. My hunting leathers feel too tight.

I taste fayte on my tongue, feel it pulsing through my forearms. I don't know why, but something deep inside urges me to raise my hands. I shield my face, throwing my palms up in front of me, bracing for the fire's impact.

It's too late. The fire reaches me, searing through the air and slamming into my hands. The heat is unbearable, the burn of a thousand suns. My skin blisters, the pain explodes through my fingers, but—

It's not the fire's heat. It's my own. I'm half-aemortal. I can feel the heat surging from my palms, the power coming from within. My eyes snap open, just enough to see gold flashing around me, the intensity of the fayte overwhelming my senses. The fire burns, but it's my own energy, the same brilliant beams of murderous sunshine that lit the torturous cellar at the palace, blasting from my palms.

I try to catch my breath, blinking through the stars in my vision. My hands shudder, my arms feeling as if they're splitting apart and re-healing, and that laugh – that terrible, ancient, cruel laugh – is leaving my lips again. I clamp my mouth shut, and divert my attention away from the soldiers. The fayte falls away, scattered into the air in fragments of moondust and ash.

When the bright lights that spot my vision finally fade, the Sable Legion patrol is gone. All that remains are silver helmets scattered above piles of charred, prune-like bodies. The air crackles with the fading blue sparks that dance across their remains.

I stagger forward, nausea rising in my throat. My stomach churns and twists as I retch, vomiting until my body is empty. I whisper a prayer to the Divinities, hoping the souls of the Sable Legion find their way to Thekla, to death, and beyond. Because they are not redeemable, not in this state. They have been drained of blood.

From behind me, I hear Tryx's light footfalls. He skips over to me, his voice filled with amusement as he looks at the smouldering remains.

"Nice," he says, inspecting the shrunken corpses. His tone is pleased, almost proud.

CHAPTER THIRTY-FIVE

Despite the hours—no, the eons—we spend searching the dense, muddy forest floor, I can hardly believe that I'm actually here. Every step through the underbrush feels like an eternity, and the air grows thick with exhaustion, the weight of it pressing against my chest. The suffocating humidity of Xandryll swirls around me, coating my skin in a clammy sheen, but it's nothing compared to the tension coiling tighter within my chest, the frantic pounding of my heart. I am so close now.

I couldn't have done this alone.

I didn't even know what I was looking for when we first entered the forest, the overwhelming darkness pressing in from all sides. Tryx is the one who guides me, his sharp eyes flicking back and forth, always scanning. "Wolfsbane," he explains, "a red root, speckled with tiny soft thorns. And it stinks—rotten eggs, like death itself."

The thought makes me shiver. A plant that smells

of decay. Lovely. I rely on my senses—my eyes, my hands, and most of all, my nose. The stench that wafts through the forest is pungent, thick, almost nauseating. I gag slightly but press forward, hoping—no, praying—to the Divinities that this is not the scent of a decaying animal.

And then, through the haze of doubt and dread, I catch a glimmer of colour. There it is. The unmistakable red sheen of the wolfsbane root, glowing faintly beneath the moonlight. My heart skips a beat, relief flooding my chest. The knot of anxiety loosens slightly, but my limbs still feel like lead, stiff with fatigue. My head is somewhere else; visions of the shrunken guards keep attacking me and plunging me into a nightmare as we delve further into the scat-scented forest.

And then I see it. I fucking *see it.*

I stumble forward, reaching out blindly, my fingers trembling as I grasp the plant and yank it from the earth. I don't realise I'm crying until the first tears hit my dirt-streaked cheeks. I can hardly catch my breath as I clutch the root to my chest, blood singing in my veins. My body is spent, my heart pounding with relief, and yet I can't stop the tears.

I've done it. I've found it.

But before I can take another breath, the attack comes.

A rustle. A shriek.

Before I can react, three forest durlems—long-tailed, clawed creatures—drop from the trees above, their talons glinting in the low light. They come at me, slashing with ferocity, claws raking across my skin. Pain explodes through me, and I scream as one rips across my face, leaving stinging, burning gashes. My vision blurs as I stagger back, struggling to stay on my feet.

And then—then it happens.

A surge of power. A roar. My body jolts with energy as the fayte reappears. I don't have time to think, only to act. With every fibre of my being, I release a shockwave of energy that sends the durlems tumbling back into the forest. I see their bodies twist, their limbs go limp as they crumple. One of them smashes into a tree, its broken form sagging. Others scatter, retreating into the shadows of the trees.

I collapse to my knees, my hands shaking violently as I clutch the wolfsbane root, pulling more from the earth. Soil and clay stain my palms, but it's nothing compared to the pulsing fire in my veins. I shove the root into the pockets of my borrowed leather jacket, and press it tightly against my chest as if it might disappear, my hands shaking.

My body is alive with the aftershock of fayte, my pulse hammering in my ears. But it's not enough to quell the exhaustion dragging at my bones. My legs tremble beneath me as I push myself to my feet. There's no time to rest. This place stinks like rotting flesh.

"Come on," Tryx urges, sounding a little spooked out. I don't think he was expecting the durlems. "We need to get out of here."

The forest feels endless as we continue our trek. Every tree and bush blurs together. We've already passed the same pink stream twice, but I can barely remember where we've been. My mind is foggy from exhaustion, and my stomach twists with hunger. My lips are dry, cracked from the lack of water, and yet, every step forward feels heavier than the last. This forest is *endless.*

Tryx stops. He doesn't say a word as he studies the ground. A flick of his wrist, and a glowing map forms on the dirt, illuminating our location. His paw sweeps over it, tracing a path out of the forest.

I look at him, my throat tight with frustration. "Why didn't you just do that from the start?" The words come out sharper than I intend, exhaustion making me rasp.

"Fayte is finite," Tryx replies curtly. "You don't always have enough to waste it."

Tension hangs in the air between us as we continue, the weight of it pressing on my chest. Every single exhausted, filthy part of me is struggling to keep it together.

Finally, as the sun begins to creep above the horizon, the first remnants of light waking, I manage to push the weariness aside long enough to focus. The wall is ahead of us.

The wall is ahead of us.

I glance at Tryx, who looks at me at the exact same moment. "You've done it," he says softly, his voice filled with a kind of pride that makes something stir inside me.

I blink back tears. Whisper, "Thank you. For helping me."

We've got the wolfsbane.

CHAPTER THIRTY-SIX

The sunrise bleeds into soft pinks and purples on the horizon. Grim Municipal must be waking up by now—window shutters thrown open, cooking pots heating over the first embers of the new day. Citizens are likely soaping pyjamas, elbow-deep in suds, before heading out to work, the first productive breaths of the morning ticking away in that familiar, reassuring rhythm. The humdrum of everyday existence, the reassuring repetition of thousands of lives unfolding in proximity to one another.

I spit into the sea of white flowers. My body feels broken. My hunting leathers are torn, my face streaked with berry stains, my hair in a messy updo, half trailing down my back, now matted with mud and coarse as bristles.

We can see the palace gates in the distance, yet I know I'll never make it that far.

He comes to us.

Tryx must have summoned him somehow. Or else he was waiting in the grounds, watching for our return. He is wearing the same suit trousers from last night, something bulging in his pocket. I'm too tired to try and guess what it is. I throw the wolfsbane in his direction—the forbidden substance.

I force myself not to notice his windswept hair, his wrinkled trousers, his mud-smeared, topless torso. And is that blood on his wrists?

Tryx slinks off toward the castle door, his movements smooth and deliberate.

Now, the prince falls to the ground beside me. His deep voice rumbles in my ears, full of warmth, as he pulls me into his chest. His strong arms wind around my back, under my legs. He's shaking—or perhaps it's me.

I'm only like this because of him.

"I nearly died," I whisper, my voice barely a breath. I have no strength left.

"Tryx bound me," he whispers back, his voice soft, apologetic. He kisses my forehead, and my skin burns with the touch. The warmth of cedar bonfires, the smell of moss, summer evenings by the fire, crackling logs on a windy beach—all of it floods my senses, soothing my pain, calming the ache in my chest.

In fact, the kiss has genuinely soothed much of the physical pain, but I can still feel the ache inside, the gnawing emptiness. This is the sort of pain that doesn't stop at an aching throat and torn palms. My soul feels split apart.

"I tried to follow," Kaelion whispers.

I mumble something non-comprehensible. There are aemortals leaving the palace ball, echoes of laughter and merriment echoing around the grounds. Through blurred vision, I see splashes of ballgowns, suits tugged loose. Someone wields a green bottle, likely sparkling elven wine from the hills of Casus. We've only been gone one night.

"I'll make you better in no time, Elira," Kaelion promises, his voice thick with determination. "I'll heal you if it's the last thing I do. And then we can go to the Divinity of War."

He smells nice. And I like his voice. It's soothing, lulling me into thoughts of bonfires and secrets, nightbirds and calming seas. I wonder if the durlems stole my sanity. Or perhaps it's the memory of the Sable Legion's faces—their shrunken, mummified forms.

"Tryx bound me with fayte. I wanted to run after you... I wanted to follow you to the border, but I couldn't. We true aemortals cannot cross without clemency. It's cursed; we die as soon as we try to breach it. Only a half-blood, still with mortal traces, or a powerful new aemortal, can come near the wall. I'm sorry I couldn't be there."

His words barely make sense. My whole body feels spent, like I'm drifting in and out of consciousness. As I look up at him, I see his stubble up close, tan and russet hairs that hide a dimple in his right cheek, toothmarks along his fleshy lower lip.

"Tryx told me," he continues, his voice thick with regret. "He entered my head, told me you'd be okay, but

I couldn't... I drove myself mad. I ran for the border, but every time it threw me back. I was miles away from where you crossed, if the Legion's morning update is correct. I tried, Elira. Not to save you, I know you don't need saving, but to be there for you when you needed me."

How does he know I always insist I don't need saving? Sometimes it feels like he can read my mind—like we've stumbled into each other's lives for a reason, beyond just me being a monarchy-hating rebel, and him being the monarchy at which my sword is pointed.

"What happened after that?" I mumble, trying to make sense of it all, wondering why he's covered in blood.

"I... tried. But the wall threw me off, and eventually, two village healers heard me and dragged me away." His voice falters. I'm too tired to push for more. Too tired, and consumed by the poison of Tryx's revelation. I'm a half-blood. The fact has consumed my mind and plunged me into raw, painful shock.

Kaelion lifts me into the air and starts walking, the early morning breeze lifting my hair and cooling my scalp.

"I killed people," I whisper, burying my face into his chest, where shoulder blade curves to collarbone curves to tanned pectoral, the calm of his bare skin soothing me. It's so soft, and yet unyielding as I press my face and inhale. "I destroyed a border. I murdered members of the Sable Legion." Pain rises in my chest, sharp and suffocating. I swallow hard, trying to breathe through it. "I hope it was worth it," I murmur.

He climbs the steps toward the palace door, the firelight from the torches flickering, catching my eyelids. His body is warm against me, his chest slick with sweat. I can smell him—animalistic, raw. Why is he topless?

"Me too," Kaelion mutters, his voice heavy with a mixture of pain and something softer, like starlight. I feel a drop of water fall onto my cheek. I don't open my eyes to see if he's crying. I don't need to.

The midday sun wakes me, my forehead burning. I open my eyes and start at the figure in the corner of the room, but it's only Elrind. He wrings a washcloth above a bowl of water, and I can hear the clicking of ice in the bowl. I am still exhausted from our mission, my whole body aching, but it is with something like relief that I see Tryx stretched out in a ray of sunshine along the tattered rug on the floor. His tail lazily flicks as he watches me with half-lidded eyes. I'm getting tired of his nonchalance, but I need answers, so I bite back my impatience.

"Elira," Elrind says. Relief cascades across his face as he drops the cloth.

"Hey." I rub my face. I wonder where the prince is. Did all of that really happen? Did I really break into Xandryll? Steal wolfsbane?

If so, then we now have what we need. Or, what the prince needs. The same tincture that mother fed me when I was an infant.

"I still don't understand," I say, looking at Tryx and blinking away sleep. I'm tired of small talk. I've been sleepwalking through life. I have woken with a burning forehead, yes, but also a sense of vehemence. "If wolfsbane hid my status as a child, why does it have the opposite effect now? I'm just supposed to take it and —boom!—I'm a half-aemortal?"

Tryx snorts, the sound half-laugh, half-cough. "Ah, you're thinking like a mortal, Elira. Not everything in this world is so straightforward. Wolfsbane's a curious thing, you see." Elrind itches his shoulder as Tryx pauses to yawn, and then continues, "It's more than just a herb. It's a tincture of change, a kind of... alchemy, if you will. When you were a baby, your mother used it to suppress your fayte abilities. It's like a lock—keeps your potential sealed away, dormant. It stops your blood from recognising its true power, my dear."

I furrow my brow. Move my legs under the covers, to get my circulation going. "So, she used it to hide me from my own nature... but that doesn't explain how I can reverse it. How does something reverse that?"

Tryx's tail twitches again. He doesn't seem to care that my whole world is shifting, but Elrind has the grace to look towards his feet. I must look like shit.

"Wolfsbane's a suppressor, but it's not permanent. Well, it's only permanent if you never try to unlock the door again. You see, when a baby takes wolfsbane, it prevents them from being able to access fayte. The effect is, in essence, a blocker—stunts the growth of their inherent abilities. But the thing is, once you're an adult, you can take a reverse tincture. Something that uses an opposite compound—a kind of activator for the dormant fayte within you."

Tryx rolls his eyes. "It's not expert science. The reverse tincture is a concoction made with wolfsbane, fireroot, and a few other bits I'm not going to explain because I'm not your tutor. Think of it like... untangling the magic in your veins. You drink it, and it stimulates what was once stifled. It helps the body recalibrate, unlock what's been held back since you were young."

I blink, absorbing his words. "And you think this will work? Turn me into something I'm supposed to be?"

"Elira, you've already been walking around with half of yourself hidden. You're not just mortal. All that wolfsbane did was put the brakes on it for a while. This reverse tincture? It'll give you the keys to that locked door. Whether you'll like what you find on the other side is another matter."

I stare at him, feeling the weight of everything he's said settle into my chest like an anchor. I was never meant to be ordinary. And all along, I've been kept from my destiny—only to walk into it now, blindly.

The betrayal exhausts me. I fall back onto my pillows, my eyes weighing down.

The afternoon wakes me again. I feel weak, but sleep has finally helped me to untangle my mind. Did the conversation with Tryx really happen? It feels like a dream now. Kaelion sits on my bed, staring blankly at the wall. As I stir, he does too, shaking his head slightly as a smile appears, tight around his tired eyes. He reaches out a hand to touch my cheek, and then lets it fall.

"How are you feeling?" he mutters. My heart picks up and starts to rage in my chest as I glance at the window. It feels strange to be back in the palace with Kaelion, as if I never left. Perhaps Xandryll was a dream. Perhaps adding yet more names to my murder roster was all just a dream.

"How's your mother?" I croak, my tongue dry. I can accept that Kaelion was bound by Tryx, that he couldn't come after me. But it's harder to accept the shocked look on the queen's face when she thought her son might be dating me. "Still devastated that I was invited to the ball?"

Kaelion looks ahead to the wall again, as he sighs.

"She doesn't know what you might be. I haven't told anyone about your... Gift."

"So, as a mortal, I'm not *good enough* for you. But as a half-blood, or whatever, she might think twice?" I don't mean to sound so bitter, but half of me is still fed up with all of them. I refuse to feel ashamed about being mortal, even if I was born differently.

"You think you're a half-blood?" Kaelion asks, his eyes burning into mine. "Can I ask why?"

I look at him for a long moment. Can I tell him? Can I trust him not to immediately execute me? His face softens as if he can read my mind, and I decide that I really don't have a choice. He deserves to know.

"Tryx told me that my father's aemortal," I mutter.

He looks at me for another long moment, and then looks down to where he's laced his fingers over his knees. As if he's thinking. And then Kaelion looks up again, and says, "So you truly do have a Gift. It's an honour to meet you, Half-Blood Elira." He tugs one side of his mouth into a smile. His eyes are kind. They melt my heart.

My parents better have a very good reason for changing me when I could've spent a whole lifetime stronger, using this Gift – whatever it may be. A whole lifetime in this aemortal town, talking to him.

Except his mother might have judged me anyway. "And what of your mother?" I ask. "She was already horrified when she thought I was mortal, let alone now."

"My mother has been through a lot in her life," he says sadly. I try and ignore the streak of sympathy that courses through my chest. "She likes... control. It is hard for her, finding out about you from Disryn. I rather think she would like to hear it from me, if this... if anything serious happens."

I look down to where his fingers linger. "But she doesn't think I'm good enough for... to be here," I breathe. "And that won't change with the wolfsbane, Kae. I'm still a poor woman from Grim Municipal."

"She will be happy for it. If anything happens."

"How can you be so sure?"

"Because I'll make sure of it."

I snort out a laugh. But I have to admit that he's made me feel slightly lighter.

And I didn't tear up my fingernails for nothing. I didn't go through all of that for nothing. And so Kaelion agrees, even though his voice is heavy with pain when I finally ask him.

Perhaps he doesn't want me to change. It will make it that much harder for him to entertain his many wenches if he has an annoying new woman hanging around more, learning how to be aemortal. All I can think about is how it's the only option I have right now – to get information about my family. And that is really the beginning and end of everything.

"If I change, will you kill me for being a half-blood?" I mutter after the request, as sunlight dances around my room.

"Idiot," he murmurs, looking at the fayte-imbued window. "But we will... I will need to explain to the Major General. He's not... fond of breaking the Legion Manual. I think it might be in Volume 1: never allow half-bloods. Some old grudge from an Archon who was dumped by one, no doubt."

"Why's he still alive? He tried to kill me," I rasp.

"My parents stepped in," Kaelion mutters darkly. "The other guards were slain, sent to Thekla. But you did... they are saying that you stabbed a guard."

"I did."

"Okay. So I think my parents consider his retaliation justified. I'm sorry. He knows so much, his Gift has been so useful for our land. And if he does try to have you executed, I'll break every bone in his body." Kaelion sounds light as he says this, his usual sunny murderous streak taking hold.

"Hah! Why not seek out the Bone-Wielder for

such a task."

The prince tenses, just slightly, just enough to tell me that even he fears the one with the ability to break bones without moving. Wielders are a nasty breed of Gift-holder.

"Take me to your Divinity," I mutter, as thoughts of the aemortal kingdom thunder around the insides of my skull.

CHAPTER THIRTY-SEVEN

The chambers of the Divinity of War are dark, heavy with ancient power, the air thick with the mingling scents of incense and steel.

We wisped here—my body pressed against Kaelion's as we slipped beyond the palace—and I have no idea where we are. Only that we seem to have arrived in a glamorous cavern, where glints of gold and towering ancient weapons catch the dim light. The only illumination comes from glowing antechambers carved into the stone above us, curls of incense rising like fire smoke in every direction. Weapons of all ilk are embedded into the cavernous walls, hoisted on plinths, burnished under stray sunbeams.

I suspect—though I do not know for certain—that only those with a Gift can wisp into a Divinity's chambers. The servant who ushered us in, wearing nothing but a gold breechcloth around his waist, his coryns cropped and gilded, seemed to recognise Kaelion. He didn't pause to question why we were here.

We have been led to a dais in the grandest of all the chambers, brilliant sunlight breaking through an opening above.

The Divinity of War sits upon her throne, a vision of power and grace. Her molten eyes burn with an intensity capable of incinerating entire worlds, their heat radiating from deep within her being. To an observer, she may appear as any aemortal—but her irises shimmer gold, and her body is encased in ancient, unyielding armour. Her shoulders are broad and battle-worn, carrying the weight of countless wars fought. A symbol rests at the centre of her forehead—the transformist symbol for War—glowing faintly in silver, visible with every movement of her head, as if the very act of thinking brings that power to life.

She is both ageless and youthful: her face etched with the lines of time's passing, yet her lips, full and unblemished, speak of unyielding vitality. Her form embodies the paradox of war itself—an eternal, fierce presence clothed in the flesh of a goddess who remains untamed by time.

And normally, I would be scared shitless.

I am standing in front of a Divinity. A goddess. One of the seven most powerful beings in the empire. It is overwhelming. To a normal mortal.

But that is no longer me. Even as exhaustion drags at my limbs, I feel Tryx's fayte surging through me, forcing my chin up, making me stand firm. I still wear my hunting leathers, tight against my skin, cupping my arse, gripping my hips, cinching at my waist where Kaelion held me on the way here—his hands firm, possessive.

He didn't have to hold me that tightly. Didn't need to stare into my eyes like he was about to devour my soul—sexier than it sounds—to cling to me as if I might disappear into the ether. Something troubled him—his feelings, his thoughts, whatever it was—but even now, standing before a goddess, he can barely tear his gaze away from me.

Fancying a half-blood who should already be on death's row? Probably not an ideal predicament. At least he had the sense to throw a leather jacket over his bare torso.

"You seek my counsel?" the Divinity asks, her voice a low rumble, regal and untouchable. Her gaze slides to me, assessing, weighing. "Corpuseus's bestowed," she mutters, almost to herself, amusement flickering in her golden eyes.

Kaelion steps forward first, his voice steady but edged with tension. "I bring Elira Corvannis, a mortal from the Eryndal municipal. We seek your help."

The goddess flicks her eyes briefly to him before settling them back on me. She doesn't speak right away —just studies me, as if she's deciding whether I'm worth the effort.

"And why," she finally asks, her tone cold, measured, "should I help you?"

I swallow, forcing my racing heart to steady. This is it. The moment I risk everything. For answers. For Mother and Seren. I step forward. My voice trembles at first, but I force it steady. "I will offer you something in return," I say, my words falling like stones into the heavy silence. "I will take wolfsbane and allow myself to change. To become aemortal. I know it will entertain you—to see me change."

Kaelion stiffens beside me, his hand twitching toward mine, but he doesn't say anything. He's waiting. Watching. His silence urges me onwards.

"I will take the wolfsbane and transform—to get the information I need. To find out where my family are," I say, my voice stronger now, more certain. "I know it will amuse you. I can feel it. The challenge of turning a mortal into one of your kind." This much is true, at least. I see the glimmer in her eyes, the way that she has aemortal and mortal playthings filling her palace as servants. And yet, I also see how bored she is. How she longs for something to happen. And turning a mortal into a half-blood can't happen very often, if at all.

The goddess tilts her head, studying me intently.

"Ah," she says slowly, amusement creeping into her voice, "you would offer yourself for information. How quaint. How… desperate."

I don't flinch. This is the offer. The bargain. The price I must pay for the truth. Servants—semi-naked, their skin streaked in gold—move silently through the chamber, carrying out Divinity business. The one who led us here, an aemortal man adorned with a tiara, stands at the goddess's side, as if guarding her. She glances between us, making a thoughtful, pondering sound. "How fares the fight for your kingdom, Kaelion?" she asks, her voice laced with quiet amusement. "That you might risk my repulsion just to aid a mortal?"

Kaelion's voice is rough, edged with something I

can't quite name. "I cannot consider mortals lesser than us," he says, his tone hoarse, heavy with pain. I whip my gaze toward him. "With one exception," he continues, his voice quieter now. "Where love is concerned. It would not be fair to my heart; if I fall in love with a mortal, I will not have long enough."

Sorry, what?

What did he just say?

Heat prickles down my neck, curling at the base of my spine, sending waves of something dangerous rippling through me. I breathe in deeply, my leathers tightening around my ribs. Did he mean that? He refuses to fall in love with a mortal? Or is he playing the Divinity—feeding into her love of romance and spectacle?

For one who incites war is one who loves—rarely has a war begun without the fire and fury of fighting for something, someone.

Perhaps she hopes we will burn.

The Divinity is speaking again, barking orders to a servant, but I can't focus. My whole body is alert, my senses aching, waiting—praying—for him to speak again. Could he fall in love with a mortal, if he had to? Or is he only disinclined because of the inevitable end—the fact that, in aemortal terms, it would be over too soon?

Or does he believe in it so fiercely, so deeply, that he would never let himself? As if he hears my thoughts—or simply notices that I am blatantly staring at him, my questions painted across my face—he growls under his breath, "Don't test me, Corvannis."

I gasp—and quickly turn it into a cough.

Fayte, I hope the Divinity cannot read our minds right now.

She pulls her attention back to us, her molten gaze sharp, assessing. It seems that some of her minions have disappeared to fetch her food; a dish of rabbit and oysters, to be enjoyed with a plum sauce.

"But your other request, Kaelion…" she murmurs, her golden lips smooth as silk. "To alter Solthera's silly little map. I cannot grant you two favours. Surely, you can see that?"

Oh my gods.

My whole body freezes.

Prince Kaelion has already asked a favour of her —to add his name to the Map of the Monarchy. Was he planning to use my change as his bargaining chip for this favour?

I can't speak. Can't look at him. I try to steady my breathing. Of course, he has his own agenda. He does not want to watch Dismal take up the mantle and run his kingdom into the ground. He barely knows me. Or— at the time when he presumably made this request—he barely knew me.

And yet…

Something inside me wilts. A quiet, unfamiliar wound. Have I been enlisted as entertainment, just so the prince can reclaim his kingdom? Was this his plan all along—to ensure that I change, just to secure his ego? Perhaps that's why he was so eager to tell me about his paternity, when he is usually rigidly stoic.

"I do not wish to seek this favour any longer," Kaelion says, his voice measured. "I wish to withdraw that request. It is more important that we find Liora and Seren Corvannis, wherever in this empire they might be."

My eyes flame, his gaze searching for mine. I refuse to look at him. I don't know why I'm so bothered.

The goddess watches, her golden stare burning through my resolve. "Very well," she murmurs. "I will consider your offer. But know this, Corvannis —you will take that promise seriously. If I help you find your family, you must honour your word. I would like to dine with a half-blood, and I miss Corpuseus."

I nod, my throat tight, not knowing what else to say. I've already given everything. I don't know who Corpuseus is. I will not rock the boat, now she has agreed. She's going to find my family.

Kaelion steps toward me, his hand brushing gently against my shoulder, his voice a low murmur. "You don't have to do this, Elira," he whispers, his words laced with concern. "Just the promise will be enough. The goddess will help us. She'll look into your mother and sister's fates without you needing to sacrifice your mortality. If you… if you become half, I don't know what life will be like. There haven't been enough studies on half-borns. I can't promise eternity."

I look up at him, my heart hammering in my chest. The fear in his eyes is unmistakable—the fear that I'll go through with this, that I'll give myself to something neither of us fully understands.

"No," I say, my voice barely above a whisper,

though I'm not sure whether I'm speaking to him, to myself, or to the Divinity. "I have to. I made the promise."

And I will do anything for my family. I feel my eyes blaze as I return Kaelion's stare, meeting his anguish with challenge. I turn back to the goddess, my whole body humming. The Divinity watches us for a long moment, her expression unreadable. Then, finally, her lips curve into something almost satisfied, as if she has seen something she likes very much.

"Very well," she says at last. "I will look into your family's fate. But remember, mortal," her voice sharpens, "the price of power is never what you think. Changing your essence will alter you in ways you cannot yet understand."

I just nod, my heart heavy with the weight of my promise.

The air is charged as Kaelion turns, leading me away. His hand barely brushes against mine, and yet the touch lingers, like static in the space between us. We walk in silence, tension thick and unspoken, until we step outside the goddess's chamber. The antechamber is cavernous, lined with rusted muskets and old military uniforms, the air thick with dust and something metallic. Kaelion stops abruptly, turning to face me.

His eyes are darker than I've ever seen them, filled with something raw, something real.

"Elira," he whispers, barely audible. "I didn't want you to make that promise. I didn't want you to sacrifice so much just for answers. I planned for us to say you might one day. We needed the wolfsbane to prove it could happen, but I would never force you to change. And now... now, I'm afraid it won't be easy to undo the promise. Not impossible. But hard."

I take a deep breath, my heart fluttering painfully in my chest.

"I know," I whisper back. "But I have to do this. For Mother. For Seren. The Divinity would not have been swayed by maybes."

And perhaps Tryx is right. Maybe, sometimes, the lamb wants to play at being a lion. What if this is my only opportunity to do so? After this event, after we've saved my family, I might not be given another opportunity. Wolfsbane is almost impossible to get.

Kaelion's expression softens. For a moment, I think he might say something else—something more. But instead, he just watches me, then reaches out, brushing a loose strand of hair from my face. His touch sends a shiver down my spine.

"Will I lose my soul?" I ask, my voice barely a breath. "Will I lose who I am?"

Kaelion exhales, slow and measured. Then, closing the space between us, he brushes another frond of hair away. The warmth of him, the quiet weight of the moment, grounds me and unravels me all at once. His breath tastes sweet on my lips.

"I'll tell you what will happen if you become aemortal, Elira," he murmurs, the air between us humming and vibrating. "You will be the most driven, unrelenting woman I have ever known. You will be so stunning that people will stop in the streets, and men will fall to their knees—especially foolish princes.

You will have a heart too large for this world, a fierce loyalty that will shape empires. And you will wield both whenever you need to. You will make the world fall in love with you just by being yourself. And you will have power beyond your wildest dreams."

I swallow. "All of that will change, just from becoming aemortal?"

Kaelion lifts a hand to my chin, his rough thumb tracing the curve of my lip. Gentle. He is so gentle. "My point is," he murmurs, his gaze fixed on my mouth, sending all sorts of feelings shuddering through me, "that very little will change. If anything."

My heart burns. I can barely breathe.

"Except I'll live forever," I whisper.

"Except you'll live forever," he agrees, his voice laced with caution. "That might change. But we have never... we have never done it before, Elira. The Shattered Isles healers have changed our kind before, but it has never been achieved in Eryndal. It is a first for our soils."

I meet his eyes, and something shifts inside me—something fragile, something uncertain, but something there nonetheless. I've kept my distance from him. Mentally. Emotionally. And yet, my borders are starting to weaken. There is an unspoken bond between us now, deeper than duty, deeper than mere survival. We've been through too much together —murder, Divinities, promises—for me to pretend otherwise. I think I might be falling. And I think it might be dangerous.

"How would it happen?"

"If you... if you wanted, then the best changeling healers from the Shattered Isles are staying in Eryndal palace right now," he murmurs. "I brought them over so that I could ask... could check what your Gift might mean."

"What?" I furrow my brow. "When did you ask them to visit?"

"Well," he looks at me with dark eyes, "the other evening, I was out on patrol, when I bumped into the most devastatingly beautiful postmistress that this empire has ever seen."

"Right." I swallow.

"And as soon as I sauntered home that night, I sent a message to the Queens of the Shattered Isles, asking them if they could spare some very specific healers. They said yes."

"You knew that I might become aemortal, might change, that first night?" I ask, my lips feeling slightly numb. And he asked the Queens of the Shattered Isles, two of the most powerful women in Orynthys. Oh, heavens.

"I did," he sighs, glancing around, as if someone might have followed us. And indeed, there are several gold-clad guards either side of our antechamber, but perhaps the Divinity knew we needed a moment alone. "It is very rare, Elira, to be given a Gift. I thought, perhaps, you might decide to accept it."

"What is it?" I ask, knowing I should have asked much, much sooner. But until right now, I hadn't decided that I wanted it. That I wanted their life. Only aemortals can hold Gifts.

"I actually don't know," he admits.

"You don't know?" I blink, stunned. "What if you're wrong? What if I'm not even a half-blood? My father might well have been the mortal salesman that Mother always told us he was!" It's a big bloody thing to get wrong. I stare at Kaelion, but to my annoyance, the only light that dances in his eyes is amusement.

"I can see that you have a Gift," he says, simply. "I can't always see what the specific gift is. Divinities aren't that stupid. Some of them make it impossible to tell what that gift is, which is best for everyone. You know that rare Gifts are seen as collectable items? And I'm not the only Giftseer in the kingdom."

"Hmm."

He's tugged on my curiosity. They all have. Our kingdom is split into the towns and the arable land, the houses and the wastelands, and I've spent my whole life living in the shit, drowning in poverty. As long as becoming aemortal is only a physical change, it's pretty bloody appealing. To know that there's potentially a Divinity out there who has given me a Gift, who's been waiting patiently for me to use it…

"Could she be lying?" I whisper. "Could I change, and she tells us nothing?"

Kaelion drags his gaze away from mine for a moment. "War's mercy is stronger than her desire for vengeance. Otherwise, these chambers would not be packed with servants choosing to work for her."

The reminder of how far away we are from Eryndal sobers me, and I feel the twinkle ebb from my eyes as I nod.

"Let's do it." I swallow. "Let's reverse the tincture."

And in that moment, I know. It's the right choice. Because whatever happens next—

I won't be a lamb any longer.

CHAPTER THIRTY-EIGHT

Their voices come and go, fragments of vague information drifting into my consciousness. I've done it. I've let them change me.

I can't move. I feel as if I died at the border and have been transported to some strange version of Thekla. A kindly nurse with a Shattered Isles accent forces spoonfuls of something thick and foul-tasting past my lips—a bitter, metallic tang of iron. The wolfsbane has been cooked into a paste, prepared by healers from the Isles.

Substances drag me into a dreamlike state. Sometimes, I feel pain. Mostly, I feel nothing. As if I have died.

When I next stir, I smell the sweet, crisp scent of ice and jasmine. Bangles clink and jangle as a cool, damp cloth is pressed against my forehead. The queen's touch is delicate, as if she's afraid she might shatter my skull. Other voices filter in, murmuring from near the window. The two princes. I can hear them, but my body feels so tired that I can't even peel my eyelids back from my eyes.

"She looks so small," the queen sighs, as heat runs through my body. I have a fever, and the cold cloth the queen presses to my face is heavenly.

"Yeah, be careful when you do the deed, bro," Dismal murmurs, his tone leering. "You might crush her."

"Hush." The queen dabs my forehead.

"How could you, Mother?" Kaelion breathes. I hear his footsteps approach. Then his hand finds my ankle, his fingers rough on my bare skin. Warmth spreads through me like an ember catching fire, sending uncontrollable sparks through my lower stomach. "You know not to mess with the dead," he says softly.

"You don't know what it's been like." The queen's hand pauses. "All the... all the stillborns. Every time. I wanted a daughter. I just wanted a daughter."

The cloth trembles against my skin.

"I can't believe we're such a disappointment as sons that you felt the need to raise the dead," Dismal drawls, his voice slipping back into bored indifference. "You know we'll have to execute her. Properly this time."

The queen's hand shakes.

"We had the Pathseer and the Necromancer right there," she whispers, her voice so low it feels like she's speaking only to me. "The Pathseer saw the possibilities. The future this child might take. It was there—laid out before me like a Gift from a Divinity."

"It was stupid," Dismal retorts.

"It was unwise." Kaelion sighs, and lets go of my ankle. "Tensions are already high between us and Fjaldorn. If they find out we've started bringing mortal children back from the dead... They may choose to make a public spectacle of us. Use it to cause further harm."

My lungs contract, my skin shivers. Bringing mortal children back from the dead. The queen must have raised the dead mortal child, the one Elrind mentioned when I first saw him. Mother told us stories of Necromancers when we were children, but only in an abstract sense; I never believed them to be real.

There is really an aemortal who can resurrect the dead. Somewhere in this castle, a little girl has been reborn. My forehead prickles, but still, I cannot move.

"Politics is so fucking boring." Dismal's words and subsequent yawn break through my horror.

"Consider yourself lucky that your brother is around to take over the throne when we abdicate," the queen hisses. "If he hadn't agreed to continue despite the map's dangers being revealed, you might not have been able to run off to the Shattered Isles to study seaweed."

"Mother, I'm hurt," Dismal says, but he laughs. "I'm very grateful my big brother is taking over. And now you have a daughter who can help him."

My chest tightens, and Kaelion growls but squeezes my ankle. Does Dismal mean me? Am I this new daughter of which he speaks? A daughter-in-law, mentioned when the queen is already shocked about her son potentially dating me?

"I mean the undead child, obviously," Dismal drawls, before letting out a loud guffaw of a laugh. "The mortal girl you've brought back to life."

The queen pulls the flannel away and strokes hair from my ears, her fingers tender, but still shaking. "She will make a beautiful aemortal," she whispers, her voice resigned.

There is a noise in the doorway, and then I hear the king speak: "We have received word. They are, as expected, furious. They got it wrong, their scenting based on lingering scents of another."

"Are they threatening all-out war?" the queen whispers.

"Fjaldorn are cleverer than that," the King breathes. "And she will do anything to claim power. We have held off enabling the Fjaldorn royal marriage, but she will kill Elira at the first opportunity. You have made the right decision, changing her. She wouldn't stand a chance as a mortal."

My legs prickle. My eyeballs burn behind closed eyelids. Kae let me change so that I could protect myself? What?

CHAPTER THIRTY-NINE

I wake up in the dark.

The room is still, silent, and smells faintly of jasmine and cedarwood. I've been asleep for what feels like forever. I feel... different. As if I travelled somewhere during my change. As if I can taste blood on my tongue, can smell flowers from the palace gardens on my nightgown.

I suck in a long breath. My body feels lighter, almost weightless, but it's not just that. There's a power in me, thrumming beneath my skin, and it's not the same as the energy I'd felt when I was full of fear and adrenaline. This is something else entirely. It's something alive, something mystic. I sit up, slowly, cautiously, and swing my legs over the edge of the bed. My feet touch the cool stone floor, but it's not the cold I expect. No. There's an odd, disorienting warmth under my skin, like a furnace just waiting to be stoked.

I reach up to rub my face, but my fingers stop. I freeze. What the hell...?

I know what this is. There's something in my scalp, something that wasn't there before. A pressure. A sharpness. I move my hand up, slowly, cautiously, and touch the points. The points. I feel the delicate curve of something soft and slick beneath my fingers, and I realise they are my coryns. My horns.

I pull my hand away quickly, staring at my fingers, half expecting them to be marked somehow, but there's nothing. Just a new sensation—a strange connection to the energy around me. The moment the realisation hits, I feel it flood me—fayte. Magic. The raw pulse of it thrumming through every vein, every nerve. It's a sensation so rich, so vibrant, it's almost intoxicating. For the first time in my life, I feel relaxed, as if someone has given me an antidote to my anxiety, the creature that clawed from my skin at first light each day.

I stand, take a tentative step forward, and the ground beneath me feels... not just solid. It feels alive, like everything in Orynthys is humming in tune with me. My new power courses through me, threading its way into every inch of my body. I can breathe properly, great gasps of cool air dazzling my tongue and stunning my throat.

I want to panic. I want to fall apart. The reality of it hits me—this is permanent. I will never age again. I will live for centuries, maybe longer. There's no going back. I can never go back to my old life.

But then again... I'm not sure I want to.

I stare at my reflection in the polished stone beside the bed. I look different—more... vibrant. There's a glow to my skin that wasn't there before, a shimmer in my hair that looks somehow more alive. I look better. I look stronger, more confident. My horns look pure and unmarred, tangled in my hair. I'm no longer a mortal woman. I don't know if I feel relieved or scared. Maybe both.

I move closer to the window and look out at the night sky. The stars glitter above, infinite and vast. I could live forever under this sky. I could live and learn and love and fight and survive for centuries, while everything I know fades into dust. Grim Municipal, my family, my old life... they'll all be gone eventually.

Is there a place for me now?

I glance down at my hands, flexing my fingers. I could use my power. I can feel it in me, just under the surface, waiting for me to let it out. But I don't dare. I don't want to risk losing control and becoming something even worse. Burning down the whole palace accidentally.

I touch my horns again, and the feeling that surges through me isn't fear, but curiosity. I want to know how far I can push this power. How far I can go. And, in some small part of my mind, I want Kaelion to see me. I want him to see what I've become. Nerissa would be horrified. I crave the familiarity of Kaelion, even though I know a part of him dreaded me changing. I mutter his name, knowing there to be a guard outside my bedroom. I can see his shadow in the gap under the door.

It takes him less than a handful of breaths. However the guards, Kaelion, and Tryx communicate, seemingly telepathically, it is instant. And with their ability to wisp – or at least, the ability of some of them – this world moves hella quickly.

The door opens behind me, and I turn.

There he is.

Kaelion, looking as composed as ever, but I see the flicker of something in his eyes as they rest on me. The shock. The awe. His gaze rakes over my body, taking in the change. I watch his eyes narrow slightly, his mouth opening as if to speak but no words come out. I cock my head at him and smile. It's rare to see the prince entirely speechless.

"Elira," he says softly, almost too softly. The name on his lips feels like a confession. He still looks guilty, as if he thinks that he's made me do this, and yet, there's a softness there too.

I meet his eyes, my heart pounding in my chest. "I'm here," I whisper.

"Are you?" His voice is strained, filled with that same hesitation, that same uncertainty I felt earlier. His gaze softens just a little. "Are you really here? Do you feel different? I can't tell if you are half- or fully-aemortal."

I swallow. For the first time, I don't feel the weight of my mortal limitations pressing down on me. He is asking if I am still Elira, if I am still the nerdy, weird postmistress who makes laundry lists and queues for the best goat kidney each butchers' day.

And I am. I am still me. I am scared – I can't even begin to think about the concept of forever – but I'm also relieved. I was so afraid that I might lose my core, my essence. But now, I'm filled with power. I can taste it, through my whole body. I have coryns, I have a vitality that doesn't feel half of anything.

"I'm here," I repeat, voice firm. "And I'm the same as ever, inside. I think... I think I might be fully aemortal."

He takes a step forward, his eyes never leaving mine. "Careful with your new power," he mutters, "I can feel it rolling off you."

I grin, as he half closes the distance between us.

CHAPTER FORTY

His eyes are urgent, his tanned skin almost glowing with beautiful, golden fayte. I stand next to the bed, my hands skimming over the newly muscled curves of my waist.

The smell of fresh bread and squeezed oranges creeps through the doorway as he takes a moment to gently close and lock it, as if he's hoping not to disturb the rest of the castle, even though they are clearly readying for breakfast. He looks at me, his hulking form taut, his eyes shadowed.

"Fayte only knows," he whispers, throwing whatever he's holding into the corner by the door. It looks like a weapon. The expression on his face causes me to forget everything I intended to say to him. He is so dangerously handsome, and he looks at me like he wants to devour me.

"Why do you have a weapon?" I ask, inwardly groaning as his eyes sweep from the muscled curve of my waist up over my sweeping, soft curves.

"Why do you look so…" Something in his tone makes me want to buckle at the knees. His gaze continues to rise, fixing on my forehead, and I tremble as I wait to be assessed. "Capable of breaking a heart," he finishes.

I breathe in, disinclined to let him see how much his words affect me. We are too tumultuous; there are too many things going on.

"I am quite the dallying type," I agree breathlessly. "Always flitting from one heart to the next."

In an instant, he has moved to stand right in front of me. This is how fast he can move; how fast aemortals move. He's been holding back so far, walking stiffly, trying to look mortal. But now... Now, the animal has been unleashed.

"Where have you been?" I repeat, glancing over at the weapon by the door.

"Negotiating," he growls, his eyes eating me alive.

"Sounds like a waste of time," I dare to breathe.

"I agree. They're coming one way or another."

"And you still won't tell me what for."

"I am bound," he says carefully, his eyes flashing at the word 'bound', "to keep royal secrets. Now, if you were to become my noblewoman, I would be able to tell you everything. I am physically bound to keep royal secrets from all but my noblewoman. If I told you things now, if I even tried, the Divinities that protect my family would rip my tongue from my throat."

I blink, dazzled and amused. I cannot become his noblewoman, joined in eternal marriage. There are wives, and then there are noblemen and -women – the husbands and wives of royals, who give their entire soul for their partner. While a typical marriage can be dissolved, a noblematch is something more, something given under the gods, something that is impossible to undo, a promise for life, a bonding of souls.

"We've already been sent a ceremony present." He mutters the words, his eyes drifting down to my lips. "It seems the Lesser Divinity of Language thought us to be soon wed."

The way he's looking at my lips sends zipping ropes through me. I ache, even as I say, on trembling lips, "The quill."

"The quill," he murmurs in agreement. He leans forward, his breath caressing the space between my lips as he whispers, "It seems no one in the palace vaults is able to touch it. It is intended for myself and my noblewoman."

"Your noblewoman," I breathe, trying to control myself. Can it be true? The Lesser Divinity of Language sent us a wedding gift, already? It seems this aemortal universe is always out of step with me; first Kaelion requesting the healers after we first met, and now the Divinity of Language sending a wedding gift. A gods-forsaken *wedding gift.*

"Elira," Kae says softly, reaching up to trace the back of his fingers against my cheek. His eyes are a molten mix of amber, speckled through with sapphire and ruby. His lips tug into a half-smile, even as his breath becomes ragged, tearing from his vast body. I think he was holding himself back when I was mortal. My change has wrought a change in how Kaelion's allowing himself to see me. And the new Kaelion, the one looking at me like he wants to devour me, is truly, thoroughly impressed.

I am aware of every inch between us. Of the hard muscles beneath his military leathers, the rolling contours of his vast shoulders, the hungry way he looks down at me, waiting for permission. I reach up and graze the skin of his jaw. My hand shakes, my breathing shallow. His face above the stubble is warm and soft, cedarwood and heady sweat rolling off him as he groans, his lips parting, taking my movement as permission, a sign I want this as badly as he does.

Kaelion. I haven't been able to stop thinking about him, not been able to sleep, not been able to *focus* since we met. That was the worst thing I could think of before—becoming foggy, losing my senses—and yet, it seems that in the face of feeling so alive, it is worth it.

I tilt my head back to help close the distance between us. He is so much taller, a full head and shoulders, and yet as he leans forward, his fingers find the thin fabric at the back of my palace nightgown. His touch is rough, but warm.

"What are you thinking?" I whisper, as I put my other hand on his chest, languishing in finally feeling all that muscle, the solid beating of his heart. His other hand slips around my face and lands at the base of my neck, his fingers lingering in the sensitive space below my ear.

"I'm thinking I've waited for you for far too long," he says quietly, his gaze heating.

My own gaze heats in response, as I blush at how

much I've changed since being a loveless postmistress. He doesn't notice my blazing cheeks, instead letting out a breathy laugh, as if he can't believe what's happening. And then he leans in, holding my face up to him.

He brings his lips fully to mine and kisses me, hard. Fierceness takes over; I slide my hands around his neck, as he works his down my back, grabbing at me, ripping at me, in every way he can. He lets out a low groan as his hands wander lower, and he pulls me up to him, his hands grabbing my curves, opening my legs around him. Oh, fayte. This is *everything*. He tastes like mint and honey, like royalty and importance, like danger and freedom. He bites my lower lip, and I groan into his mouth.

"Do you want me more now that I'm aemortal?" I murmur against his lips, my heart leaping and soaring in my chest.

"I want you with or without pretty horns," he growls. His hands move, exploring, undoing me with every place they go.

It's lightning. It's thunder. It's the Divinity of Sun and the Divinity of War and the Divinity of Wrath roaring around the bedroom, sparking fires in their wake, active through my veins, panting through the hot breaths that we taste in each other's mouths. The castle walls seem to crumble, the earth seems to be ripped from below us, thunderclaps roar from a distant wind, heat rips through my body. Time shudders through the Temporal Bastion, moments clashing together like crashing drumbeats, waves of pleasure overtaking the sunrise, friction and desire pounding through me as he yanks my nightgown up and grabs my bare buttocks.

Reality takes on a new meaning, and then bounds around the room. There is no reality without this man. I am not someone who can sit in a dark room, being good. I am sunlight, my flesh devoured, my body heating for him. Lust makes my heart pound. Something more makes my chest ache. And then I pull back, my whole body trembling. Breaths still rip from both of us, as a wave of emotion runs over me.

Well, good. I'm glad I haven't lost my emotions. Lost my ability to feel. Lost my *personality*.

"What is it?" he whispers, his lips glistening. His hands drift back up my spine, dropping the nightgown, and then he pulls back, stroking my cheek, as if worried that I already regret this.

"It's just…" I glance towards the window, trying to swallow down all of my feelings. The sky has shifted into shades of hazy plum and orange spice, streaked through with gold. "Seren told me that I'd let my… my issues drown out my personality. And I resented her, I resented that." I turn back to him, once again caught by the depths of his eyes, his straight, perfect nose leading to soft, pink lips. "I didn't understand, because I couldn't see that this is a part of life. I didn't believe that I needed anything else, didn't understand that I was missing something. Something huge."

I daren't say what that thing is, but he understands. I swallow, nerves juddering through me. "Until now," I whisper, not daring to look back up at his eyes.

He swallows as well, his neck moving and contracting. And then he pulls me to him, urgency rife on his hot lips, his strong arms lifting me. Our mouths become one, hurried, intent. He is saying everything he wants to say through his body, and I find the courage to push him onto the bed and climb on top of him to continue the movement of his tongue against mine. Fire roars from both of our bodies, the tang of fayte filling the air, as if we have brought our magic into bed.

His hands drift, my mouth roves, and I ignore the excited voice in my mind that's telling me: You're making out with *Prince Kaelion!*, even as his hand explores. He spins me onto my back and pins my hands above my head with one of his vast palms, kissing my neck, as if knowing I need to spiritually make myself vulnerable even as I physically do. He explores further, increases his strokes, until I finally relinquish everything.

As I let go of control, of repression, of everything that's held me back for my entire life, my body tips to crashing before I even fully feel him. He breathes into the shell of my ear, pride trembling from his lips.

The sunrise soon warms our bare skin, sweat shimmering on his shoulders as we move. In the face of an uncertain future, in the wake of destruction and pain, we are rebuilding.

He pauses only to pull back and look deep into my eyes, his expression wild with happiness. He murmurs, "I could make love to you forever, Elira."

I don't think I have ever burned so brightly.

CHAPTER FORTY-ONE

I don't care that I'm wearing a nightgown. I don't care that my hair is unravelled, spread out around my shoulders. I run my hands over the muscled curves of my waist, trying not to smile. Sensations still pulse through me, radiating from below my stomach.

Kaelion left mid-morning, called away for some negotiation or other. He was pained to leave, but I sensed that Elrind was waiting on the other side of my bedroom door, patiently. And fayte knows, if Elrind could have read the prince's mind as he hurried out into the hallway, skin fresh with sweat, then I might never look the messenger in the eye again.

Now, I notice a faint glimmering shield around the door. Kae's set a protection. It's a small detail, one he no doubt hoped I wouldn't notice. Perhaps it's my new vision—everything feels clearer, sharper, almost in higher definition. I can see the way he's stitched the transformist symbols together to form the shield, enclosing this space.

I want to be annoyed, but my heart swells. Oh fayte, I'm in trouble.

I'm ravenous, and I don't have any other clothes. I can't find a maid, and the leather jumpsuit I arrived in hasn't made an appearance since it was whisked away for laundering.

I follow the smells of freshly baked pastries and sweet oranges through the palace. As I arrive at the sunlit breakfast room, I blink, my eyes adjusting. The King, Queen, and Dismal sit at various points down a long table, the lace tablecloth laden with dishes of every ilk: silver bowls of bright berries, platters of steaming meats, boards of thick-crusted bread. A steaming pot of coffee has recently been refilled, tendrils swirling in the sunlight.

"We have peace talks with the Culu captains later today, darling," the Queen murmurs.

"Damned pyrates," the King snorts. "Ask Saida to check their pockets when they leave. I've had enough of them."

The royal family are already dressed—the King and Queen in their spotless robes, Dismal in his tighter black dress, his wet hair indicative of a morning bath. They're reading news reports, yellow-stained scrolls delivered by royal couriers.

I have never handled such a scroll, despite having met royal couriers. While we receive watered-down versions of the empire's broadcasts at work, this is only because we're seen as distillers and sharers of information. How I would love to be able to read the royal broadcasts—the brutal, the ugly, the honest.

Elrind hurries in from a nearby doorway, a thick wad of post under his arm. He starts to distribute the letters, though the royals don't look up from their news reports.

"Any response from the Celestial Bastion?" the King grunts in Elrind's direction. Without looking up, His Majesty reaches out and grabs a gold letter opener.

A gold letter opener. It glints up at the ceiling and pierces my heart. Oh, to have a gold opener. Less effective on beasts, of course, but I only bought silver as it was all twenty sigils would afford me. Given the choice, would I swap the fifty sigils in my secret store for a gold letter opener?

Of course not, I tell myself. Buying my own house, a little cottage with winding flowers and room to knit and draw, organise and revamp, is all I want. Everything else is just vanity.

"Can we not make enemies of the entire Celestial Bastion?" Dismal whines. "When I'm a healer, I want to be able to visit the Cecedits and the Lands of the Forgotten. You know there'll be cures for a whole load of stuff in both."

"You can never be a healer," the King says shortly, rubbing his tattooed nose. "You know that. It's too dangerous for our people. You are permitted only to study."

"Remember when Kaelion wanted to be a musician?" the Queen sighs, reaching out and finding her delicate teacup. "Oh, how beautifully he played the lute, as a child. But it could not be."

"Of course it could not be," the King snaps.

"You did not have to smash his lute and ban the instrument from the palace," the Queen mutters.

"Kings do not play lutes."

My hands tingle. I tell them to stop. It's the thought of Kae, as a small child, having his instrument smashed to pieces because *Kings do not play lutes*. Dismal has been able to follow his dream path, going to college to study healing, but where does that leave Kae? Unable to pursue any passions outside of his future king status? I can't help feeling that Kae needs to break the rules at some point in his life. It seems he's always had to follow the strictest instructions. What kind of life is that?

He could do with something to make him smile.

"Elira?" Of course, it's Elrind who notices me. He looks at me, and this time I feel it. Him grasping through my mind, reading it. I think he can only read my mind when I meet his gaze. Which must be why he is the only servant I can see wearing blinkers. He smiles, genuinely, his feathers waving. Dismal instantly looks delighted by my attire—or lack thereof—while the other royals squint at me.

"Have you ever heard of clothes, mortal?" Dismal demands, his eyes shining and dancing, focusing solely on my gown rather than the coryns that tangle through my hair.

"Have you ever heard of manners, aemortal?" I shoot back. Elrind sighs.

"She is no longer mortal," the Queen whispers. Her lips are tugged up into a smile, and I can tell from the look that she's giving me that she is begging my forgiveness. I send her a small smile in return, not yet ready to completely forgive her earlier reaction. Even as a mortal, I was not beneath her son.

"I'm not happy about this," the King spits, looking behind me, as if his eldest son might be there with a gram of wolfsbane and an apology. "Why can no one stay with their assigned condition around here?"

"I was born like this," I say, as Dismal's eyes finally reach my actual face and then my horns. He lets out a loud guffaw. "I have only been returned to what I was supposed to be."

"Your horns are whiter than Kae's," Dismal cackles.

"She is beautiful," the Queen sighs. A lump tickles my throat as it tries to form. Perhaps, just perhaps, the Queen will do anything for a daughter.

"I'm not happy about this," the King growls. "Not satisfied at all. What if other half-bloods start crawling up from the city? What then? Are we supposed to look the other way while our sons defile—"

"I have defiled no one," Dismal announces with mock horror and shining eyes.

"You speak out of turn, Aestos," the Queen suddenly snarls, her voice snapping out of its usual pleasant lull. "You shall not speak of Elira this way again. She is invited here by our son, under Divinities who know much more than you."

Dismal and I look at each other. My lips tug upwards, as my chest bubbles, and he bites his lip. I think we both want to laugh, but we hold it. The King starts to bluster, but has no argument in return.

I stride forward and grab a piece of fresh bread from the basket on the table. I rip a hunk off with my teeth, without sitting on the chair that Elrind has swept from under the table. I see Dismal's delighted grin from somewhere in my peripheral, but I really don't care. I'm famished. Famished, and newly aemortal, power coursing through my whole body, as the King and Queen pretend not to be horrified by my mortal city manners.

CHAPTER FORTY-TWO

Tryx and Elrind wisp me to the palace grounds, to a vast open space surrounded by thick trees.

I keep reaching for my coryns, but I can barely feel them as I move my head, as though they are part of the bone, as if my skull hasn't gained any weight. Yet, I'm acutely aware of them all the time. When the wind picks up, I feel it first in my coryns. When I'm happy—like when Kaelion walks into the room—I feel a purr of contentment ripple through my horns. They've become conduits to the world around me.

"Right, so we need to teach you fayte," Tryx muses, slouching on the grass. The day is fresh, but sunny—winter still lingers, but the warmth of the new season pushes through. "Rumour is that you have a Gift, but until it reveals itself, we can't teach you how to use it."

Something in the way Tryx speaks makes me suspect he knows very well what my Gift is, but I know he wouldn't tell me if I asked.

"We shouldn't be the ones teaching her," Elrind sighs, parting his feathers and watching me. He seems more relaxed outside, the sun playing on his pale skin. His sense of duty is still there, tight in his shoulders, but there's a sense of ease about him. It suddenly strikes me that he is a messenger, and I am a postmistress—we both thrive on communication and duty. "She should learn on the Isles."

"Fine, fine," Tryx mutters, his tone dripping with boredom. "I'm sure it'll be something dreadfully tedious. A Plantseer, perhaps. Someone who can tell when a flower is about to bloom."

"Does such a Seer even exist?" I scratch my forehead, feeling uncomfortable with the idea of harnessing fayte. I'm only just getting used to my horns, to the way my lungs now fill with new strength, to the power that courses through me like heat.

Elrind hides a smirk and straightens his shoulders. "We typically learn this as juniors, but you're obviously... umm, delayed."

"Achingly backwards," Tryx adds. "Just telling it how it is," he says sweetly, earning a scowl from me. Elrind coughs, and we turn back to the messenger.

"So, where does fayte come from?" I ask, genuinely curious.

"It's a type of fay magic, descended from the faeries that died out long ago," Elrind explains. "When the first aemortals were born, it seemed they were descendants of both fay and mortals—able to be destroyed, their powers weakened, but still far stronger than the mortals who survived in Orynthys."

I nod slowly.

"When do we get to the part where Elira sets fire to herself?" Tryx asks lazily.

Elrind ignores him and continues, "There's willed fayte, and created fayte. Willed fayte is unpredictable—it appears when the mind bends fayte to its will. But we can't teach you this."

"Right," I murmur, feeling a little overwhelmed.

"That's what you released at the wall," Tryx comments, his tone almost approving. "That was pure will."

I swallow, wondering if there's a touch of pride in his voice.

"The first transformist symbols were transcribed, taught by the very Divinities we worship today," Elrind continues. "Through these symbols, aemortals were able to create fire, hunt, swim underwater, change a rock into a drinking vessel. They soon realised that transformist symbols are loosely split into elemental control, water breathing, transfiguring, and... things."

"What are things?" I ask politely, still trying to understand it all.

"Good question," Tryx yawns. "A stupid name for it."

"The Things were originally a type of aemortal who could perform small magic—sew without a needle, write without a pen, cook without needing to chop or stir. And then the Things discovered wisping."

"Ooh, am I going to wisp on my own?" I ask, looking around the vast field, hoping for some miraculous sign of progress.

"No," Elrind and Tryx say simultaneously. My heart sinks. I can feel my face fall, deflated by their unanimous dismissal.

"Today, you are going to attempt the first transformist symbol," Elrind continues, as Tryx yawns again. "That of fire."

"Fire?" I echo, my mind racing. To create or control fire is a weapon in itself. I could set fire to enemies, build a blaze that would take down kingdoms. The power is intoxicating just to think about.

"You'll be lucky if you can create a spark, Elira," Tryx interjects, his tone dismissive. "You're far too old to be starting your fayte training."

I fight the urge to scowl, trying to keep my face neutral, but I feel my features twitch with frustration. Why is he even here? What's the point if all he does is mock me?

"First, you need to summon your fayte. Then, we sketch," Elrind instructs, rolling up his sleeves and blowing his feathers back, a silent motion of readiness.

It is, of course, a disaster.

I manage to summon fayte—the energy surging through my body, intense and overpowering. At first, I mistook it for the kind of anxiety that made my chest tighten and my breath shallow, but now I realise it's the magic, coiling beneath my skin, begging to be released.

"It gets easier," Elrind reassures me when I voice my discomfort.

On my fortieth attempt, I manage to summon a flicker of blue flame—just a spark, but enough to make Tryx stir from his lazy slump. His eyes snap open, and for a moment, I think he's going to say something encouraging. But he doesn't.

Instead, I falter again. My fingers are sore from sketching the shape into the air, trying to copy Elrind's swift, practised movements. Every time, the symbol aligns for only a fraction of a second, slipping away before I can commit it to memory.

"If I had a quill and scroll, this would be easier," I mutter, but Elrind shakes his head.

"To do so would bring terrible luck," he warns. "It must come from you, not from the page."

"If you can't remember it, you're not worthy of it," Tryx adds, his voice as flat as ever, his eyes now closed again. The weight of his words hangs in the air, but I grit my teeth and push forward, determined not to be defeated. I won't let this be the end.

Finally, as the sun begins to dip below the horizon, the last sliver of daylight casting a golden glow over the field, I manage it. A single flickering flame appears from my fingertip and vanishes almost as quickly as it came. But it was there. I saw it. I did it. I look up, and to my surprise, Elrind is smiling. Not a smirk, not a mocking grin, but a genuine smile.

"You've now controlled fayte," he says, his voice warm with approval.

"And she didn't spontaneously combust," Tryx adds with a sigh, his tone heavy with disappointment. But I can hear the faint edge of something else in it—

perhaps grudging admiration.

I stand for a moment, my body trembling from the effort, the energy coursing through me like a live wire. Goosebumps roll down my arms, and I feel a strange sense of accomplishment settling in my chest.

"Practice summoning the fayte inside you," Elrind advises, his tone soft but firm. He sketches the transformist symbol for fire in the air again, and each of his five outstretched fingers produces a single flame. They dance in the air, lighting up the dimming field like tiny stars. "And then we can move on to the next basic."

"Basic," I mutter, feeling the exhaustion in my limbs. My arms feel like lead, and yet, there's a flicker of something more inside me, something that drives me forward. It's all very well learning to summon a flame, but I can't help but feel that I'm not yet useful. I want to be more than this—more than a flickering spark in the dark. We need to move faster, and yet here I am, still learning the basics.

With the attacks growing closer, time is running out, and I know we don't have the luxury of wasting it. But for now, I've taken the first step. And that's enough. For now.

We trudge back towards the castle, my companions clearly preferring the slow sunset stroll over the faster pace of wisping us the distance.

"Why do you wear the band, if you have the ability to See?" I ask Elrind, as Tryx bounds ahead, distracted by butterflies and soaring birds. "Surely, as a Gift-holder, you must be worth something to our armies?"

Elrind slips his hands into his pockets, his voice quiet, almost melancholic. "Do you know what my Gift is?"

I hesitate, my voice barely a whisper. "Mindseer." I've heard of this rare type of Seer, but I never imagined meeting one in person until now.

"Mindseer," Elrind confirms, his gaze fixed ahead, his voice tinged with something raw. "We are banned. Much like half-aemortals." He flashes me a small, sad smile. "My father made a deal with the King. I was to be kept secret, adopted by the palace, in exchange for my continued life."

The weight of his words sinks in, and I remain silent for a moment, stunned by the injustice of it. It's incomprehensible to me that someone gifted by a Divinity should be forced into servitude, hidden away for fear of their power. A life saved at the cost of everything else.

At last, I break the silence, my voice strained. "At least your father did something to keep you alive," I mutter, though I know bitterness creeps in. His father essentially handed Elrind over to the palace.

Elrind's shoulders sag slightly, the weight of memories in his eyes. "I think he was planning on abducting me when the time was right."

The sharp taste of anger rises in my chest, and I feel helpless. How could anyone live with such cruelty? I swallow hard. "One day, you'll be free," I say softly.

He looks at me, a hint of something breaking

through the layers of his calm. "One day, I'll be free," he agrees, his voice steady, though there's a sadness there. "But it's not all bad, you know. I grew up in a rather... unpleasant household. When my Gift manifested, I was kept in a cage, in case I tried to run away. My father took me gambling, won a lot of sigils. Until someone realised what I could do, reported it to the royals. It was... all rather unpleasant."

I feel a lump form in my throat, and my heart aches as I watch Tryx leap and dive after a dragonfly.

"I get three meals a day, a sumptuous chamber, and generally, I am respected here. To be honest, if I left the palace, I'm not sure what I would do. My ex-boyfriend once suggested I take up painting again, but I think it would be lonely."

I look up at the sky, a canvas of deep oranges and reds that curl beneath a veil of golden clouds. There's a dark undercurrent to the sunset, a blood-red streak, hinting at something more threatening just beyond the beauty.

The days pass quickly, and the lessons are relentless. Over the next moon phase, I attempt and fail, learn and burn with frustration, until I finally summon a flame that stays. Another day brings with it the shocking discovery of gills sprouting from my neck, only for them to fade after moments, leaving my spine aching from the effort. Slowly, the symbols for fire and water lodge themselves in my mind, and Elrind moves on to teaching me the symbols for heat, ice, controlling small pieces of metal, and bending the tiniest shadows.

"You're an average student," Tryx says with his usual dry sarcasm. "Which, given your advanced age, is an achievement in itself."

I can't help the small smile that tugs at the corners of my mouth. Despite the difficulty and the bruises to my pride, I feel something else growing inside me. It's as if the magic is finally awakening, like a long-dormant ember catching fire.

I glow.

CHAPTER FORTY-THREE

It's not that I'm his mate, nor some noblewoman, nor any other such romantic title. As Prince Kaelion takes me around his local towns – the three primary towns of the aemortals – we don't discuss rubrics nor dwell on the formality of the situation.

But others do.

We're often accompanied on our trips by Elrind, who purses his lips and tries not to smile every time a confused denizen asks, "Is this your fancywoman, Your Highness?" or leans in to examine my coryns – mostly white, as opposed to the streaks of silver adorning those in the Eryndal aemortal towns – asking, "Is this lady to become a royal bride, sire?" Their attitudes toward the prince range from utmost respect – some locals physically shaking when Kaelion walks into their establishment – to something akin to parental fondness, as though they've watched him grow from a small boy to this enormous man who takes up doorways and casts long, imposing shadows as we walk.

Kae stops mumbling a response and starts to look at me during such infringements on our privacy. His lip twitches, his eyes glinting with something unreadable. And I, with the sweetest honey my voice can muster, say something like, "Oh, if only the Prince would realise I am his one true mate, we might put an end to this flirtation," or "I'm not sure he's convinced me yet." Such a response tends to draw a smile from whoever has approached, and I notice the way people's gazes soften toward me, their wariness giving way to respect.

"Isn't her hair beautiful?" a few people croon, while others marvel at my green eyes.

"Come now, Elira isn't a show animal," Elrind claims, sweeping the gathering crowds away as we move. "More's the pity, then we might actually gain some gold from putting up with her," he mutters afterward, though I catch the twinkle in his eye.

Kaelion and I stop at a wine bar atop a jetty over the Xandryll-originating Rotgut River – which Kaelion calls Blue Salmon River – sitting downstream from the imposing Xandryll glacier. Even here, the air is somewhat fogged and sulphur-scented. But it doesn't matter. We share chilled elven wine, served from a carafe that beads condensation across its surface. I don't think I've ever tasted anything so delicious.

The waiter, a young aemortal boy with short, silver coryns, bows every time he brings something to our table. Soon, it is laden with boar galette glazed with orange, lemongrass almond paste atop fleshy pink salmon, a skillet of aromatic potatoes, vivid green gratin, cream-dolloped muffins, and wild-garlic-soaked mushrooms. My hand trembles as I help myself to the food, guilt gnawing at me for not taking some back to Grim for Nerissa and her family.

I taste the first bite of the salmon. It falls apart on my tongue, the lemongrass and almond touching different parts of my palate, and I seem to fall apart with it. There will be time to share. There will be time. I'll make sure of it. But for now, I'm enjoying whatever bizarre ride the prince is taking me on. My belly has never felt so satiated; for the first time, I don't feel an ounce of hunger.

As we walk along the river afterward, I sigh.

"The aemortal towns are lovely," I admit. Houses rise from the river itself – tall buildings with white window shutters and clusters of flowers. There are plants everywhere, but not tangles of poisonous weeds or dried husks of grass. These are actual, vivid green plants, bright yellow blooms, and long pink fingers of flowers releasing their fragrant fervour into the air. It's like a different world, one that feels safe, calm, and thriving.

I'm all too aware of Prince Kaelion's hand so close to mine as we walk. The back of his fingers occasionally graze mine, and though he pulls away each time, as though he's overstepped, it makes me smile. I bite the inside of my cheek, amused by the thought that he can run me ragged in the bedroom yet pretend to be a perfect gentleman on the streets.

"Yes, the people do their best to have something to come back to," the prince agrees, his deep voice rumbling. "Most of the population here are part of the Sable Legion in one way or another. It's a life spent on the battlefield. When they come home, if they come home, they surround themselves with beauty."

It *is* beautiful. And so peaceful. The river flows gently, casting sun reflections onto the buildings. Shades of aquamarine flicker and dance on the water's surface, shimmering with the movement. As we pass the people on the street, most of whom openly gape at us, I see traces of battle-worn lives. A missing arm here, a limp there. A woman with dark hair bears a jagged scar, marring one entire cheek, pulling her eye downward toward her ear. I shoot her a fleeting smile, and she grins back, her smile wide and toothy, as though she's seen enough of the world to wear it proudly.

"Do you... ever fight?" I ask, unsure how to phrase it, but Kaelion doesn't miss a beat.

"Of course." His voice carries an edge, almost offended. "I don't spend all my time taking pretty women to wine bars, Elira."

"I should hope not."

"I'm trained to fight."

"I should hope so."

"I killed fifteen enemy soldiers on my last station at the Claran border."

"Lovely."

"Each morning, I review our formations, sustain our borders."

"Well done, Kae," I say with all the emotionless platitude of a parent admiring a child's painting. "That must be terribly gratifying."

Before I can stop him, he moves like lightning. One moment, we're walking along a shiny-patterned walkway by the river, and the next, he has swung me into an alleyway. His cedar-scented warmth pounds down on me, his face almost snarling right into mine.

"You can stop with the sarcasm." His voice is low, dangerous, his eyes locked onto mine with intensity that makes my heart wedge itself firmly in my throat.

My breath catches, but I manage to lift a hand, my fingers trembling as they trace the side of his jaw, his skin warm beneath my touch. His stubble teases my nails, and the sensation shoots through me like lightning.

"I'm just glad they make Big Boy Leathers in your size," I breathe, trying not to laugh as his eyes silently burn with annoyance. "It would be such a shame for the battlefield to miss your prowess."

"Don't challenge my prowess," he growls, leaning forward, his lips barely brushing mine. His body presses into mine, and his heat envelops me completely, making me dizzy with the overwhelming closeness.

"Or what?" I breathe out, my body trembling under his proximity.

He cocks his head, the faintest shadow of a grin forming on his lips, even as aemortals start to gather at the mouth of the alleyway, their whispers rising like a hum in the background.

"Or I'll be forced to show you my *Big Boy Leathers*," he growls, his eyes dark and playful, as he leans forward and sucks my lower lip into his mouth.

So, it seems like everyone in the aemortal towns knows about Prince Kaelion and me. Dismal mutters about it loudly at breakfast, waiting for someone to bite. The Queen has started pouring my coffee each morning, perhaps as an apology for her earlier scorn. The King largely ignores me, though I catch him turning slightly red when Kaelion casually drapes his arm around my shoulders one morning.

I try to ignore the giddy flutter in my chest every time Kaelion walks into a room. I force myself to push down the blissful warmth that threatens to engulf me whenever he visits my chamber, always leaving before sunrise for some important meeting or another. When he lets me loose in the palace library, I devour three books in one sitting, almost tasting the pages as I lose myself in stories of battleships and hopeless love.

No one mentions my status. I half-expect the Sable Legion to appear any moment, demanding my parentage, ready to arrest or execute me for being a half-aemortal. Though I catch strange glances when I dare to meet a soldier's eye, everyone remains controlled. I am watched, yes, but I am free to roam the rooms, the grounds—Kaelion has even offered patrols to accompany me back to the city whenever I wish.

But I don't wish it. Not yet. Let me live in this heaven for a little longer.

And then, one morning, a scream pierces the air.

CHAPTER FORTY-FOUR

Elrind and I run through hallways, while I yank my hair up into its bun. Kaelion left before sunrise, to meet a battalion. It seems to be only Elrind and I who heard the scream, that pound from the hallway of my chamber towards the outer doors. There are no further sounds. Most likely, it was a bird, cawing. We don't slow, but I notice that we both relax slightly as the silence stretches on, as we approach the vast castle exit.

We stride to the steps. To my left, a gargoyle gapes with broken teeth; to my right, a heraldic beast pulls from the stone. My eyes instantly spot the incongruity —vivid crimson staining an otherwise serene landscape of white. A body, sprawled on the ground. She is half-hidden in a sea of white flowers.

I run.

The flowers are soaked so much that it's all I can stare at for a moment—the smell choking me as it floods my senses. Something tugs inside me, an insistence that seems to have nothing to do with anything. A splay of roiled cherry flows from her ruined body. I fall onto my knees, push her onto her back.

    I don't know what happens to me. I don't know where my mind goes as I look at her face, fresh blood collecting around her white ringlet hair. Her blue eyes are swollen, her cheekbones bruised and beaten, her usually immaculate eyebrows smudged with blood. Her body has been sliced horizontally, as if by claws. The blood is so damn bright on the white flowers. I stand and stumble a few steps backwards—and thump into something hot and solid. I spin, hands rising instinctively to defend myself, but Kae murmurs, "It's me," and I close my eyes.

    It is him.

    "What the fuck," he whispers as I try not to shake.

    "She's been savaged," I mutter, my tongue swollen. "She's been torn open, she's been..." I can't stop panting, anxiety rolling through my head, stars appearing.

    "Elira, you will be okay..." Kae briefly holds me at arm's length. His gaze–so steady, so present–calms my breath slightly.

    Isolde. *No.*

    I look at her again, bleeding onto the flowers. Elrind is checking her pulse, as Sable Legion guards rush to join him. If I see Major General Drystan, then I might just rip his head from his body. Was it a random attack? Or was it planned? Is Fjaldorn determined to destroy everyone in my life, or is it simply pure coincidence?

    "She's Seren's girlfriend," I say, my voice barely working. "My sister's girlfriend. Perhaps whoever has... Seren – if she has been taken – has found out Isolde's name. Is she dead?" I can't cope. My lungs constrict, my eyes burning. It can't be a coincidence. The attackers must have gained Isolde's name from somewhere. Which might mean that Seren is still alive, that they have discovered Isolde's name from my sister's lips.

"No." A heated anger laces Kae's voice. "She has been attacked by silicrites, and left to die. But she is not dead. Her breathing is intended, no doubt, to scare us more than slaying her would have."

Footsteps and other voices rush towards us. "It's gone," someone calls out. Sable Legion boots crunch against frosty ground, their helmets glinting in the sunlight, casting bright spots that dance as they move. I hadn't even considered the possibility that whatever did this, whatever attacked Isolde, might still be nearby. It could have watched me fall to the ground. Making sure we found her.

"They've stuffed a note into her jacket," Elrind says, holding up a torn piece of notepaper, smudged with blood. My stomach clenches.

"It's on headed paper, printed with Fjaldorn," the messenger reads aloud.

"Fjaldorn," Kae and I snarl at the same time. That kingdom again. The one across the Thealean Sea from our bastion. Only the most adept sailors could make the journey from here to the Shattered Isles and onwards to the Celestial bastion. Fjaldorn is ruled by a silly, gullible king, I remember Tryx saying.

"What... what have they written?" I choke, trying not to look at Isolde's ringlets, saturated in the fresh blood that drips from her neck. Kae moves closer, standing at my side as Elrind carefully wipes the paper. Healers have managed to manoeuvre Isolde's body onto a stretcher, her arms lolling off the sides, her eyes open, unblinking. I force my gaze to shift away from her milky irises, focusing instead on the note.

"'You know what we want,'" Elrind reads aloud. "'This is only the start.'"

"They're brutal slayers," Kae spits. His ears are flushed, fury burning in his eyes. I glance at him quickly before looking back toward the violent scene, my thoughts swirling. "They can't come here and speak to us like honourable contenders. They are cowards, and we shall not yield or agree."

"You know what they want?" I ask, as I scan his face.

His eyes flicker briefly toward Elrind. Tension thickens the air. "Let's talk over here." His voice is low as he slips his hand down, lacing his fingers through mine with a gentle tug. He pulls me away from the body, towards the gates, as if he needs a moment to collect his thoughts—or perhaps to gather some bullshit words to keep me happy.

I pull my hand away as we walk.

CHAPTER FORTY-FIVE

The morning sun gilds the flowers as water is thrown over the blood. The splash cuts through my mind. Heady smells of iron creep through, followed by fire smoke from the chimneys. Someone has started up the kitchen fires. Someone is preparing for a normal day.

"What shall I do about this message, Your Highness?" the messenger calls, and I swallow the fury that rises inside me. Kaelion knows what Fjaldorn wants; he knows why my sister's girlfriend has been maimed and left for dead.

I have dined with this girl. Giggled with her. Watched as she finally made Seren happy. And now, her many wounds are being poked and prodded by the palace healers. I follow Kae to the gates. He calls something back to Elrind. I don't hear the words over the whirlwind of horror and shock that's still making dents in my skull. I feel cold.

Kae places a hand on my shoulder, steadying me as I falter.

"To break through the spelled gates, to tear her body open right here on royal soil…" He clutches my shoulder tighter. "It's not like the King of Fjaldorn. It's not like him at all."

"Don't be naïve," I hiss, anger rising. "He's the devil. Look at what he sent." Kae goes still, his hand firm on my shoulder. "What do they want?" I ask, my voice tight as I look up at his face. "Why won't you tell me?"

"I cannot always share royal business." He pulls his hand from my shoulder. The sudden loss of contact sends a cold shiver through me. "I wish I could, but…"

"I know," I snap, glaring at Elrind, who is studying the blood patterns. "And I suppose he won't say anything either? Is it connected to my sister being missing?"

"Yes," Kaelion says quietly, his voice still thick with suppressed rage. "I expect they are connected. They want us to know they're prepared to go to war. They've shown us that our battalions can fall, that they can break our royal wards." I close my eyes again, trying to shut out the cold dread creeping up my spine. I must look horrendous, because Kae mutters softly, "I won't let anything happen to you." The intimacy of his tone, the softness in his voice, touches something deep inside me.

"Kae!" Two voices shriek his name in unison.

We turn slowly, as if made of ice, to see two women running towards us through the palace gates. They are immaculate, thick hair cascading in waves around their faces, their cream robes billowing around them, practically glowing. If there were such a thing as angels, I would think it to be these two, and they barely pant as they close in on us, their pure silver coryns catching the sun. Their gowns are those of immortal healers; creamy fabric lined with gold, spelled to stay clean.

I blink. I have Isolde's blood on my knees. I'm wearing my nightgown, my hair a tangled mess, my eyes stinging with exhaustion and grief. Are these women real?

"Oh, Kae," the blonde gasps, grabbing his arm and winding hers through his before he can stop her. "We heard there had been a disturbance."

"And after we found you at the wall," the redhead adds, "and you were so tired, we thought we should check on you."

The way they simper. The way they look at him. The way they both cling to him now, as though he's a tree to be climbed.

Kae's brow furrows, distracted by the newly emerging guards, who are furiously throwing buckets of water over the bloodstains. *Splash.* Can't they just fucking magic it away, for Divinities' sake? What's the point in being aemortals if you have to clean? Elrind is talking quickly, his words indistinguishable amidst the chaos.

"You found him at the wall?" I ask, my voice steady but sharp. It's the first time the women have acknowledged me. I notice their eyes flash coolly as they take me in.

"We did," the blonde croons, her tone laced with sweetness. "We dragged him to our house for a hot meal. He was soooo sleepy." She reaches up and strokes his face with the back of her fingers, the touch too intimate.

A fire ignites inside me. I can feel the heat building in my fists, my body tensing as I try to control it. Kae opens his mouth to say something, then closes it, looking at me with confusion. Blood splatters across the ground, some of it flying dangerously close to us.

"Quit splashing me," he mutters, his eyes locked on my hands. They glow faintly in gold, the scent of fayte rolling off me and filling my nostrils with the heavy scent of iron ore. Am I doing that? Redirecting the blood to spatter his legs?

"Be careful with your new power," he mutters, leaning in so that only I can hear. "If you're not careful, you'll harness darkness. You haven't learned how to manage the light yet."

The burn of the invisible poker pricks up my spine. While I was risking death in Xandryll's endless forest on a mission set by the man in front of me, he was frolicking with these beautiful healers. Most likely sleeping with these healers.

Fuck harnessing the light.

"What a strange woman," one of them remarks, squinting at me. "Is she a relative of yours, Kaely?"

"Kaely?" I snort. Betrayal—hot, thick betrayal—roars through me. Isolde's broken body is barely gone; I can still hear the groans of the healers as they navigate the palace steps.

Elrind calls to a butler, asking for more water to wash the blood.

"We have decisions to make," Kae mutters, looking up at the sky. He doesn't pull his arm away from the women. "We don't have the resources to invade another land right now." He sighs and rubs his cheek with his one free calloused palm.

"You were scared of falling for a mortal," I say, slowly, thinking it out. "You wouldn't sleep with me when I was mortal. And your mother was horrified."

"What are you saying, Elira?" Kaelion sounds wary.

"Is it true, you wouldn't sleep with me when I was merely mortal? These aemortal women are more your type?" I bite the insides of my cheeks, thinking.

"Yes," Kae agrees, far too quickly. "I would never sleep with a mortal. Historically, my taste has been for those with horns." He smiles, as if he's joking, and I remember what he said to me in bed: he wanted me *with or without pretty horns*. Kae drops his hand slowly, and the air between us becomes thick.

"Wait a breath," one of the women says, her voice a mix of confusion and disbelief. "You're dating this woman, Kaelion?"

"No," he says, confused, his eyebrows drawing together.

"No," I say, not really a question, nor a statement. What is happening?

When I was a mortal I wasn't good enough to have sex with. And now, it's become clear that the very night he sent my mortal arse to the Ancient Forest, he went home with these two women.

"Your Highness," Elrind calls sharply, his tone urgent. "We need to mobilise the Sable Legion if you're truly planning a full-scale defence. If an attack is coming, we should prepare."

"Attack?" A chill runs up my spine, even as my heart shatters into a million pieces. I remember all the stories my mother told me about the Thousand Cycle War: hunger, violence, locking the shutters, praying to the Divinities.

"We've tried the nice approach." Kae's voice is grim. "Mother sent them a letter, spelled to allow them access to visit here without weapons. It was an invitation to talk. They never replied, nor acknowledged receipt."

A letter.

I fall into a crouch, my hands meeting the cold petals of the white spray. I am not near enough to the slaughter site to touch the blood, but the scent of it clings to the air and fills my throat. My hands shake as I press my palms onto the grass, grounding myself.

The letter. The letter to Fjaldorn. The letter I burned. It was spelled. It was more than just the words. Holy shit. I've caused this war.

The weight of his words settles over me like a stone in my stomach. The letter I destroyed, the one the prince's family sent in peace, thinking it would end in a quiet resolution, is now a symbol of failure. I feel sick.

"I tried to break into Xandryll," Kaelion says, his hand reaching out as if to touch my arm. But he stops himself at the last moment, his hand falling awkwardly by his side. He coughs lightly, as if to clear his throat. "I have clemency to travel, but not freely. Not without seeking the permission of the King of Xandryll. I tried to summon a meeting with him, tried to send word, tried everything I could to get to you, once Tryx released me from his binds."

I'm still stuck on the letter. The one I burned.

I stand up suddenly, just as one of the women bursts out: "I can't believe you're seeing someone, and you didn't tell us."

The beautiful aemortals, Prince Kae and the women, look at each other, clearly stunned, and my anger rises again, spiralling out of control.

"Did you *bed* the prince?" I snarl at the women. My words are venomous, sharp, and they cut through the tension like a blade. I shouldn't be angry—not really. But there's something about seeing these women hang off him that makes my blood boil.

The women's faces flush. One of them looks at Kae, her lips parting in surprise, while the other glares at me, her expression cold. "I—I'm sure the prince didn't —" the blonde woman stammers. My heart is pounding, my thoughts a jumble of confusion and betrayal.

"Prince Kae is a passionate man," the colder one says, her eyes flashing as she looks at him. "My sister and I have had many a night with his wicked tongue."

"And his wicked other thing," the first one chimes in, cackling with laughter. The sound is sharp and mocking, in stark contrast to the fury simmering inside me. I can barely breathe. My chest tightens, a mixture of jealousy, disgust and betrayal curling into a knot.

"He is well-known as a generous lover," the blonde healer advises.

I burn. While I was risking my life, crying over a fucking tree root, the prince was being a *generous lover* to these two.

"The night of the wall," the prince growls, his voice low and edged with anger as he shifts between them and me. "She's asking if you bedded me the night of the wall. We did not fornicate that night." It does nothing to quell the fire surging inside me. He asked to kiss me that night.

"We nearly did," the redhead flirts, her tone like honey. "You were half-dressed, if I remember rightly. You popped off to get the contraceptive elixir, and never returned, you naughty boy."

"Got stage fright, did you, Kally?" the blonde asks.

I'm suffocating, every word a knife digging deeper into me. While I was fighting to survive, dredging poisonous roots from a forbidden forest, the prince was... with them. That's why he was topless when he found me. Why he stank of sweat.

I stand on my own now, my chest tight, and I force myself to turn away from Kaelion. He owes me nothing. Nothing. We are nothing.

"Elira, please," he mutters. I hate the pleading in his voice. As a mortal, I wasn't *good enough* for him. He sent me across the wall, after asking to kiss me, and then disappeared to the house of two women he's slept with multiple times before.

"We need an army," I say, my voice rasping.

"It might be an empty threat," Elrind replies, his tone steely. "They might have an army, but they'd have to cross the Cecedit Mountains to get close. And even then, they'd have to get past the Elemental bastion, who wouldn't take kindly to an invasion. Fjaldorn knows they can't risk attacking us without starting a full-blown, inter-bastion war."

"They could come by sea," I say, through gritted teeth. My fingers tug sharply at my hair, pulling it free from its messy bun. As it cascades down my shoulders, I see the prince's eyes light up. But I don't care. Not even a little bit.

"It won't come to that," Kae says. "We all lost soldiers during the war. The Celestial Bastion, Fjaldorn, lost as many as we did. King Vaelthorne won't want to revisit that time."

"King Vaelthorne," I mutter, the words tasting bitter on my tongue. How strange it feels to say his name, like a forgotten memory slipping back into my mind.

"He's not a bad man," Elrind says gently, causing me to startle. "Just a weak man."

The image of Isolde's body flashes before my eyes again—her broken, blood-soaked body. My hands tremble. "Did you see her?" I hiss, my back bristling with anger. "How does one person have that much blood? They're still cleaning it from the garden!" I take a deep breath, forcing my voice steady. "She might be dead, Elrind. And how do we even know that this king hasn't taken my family? Perhaps he enjoys tormenting the women of Grim Municipal. Maybe he has some ancient grudge, some reason to hate our city."

"King Vaelthorne is very handsome," the blonde woman says, her voice light, almost absent. "When he came to visit Eryndal, my mother took me to watch him outside the palace gates." I blink at her, taken aback by her casual tone, and her sister chimes in.

"I suppose he was apologising for the Thousand Cycle War."

"He was," the blonde one says with a sigh. "Four cycles too late, but I suppose a thousand and four cycles too late is better than nothing." She laughs lightly, the sound tinkling like glass, delicate and distracting.

My hands clench into fists, but I say nothing. The idea that Fjaldorn, so far across the sea, holds my family is enough to send a cold knife of dread through my ribcage. Not even Prince Kaelion, bound by the rules of clemency, could cross those borders without ramifications.

"Pay them," I say, looking up at Kae. "Whatever it is they want, give it to them. And get my family."

"I can't do that." His voice is steady, but I see the tension in his fists. "It's not my decision. If I do that, people will die."

"Just give them what they want," I hiss, yanking my shoulders back. "After that, I don't care what you do. If you bed every woman in Orynthys. I just want my family. After that, you can have your wish."

I pause, my chest tight with the weight of everything I'm saying. "I'll happily plead with the Divinities to add your name to the map, if it will put an end to everything you desire. After that, I don't want to maintain this friendship any longer. I want only to return to my old life."

His amber eyes are tormented, his brow furrowed

in a way that makes him look both beautiful and tragic. "You weren't happy in your old life," he murmurs.

"I was happier than I could ever be here," I hiss, my anger rising, jealousy swelling, causing me to say things I don't mean. "I regret everything. You are no more heir to this kingdom than I am, and if you must satiate a Divinity so, then you lose my respect, Your Highness."

He flinches, the words cutting him, and Elrind sighs.

"Lira," a voice calls. We turn to see my best friend, her pale face peering through the iron railings.

CHAPTER FORTY-SIX

"He was nice," Nerissa says, as we settle into a cosy round turret room. A fire crackles merrily from a grate, beneath two swords that have been pinned to the wall.

"He's a prince," I say sourly. "He's trained to be nice."

And he had been. As soon as Nerissa had appeared, Kaelion hurried to welcome her in, recognising her from *The Dwarven Bombard*. He'd escorted us into the castle, strategically angling his body so Nerissa didn't see the full force of the blood on the grass. But it didn't matter if she did, because she saw the silicrite take Isolde. They all did, an unwarranted attack, dragging the girl from her parents' home as the people of Grim Municipal shrieked and hid again. Nerissa finally ran for the palace, to find me. Apparently, the prince taking me wasn't enough of a reason, but *yet more* silicrites bolstered her need to come up here, to find out what was going on.

I swallow down these mad and toxic thoughts. I'm blaming Nerissa for the prince.

"What have they done to you?" my best friend whispers, as soon as we're alone. Her eyes well with tears, her gaze fixed on my coryns. "You've become... one of them."

I take a deep breath in. This is the moment.

"I think I was always one of them." I look down at my hands, half-hidden in Kaelion's hunting jacket, which he slung across my shoulders before ushering us in here. "It appears... it appears my father was an aemortal."

"You're a half-blood," she whispers. She lifts her hand, subconsciously rubbing her own hairline. "Can they tell?"

"They think that Kaelion has changed me for his own bidding," I mutter, knowing that Elrind doesn't believe this—he was able to read my mind, he knows Kaelion has only changed me back. "No doubt he'll get in trouble for that."

"And so they will not kill you? For being half-blood?"

"I hope not." I swallow, the weight of everything pressing down on me. By drinking wolfsbane, Mother saved my life. Even if I've chosen to reverse her changes, to become this... this monster, that Nerissa can't stop staring at. Shame runs through me, and I shiver inside the thick hunting jacket.

Have I rushed into this? This huge physical change? I suppose I wanted to feel powerful, in control, but is this just another manifestation of my obsessive tendencies? I needed to feel more in control than the aemortals I've been spending time with, so I changed my entire destiny?

    The goddess did not need me to change. Kaelion only promised that I might, one day. Except every cycle, I would have aged in mortal time. I did not want to render myself elderly for the rest of my existence.

    I will never die, unless I'm destroyed. Pulled apart, my body burned, or starved until my mind is lost and only my aemortal body remains. I've become something that mortals fear, something the group in Bombard plot to kill.

    "Hey, look at me," Nerissa whispers, her voice back to its usual soothing tone. I look up at her, and she's blurry behind my tears. "You were always meant to be more than the city postmistress, okay? We've all known it. I think that's why Liora and Seren have always been so keen to see you do more. Because we've all known you're more powerful than you let yourself be."

    I wipe away a tear from my cheek. This hunting jacket really does smell delicious.

    "And we'll all support this, okay? You look fucking stunning. Like, beyond beautiful. It was worth it for the looks alone. If you fancy changing me one day, feel free, yeah?"

    I laugh at her attempt to humour me. She still sounds weirded out, but Nerissa is great at rolling with changes. She's the opposite of me, quick to move on, to change her life, to fall in and out of love. Nerissa bites her lip. "You know, when I slept with… with Riven," she breathes his name, "I realised, they're just like us. We're all the same. He was… nice. He was caring."

    "Nerissa, I'm so sorry," I whisper. She hasn't been

the same since the awful ramifications of her night with the aemortal soldier. I look at her with my brow furrowed. "I'm sorry I've been gone, Nes," I say softly. "Sorry I haven't come back to the house. It's been... well, I've had this change," I gesture down at my new, stronger body. "And there's been a lot going on. I still haven't heard word of Mother nor Seren, and now Isolde... but I miss you. I really do."

"It seems I have a lot to catch up on." Nerissa cracks a weary smile. "What are the chances of getting a mug of tea in this place?"

I smile, relief coursing through me. We're okay. We're going to be okay.

CHAPTER FORTY-SEVEN

"Holy shit." She raises a shaking, ring-clad hand to her chest. "You swear?"

"I do."

"You slept with a prince." Her lips part as she inhales a low whistle of a breath. I bite the insides of my cheeks as storms of emotion flicker across her face: judgement, surprise, envy. I see her land on envy for the sake of our friendship, and she bites her lip as her eyes sparkle. "Tell me all about it. That prince looks like he knows his way around a woman."

I breathe out. I appreciate her effort to keep things normal, and I blush, despite myself, gratitude flowing through me like sweet fire.

"It was just sex," I say, the lie burning hot against my cheeks. "But yeah, it was good."

"Good?" Nerissa raises an eyebrow, and I feel my face practically combust. "It seems it wasn't just sex, my shrewd little friend."

"I told you, it was just sex," I repeat, more firmly this time. "Was it the best sex I've ever had? Yes. Is he the hottest man I'll probably ever meet? Yes. But he's insufferable. He's so damn controlled that he lives his life by duty. He can't tell me anything, and he has so many secrets I can't even keep up!"

I throw my hands into the air, my voice rising, but I can't stop it now. "One breath, he tells me that he wants to kiss me, and the next he's off with two gorgeous sisters, getting undressed! He talks about making me his noblewoman one day, but he'd sooner send me into a dangerous forest than risk telling me what I need to know or pissing off his precious goddess. And by the way, we still haven't heard a damn thing from her! It seems like I have to do everything myself around here!"

I've spoken louder than I intended, and the adrenaline pouring from me doesn't stop. I sit up straighter, my face blazing.

"I've had the best sex of my life, but he only did it because I've become aemortal! I wasn't good enough as a mortal, and his mother even thought so too. He acted like he wanted me to get my powers back—whatever that even means—and then, as soon as I become aemortal and these damn horns appear, he doesn't teach me how to even use this insane new power, just leaves it to Tryx and Elrind. He warns me that I might start to show darkness, but what does that even mean? We're running with wolves, falling for each other, sleeping together, but can a girl from the Heartlands ever be with a prince? We're so, so different."

The words fall flat as I lose momentum, and

my frustrations start to feel smaller, less important. I sink back into my seat, hands still buzzing with power. That's when I realise. That's where the fayte comes from; my anger, my energy. It's a force that's created by internal vigour; every time I get angry, or upset, or overwhelmed, I feel it. And I've always felt it, just I didn't realise what it was, the beast inside me waiting to escape. It was my magic, waiting to be fully realised.

I'm not the same person I was. I'm no longer the helpless mortal I used to be. I've become an aemortal, and I've barely stopped to think through the consequences of this change.

"And besides," I mutter, the darkest thoughts slipping out before I can stop them. "I've left behind certain mortal death in exchange for an unknown eternity. I've purchased immortality just to entertain a goddess who hasn't delivered." I reach up and touch my coryn, the sensation flooding me with golden light. Relief. Perhaps they're not such a bad thing after all. I know that, should I ever truly want to, there are ways of ending an aemortal life. We don't die in the traditional sense, but we can be destroyed—certain weapons and powers can tear an aemortal body apart.

I find the thought oddly soothing, even though it is something I will never voice to anyone.

"I'm attracted to a prince," I sigh, my mind flashing with images of amber eyes. Tanned skin, calloused hands, thick, bronzed hair. The smell of cedarwood and nights beneath the stars. Thoughts race through my mind, as vivid as the touch of his fingers, the taste of his lips, the press of his body against mine. How slow and tender he was, and yet how he seemed to own me, pinning me down so I could do nothing but surrender.

And then the consequences. They run through my mind, too. I'm just another name in his catalogue, another entry on his no doubt much longer-than-mine list. "It appears he's slept with every aemortal woman in Eryndal," I say sourly, trying to push down the betrayal that's crawling across my face.

"When you're our age, every man comes with baggage," Nerissa sighs. "Don't hold it against him. The past is the past."

"Hmm." I bite my thumbnail, listening to the distant sounds of the palace grounds: wind through branches, iron gates rattling, voices calling on the breeze.

"It's nice to see you like this," Nerissa says softly. She curls her legs under her in the armchair, scratching her chin with long, slender nails. The pot of oolong tea that we have been brought gently steams into the air between us. "I feel like this version of you has been waiting to come out." We share a heavy look, her face etched with love and pride. My face scrunches in response. "I have a feeling you're going to be very powerful, Elira Corvannis," Nerissa sighs, resting a hand on her abdomen. "A mortal lifetime was never going to be enough for you."

"An aemortal marriage might be too much for me, though," I joke.

Her eyes turn serious. "Have you thought about what happens if it does become something?" she asks, her voice quieter now. "You'd become part of the royal family, thrown into this world of..." She looks around, searching for the right words. "Danger. You love The Courier's Keep, Lira—the humdrum of everyday life. Wouldn't all of this stress you out?"

"It won't become a problem," I say, though my brain whispers, *It is a price worth paying.* I purse my lips and mentally tell myself to shut up. It wasn't long ago that I wanted our monarchy dead, or at the very least to step down and encourage democracy.

And all of that is still fresh in my mind. No matter what, I plan to use my new status to ensure a fairer world for aemortals and mortals. There is no version of Eryndal in which I could happily now sit on my arse and look the other way. I have known poverty, and now I know power, and I plan to even out the durvelball field. Just as soon as I've found my family, reassured myself that I'm not a monster, and done some serious recovery-slash-soul-searching.

"Look, Lira. You must do everything you can to find your family," Nerissa says, tipping her mug to finish the last dregs of the tea. She swallows and sets the mug down. "Explore every avenue. Find a way into Thekla if you must, just to make sure they're not truly gone."

She snorts at her own joke, and I resist rolling my eyes. There's no way into death. Not for an aemortal, and certainly not for a half-blood like me.

As if she can read my mind, she asks, "Are you sure they are not going to destroy you? If your father is an aemortal, like you say, then you're not allowed to be... one of them. You're a half-blood. The Sable Legion—"

"I do not look like a half-blood," I say, reaching up and carefully feeling my right coryn. It feels sensitive to the touch, like skin, and I'm flooded with a memory of them both fizzing as Kaelion sent wave after wave of pleasure through me. I swallow down the blush that threatens to rise. "I do not think anyone dares to ask. This is a family of secrets."

CHAPTER FORTY-EIGHT

As I show Nerissa out, Elrind and a guard follow us from the tower room to the front doors, a journey we take in comfortable silence. Nerissa gapes at the tapestries and artwork as if she has never seen anything so grand, and I feel a shard of guilt that I'm yet to be truly impressed by this palace.

As the cool late winter air hits our faces, I start. At the top of the steps, Kaelion stands, looking out at the gardens and beyond, at the wall separating us from Grim Municipal. My heart lurches into my throat at the sight of him, but as he turns, he doesn't meet my eyes, his expression moving into one of civility.

"Lady Raven," he says, nodding at Nerissa. I'm surprised he managed to learn her surname—her original one, not the surname of her adoptive parents, the Zephyrs—but I show no such surprise. There's a kindness in the way he holds her gaze, knowing that it must have been a shock to see me looking like this. He's used to holding people together, to being there when others need him.

I don't know where we stand anymore. The last thing I said to him was that I regret everything.

"Your Highness." A guard strides up behind us, and it shoots a dagger of fear through me, but I don't recognise his ruddy skin, his bright eyes. I need to hunt down the guards who forced me into the cell, who left me to die. All in good time.

This bright-eyed legion member is accompanied by four more guards, crowding the stone entryway in their leather uniforms and thick boots, smelling of gunpowder and cologne. The lead guard takes a deep breath, as if ready to reel off the latest news. "The mortal woman is showing signs of improvement. It is most likely that she will live."

I close my eyes and grab Nerissa's arm, overwhelmed by the rush of relief that courses through me.

"But you should know," the guard continues, his tone graver, "that we see silicrites on the horizon, from the direction of the Elemental Bastion. The King of Claran has readied his troops and requested a fleet of golems from the mountains."

"Good," Prince Kaelion says, his voice commanding. "I shall meet Major General Drystan on the far side of Grim Municipal to further ward the borders."

Nerissa squeezes my hand.

"Word has been sent by your goddess that she is still considering helping your guest. She sent word via Tryx and advised that you give her time." His tone remains official, as if he's merely reciting the weather. My heart sinks as quickly as it rose. The Divinity of War knows not time as we do; she doesn't understand the urgency of this. Fjaldorn is sending more silicrites, more golems, more war in our direction. Finding Mother and Seren might provide clues about what they're after or, at the very least, convince the prince to give them what they want. Nerissa squeezes my hand even harder.

"The Sable Legion have informed their royal majesties of the incident at the Xandryll border," the guard continues. As I open my eyes, I see him glance at me uncertainly. "They are most displeased. They have apologised to the King of Xandryll, to whom the border patrol belonged, and sent sigils as compensation for every lost life."

"I didn't mean to kill them all," I say through gritted teeth, but only Nerissa looks at me, her eyes carefully guarded.

"We have also been informed that Her Majesties'... project," the guard says carefully, "has been settled in her new bedroom. The child for whom the funeral proceedings were organised has returned from Thekla to live at the palace." He turns a delicate shade of green, while the prince arches an eyebrow. Nerissa lets out a small squeak, her face going pale. "Unfortunately for the child, Her Majesty is distracted organising a congratulations party for His Royal Highness Prince Disryn. He has been accepted onto a prestigious course and shall set sail for the Shattered Isles in a quarter moon."

"Oh, well, as long as Disryn's got his place at the academie," Kaelion mutters.

"The quill that the Lesser Divinity of Language mistakenly sent for your royal nuptials has been stored in the art gallery, for your collection when you see fit," the guard continues. I don't look at Kaelion, and he doesn't look at me. A present for our nuptials. From a Lesser Divinity who obviously hasn't heard that we are not meant to be. That the prince only used me to entertain his goddess. That he lied to me and told me I could use the Divinities' favour to find my family.

Nerissa breathes in through her nose and out through her mouth. I've told her the whole story, and her sympathy rings like a siren song in the grounds.

"Regarding the undead child," Kaelion mutters, "is she showing unusual skills? Gifts that have awoken now she has become aemortal?"

"You can See Gifts, Your Highness." Elrind looks at the prince. "You should—"

"Please have the maids make sweet tea for everyone who has dealt with the morning's trauma," Prince Kaelion interrupts, voice loud, his face paler than usual. He lowers his voice and mutters to Elrind, "My ability is a palace secret. No one else is to know."

Apart from me. My shoulders twitch. I don't have time to stand here.

"Saida, send word to Major General Drystan that I shall be there shortly," Prince Kaelion snaps, straightening and commanding power. Fayte crackles off him, his whole body alight, and I take a step back. This is the man I first saw, the one arguing with his parents in the throne room—master of his kingdom, unwavering and resolute. Fayte's alive, he's hot when he's angry.

"Ensure Tryx tells the Divinity of War that we do not have the luxury of time, and that we—respectfully—request information on both captives. Now. Send word to the King of Xandryll that I will visit to apologise in person at first light tomorrow, and ensure the resurrected child is not housed near anyone else."

"Yes, Your Highness." Saida, a female guard, salutes.

"Lock the quill away in the underground crypts. We will not be needing it, and I do not know how we can dispose of it safely," he says. A spear stabs my heart. A wave of cold, sharp pain. It feels as if my chest might cave in. Nerissa finds my hand, her fingers curling through mine, offering a small comfort as I struggle to hold it together. Prince Kaelion doesn't look at me.

We will not be needing it. His words echo in my mind. I swallow hard. It was inevitable, obvious, that it would end like this, but still. To destroy a *quill*.

"Send Isolde's family royal condolences and clemency to visit the palace gallipot as soon as they wish. As for Disryn, tell him he must delay his party. We have enemies on the horizon, and I cannot have my mother and father distracted with table décor."

"Yes, Your Highness. Will that be all?"

"One further thing," the prince snaps, turning to face his kingdom. "Deploy two guards to see Lady Raven home safely. Station an additional guard outside her abode, and an addition outside the current abode of

Oswin Azba, until this enemy situation is dealt with."

My mouth has gone dry. I want to speak. *Sorry for saying that I regret everything. Thank you for keeping Nerissa and Oswin safe.* But I can't. I am just a guest in this palace; I have no right to claim any more of the Prince's attention. He has enough to deal with.

"Done," Saida calls, turning and doling out instructions to the remaining guards. Two come to stand by Nerissa and me, while the others file off to complete their tasks. As we step forward, towards the stairs, we are forced to pass the Prince, who is still looking at the horizon, as if expecting to see silicrites hurling in on bloodless wings. I open my mouth to speak, but it is Nerissa who finds the words first.

"Kaelion," she says, drawing herself up to her full height and gripping my hand protectively. "I do not like this life for Elira. I think she deserves better." With that, she yanks me forward, and we descend the stone staircase. I don't dare to turn and see the look on the prince's face. I keep my focus ahead, keeping my self-pride afloat as much as reasonably possible, given my best friend has just denounced the man I'm falling for.

I lead her to the palace gates, where I instruct two Sable Legion guards to escort her home safely, my voice stronger now, as the proximity between the prince and I has widened. As both guards bow towards me and exchange orders, Nerissa gives me a strange, lingering look. As if she's seeing me for the first time.

I wonder how I must look—enveloped in a man's jacket, my coryns proudly adorning my head, my posture confident, my instructions clear. She glances behind me, no doubt seeing the Prince, my wasted conquest—a prince who has stated that our nuptial present will never be needed and must be destroyed.

"Come home as soon as you can," Nerissa urges, before leaving.

Her words stir something funny inside me. I could ask an army patrol to escort me home right now; certainly, I'm strong enough now to feel safe, unlike last time. But still, I feel strange. Perhaps it's because the concept of home has evolved so swiftly that I've forgotten what it ever meant.

CHAPTER FORTY-NINE

It's all action in the castle.

The prince wisped away before I even returned to the steps, no doubt above such laws that stopped Elrind from wisping inside the palace gates. The hallways are abuzz with activity—Sable Legion cadets and palace staff running around, enacting the prince's instructions. I spot Dismal stalking down a corridor, his shoulders tight. I quickly turn the other way, not wanting to get into a conversation about his stalled party. Is he really so deluded that he thinks the celebration can continue, even with beasts on the horizon? Perhaps the King and Queen have had to focus on controllable matters to avoid the fact that they can't partake in the outside wars.

I turn over Nerissa's earlier words as I stride along. She's right. I must focus solely on finding Mother and Seren. No more dalliances with the prince, no more wasting time. *Find a way into Thekla, if you must.* But entering death is impossible.

I trace the journey back to my chamber, trying to ignore the ache in my chest—the guilt from the words that scraped from my tongue in the palace grounds. I told him I regret everything, and now he's having the quill locked away. Just because he half-stripped in the presence of women who've felt his wicked touch doesn't mean he owes me *anything*.

Yes, I was stealing a herb he'd asked me to steal, but that didn't suggest romantic intent. Not even slightly. I have spun myself a story that spoke of something more, that suggested that when a prince asked to kiss me in the palace grounds, that inferred he might not run off to bone two beautiful women later that night.

And, to be fair, he did say he wanted to distract them so he could steal something. They're both healers, with access to many herbs, the likes of which I know not.

I regret what I said to Kaelion, but still, I must focus on the most pressing matter at hand. A semblance of an idea is starting to form in my mind. I desperately need to find out if my family are alive, and now there is finally a way to do so.

I need to find the undead child.

It's nightfall before I get a moment alone. Whether by design or not, there always seems to be Sable Legion soldiers near me, watching my every move beneath shined silver helmets, bone-white faces unnerving. I feel sure that I could counter-attack if one tries anything – if my soldier-murdering tendencies have sparked more need for revenge – but it's almost as if they know this. They keep a respectable distance, but still, they are there on the castle air, cologne and gunpowder, rage and retaliation.

By the time I settle into my chamber, the only thing left to contend with is the shield Kaelion placed there. It is time to test my mettle.

I take a deep breath in, and with the door closed, but the shield visible, I raise my hands. Nothing appears. I feel ridiculous. I glance towards the window, where the new moon is growing outside – Afluenta, the moon that aligns with the Divinity of War – and it shines bone white onto the floorboards. She is taking her time to decide whether to help me. She is delaying, with no concept of the mortal lives that are at stake.

It appears. Not quickly, not dramatically, but with a slow trickle that winds itself around my fingers, releasing a taste of ancient metals into the air. This is *willed fayte.* Unteachable. I do not wish to do anything complicated; I only wish to undo the over-protective shield from a man I no longer wish to know.

Perhaps the Divinity of War helps me – her power surges into our land under her moon – or perhaps my intuition takes hold, but the fayte I release from my palms makes quick work of untying the shield, a faint golden shimmer in the air as each transformist symbol is highlighted and then undone. A second later, I pull the door open; I have successfully removed the shield, without understanding how. I am ready to find the undead child, to ask if my Mother and Sister are in Thekla.

I put a little weight onto my front foot, still

testing, but nothing happens, and there is no one in the corridor. They have been convinced of my safety behind the shield. No doubt guards have more important residents to protect, than the half-aemortal who seems to be having an endless sleepover. Kaelion's boar skin jacket weighs down my shoulders.

I creep along the familiar corridors. The suits of armour, the rich paintings, the emerald runners along each hallway. My bare feet pad quietly on the floor as I move, hoping that no one else is awake. Perhaps Kaelion.

I push the thought away. I can't think about him now. I have one goal. To find my family and return to the life I once knew. I was *happy*. Well, maybe not happy, but secure, which is essentially the same thing.

There is no one around as I progress. Where would one keep an undead child in a castle of this size? I try every room in my turret, but it's not until I reach the ground floor that I hear it. A child singing. The haunting melody slips through the darkened hall and sends a shiver down my spine. My feet prickle, as though wading through near-freezing water.

The undead child continues to sing.

It scrapes against the walls as I creep forward, inching toward a lightly parted door, a shard of moonlight drawing a finish line across the hallway floor. I start to make out the words of her song, a rhyme about power and royalty. "An heir to a throne, a gold target to those, watch as their arrows run, run little thing, run, run little thing, run."

Bile burns in my throat. What kind of fucked-up nursery rhyme has she learned? I hover outside her bedroom door, my confidence shifting to fear as a breeze tickles my face. And then the singing stops.

"Hello," the child says. Through the gap in the doorway, I can see her sitting in shadow, staring into a mirror.

Only the back of her head is visible. Because the mirror, which faces the rest of the room—and the doorway—is empty. Her reflection is nowhere to be seen.

What am I doing?

CHAPTER FIFTY

"Don't be scared, Elira." She turns towards me. I take a step backwards, but her face halts me. She looks... normal. A little like Seren as a child, all glossy hair and chubby cheeks. No coryns sprout from her scalp, no aemortal energy hums from her skin. "I'm sorry you're sad," she says, scratching her nose.

I'm not surprised that she can see my sadness. Ever since my family were attacked, and my heart was torn out, it feels like sadness seeps from my pores, permanently. It's etched across my face, like a tattoo.

"I'm sorry you..." I can't say *died*. I just can't. I look away from her face, away from the mirror, towards the child's bedroom. It's packed with toys and futons, and animals that seem to rise from the gloom. I need to pull myself together. To accept that in a world full of talking cats and murderous silicrites, I've already pushed too far beyond my old life to look back. This is my new reality. I must adapt, or risk someone else being slain on the palace lawn. A fleeting image of Nerissa lying there flashes through my mind. I can't let that happen. I can't let silicrites slaughter my kingdom.

"I need to talk to you," I say, steeling myself. All these reminders of Seren as a child—*my little sister*. I still think of her as a child, even though she's well into her twenties and has a serious girlfriend.

Her girlfriend. My heart aches. A shiver crawls up my spine.

"Of course you would like to talk to me," the girl says, getting back onto her stool. It's too tall for her, and she has to climb across the top before she can settle.

"Why... why of course?" Pain sings from somewhere in my chest, but I swallow it down. It wasn't long ago that this girl was *killed*. In the grand game of suffering, she wins.

"The queen thinks we are her children, doesn't she?" the girl muses. "I think she likes you better than me, though. I haven't seen her in days."

I breathe softly. Another thing I have no real knowledge of: the extent of the queen's grief. Has she taken us both in? I've never fully understood why they're letting me stay here. Perhaps we've become possessions for a queen who wants a daughter more than anything else.

"I need to know if they're alive." I walk further into the room, toys strewn around my bare ankles, my feet skeletal in the moonlight.

"That's fair," the girl says matter-of-factly, tossing her hair over her shoulder. "I don't sleep. They think I sleep, but I don't. I just sit here all night, on my own. It's nice to have company." The glow of moonlight fills the fayte-imbued window, casting shadows across the room.

"I'm glad," I say cautiously. Did she hear me? Does she understand that I want my family found? The back of my neck prickles, but I push my fear aside.

"It's different, now." She grips her lips together, rubbing her hands on her knees as if lost in thought. I know what she means by *now*. It's different, now that she's been resurrected from death. I push stray hair from my forehead, ignoring my shaking hand. "Sometimes, I hear their voices. There's a man on the Cecedit Mountains. He wants to collect us. It's hard to decide which is the real place." Fear gnaws at me, but I force myself to stay relaxed, loose. A bird streaks past the window, flashing in the moonlight. Otherwise, all is silent. "But I can find people. I couldn't find my parents because they're long gone, but if your family are recently gone, I can find them."

My breath catches in my throat. I rub my hands on my sides, on my newly-muscled hips, and swallow. The weight of what she's offering hits me, and my heart races.

"I want to help you," the child says, her voice sweet, and she smiles. It's a smile that makes me breathe a warm breath. She's going to help me. "If you do one thing for me." She cocks her head to one side.

I bite the insides of my cheeks. As always, this aemortal kingdom demands bargains.

CHAPTER FIFTY-ONE

She hums until she is thoroughly in Thekla, and then her body seems to freeze. Stills. Moonlight beats through the window, turning her figure into a chalk-blue statue. Panic rises in my chest, and I struggle to resist grabbing her to check that she's okay. She has entered death, on my behalf. I have sent a small child into Thekla to do my bidding.

I grip my hands together. There is nothing I can do now. Not a single emotion touches the girl's face as she sits in her meditation, her body present but her soul elsewhere. And then her face ripples. Her expression tightens, faint lines appearing where her eyelids close. Her eyelids flicker. If she is thoroughly in death now, then it's likely she's searching, or calling out my family's names. I swallow to try and dislodge the cold stone in my chest, the one that can't bear to wait for her to return.

What happens if she finds them? If death spits out their names like it's reading a roll call in a morning assembly. I stride around her room, pumping my arms and legs as much as my aching chest will allow, trying to keep my circulation going, even as my new body is stronger, faster, capable of terrible things. Thirty cycles worth of playing it nice, getting up early to comb my hair and shine my sandals, weighing up potential suitors to try and find someone safe, someone who will make life easy. And it's all led to this.

Pacing under the moonlight with my new horns, my hair everywhere, my feet bare, while I wait for a child to return from the underworld.

She starts to whine, the sound leaving her nostrils, a high-pitched scream that's hampered by her clenched-shut lips. I leap, lithe, quick, so that I'm crouched in front of her, as the whine becomes longer and longer, and she doesn't take a breath.

"Wake up," I urge under my breath, reaching out and letting my hand fall. Should I touch her? Will that create issues for her, in there? I shouldn't have let her go. A chill of fear runs down my spine. "Wake up," I urge again, as her body starts to twitch, as if she is running in another life, as if she is in pain.

"What's happening?" I breathe, confusion and helplessness starting to pound through me, as the girl shakes, her whole body trembling as that whine goes on and on, a siren's call of warning, a death toll above a city temple. What's happening? My palms turn clammy, and I reach out, hovering a hand above her arm. Touching her is the last thing I want to do, and yet I can't bear to see her tortured under the Divinity of War's moonlight. She lets out a whimper, a moan, and it's the final straw. I curse out loud and grab her arm.

It feels as if my forehead explodes into smoke and embers. She rears up, and I swear again as I fall backwards, crying out loud and sucking in precious air as the bottom of my backbone lands awkwardly on her floorboards, my coccyx sending shards of stinging pain up to my skull.

I can't see for white dancing spots of pain.

I can't even breathe.

I sure as hell am not prepared for what I see when the spots clear.

Her eyes have snapped open, tremors eating up her entire body, her arms outstretched as they create violent moving shadows on the ground.

I don't know what to do. There isn't time to think. The girl isn't breathing anymore, her mouth opening and closing, choking sounds gurgling from her mouth, her eyes wide, unblinking. I jump to my feet, my own fear replaced by the need to protect – protect this child at all costs, even if she looks like a demon possessed. What's that sound? It's coming from her.

"She's there, she's coming, I'm not dead, I'm not dead, what is that sound?" she whispers, and then she opens her mouth fully, tilts her head back, and screams at a shattering, blood-curdling volume: "RUN, ELIRA. RUN FOR YOUR LIFE!"

Panic claws at me as I sprint away from the blue flames, the sound of the child's screams still tearing through me as my heart pounds against my ribcage, even though she's been sent onwards. I didn't have time to ask why she told me to run, didn't stop – I carried out what she'd asked me to – I had to – and then I–

FUCKING

RAN.

What did she meet in Thekla? Who was the 'she' the girl talked about? My feet hit the floorboards as I reach the turret stairs, and barrel up towards my guest suite. It's dark, the moonlight barely breaking into the turret, the corridor I fall into seeming to shake with my own blurred vision. I am wearing Kaelion's jacket over my nightgown, the thick cedarwood scent chasing me, or leading me, I'm not sure.

The moon is at its highest, and I hear a moan coming from my own body – not just the child's reaction – the fucking terrifying feeling of something screaming RUN at me – but the action I had to undertake afterwards, the vision that's seared into my eyeballs. I had to. I had to, I had to. It was her one condition.

I'll lock myself in my bedroom and think what to do.

But I can't decide right now. I don't know where to go. I don't know what just happened–

My bedroom door is ajar. I can't remember if I left it so. I freeze, watching the opalescent light on the floorboards of my bedroom, cast there by moonlight through a fayte-imbued window. Shapes and creations, flowing eerily. Is Kaelion inside? Has he come to see me? Thank fayte, I can't be annoyed at him any longer, I need him. I fucking need him, more than I've ever needed anyone.

I run forward, but I can't hear him, nor smell him.

His cedarwood usually carries around him, a sense of power, a sense of him just being there that I always seem too aware of, as if I have him on my permanently etched internal radar, showing up blank. He can't be here.

I must have left the door open. It would have been madness to close the door behind me when I was trying to be silent. But a creaking from behind me has thrown me off. It feels as if I'm caught between worlds, unsure which has an Elira-shaped space ready.

I step forward. Press my hand to the door until it swings away.

The robed figure inside faces the window.

"Don't go in," a voice behind me cries, as the robed figure leans their head back.

I spin. "King Aestos?"

He'd been following me. I don't have time to be flattered. "Kae had me monitor you," the king gasps, drawing his shaking hand in the air. Drawing transformist symbols. Summoning power. "He didn't trust the Sable Legion to protect you. But I will, Elira, I'm here, and I can taste... I can taste someone in the air, a most terrible fayte. Can you taste it, Elira? Can you taste the swamps?" He sounds a little delirious, and he is slow. He hasn't fought in numerous cycles, hasn't left the palace in many moons.

It happens too quickly for me to register. I whip my head back to the robed figure–never turn your back on an enemy–and a face of blinding light's revealed. The golden figure lifts a hand, as the King cries out, hurls a shield across me—a film of gold light–but–

The monster in the bedroom has already

retaliated. Light—red, blinding, fleeting—skims my side as it strikes.

I lift my hands, pray to the gods, and fayte actually *leaves me*. Blasts the inside of the shield – the shield the King created to protect me, instead of himself. It reverberates around my bubble shield, hitting me with pure heat, overwhelming metals, light that quickly falls as I drop my hands.

My fayte might have been useless, but hers hit true.

The King lets out a sigh as he slumps to the floor, his skull cracking against the doorframe. It's all too quick, the smell of fayte burning my tongue. The shield disappears. His skull has split open. The smells of iron and sulphur fill the hallway air. My lips feel numb. My palms burn.

The King is dead.

I look up.

"That wasn't a very nice greeting," a woman drawls, her voice terrible, her golden face shimmering.

CHAPTER FIFTY-TWO

"Who are you?" I step back. I'm aemortal now. Coryns adorn my hairline. And I can ignore them no longer.

Because they are *burning*. They are the source of my power. They will birth me great fayte, and enable my new status as half-aemortal. I can see the reflection of their glare in the air around my face, feel them humming to life as my heart cavorts in the white-hot grip of pure fear as the *being* looks at me, her smile stretching across her terrible, golden face. I take a deep breath, trying to calm my mind. I am powerful. I am no longer a mortal.

"I'm going to have to bind you, Elira, darling," she trills, throwing yet more fayte forward. This time, it takes the form of a blue net, capturing me before I can retaliate. The net binds me tight, clutching at my hair, suffocating my lungs.

Okay, maybe I can't defeat this monster. Fucking lion pelt.

"When the Sable Legion find out you're a half-blood, they will execute you anyway." She lets out a cackle of a laugh, one that chills me all the way through. She's right. But how does she know what I am? "I must say, I was very impressed with how deliciously you killed my silicrite," she drawls, still sitting on the bed, robes spilling around her, her face a mask of molten gold. I struggle against the binds, but it's no use. I focus on breathing, the binds engulfing me. "And how mercilessly you killed the army boys. You do have the Vaelthorne spark in you."

"I'm a Corvannis," I gasp, as the king's head spills blood onto the floor. It cascades towards me—and then stops. My feet have created an invisible barrier. The blood won't travel beyond.

"Your sister is an interesting character," the woman purrs, standing from the bed and stretching her arms above her head. There's a crash as a few beads from her wrists fall to the ground. "Keeps us on our toes."

"What?" I choke, my jaw locked in a bind.

"Seren. Now, she's a Corvannis. Thick, pig-headed, feisty."

"Elira!" a voice cries. My heart leaps into my throat, but it's Elrind. As he sprints down the hallway, I feel a jolt of energy surge through me. He's released me, thrown his releasing symbols in my direction. I am free of the binds. I rip my arms up, my jaw liberated, fayte sparking from my fingertips. But I don't attack.

This woman knows where Seren is.

I raise my hands toward Elrind, in a stop signal. I need to stop him from walking closer. I can't let her see him. He should not come any nearer. He halts mid-stride.

Glowing, bright fayte bursts from my palms. Something starts siphoning from the King's body below where my fingers tremble. The foe in the bedroom lets out a short, sharp sigh, as if she now has to kill the messenger as well as the king.

I can barely see his corpse beneath my glowing hands, but something is rising. I'm *pulling it* into the air between Elrind and I. I can no longer see the king's cracked skull as black liquid siphons from the crack and rises, hovering in the hallway air.

I can't stop. My hands are siphoning, and as I look back at Elrind, I see only horror in his ash-coloured eyes behind the feathered guard.

"Stop it," he croaks, looking for the first time, afraid. I don't think he's seen the enemy in the bedroom. I think he sees only me, and the dead king—and as understanding flits through him, Elrind stumbles backward, falling into a suit of armour. The helmet is knocked off, and rolls like a severed head between us, casting silver shapes of light onto the walls.

"I didn't kill him," I breathe, glancing beyond Elrind, my gaze flickering to the empty hallway. Where is Kae?

A prince does appear, alerted to the noise. Dismal steps up behind Elrind, his face pale, his black hair trembling at his forehead. "What are you doing, Elira?" His usually jovial voice is afraid. He hasn't seen the king's body yet. It's almost entirely covered by the wall I've started building in the corridor. And it's not black liquid forming this barrier. My heart sinks in horror as I realise the truth.

It glints red in the light from the nearest fayte-imbued window.

It's *blood*.

I am using the king's blood to build a wall, to stop them nearing me and the demon in the bedroom.

Prince Kaelion's voice echoes in my mind: "If you are not careful, you will harness darkness because you have not learned how to manage the light."

"Enough," the woman in the bedroom snaps, standing to her full, blazing height. She clicks her fingers. And then we are moving. Not disintegrating the way we usually do when an aemortal forces me to wisp, but sinking.

I only have time to release the fayte that burns in my hands, watching in horror as the blood wall drops and splashes across the hallway, across Elrind's feet, over his trousers. The messenger stares at me.

"Thekla," Dismal whispers, his face nearly as pale as Elrind's. "She's going into Thekla."

And then we are gone.

CHAPTER FIFTY-THREE

Thekla is a place of nightmares. Thick fog clings to the air, black treacle wraps around my ankles, strange shapes loom from the mist like the gnarled fingers of heaven-high skeleton trees. Under the scent of fog and marsh, there is a strange smell of worn leather and well-worn boots. Sounds—eerie echoes, pained sighs, indistinguishable whispers—fill the fog.

I am in death. Have I died?

The woman is no longer glowing. Instead, she has become just a shadow, dragging me forward towards a murky-edged black hole that sucks light in the distance. "I had to pay the Divinity of Death to let me bring you through whole," she hisses.

"Where are you taking me?" I glare down at my hands, which have decided to be useless since creating the blood wall. Why does fayte only appear when I barely want it, and disappear when I *need* it? I am still wearing the prince's boar skin jacket, the sleeves rolled up to reveal the knobbles of my wrists, my useless hands coated in shadow. And yet. And yet I will not stand to be *stolen* from the palace, not after my family have been taken, not after everything we've been through.

It's the look on Elrind's face that does it. I refuse to be looked at like a creature of the night, a prowling king-murderer, cracking skulls under a full moon. I may have once plotted against the monarchy; I was once the first to call them a waste of a perfectly good palace, a waste of *air*. But not anymore. Now, I know them to be just as flawed, awry, faulty as anyone else. As *mortals*. They are not superior beings; they are just as fucked up, just as likely to drown their sorrows in the taverns, carry a hipflask in their pockets, just as likely to fuck around and fuck up as mortals, but they look better doing it.

And so no, *Elrind*, I did not kill our king on purpose, no matter how much I once might have dreamed of abolishing him. And it's that, the unfairness of the situation, the need to *fucking justify* myself to the messenger, to make sure he doesn't think me a cold-hearted killer, that leads me to my next thought.

I'm not fucking going.

I *am not* fucking going.

I do not *obey*.

Before she can react, I attack. My knee swings up and catches her in the hip, sending her staggering, as I yank my hand away. I form a fist, lunge forward, pound it right into her face, knuckle cracking cheekbone. For a shadow, she is still solid, as solid as I am in this place, and her scream bellows around the thick fog, a shriek that eats the very air we breathe.

Fuck, yes.

She scrabbles back to fight me, but her fayte doesn't work here either. We are in neutral ground, and as she grabs me around the neck, her shadowed form pressing into my skin, I choke. My vision blurs, my heart blocking itself in my throat as I scrabble to breathe, just a half-aemortal about to be killed in death itself.

I manage to hit her around the face, jam my fingers into her left eye socket until she lets go, baring her shadowed teeth, hauling her legs through the thick liquid as she steadies herself and then launches for me again. We stagger through death, overtaking the mist, shrieking, cursing. Pain sings from my knuckles, blazing up to my shoulders as we grapple, kicking whatever I can grab, aiming to push her into the deathly swirl around our feet as cold fog clings to my skin like drying sweat. I grind my teeth, finally getting purchase on her shadowed robe, slipping my hands around her neck, and then–

She puts her hand up, just as I go in for the final kill, my new strength promising me that I can snap her neck, even in death, even though she is a shadow of her body outside.

She gasps, "If you run now, you doom them all."

I pause, my breathing heavy. "What?" I won't listen to her. Won't listen to this cruel creature that's just *murdered* my king, left him for dead. Cracked his skull, ruined a family, ruined a kingdom.

"I have an army." Her voice turns from a gasp to something wilder. "They are ready to invade Eryndal, kill everyone. You think the hundred silicrites we sent before was hard? Wait until it's a *thousand*, and they're instructed to *slay en masse*."

Why would she go to all that trouble for me, a postmistress? No. Following her would cost me something far more valuable than my own life, it would kill my ability to find my family. I'd rather rip my own eyes out. But it's not just about my family. Fear prickles at the back of my neck. She's got me hooked, my heart a painful pendulum, and she knows it.

"That's right, Elira. Come with me." She reaches out. Grabs my arm.

It's not just about my family. There is a whole kingdom at stake here. And to torch Eryndal, just so I can avoid going with her... Just so I can save my own skin.

She pulls on my arm, her hand cold around my skin, stinging the inside of my elbow. And I let her. The liquid below splashes, a resonant song that seems to mourn with me. Because I have to go. I can't let them invade Eryndal. Can't let her army of silicrites take over the city. The slums, barely protected, the farmland, the districts, all packed with hunger and gore already.

A hopeless city rendered even more hopeless.

I submit.

"Come, stupid girl." As she strides, yanking me with her, she announces, "Your mother slept with the King of our empire, and thus produced you, an unwanted, festering half-breed. You do not deserve the horns that adorn your head. You have not earned them as a fully-fledged aemortal, and as such, barely deserve to breathe the air of our kingdom, let alone oversee it.

It is only right that you join me, and you can apologise when you're ready."

What. The. *Fuck?*

"What did you just say?" My voice is blank, my lips numbed, as I follow her through death, waiting for a miracle. "My father isn't a king." I breathe, but it's shaky. My whole body feels like it's fizzing, pushed past the point where I can contain anything. I am a neat, apathetic postmistress with a schedule for every week. I cannot take on this much information at once.

I cannot be an heir. It's as unlikely as Nerissa deciding to join the Sable Legion, or Rhett signing up for an aemortal fan club.

"Trust me, I've read and re-read your name a thousand times," she drawls, as we progress. "I have had my best men try and break the map. I have had dwarven cartographers verify every inch of that damned thing. It is you, and you don't deserve a single inch of my kingdom. Filthy half-blood."

"That's why you sent the silicrites," I say, my voice still strange to my own ears, as if someone else is talking. That's why Elrind asked me, the first time I saw him, how the silicrites found *me*. The beast was waiting outside my place of work, waiting for me to turn up. And I did. I just walked straight into his path.

Which means that it's true. Or at least, these people think that it's true. And if they think me to be an heir…

My pulse jumps as I speak. "Do you intend to kill me?"

Shadows rise, darker than the palace hallways, curling around us. The fog lingers in my peripheral, grey as silicrite flesh, as unrelenting as the end of time.

"I need only a favour from you, Elira," she hums through the growing darkness. "Grant me that, and I might let you live."

Oh, fayte. Another favour.

Why is the aemortal world full of bargains, deals, pleas, and punishments? We do not live like this in Grim Municipal. We do not sell our souls, our pride, to the highest bidder.

"How did you get into the castle?" I hiss, as we near a black hole.

"You have your Queen to thank for that," she croons, her voice dripping with delight as death splashes around my ankles. "When Her Majesty opened the gates of Thekla to pluck the child's spirit out of the fog, she opened all sorts of avenues for us."

"The Mancer rebirthed the child," I say, confused. After that first silicrite attack, the necromancer must have brought the mortal child back from the brink of death. Which opened the gates between the palace and Thekla... I close my eyes briefly, the truth dawning. By bringing the child back, they have let the monsters in.

"Your Queen did not seal the entrance to Thekla, so to speak, upon her exit. It made it far too easy for my soul to slip through the doorway at one end and enter at this end."

"But the undead child is dead again," I say, swallowing hard as pain pulses through me. "I made sure of that. I burned... I burned the body."

She had told me how. The correct way to summon the right fire to destroy her. That had been her only term: she would enter Thekla, if I sent her on thereafter. She did not wish to live a sleepless life. She granted me my favour, and I granted her hers in return. Guilt burns me.

"This does not matter now." My captor's voice sharpens. "The gates were not closed. I had to sell a Seer to the Divinity of Death to allow you to pass through in full form. It is a loss I already mourn, and you will make it worthwhile."

My stomach bottoms out. Why is this empire riddled with corrupt gods? The Divinity of Death accepted a *Seer*?

"Perhaps your beloved prince will save you," she breathes, her voice rattling through the air. "When he *begged* me not to attack his kingdom nor steal you, I must say I saw why you're *enraptured* by him."

I stop walking. Clench. But she doesn't pause, continues dragging me through thick, suffocating treacle. "Prince... Kaelion," I say, throat raw with pain.

"Of course. He took azizova petal, I would guess, to talk to me. Negotiate. It seemed he saw a *future* for the two of you. *Begged* me to leave his woman alone. Said he would pay any price."

My jaw flexes, my breath catching in my throat.

"Of course, the only price I needed was you, one thing he wasn't willing to grant me. A shame, to have a Gift-holding prince on the roster..."

I've never hated anyone as much as I hate her, pain burning through me with the heat of all major Divinities. And yet. Her words give me life. Which is just as well, since we've arrived at the next door: a hole in the fog so black it seems to suck the shadows from her form.

The prince begged her to leave me alone.

I can get over the fact that he has been some sort of aemortal lothario. Like Nerissa says, we are thirty cycles. Even the mortal men our age come with baggage. My heart somersaults, and I stumble clumsily forward, drawn towards the black hole that devours the shadowed woman's form. It pulls at her like a hungry beast, gutting her sleeve, dragging her deeper into the abyss. Am I really going to do this?

As she grabs my wrist, the darkness swallows her, dragging shadows at an odd angle, yanking me along with her, even as I stand my ground, lost in a momentary need to fight, and I hear a sickening crack above my hand. I hear it before I feel it.

Yank–Yank– FUCK!

As my wrist breaks, my scream rings out, echoing through the empty, ghostly expanse of Thekla.

CHAPTER FIFTY-FOUR

I track time by the nights that unfold outside the small, high window of my cell, a blanket of stars shaken out as if for my own amusement. Two nights, both so beautiful they almost numb the unbearable pain in my broken wrist.

When I stagger to the window, I see the mountainous kingdom spread before me, mountainsides and luscious forests expanding into valleys and divots, a haze of mist seeming to rise from the endless trees. The air feels thinner here, but my lungs are starting to adjust.

I eat the rancid food that's pushed through a hole in the door: mushy greens, grapes with a rind of mould, molasses with strange clogs floating in it. Though I ask for a pot, I'm told to empty myself in the corner of the cell. I hear noises – people screaming, shouting for help, from other cells, cells that sound distant, voices that resonate and rebound like hungry wolves around my cell and past the window bars.

I squint as I hold my arm up to the new sunrise, which bleeds purple through the window. The pain hits me, waves crashing through my body—white-hot, unrelenting. Aemortals do not heal any quicker than mortals without a healer or elixir. That's why we can be destroyed, our bodies broken, our minds eventually going mad without the sweet release of being sent to Thekla. I slump to the floor, nursing my arm in the comfort of the prince's jacket.

I am an heir. I am the heir to the throne of Fjaldorn.

Who knows about this? Mother, presumably, and my father. I don't think Seren knows, nor Nerissa. Did Prince Kaelion know? He must have, to have begged. He knew I was *heir*, and he said nothing, bound to secrecy. No wonder the royals were so keen to keep me at the palace, to enable me to stay. I might have been kidnapped within mere breaths of stepping foot in Grim Municipal.

I am heir to a throne. And, technically, Kaelion is not, because another child has been born under his King and Queen. What a strange pendulum dance my mind undertakes, as pain sends delirium through me.

The cell door opens.

No visitors in days, and now two enter. The first causes me to inhale sharply, instinctively waiting for my fayte to rise. But it doesn't.

"You've eaten an elixir that counteracts fayte." My captor leans against the wall. She's dressed in smart, fitted cream leathers, her skin a deep, rugged tan. Gemstone-studded hair is piled atop her head, either side of deep brown coryns, and her lipstick smile splits into a warning, the bags under her eyes betraying her weariness. I preferred her as a shadow in death. It was her soul, it seemed, that entered Thekla and took on a golden form in the palace. But as soon as we returned here—this prison building in Fjaldorn, by the looks of it—she assumed her normal form.

A smiling aemortal bitch.

The girl standing with her is aemortal, but still young, not yet fully enduring the slow aging process that aemortals undergo after eighteen. She has dark hair, and her fear is palpable.

"Fuck you." I spit onto the ground, a wave of pain breaking through me as my dried mouth barely forms enough to create a sigil-sized splat of phlegm on the floor.

"Now, now. We haven't properly met, Elira. I'm Draevena Hrox, and I'm all set to be your father's new wife. I've started to tidy up this kingdom already."

I close my eyes. My captor is my father's bride-to-be.

"I've locked you here for your own protection," Draevena continues. "I heard about your recent change and your tryst with the Eryndal Crown Prince. We can't have you running loose in our kingdom, and we certainly can't have him coming here and causing trouble. I'm here to show you what could happen if you do as I ask."

"Which is what?" I gasp, struggling to keep my chin held high. Every instinct, every part of me that is both mortal and aemortal, screams to rise up and attack. She's unarmed, and the girl looks harmless. But she has magic, and I do not.

"Have a look," Draevena croons. The dark-haired girl steps closer. Her eyes turn milky as she holds her hands out, cupping them so a small hole forms between her thumbs. Despite every warning in my head, I lean forward. Gasping against the pain in my wrist, I press my eye to the hole in her hands. It displays a scene, where her curled palms should be. I can see the breakfast room at the palace.

I jerk back, as if stung. The cold stone of my cell still surrounds me. Nothing here has changed. The girl is showing me a vision.

"She's a type of Seer." Draevena's delight is clear. "She can show *futures*, Elira."

I lean in again, my heart racing. Sound hits me first: birdsong, the clink of glass as orange juice is poured, Elrind muttering to a servant. Elrind. My heart leaps. And then I see him. Prince Kaelion, sitting at the table, looking... glorious. His tanned skin glows, his hair shines from his coryns, he smiles as he speaks. He looks effortlessly happy. I wonder if I've ever seen him this at ease, this pleased.

Across the table sits a beautiful woman. Her coryns are pure white, her skin like fine porcelain, her hair long and opalescent. It tumbles down her back. I always wear it in a neat bun, always pulled up so it doesn't get in my way, but now...

I'm wearing it down.

It is me. A version of me.

I swallow hard.

"At least we're prepared," I hear myself say, responding to something he has just mentioned. I reach for an ornate hilt. The hilt of the sword that is leaning against the table alongside me. The imaginary me fingers the hilt and then pulls her hand away, satisfied that it is there, waiting.

In the present, my heart lurches painfully. I hadn't known I wanted this — not truly — until I saw it, and now I can't look away from the image of myself: my robes, the silk of my hair cascading over one shoulder. I look *powerful*.

"Disryn insisted on helping the queen with the Cyder Festival soirée." Kaelion laughs, reaching across the table to take my hand. He is so happy, it almost blinds me. As the other me reaches out, symbols shine from our hands.

The symbols of bonded noblemates. The very highest order of marriage. He clutches my hands between his, and I angle myself to get a better view of my face. I look so free. So clean. So happy. My cheekbones glow, my green eyes dazzling in the early morning sunlight.

"Elrind, some orange juice for my new bride, if you will," Kaelion calls, and instantly, the messenger appears at my side, his face flushed. I notice he was flirting with the servant in the corner. The servant hurries off, but I don't miss the gleam in Elrind's eye as he pours the juice.

"You know," the fake Elira says, looking between Kaelion and Elrind, "when Mother and Seren visit later, you must let me take them to the training grounds. I would love to teach my sister proper swordsmanship."

"Of course, Your Highness," Elrind replies. My pulse quickens, caught between jealousy and longing. The warmth, the tenderness — I could have this. I *want* this.

"That's enough," Draevena snaps. I jolt as she grabs the Seer away. The full dankness of my cell hits me like a slap to the face. The harsh brick, the stone door, the tiny barred window. The oppressive grey of everything, the only colour Draevena's bright lipstick as she grins at me, mockingly, against the cold, miserable backdrop of my reality. "That can all be yours."

The Seer looks miserable. I nurse my wrist, wrapped in Kaelion's jacket, and glare at them. The room reeks of filth.

"I require only one thing from you, dear Elira," Draevena continues, her smile grotesque. "Relinquish your rights as heir to the kingdom. That is all. You've never been here before, you have no relationship with your father. You shouldn't manage this land. All can see that." Her smile widens, the words hanging in the air like a noose around my neck. "Just sign the papers," she continues. "Agree to surrender your position, and I will let you and your brethren go."

Brethren.

"Where are they?" I rasp. "My family."

"I expect you'll be seeing them soon. They're being brought up from the underground cells." *Underground cells.* The playrooms in our city gaol flash through my mind, stories of chambers that are so filled with screams a prisoner can't hear themselves think.

"Fuck. You," I hiss, pain slamming into me, stars flashing across my vision. "How dare you—"

"Silly woman," she hisses, striding towards me. Her hand darts out, grabbing my injured wrist. The pain is white-hot, flooding my body until I can't focus on anything, the sting *unbearable*.

"The empire was built for dick-swinging men," she snarls, her grip tightening, her voice dripping with venom as spots cloud my vision. My throat tastes of bitter bile. "If the king dies, I sacrifice my rights as his heir, because we are not yet wed. The rest of the empire is taking its time in organising our official union, as our wedding must have all royalty present to be binding. Which means that I am not eligible for anything if he dies now. It will go to you, all to you, and if I cannot speed up our wedding, then I will eliminate the risk."

"If I die," I gasp, my arm shooting pain up to my shoulder, "you will still not be queen. You will still need to wed him." Her words make me think though; does my father know I'm here?

"The Divinities shall take pity on his *loyal* partner, will crown me within the week."

Even through the agonising pain, my mind flashes to the sight of the king's head split open on the floor, blood pooling. What of Kaelion? What of his real paternity, and the didactic laws that my torturer actually *is* correct about; the queen's offspring is not as powerful as the king's offspring. My captor speaks some sense, even if she is deranged.

"Then why not just kill me?" I hiss, wishing I had

the fayte, the power, to burn her from the inside out. She pauses, her breath parting the stale air. And I know the answer. "Because there's no guarantee, is there?" My own breath rips from my body. "You cannot be sure that the Divinities will grant you your status as queen. But if I sign the kingdom away to you, list you as my replacement heir, you are certain to inherit it."

"If the king dies," is all she says, her words doing laps around the dank cell. She needs me to sign away my rights as heir because the rest of the kingdom will not allow them to marry. It is the next best way that she can make sure she will rise to power. Which also means that she is probably going to kill the king, just as soon as I sign. And even though he left, even though he betrayed me, I don't want him dead.

"I'll let you think some more, shall I?" Her breath burns my face, hot and taunting. "I've assembled our court as witnesses, and you'll be expected on the dais tomorrow."

She turns for the door, her heels clicking sharply against the stone floor. A guard appears, stepping aside to let her pass.

"You'll be lucky if she leaves you alive," the dark-haired girl whispers, her voice so quiet I wonder if I imagine it. "But you can't let her rule. You just can't." And then, just like that, she's also gone. The door snicks shut behind them, and I'm left alone in the silence of the cell, pain still rattling through me.

With shaking hands, I drag myself to the privy corner and vomit, my body heaving.

CHAPTER FIFTY-FIVE

I drift in and out of sleep. Each time I wake, the sun has hauled itself higher in the sky, oblivious to my pain. The strange purple hue of the heavens shifts each time it climbs, and through my small window, I catch glimpses of Fjaldorn, the kingdom that keeps me hostage. The sky seems tinted by twilight even under full sun, as if a candlelit dinner party in the heavens never quite ends. In the distance, mountaintops loom—clouds or smoke, impossible to tell, rise like mushrooms, spreading an undulating sweep across the purple sky.

Stale meals are pushed through the slot in the door at regular intervals. When a cup of water is offered, I snatch it up, glugging it as quickly as I can without spilling, trying to satisfy the relentless thirst that has become part of me, mixing with the ever-present pain in my wrist.

The two sensations blur into one.

If what Draevena said is true, and the king's passing means his heir must take his place, then—

though I hate admitting it—she has a point. Why should she sacrifice her kingdom for me? A woman who's never stepped foot in this land? What really gets me, though, is why in fayte's name she thinks locking me in this cell with a broken wrist will convince me to help. If she had simply asked—if my father had asked—I'd have been more willing. Instead, she seems set to kill me.

Kaelion's father killed Kae's biological father so that he could keep a family secret, could pretend to his kingdom. A voice of doubt whispers in my mind, *Perhaps Kae was able to ask her to change the map. Perhaps he's leaving you here to die.*

A flash of movement catches my eye, and my heart leaps into my throat. Something has flown past the turret window. Could it be a messenger from Eryndal? Maybe a new form of flight, something imbued with fayte, capable of crossing the border? I totter to my feet, dizzying under the pain in my wrist as I stumble toward the window. Pressing my face to the cool air, I squint.

I immediately recoil. *Silicrites.*

They circle like a committee of vultures. Their wings flare, their legs tucked into their bodies, streaks of brown and lavender. Their grotesque, human faces twist into malicious grins, as if they are savouring the freedom of flight, the hunt.

Terror claws into me.

Are they here to kill me?

Where is my father? He may regret having a child with my mother, may not care for me, but *surely* he can't want me dead? I am his bloodline. And yet, dead I will be if I don't escape this cell soon. The pain in my wrist has sharpened. The swelling is sizeable, the broken bone unable to heal. Infection creeps in, hot, suffocating, sending waves of fever across my body, thick sweat sticking to my skin. I need healers or medicine, before it overtakes me.

Outside, silicrites call to one another, harsh voices carried on a goading wind.

The only thing I know for certain, as my chest aches in a way that has nothing to do with my wrist, is that the smell of cedarwood from this thick boar-skin jacket is grounding me. Its scent is like a tether back to reality when everything else is trying to pull me into madness.

Tomorrow, I'm expected to sign a treaty in front of Fjaldorn's aemortal legion. I'm supposed to hand over control of a kingdom I never asked for, to a woman who will likely ruin it with her torturous ways. If I sign that paper, she might rip my throat the moment the ink dries. But the thought that keeps gnawing at my mind isn't the treaty or Draevena or any of this twisted power struggle. It's that *vision*. The Seer's vision.

It's *my* face. I barely recognised it. She was relaxed, peaceful, *content*. And that terrifies me. Because I've never looked like that. Not once in my life. I've never been at peace. Always rushing, always looking for something to fill the void, burying my loneliness in routines, tasks, keeping busy. But that woman in the vision… she wasn't buried. She wasn't running. She was *living*.

I want that. I want that so badly that, for a moment, the dream steals my breath and tucks it beneath leaden weights. I can't remember the last time I wanted anything this much.

But I might be dead before I have the chance to tell Prince Kaelion the truth. I want the chance to get to know him, to turn the vision into reality. I would gladly take this punishment, this life of pain and imprisonment, ten times over if it meant sparing him from having to step foot in this kingdom. If it meant he didn't have to beg Draevena. If it meant he didn't have to risk his life to save mine.

His jacket soaks up my tears.

CHAPTER FIFTY-SIX

"ELIRA," a voice shrieks from the corridor, cutting through the stillness.

The sudden burst of noise explodes into my cell. Seren's shouting. Sounds of struggle. My mother's voice, frantic and laced with worry, barking at Seren to calm down.

I blink. Force myself to sit up. This can't be real. When Draevena said they were bringing them from the underground cells, I assumed it was to place them somewhere else, somewhere safer. Not–

The door creaks as the fayte-imbued lock is painstakingly disassembled. A sob heaves from me, as I struggle to stand, my broken wrist sending pain rolling down my body. Kaelion's jacket slips from my shoulders. My vision blurs as my balance dances across the inside of my skull.

They're here. *They're alive.*

"Get the fuck. Off. Me." Seren snarls, her voice

choked. Sunshine breaks out in my chest. My throat clogs. Relief tastes like salt, fresh on my tongue, as my eyes prick and sting.

"Get off her!" I rasp, my voice cracking as I stumble blindly toward the door. It swings open with a groan of protest, and I shrink back, half-expecting to find more soldiers, more terror waiting behind it.

It's worse than that.

The room is filled with a presence that makes the air around me turn to ice. I can't stop myself from gasping, a scream bubbling at the back of my throat, as he steps in. A silicrite. It stands tall over me, looming like a nightmare made flesh, its many legs skittering across the floor with a sound that makes my stomach churn. This is it. They've brought Seren here to watch me die.

"You murdered my cousin," the silicrite declares in a voice that sends a wave of cold through my veins. I sense movement behind the silicrite, and my heart leaps into my throat as Seren, her hands bound, is shoved into the doorway. My eyes devour her, relief flooding through me. If I'm about to die, at least I've seen my sister one last time. Her face is pale, her grey robes torn and soiled, smeared with filth. Her red hair tumbles around her sharp cheekbones, but her eyes are wild and alive with energy.

"I did," I whisper, my voice growing. "Murder your cousin. I had to protect my life."

"You killed a silicrite." It's my mother who croaks the words, her voice hollow. She is shoved into the doorway next to Seren, her robes stained and ragged.

Her hair is a tangled mess around her face, her eyes wide as they take me in. They both have golden binds around their wrists and ankles, shackling them into submission.

Fear rattles through me, cuts out my tongue.

"I am here to warn you," the silicrite continues, leaning down so that his putrid breath hits my face, stale and foul. "If you try anything at the signing ceremony tomorrow, I will tear you apart. First, your arms." He snarls, eyes narrowed, a sickening grin spreading across his lips. "Then your legs. And then we'll all watch as you bleed to death. And if that doesn't work, we have *collateral*." He glances at Mother and Seren.

My stomach churns. The words land like heavy stones, dropping into the pit inside me. He straightens, eyes glinting with malice. And then he strides out, passing Mother and Seren without pause. I can barely breathe, the weight of everything – fear, relief, fear – pressing down on me like a vice.

"You're alive," I whisper.

And then Seren shrieks, "WHAT HAVE YOU DONE TO HER?" Her voice slaps the silence like a paddle. My heart skips a beat, and I inhale sharply, an unknown pain clenching my throat. She means me. Her eyes are locked above my forehead. "You've turned her into a monster! Don't LEAVE US here with her!"

The silicrite chuckles from the corridor, the sound ringing like a bell. "Lock them in. They should catch up before tomorrow's *occasion*."

The occasion. The ceremony. My signing away of

my rights and, no doubt, my slaughter before an entire empire. My legs weaken beneath me, and I stagger forward, my head spinning. "Do not be afraid," I say, voice trembling. "I'm still the same person. Still Elira."

The words are empty, a desperate plea thrown into a void. Seren's eyes, wide with horror and disbelief, meet mine. Shame slices me like a blade. I want to scream, to tell her that I am still her sister, still the person she's known all her life, and I've been *fucking searching for her.*

But the words get caught in my throat. The door slams, echoing through the cell, through my bones. The golden binds fall away, leaving them free to move. But they don't.

"They take the good water," Seren hisses, her face bone-white, her eyes shining. "They take the good grain. They take *our money*. They patrol our *streets*. They use our *sex workers*. They see themselves as *superior*. You are now *one of them*."

My arms hang at my sides. I feel like a stranger to myself. The stench of waste clings to the air. I glance at Mother, her eyes hollow, her face drawn with exhaustion. Our captors have dressed them in simple robes that clutch their ankles, grey slippers on their feet. Given the cold, it's a small mercy.

Tears spill down my mother's cheeks, and my heart clenches painfully. She stumbles forward, and before I can move, she's in my arms, her face pressing into my collarbone.

"I never wanted this for you," she gasps, clinging to me desperately, sobbing. Something inside me releases itself. The annoyance, the *betrayal*, I'd been holding for her snaps, and the warmth of her body makes me ache in places I didn't realise were tender. I close my eyes. This might be the last time they see me alive.

"So, let me get this straight," Seren says, looking out of the window. "Mother, you knew that you were sleeping with an aemortal king, and yet you chose not to tell anyone." She has calmed down slightly, as Seren always does after an initial blowout.

"It wasn't for me to tell. I knew nothing of this land in which we now find ourselves, and the king could not live in Eryndal." Mother has repeated her version of events enough times that I could almost recite every word, but still, it's a shock.

He wasn't a client. The King of Fjaldorn had been in Eryndal celebrating the end of the Thousand Cycle War. Exactly as the beautiful healers had said. One evening, Nerissa's aunt invited my mother to help her clean at the palace, their real plan to sneakily watch a palace ball. The King of Fjaldorn found them, bored by the party.

They snuck him into the servants' quarters, cracked open a bottle of araq, and got merry. Conversation flowed, helped no doubt by the strong mortal spirit, and they enjoyed his company. My mother stayed up with him until the sun started to rise, whereupon they made plans to see each other again. The next night, he took her dancing beneath the stars.

"And you fell in love. But you didn't want to move here, and he couldn't move to Eryndal," I surmise.

"When I found out I was with child, we didn't want either land to find out I was to birth a half-aemortal. Your father agreed with me. You would have been executed." Her voice shakes.

"Right. And were you planning on telling me, at some point?" I've waited *thirty cycles*.

"You seemed happy," Mother sighs. "Who was I to interrupt that? You had everything together. A job you loved, Nerissa. Your savings. I didn't want to introduce you to... this." She waves her hand at the dank cell in which we find ourselves. A drop of piss-coloured condensation falls from the ceiling. "Oswin and I fell in love, but he has another love: the sea. He could not commit; he didn't want to be tied to land. When King Vaelthorne came to visit you, Elira, and realised I had a new love, and a new baby, he could not face visiting again."

"That's when my father said goodbye," I whisper. Flashbacks have always haunted me: his tears on my forehead, words muttered into my hair.

Mother nods. This conversation has been so long coming that it will take a while to accept it all. There is something else for me to say.

"Seren, I have news." I inhale shakily. "It's... Isolde."

She spins to look at me so quickly that sparks almost fly. Her face turns grey. "What happened?"

As I explain, she staggers backwards and falls against the wall. When I reach the part where the army officer assured the Prince that she would live, she puts her face into her palms. We let her have a moment.

Her hands grip her face, her shoulders shaking. She's always been her own version of strong, but this is a different kind of hurt. The kind that isn't easily healed by strength alone. I want to reach out, to comfort her, but I know that nothing I say will make this better, not yet.

"I said her name, to Mother," Seren rasps. "They must have thought her a family friend. Perhaps they thought you would care if she nearly died, and might come forward."

"I would have done," I say fiercely. "If I knew what they wanted, of course I would have done. They did not need to… to harm Isolde." I swallow. "Seren, I'm so sorry. We're gonna get her healed. We'll fix this. I'll make sure of it."

But even as I say the words, I know it's a promise I might not be able to keep. Everything is out of our control now. The empire, the gods, Draevena—there's so much at stake. All three of us might be in Thekla this time tomorrow.

"If they were looking at punishing you," she eventually mumbles. "I'm glad they took Isolde and not Nerissa. She could have lost her child."

It's my turn to stare, starlight rendering her in golds and shadows.

"You didn't know?" Seren whistles. Her face is blotchy. "She's with child. A butcher's child."

Nerissa is pregnant? Why didn't she tell me?

"Perhaps she thought you had enough going on," Mother mutters.

"So, what of this Prince?" Seren demands, her vulnerability turning to anger, as it always does. "You cannot be with him. You cannot stay aemortal. Mother, who is your healer? Can they get rid of those... those horns?"

"I do not wish to get rid of my coryns," I hiss.

"You wish to stay a *monster*."

I inflate my lungs. My sister looks at me as if she might, at some point, try to end my aemortal life. I shudder.

"It is her choice to make. We will support her, whatever. I've made the choices for too long." Mother adds, as an afterthought, "Elira, that woman is no friend of this land. I have heard enough hushed conversations between guards to understand the king is bedbound. You cannot sign Fjaldorn to a woman who will rule with cruelty and bloodshed. You cannot."

"So you expect me to inherit this land that I know nothing of?" Everyone has an opinion, and yet no one realises that either way, Draevena will have me killed. I cannot live in Fjaldorn. That vision flits through my mind again – the one of us in the breakfast room – and my selfish heart *aches*. Oh, how it aches, love rippling through me like the worst kind of poison.

"She would make a cruel queen. The people deserve better."

"But..." I want to say: *If I live, I have a new life planned in Eryndal*. My father might have wanted to stay with Mother and me, but he had a duty to uphold; love is clearly not a good enough reason to shirk royal duties. He is literal evidence of my choice.

"The prince deserves better than a half-aemortal. Can you even summon fayte?" Seren asks, her pain evident in every line of her face. She is upset about Isolde. She has been trapped in a cell. She cannot deal with her emotions. I will not react. I glance towards the first stars in the dusk sky. The smells of night flowers and moonlight creep into my cell from the small window.

We still have a lot to discuss, a lot to decipher.

My festering anger is interrupted by a lazy, bored voice.

"Well, hello. You must be Elira's family."

CHAPTER FIFTY-SEVEN

Mother lets out a tiny shriek, and Seren gasps.

"Tryx!" I jump to my feet.

He is gently smoking, tendrils rising from his tiny feline body as he saunters from the closed door, looking far too pleased with himself. "The Divinity of War enabled my path in," he says languidly. "She said to tell you that your family are here."

"Is she serious?" My voice has never been flatter. "I have changed for her, and her news arrives at the most useless time."

"You changed for yourself," Tryx says firmly. "And don't pretend otherwise."

I sigh. I want to leap forward and scoop him into my arms. But he is not that kind of cat.

"Before you ask, I can't get you out," he says sourly. "And Kae sends his love, says he'll tear something or other to the fucking ground." The cat yawns.

I make a noise somewhere between a cough and a laugh. I open my mouth to speak, but Tryx interrupts: "It smells like the fayte of... well, that's interesting." He pauses, then falls to the floor, lolling onto his side with his furry belly on display. "The smell of a certain Seer fayte is drowning out all else. Have you been sent any visions?"

"I have." I add, not daring to look at my family, "I was shown the prince and I. In the palace breakfast room. We were wed. I was... powerful."

Seren lets out a noise of disgust, while Tryx breaks into a grin. "Oh, how clever the Dreamseers are," he sighs. "Always such leverage. Such dangerous, dangerous leverage."

"Dreamseer?" Mother says, her voice wavering. "Those who can show desires?"

"Indeed." Tryx looks at me. He knows what I'm thinking. That I had thought the vision delivered by a prophetess, a fate set in stars. But it was nothing more than my heart's *desire,* played as a vision. It might not come true. Kaelion might not want me the same way I want him. The whole thing was *made up.* I close my eyes, my chest sinking, aching.

"What's going on?" Seren demands. "Who are you? How'd you get in?"

Tryx looks delighted. "You must be Elira's sister." He glances between us. "I can see the obstinacy *radiating* from you both."

"What do you want?" Seren almost shouts, playing up to his teasing. "And why are we here? Are you a Divinity? Do you come to save us?"

If Tryx were a Divinity, I might think better than shouting at him, but I don't tell my darling sister this.

"Elira, what's she offered you, to sign the kingdom over?" Tryx asks, ignoring Seren. Fair enough.

The answer is easy: "Life." But I voice something else I've been thinking about, a guarantee I will ask for. "I will say that I'll only sign the kingdom over if she promises to release me, my family, and leave Prince Kaelion and Eryndal alone."

Tryx snorts, even as his ears pin back, flared by anger. "Never make bargains, Elira. Draevena will find a way to kill you and blame your own words." A chill slithers down my spine. Seren has the sense to sit, her face pale. "Let me tell you where that monster came from," Tryx sighs.

My palms turn clammy, because night has fallen outside, and I don't have long to make a decision.

"When the Archons were killed at the end of the Thousand Cycle War, royalty suddenly became a lot more powerful."

"I know," I say, bluntly. But my eyes urge him to continue. Mother tuts, even as she clutches her gown.

"This in turn alerted power-hungry aemortals from the Cecedit Mountain towns, towns that are furious because they were never considered part of any land. They were ignored when the bastions were divided, and they have no say in empire matters. They've grown and developed with the belief that their rights have been overlooked.

Hence, Draevena. She was a clanswoman in one

such mountain town, Kråknar, a place of violence, immense hunger. Draevena was admired and feared by all, the Kråknara needing a strong leader, someone to bolster them through the bitter winters. But, having the power of Kråknar wasn't enough. She wanted more. She realised that the new changes meant there would be turmoil. And so, she hatched her plan: Find an unmated king with no heir, and marry him.

She found your father, and for twenty long cycles worked as his aide, making her way up the ranks until she found herself in charge of the Sable Legion. But just managing the land's army wasn't enough. She finally found the chance to seduce Fjaldorn's dear king, delighting when he gave in. Her powers, both in will and actual fayte, are so strong that I daren't say she spelled him into agreeing to marry her.

However it happened, they are planning to wed. And everyone in the kingdom believed there to be no true heir, until she found out about you."

He smiles lazily. Seren stares at me.

"How did they find out about me?"

"The Map of the Monarchy," Mother whispers, her eyes closed. "No one but your father and I, and the King of Solthera, have set sight on it since you were born. Until now."

"It's true," Tryx confirms grimly.

"When it was stolen…" I can't finish the sentence.

"Indeed. The irony is, the map was only stolen for an art piece. It is unusual to have an item spelled by all seven major Divinities. It was brought to His

Royal Highness, the King of Fjaldorn, as an offering to cultivate Fogarty Oil from Fjaldorn's badlands. But no one thought to read the lines of heir before showing it to everyone at the palace."

I tunnel my lips and breathe out. Everyone knows. Everyone knows that I am an heir, and an entire palace knew before I did.

Mother reaches out and clutches my hand. "It's spelled to show current leaders and future heirs," she whispers. She closes her eyes. "I didn't think it would leave Solthera."

"Liora, you made a deal with the King of Solthera," Tryx hums. "King Aubade owns the map, technically."

I stare.

"You know my mother," I say, mind blank.

"I am not tied to Eryndal, Elira. I like to understand all Orynthys matters. As it happens, I was being fed a rather delicious sun-baked rotfish at Solthera Palace when your mother and father arrived."

"We wanted to protect you," Mother says miserably. "Before you were born. Before your name became known."

A chill runs down my spine. "So, you appealed to the King of Solthera, made sure the map would never see the light. What did you offer to keep this map secret?"

"Your father offered it, not I," my mother says quietly. "I did not have anything to give."

"What did my *father* offer?" My whole body is

tense, my teeth gritted. Around us, the cell presses inwards, purple darkness and muted stars filling the air.

"He gave up his Wield," she whispers, closing her eyes. "He was born under the moon of Lipe. The Divinity of Water gifted him a Water-Wield. He was capable of controlling seas, parting oceans, filling cups for thirsty denizens."

I feel sick. Like, I might actually hurl across all of them. First, Prince Kaelion begging Draevena not to take me. And now, my own father giving up his most precious Gift to keep my name hidden. So that I could live a normal life, so that he might respect my mother's wishes. Everyone, sacrificing everything.

Meanwhile, I sit here, throwing a strop because I might have to become heir to a kingdom I know nothing of. Everyone in Fjaldorn might become scared to live, might face torture and slavery, and it will be my fault.

"I will not sign it," I say, knowing that this might expedite my demise. "If I die, who is to inherit this land?"

"If you die," Tryx says cheerily, as my mother turns green, "then there will be a fight for the position. A battle thought up by the Divinities. The last contender alive will be King or Queen. Draevena very well might win."

I won't stand for this. I slam my palm into the wall, frustration eating me alive. There is no way out. Either I sign, and Draevena rules Fjaldorn with abject cruelty, or I don't sign, and she has me killed, potentially securing her rule anyway.

"And you might want to decide quickly," Tryx says lazily, before licking his belly. "Prince Kaelion has assembled a thousand warriors, and is on his way here now."

Is on his way here now.

"Kae." His name sticks in my throat, my mouth as dry as sun-baked rotfish, my tongue swollen.

"And yet, his army is much smaller than hers," Tryx muses. "And so he will most likely die the second he arrives, even if the Elemental Bastion has given him clemency to cross. Such a shame. I do like Kaelion, even if he *is* questionable on occasion. Drinks too much, has a *terrible* taste in women."

He will most likely die.

"What are you?" Seren suddenly demands of Tryx. I think she sees the look of fear that has finally taken root on my face.

"I'm not your concern, my dear. Your little battles don't much interest me, but I must say, I've taken a liking to our new recruit." Tryx looks at me with sly eyes. "She's a cutthroat empress," he purrs.

"I'm not cutthroat," I gasp, thinking about Kaelion, and the silicrites that choke Fjaldorn's air.

"Elira," Tryx buzzes. "You've slaughtered a silicrite, killed an entire patrol of the Sable Legion, murdered a scumbag in a tavern, and burned the body of an undead child. I think you ought to take my words as a compliment."

It's the look that both Mother and Seren give me that sends revolutions up my spine. They're looking at me as if they've never seen me before. Moonlight the colour of bone strokes my skin.

"You must earn your place at Eryndal Palace, Elira," Tryx says slyly. Then, with a lopsided grin, he lumbers to his feet and makes a run for the door, exploding into firesparks and smoke.

I close my eyes, tears spilling as pain lances up my body. Not from my wrist this time, but from the thought of Prince Kaelion, out there, fighting for me. His certain death on arrival.

"He will win," Seren says fiercely, her loyalty blazing. She has never seen me cry before. "We will win, Lir. We'll find other mortals, get our own army."

Drowsiness and hopelessness pull me down, towards certain fear and abject pain.
And yet, I whisper, "I will not sign. I won't let us fail."

As I speak, something glimmers against the far wall. As if they're listening.

CHAPTER FIFTY-EIGHT

Mother has taken to slapping the door and bellowing.

"She needs golemwort!" she shouts, as fever consumes me. "She'll die otherwise, and won't be able to sign your stupid deed!" Golemwort is a common herb used in Grim Municipal, but I expect they have better herbs here for an infected wrist bone.

I don't tell her so.

"Mother, quiet," Seren snaps. "You'll have us executed before sunrise." My sister is unnerved. She has always been braver, stronger than I, and yet this is too much to process in one night. I have coryns. I've become aemortal. I'm heir to a kingdom. The King of Fjaldorn sold his power to keep me safe. I take some comfort in Seren's discomfort, if only because it makes me feel slightly less alone.

Mother continues shouting until the door is finally unlocked and unceremoniously thrown open by a guard who has clearly had enough.

"She needs golemwort," Mother pants, stepping back.

The guard grunts. He grabs my mother, yanking her towards him before any of us realise what's happening. Seren and I are on him in an instant, even though fever roils around my skull, the pain seeming to come from everywhere. I can barely see as I stagger forward, reaching for Mother, but she's already gone, pulled away into the darkness of the corridor.

"*Run*," Seren hisses, grabbing my arm. Another guard appears, wider than the last. He yanks my sister away, her handprint still burning hot on my skin.

"She wants to talk to you," he grunts at me, dragging Seren with him as he leaves. She puts up a fight, as do I. I might not be able to summon fayte, but I'm stronger, fitter now that I'm aemortal. I claw at his neck with my good hand, while Seren knees him between the legs, screeching like a banshee. Clearly, he's made of absolute armour because he continues dragging my sister away until the doorway throws me backwards into my cell.

It must be spelled. No wonder Tryx was smoking as he broke through.

I hear her before I see her—the voice of Draevena, calling something cruel to my sister. I hear Seren's fists, beating against the guard as she's dragged away, as she shouts curses like spells into the darkness.

I am beaten black and blue while Draevena watches.

I lose track of time—the beatings, the pain—as

two guards, both twice my girth and a head taller than me, throw me between them. Their fists crack against my nose, and at least one rib breaks beneath their hands.

When I fall, they kick me. I have only one good arm to protect my head. They've removed Kae's jacket, tossed it aside, leaving only my thin nightgown to cover my broken bones and contusions.

They pause long enough for Draevena's sigh to cut through the chaos. "I know that Tryx came to visit you, Elira. I have been bothered by that individual before. I heard everything you all said. Did you really think that I wouldn't imbue these walls? I know your intention is to avoid signing the deed."

The glimmer on the wall. She had been listening. Pain shoots through my skull. My lips are wet with spit and bile. My throat feels caved in.

"Where have you taken my family?" I croak, but the words barely form as my coryn meets the thick end of a leather boot. Pain tears through me, blinding me, stealing my breath. Vomit rises in my throat, but I can't bring myself to spit it out as another boot stamps down on my ankle. I scream, my body writhing, contorting on the cold floor.

"I do not need your family," she replies coldly. "I'm sure we will find new and interesting ways to kill them. Unless..."

"I'll sign your stupid agreement," I cry, willing to say anything to make the pain stop, to protect my family, but my voice is hoarse, barely audible, as another stamp lands on my already swollen ankle. I can feel it cracking. Fayte, I will die here.

"Don't kill her," Draevena snaps as blow after blow rains down, each hurt melding into one. "You are only to teach her a lesson for her treason."

Food expels from my stomach, spit drooling across the floor. Agony ricochets through my nervous system. I have no fayte. No way to protect myself. I must breathe. I must survive. Prince Kaelion is on his way.

We are both so fucked.

I twist just in time to see the same guard lifting his heavy boot, ready to slam it down and break my ankle. I can't let him. I lift my hand, and in that moment, Draevena sends fayte towards me, as if preparing to bind me. Hot spittle coats my chin.

Prince Kaelion, I love you, I think, shrinking away, throwing my palm in front of my face. At least the prince is alive. At least my family are alive. I would gladly take these beatings ten times over if it keeps my family safe in another part of this prison.

Time slows as the golden streak Draevena has thrown into the air turns red. I am still screaming, my hand lifted, my eyes narrowed, unsure where Draevena's magic begins and my one good hand ends. There is a flash that blasts both guards off their feet. The cell shakes as their bodies crash into the walls.

My throat rattles as bones crunch, light engulfs.

And then it clears, and I find Draevena glaring at her hands. "What was that?" she snaps, looking at her palms. "What happened? That was supposed to maim-"

She stops mid-sentence, as we both realise what

has happened. The guards, their bodies grey and devoid of blood, are nothing but husks slumped against the walls. Their skin is grey, yellowed, clinging to bone and sinew. Great cavities around their eye sockets slip over gnarled cheekbones, their hair sprouting from shrunken skulls.

"How did I do that?" Draevena mutters, nonplussed. She has assumed it was her that harnessed the fayte, that rendered them this way. She looks between the dead guards, disgust creeping across her lips. "Pathetic, that they can be rendered this way by a mere eon of my fayte." She steps forward, and I shrink back, but she is only lifting the hair from the forehead of the guard nearest to me. His pallid, bloodless skin stares back at us.

"Chickenhearts, both of them." She drops his hair and steps away. Finally, she looks at me. There's something in her gaze as she examines my ruined face. I wonder what she sees—pain etched into my eyes? Hopelessness at being changed to aemortal and *still* not feeling powerful?

"It was interesting to learn that King Vaelthorne sold his Wielding abilities to protect the bastard daughter he did not want."

I am in too much pain to focus. I think only one rib is broken, but my shattered nose is causing issues. My face is wet, pain stabbing through my cheekbones, as if they've drilled holes into my skull. I'm glad they sent Mother and Seren out, that they didn't have to see this. My face would give them nightmares.

"Unless he didn't want you coming to be heir, no

matter the consequences," she ponders, as if we're not looking at two corpses. "Perhaps he was willing to give up his Wield to stop a mortal whore's baby from gaining power." Her voice turns harsh as she surmises, "His end cannot come soon enough."

Draevena's grotesque face twists into something resembling a smile, even as a thick vein presses out from her forehead. "So, it seems Prince Kaelion of Eryndal is arriving with one thousand soldiers."

My heart sinks to absolute rock bottom. I dig the fingernails of my working hand into my palm as I stare at her.

"And you *love* him," she continues, her expression switching to mock sympathy. "We can't help falling for men in power, can we? I trust that you will take this as a reason to sign away your rights. The thing is, Elira, you must see it would be unreasonable for you to take control of a land you've never been to."

"You will rule with cruelty," I hiss.

She shakes her head, studying me. "Every leader rules with cruelty, Elira," she says softly. "But there are those who are clever enough to make it look like mercy, and those of us who are honest. Can you truly say your land is ruled fairly? That Grim Municipal is governed well?"

The name of my city sends shockwaves through my heart. As does the sinking realisation that she's right. Have I not always complained that Grim Municipal is a place of poverty and broken systems?

"I hope we can put this aside once you've signed." She pauses. "Elira, what you're doing is what's right."

She sighs again, and then strides out, leaving me with two shrunken guards.

"You're wrong," I whisper. But it's the lack of conviction in my voice that scares me. A wave of hopelessness rolls over me as the door snicks shut. I have been rendered an aemortal, and yet I can't harness fayte. I am useless. And I have brought Mother and Seren into my universe; they were captured because of me.

If it will save their lives, then I will sign that agreement a thousand times over. If it will stop Kaelion from coming, and risking his own life, then I will rip my arm open and sign the agreement in blood right now. I have put everyone through too much already. I haven't been able to save the people I love most in this empire.

CHAPTER FIFTY-NINE

The first tendrils of sunlight break through my eyelids. And then the pain starts afresh.

I do not think I slept, but rather passed out—fever sending me to places I would not dare go otherwise. To Xandryll, digging with my bare fingernails. To Isolde's slashed body, bleeding on palace flowers. To the reborn child's body, burning in a flare of blue flame. The King's head, split in two. At some point, I must have retrieved Kaelion's jacket, and it clutches me, even as the two guards fill the air with the stench of rotting corpses. Outside, a new day dawns—birds singing far too happily, the breeze that sweeps into my cell far too sweet.

Today, I am expected to sign away my rights. I may never see Grim Municipal again. Never work in the sorting room, listening to Nerissa chatting to customers in the front shop. The sunlit alleyways I walked with my mother and sister, the bridge I sat on with Nerissa, smoking reeds, the sigils I saved.

The palace breakfast room, the guest quarters with the sumptuous bed, the place where Kaelion held me against his body.

All lost to me, potentially forever.

There is a scrape at the door. Someone unlocking it, quietly. Kae? My heart leaps into my chest. I attempt to stagger to my feet, but my body is too broken. My rib sends fresh waves of pain whenever I move. I can only slump against the wall and wait, my vision blurred.

Slowly—so slowly—I realise, with a sinking heart, that it cannot be Kae, someone creeps into my cell, her dark hair trembling.

Her blue eyes meet mine.

"Where are we going?" I hiss as she helps me along the corridors. I am too slow, and every time I stop, she winces, as if scared that my injuries will get us caught. It is the Dreamseer—the one who showed me what I wanted to see, rather than the future I was supposed to face. We pass cell after cell, doors that release the sounds of people moaning, crying, calling for help.

The girl whispers to me, "Ever since she gained power, she's imprisoned anyone who does not agree with her."

My arm rests around the girl's shoulders, and yet each step we take causes the edges of my vision to turn. Pain threatens to send me under. "Who are you?" I ask, as every inch of my ribcage screams in protest.

"He sent me to get you," she mutters, her gaze flicking to mine and then up towards the ceiling. "We'll never make it. We'll die here."

"We have to make it," I hiss, doubling my efforts to move quickly with one working foot. My nose splinters with pain, radiating through the rest of my face. "And who's he? Kaelion?"

"My brother. We don't have time," she hisses. "They're nearly here. You need to see what she's done."

"What who has done?"

"Draevena. You need to see what she's done to your father."

"Holy Divinities." Shock sends pain shooting through my nose cavity again, my eyelids slow and heavy across my dry eyeballs. The King's chambers are grand, vast windows showing the purple-blue sky. The cavernous ceiling rises into cornices, smooth stone edges beneath gilded candelabras. But I can't admire the room. Not when the sole bed, pushed into the centre of the stone floor, slams new facts into my face. The dark-haired girl lingers by the doorway, letting me progress alone.

I step toward the bed, the smells of blood and piss mingling in my nostrils.

My rescuer sent the nurses away. After one look at me, they bolted, but not before the dark-haired girl hissed something at them in another tongue. A warning to stay quiet.

"Your Majesty," I whisper, unsure what to call him. I can hardly say 'Father,' not this late in my life. But address him, I must, as his eyes swivel to me. Eyes the colour of emerald and moss. Oh, fayte. He never sent word, a card, a hint that I am a blood heir. He extracted himself from my life. And yet…

And yet, his face around those green eyes is more battered than mine. His body is enveloped in bandages. He looks as if he's been here for months. Pity beats hatred in every game of life, and I am moulded in various directions by molten hammers that prick my skin.

"It's you," he rasps, his eyes widening, lips trembling. His gaze locks onto mine, and fills with tears, a pain matched, I'm sure, in my own eyes.

"What happened to you?" I whisper.

"Bone-Wielder," he croaks.

"She had the Bone-Wielder do this." My voice is barely stronger than his. A tear drips down his cheek, and it's more than I can bear.

"What happened to *you*?" he rasps.

"Just normal guards." I attempt a smile. It doesn't go well.

He briefly closes his eyes, as if in pain. "I was a coward," he whispers. "But I knew you would become this. Strong. Powerful."

"I'm not sure I'm—"

"You must take Fjaldorn, Elira. You must. You cannot let Draevena rule." He screws up his eyes. "I would like to show you the letters," he murmurs, his eyes closed. "Every cycle, sent between your mother and I. I have your school reports, your schedules, the event poster you painted for the Eryndal festival."

My heart stutters in my chest. I think it might have broken.

"I sourced the wolfsbane, Elira," he whispers, his eyes creaking open to shine at me. "It was my... my fault. I am sorry if it was the wrong decision. I couldn't leave you there to die."

I can't do this. There is so much to say, and yet now is not the time. I look up at his coryns, the same pure white as mine. They are, at least, unmarred. A memory flits through me. Kaelion touching his coryns to apologise to his Divinity, when we were in the garden. Why have I not remembered that until now? I had always thought them simply a headpiece, a symbol, but perhaps they are something more.

Kae's coryns allowed him to communicate with his Divinity. Nothing ventured. I touch my left coryn, cringing as I do so, the pain in my rib flaring. But there is something. A feeling flits through me, something that connects me with the Divinity, that convinces me she is listening. "Please, fix me," I beg. My coryn seems to hum and heat under my hand, but nothing else happens. Sounds begin to rumble from outside. Battle cries. A horn. I hear a fleet of silicrites zoom past the window, wings ticking: *clack, clack, clack.*

"Can you ask your Divinity?" I ask my father, hoping it could help him, too. If mine even listened. "Touch your coryns and ask your Divinity to fix you. It might work, it's worth trying."

He looks at me strangely. "Only a select few can talk to Divinities, Elira."

"We need to get out," the dark-haired girl calls.

And then a Divinity answers me, whispering through my head: 'Just this once.' My skin bursts. Light blasts through me from within, and I close my eyes as pure pleasure bathes my skin. My rib tingles, my nose cracks itself back into place, my ankle warms. And then the Divinity lets me go, and I stumble. Open my eyes. Tiny light spots dance in the air.

"You still look awful," my father rasps, and I let out a bubble of laughter.

"My Divinity doesn't seem to care much for looks." I glance down at my body. Everything is in order, my ankle in far less pain. "She's said she'll only help me this once." It's not until I look up that I realise both my father and the Dreamseer are staring at me.

"What?"

"You... you have a Gift," my father rasps. "Your Divinity has spoken to you. You are a Wielder. I can tell, your fayte smells like mine did. Oh, Elira." A tear traces its way down his cheek as he closes his eyes.

"We must go," the girl squeaks. "There's no time."

I yank the jacket around my shoulders. "I'll be back," I promise, touching my father's hand once more. The irony of these words isn't lost on him, but all he says is, "You have my eyes."

I don't stay to hear more. The Divinity's power still pulses through me, but there's something else, too. Something I'd buried deep inside, something I hadn't fully acknowledged—until now. It's rising within me, battling to be felt, to be used. With both powers pushing and pulling, I make for the door. My rescuer ushers me forward, and we start down the sunlit corridor of the King's quarters.

We make it only three paces before my companion's backbone snaps.

CHAPTER SIXTY

"How dreadfully dull you turned out to be, Elira," Draevena sighs, as the girl screams sounds no one should ever make. My nemesis stands tall in a robe of crimson red.

"What have you done?" I shriek, my hand hovering over the girl's arm. I don't know where to touch, where to help. She screams, her head writhing, her arms twisting at unnatural angles, her face contorted in agony. Her cheeks are bone white, her forehead blotched red, her breathing a strangled gurgle.

"I suppose I always knew you'd be this way," Draevena sighs, and I become aware of another presence behind her—a dark figure lurking in the shadows of the hallway.

My entire body starts to hum, the air thick with a strange energy. I taste metal on my tongue, my heart tugging against my ribcage. What the hell is happening? What's that *thing* behind Draevena?

Two nurses arrive, their faces white as they gingerly lift the screaming girl onto a stretcher. It seems Draevena is invested in keeping her owned Gift intact, as she watches with a flicker of concern before they cart the girl off.

"Your father was such a bore," Draevena sighs to me. "Now break Elira's ankles." The words hit like a hammer, and I'm on my feet in an instant, stumbling backwards toward the King's quarters. The bare hallway offers no shelter, no place to hide but shadows and the eerie, predawn darkness.

He steps out from behind her.

And everything inside me fucking *sings*.

My tongue erupts with new sensations, my skull buzzing, my body feeling as if it's arching like a kitten into the warmth of its mother. I stretch my hand out, steadying myself against the wall, as my balance falters, my surroundings disorientated.

From his face, I can see he's experiencing the same overwhelming sensations. Pain ripples across his pale features, trembling through his tall, wiry body. He wears a simple white t-shirt and dark trousers that billow at his lower half. If it weren't for his coryns—deep yellow, flecked with gold—I'd almost mistake him for mortal. His hair, a dark brown, messy and wavy, falls just enough over his dazzlingly blue eyes, making his coryns even more prominent. He stares at me, confusion clouding his gaze.

An urge to move forward grips me, sharp and unrelenting. What I'll do once I reach him, I don't know. The sensation pulses in my chest like a strange hunger. I have the bizarre thought that I might bite him, just to see what he tastes like.

"I thought it was just a rumour," he says, quietly.

His voice hums through the air, my whole body *yearning*, shaking, threatening to tug apart at every skin seam, at every contusion battered into my body.

"How rude of me," Draevena trills, her tone full of delight, mistaking my confused reaction for fear. "Elira, I'd like to introduce you to the Bone-Wielder."

The Bone-Wielder.

The fucking *BONE-WIELDER*.

He doesn't break my ankles. Doesn't move. He does nothing but open and close his mouth, staring at me like I've sprouted a second head. What is this? What in the name of Orynthys is going on in this hallway?

Draevena raises a hand, the movement yanking us back into the present. She slaps him across the face, and I wince, even as the Bone-Wielder merely twitches his left eyebrow in response, his forearms flexing.

"That'll teach you to stare at pretty girls," she quips, her voice dripping with mockery. "Don't make me pay a visit to your parents. I believe their cell is nearby."

Two huge guards appear behind me, as if they've chosen to wisp right into this fucked-up mess of a situation. I don't have the strength to fight back as they drag me away.

My eyes stay locked on the Bone-Wielder, his skin still flushed. What just happened? What kind of response was that—from either of us? It must have been fear, primal and raw, manifesting in my body. I could smell the danger. That's all it was.

I am dragged through dank, empty hallways, one

after another, until they begin to change. The corridors start to resemble something grander—more like the halls I expected from Eryndal Palace. Hallways bathed in light, with window vistas, cream tapestries, intricate sculptures. Spaced-apart windows show mountains stretching under a brooding sky.

As we progress past a window, a vast stretch of sandy ground unfurls beneath the palace steps, far below. Tiny figures, the kingdom's denizens, move about their daily tasks—working in the gardens, accepting deliveries, continuing with their lives. It seems impossible that they accept the presence of the silicrites flying above, casting shadows across the pink-hued grounds. Equally impossible is the thought that they are blind to the horrors happening inside these palace walls—the girl whose back has just been broken, the king slowly being shattered.

By the Bone-Wielder, I realise with a jolt as I am dragged down yet another bend in the corridor. The tall man with disorderly hair tumbling over his forehead, the one who looked almost as confused as I felt... he's the one slowly killing my father.

And I did nothing.

To be honest, I'm not sure I could have done anything, even if I wanted to. The moment felt like a chemical reaction, like looking into a mirror and seeing myself reflected back. But now, as I'm yanked down a staircase, swallowed by the pit of darkness below, I don't have time to ponder it further.

Crowds of aemortals line the corridor as we approach the vast antechamber. Their pale coryns and green eyes are identical to my father's. Identical to mine. A slow, prickling sensation creeps down my spine under their scrutinising gazes. This is what Fjaldorn locals look like. I look like a Fjaldornite.

They watch me. Not with rage. Not with grief. Just curiosity. As if the fact that their king's daughter is being dragged here is nothing of consequence. We pass beneath the towering arched doorway, stepping into a circular courtroom. Aemortals fill the seats in a loose semicircle, shifting forward, eager for a better view. And above their heads—

My gasp shatters the silence.

My body lurches forward before the guards can stop me. They let go. I stumble. My knees nearly buckle as I catch myself at the edge of the steep steps leading to the dais.

Suspended in mid-air, held aloft by fayte, is a cage of molten gold.

Inside—curled together, pressed against the gilded bars—

Are my mother and Seren.

They have never looked more mortal. Never looked smaller. Seren's expression is feral, her face twisted with rage I have never seen on her before. She meets my eyes. Mouths the words, "Fucking kill her."

I cannot move. Cannot breathe. There's an intake of breath behind me. A voice, smooth, taunting. Draevena. "You didn't think we'd let them miss this, did you?" she asks, her tone soft, conversational. It's the final reminder. If I don't sign, she will kill them in front of me, until I'm forced to put quill to parchment.

And yet, if I do sign, she will kill them anyway. There's no escape. No way out. I stare at the gold bars until they blur.

"Hurry up, Elira," Draevena cackles, striding past me to descend the dais. Her robes swirl around her like a burst of flame. The crowd murmurs, their voices official, but there's a palpable discomfort in their demeanour, clearly unsettled by the sight of two mortals kept prisoner above them, like trophies.

I notice the crowd is split into two distinct groups, both in appearance and demeanour. Half of the court consists of mountain people, their skin ruddy, their dirty emerald coveralls far more practical than elegant. Their coryns are twisted spirals, brown and barely visible beneath their hair, as if Draevena has brought the entire Kråknar mountain clan to make up half of the court. The other half of the assembled aemortals is far less rugged, more ethereal in their presence. Their robes shimmer in pastel hues, their faces pale and serene, their coryns a pure bone white. Yet, despite their beauty, they seem less useful, less threatening.

My gaze flits across the room and settles on two Fjaldorn women who clutch each other's arms, their faces tinged with green beneath their white coryns. Why are they here? Why aren't they killing Draevena where she stands? Surely, with the fayte in this room, something could be done. Just because I can't summon it – my body numb and drugged – doesn't mean they can't. And then, I overhear someone mutter: "She brings shame on the Vaelthorne bloodline, shirking her responsibilities."

Another voice adds, "The shame is on society, for not teaching her the importance of royal duties. She has been gone for far too long."

I scan the crowd for someone who doesn't hate me, someone who might see the situation as it truly is. But all I see are accusing glances, harsh judgments. I haven't *chosen* to be gone for too long. I didn't know this fucking place *was* my responsibility.

Draevena croons from across the room, her voice cutting through the low murmurs, "Come, Elira." One of the guards shoves me forward, and I steady myself, my body shaky. I descend the stone steps. The whole room seems to hold its breath as I walk. The muttering dies instantly. I don't dare to look up at my family, but I focus only on holding my chin high, striding forward without hesitation.

I won't let them see me rattled.

From above, I can feel Seren's approving gaze. She's still watching me, still holding onto some hope.

I will be brave.

CHAPTER SIXTY-ONE

"We have all gathered to witness Elira Vaelthorne, the bastard, unwanted daughter of our dear King Vaelthorne, sign away her claim to inherit this kingdom —a kingdom she has never set foot in, never cared for until now."

"I didn't know I was heir," I mutter, hoping someone, somewhere might hear me. I feel nothing. No fayte. No connection to my Divinity. This is where I will die. I will be slain on this dais the moment I sign. I can't even send a message to the Prince. I love you, I whisper in my heart, hoping there might be a Mindseer in the audience. I've been seated behind a wooden table, the hand-carved chair digging into my lower back.

If I die here, perhaps he might stop his army. There would be no reason for him to invade—no need to bring soldiers from my lands here—if Draevena has every legal right to claim the throne. At least, if I die here, the Prince might live. And death at that cost— perhaps that's a price worth paying.

"Unfortunately, King Vaelthorne has been called away on vital business," Draevena trills, and I snap my head up. Do they truly believe that lie? Is that the story she's spinning?

"Liar," I hiss. But one of Draevena's guards, standing at attention, is ready for my defiance. He raises a hand and strikes me sharply across the back of my head. My skull reverberates from the force, and though I hear a crack, it happened so quickly I doubt the crowd noticed.

The crowd can't see the injuries they've inflicted on me, where I sit in shadows. The guards are careful now, not wanting to reveal the extent of the violence they've used to break me. Despite my clothes being soiled and torn, the horde likely think I'm just a hag from Grim Municipal—someone unworthy of consideration, fitting the stereotype of the lowly postmistress that Draevena is making me out to be.

"Without further delay," Draevena continues, her voice dripping with satisfaction, "we will now present this peasant woman from Eryndal with the official deeds." Her tone is triumphant. She's won, and she knows it. Kråknara clanspeople glare at me, hatred clear in their eyes, their faces hardened by cycles of battle. Even my father's people—the ones who should support me—look at me with confusion. They believe I've come willingly, prepared to relinquish a throne I never sought.

An elf wisps in, holding the papers, his arrival silent. I blink, my vision accepting this new addition. It's Feldrin. A postal worker who brings me the news reports, who chats to me during late nights in the sorting room. His small frame trembles as he looks around the courtroom, his ears curled into the bristled nest of hair that sits around the back of his skull.

"Feldrin," I say, my heart leaping into my throat. *Help me.* He stands just a foot away from the table, and when he looks at me, his face breaks into an expression of equal surprise.

"Lady Corvannis," Feldrin says, taking a step back. He glances at Draevena, then back at me. "Why are you here? Shouldn't you be at The Courier's Keep?"

Draevena barks out a laugh that rings through the courtroom, mocking and sharp. "You see, everyone?" she declares, her voice carrying to each curve of the room. "He recognises her because Elira works at the Eryndal postal office. She's nothing more than a postmistress, mortal until recently, her thirty cycles in Orynthys wasted by a lack of ambition. She's good for selling stamps, not ruling a kingdom."

A murmur rises from the crowd, a ripple of doubt, scorn, and curiosity. I stare at Feldrin, hoping, praying that he might help me. The elves cannot harness fayte like the aemortals, but they can wisp, travel across borders with ease. They don't need clemency to arrive in another kingdom, unlike aemortals, who risk instant death if wisping in without permission.

"Give her the deed, elf," Draevena snaps, her voice cutting through the tension, directing her gaze at the pale-robed members of the court.

Feldrin sets the deed scroll in front of me, his hands trembling as he does. "See you in the Bombard, Elira," he mutters, taking a step back, his eyes filled with uncertainty. He thinks I am here of my own choice. He has no idea that my mother and sister hang above us, their lives held hostage by Draevena's cruel hands.

"Get word to Kaelion," I whisper desperately, my voice barely more than a breath. "Tell him to retreat. I will be... fine."

He needs to leave. I won't let him die here. Not at the hands of Draevena.

Feldrin gives me the smallest shadow of a nod, his wide eyes filled with fear. Draevena opens her mouth to laugh again, but before she can, a loud crack echoes through the chamber as Feldrin wisps away, vanishing without a trace, choosing to wisp noisily, perhaps to make a point. I breathe out, the tension leaving me in one long, desperate exhale. At least I've told him. Told Kaelion to retreat. Told him I love him.

With trembling hands, I unroll the deed. It's short —perhaps two feet of parchment—and as I scan the text, the words 'sacrifice' and 'rights' leap out at me, searing into my mind.

"Now sign," Draevena orders, her tone sharp. She waves her hand, drawing transformist symbols in the air above the table. A quill, with a deep crimson-red feather, materialises beside the scroll. It's fayte-transported, but plainer than the quill the Lesser Divinity of Language gifted us. For our nuptials. The Lesser Divinity had been mistaken, had sent something the exact colours of Kaelion's eyes for no reason.

"I cannot sign this," I whisper, my voice barely more than a breath as I stare at the quill. A few people in the crowd have started shuffling, as if they are uncomfortable. I look up and see a few fear-stricken faces. They cannot do anything. Draevena controls them.

"Bone-Wielder," she calls, and the sensation surges through me again. Metal on my tongue. Fizzing across my skin. My entire body feels tethered to an invisible circuit, pulsing with power that I can't control.

He steps forward, and I look up. His gaze, fixed on me, is inscrutable.

"Break her left wrist," Draevena orders, her voice colder than ice. "And this time, don't let her pretty hair distract you."

His eyes meet mine, and I see only confusion and pain etched into his face. His body is lanky, forlorn, a striking contrast to the quiet power he holds—enough power to break the bones of every person in this room. He doesn't shift. Doesn't make any move to indicate he might be about to snap my wrist. His dazzling blue eyes lock onto mine.

"Well, I do hate to break up a party."

The lazy, disdainful tone makes my heart leap. I turn away from the Bone-Wielder, and there, standing on the opposite side of the dais, is Tryx. His tiny form jumps down the steps, a flash of silver in a dark sea of enemies.

CHAPTER SIXTY-TWO

"Elira, do not sign the deed," the cat instructs, his voice as relaxed as ever, though a steely edge laces his words. The crowd stirs, murmurs rippling through them. Some of them seem to recognise Tryx, his name whispered in confused tones, and one woman even waves at him.

Energy pulses through the air, electric, and I feel it surge within me. The aemortals around me glance back and forth between Tryx and me, as if we're allies, as if I've already earned some unseen favour.

"We thought you might try something, cat," Draevena sneers. Her voice drips with venom, sending a cold chill down my spine. "Your powers are meant to do good, aren't they?" Draevena stretches her mouth into a mocking smile. "And we're prepared to bind you for eternity, if necessary."

"I'm already bound for eternity," Tryx retorts, his eyes flashing as he steps onto the dais. "You think I choose this form?"

Draevena's patience seems to snap. She strides toward me, grabbing my barely healed wrist. Sharp pain shoots through my body, and I gasp, struggling not to cry out. I reach up to strike her with my free hand, but the guard behind me lands a heavy blow to the back of my skull, and everything goes momentarily black.

My palms are starting to fizz again, as if my fayte is returning. How long will the drugs from the prison food last?

"You don't understand what the girl is," Tryx hums, jumping lithely onto the table. I swallow, yanking my shoulders back.

"What is she?" Draevena hisses, patience thinning. She casts an impatient glance at the Bone-Wielder, her fury obvious, but he's still staring at me, his eyes an azure warning on the horizon.

"And that's your first mistake," Tryx purrs, clearly enjoying the tension. "The power to dominate this empire lies far beyond making her sign away some ridiculous title. When did titles ever equate to real power?"

Draevena's face darkens, almost puce with anger as she glances at the crowd, her control slipping. The audience is growing restless, murmurs rippling through them.

"Ladies and gentlemen," Tryx announces, his voice smooth, looking around the room, his gaze briefly fixing onto the Bone-Wielder's before moving on.

I know what he is going to say. It comes to me as the Bone-Wielder stares. Didn't Tryx once hint at a third, when he said: *"No flesh, no bone, no blood. They're the perfect weapons against the most powerful foes this empire faces."*

My mind freezes.

"Allow me to properly introduce you to Elira Corvannis," the cat calls.

The room falls into silence, hanging on his words. Then, Tryx delivers the bombshell: "Royal heir of Fjaldorn, and the Blood-Wielder of Orynthys."

CHAPTER SIXTY-THREE

Outside, chaos reigns.

I barely make it to the steps, curses and fayte swirling behind me, chasing us as we run—me, the Bone-Wielder, and Tryx.

"You don't have to stick with us," I pant, adrenaline coursing through me, my feet slapping against the stone steps. "Go save your parents." Draevena had mentioned they were in a cell, kept as leverage: he needs to retrieve them.

"I can't Wield in the cells," the Bone-Wielder responds, his voice low, pain lancing his words.

The route out of the courtroom dungeon was treacherous. But when my title was revealed, something inside me flared to life—vast and golden—blinding everyone in the room for a fleeting moment.

It connected me to the Bone-Wielder. In that single, absurd moment, it felt as though the two of us were the only ones left in the room, staring at each other through a haze of golden fire, light neither of us could control. My soul burned. So did his.

Born under the same Divinity, the Divinity of Body.

Is it possible? Can I truly be a Wielder? I can't even control fayte yet, can barely wield at all. But the moment Tryx spoke the words—*The Blood-Wielder of Orynthys*—my body responded, as if it had been waiting for a Divinity to claim me, to officially launch me into the world.

I was born between moons, between Divinities. I am not under the Divinity of Power, nor Sun, but in the space where other Divinities can claim me, those few breaths between moons when anything can happen. I rewrote post, using blood. I can fucking Wield, and I was using the limited amount of power that I could handle in my mortal state to *rewrite people's party invites.*

That's what I was doing. Controlling my own blood, in a small, fayte-imbued way, perhaps using the amount of fayte doled to a half-aemortal who hadn't allowed herself to fully grow. The *voice* inside my head, that of the Divinity who gifted me, was telling me to write with my blood *because it was the only opportunity she had to show me what I was.*

And yet, I kept it a secret. I feared what I could do, even as I delighted in being able to do something secret, something that set the day apart from the mundanity of the rest of my existence. I can rewrite with blood, yes, but I have a feeling *I can do so much more.* There's no time for contemplation. I need to get my fayte back.

"You should run," I urge the Bone-Wielder, feeling oddly protective of him. It was his fayte that got us out of the dungeon; he's the one who broke everyone's ankles.

After the blinding light filled the room, after Tryx's grin—one that said he had been anticipating this moment for a long time—the light cleared. Then the Bone-Wielder Wielded. His fayte cracked through the air like a whip, and literal bones shattered. Draevena, the guards, an unfortunate elf at the top of the stairs—all of them fell, helpless.

Screams echoed through the corridors, the sound thick with panic. Tryx laughed, his voice carrying a kind of dark amusement, while the Bone-Wielder roared, "RUN!" I followed him down corridor after corridor, Tryx streaking ahead like a silver blur, moving too fast for even my strained senses to track. A Bone-Wielder and a Blood-Wielder reigning terror down on the royal palace.

Now, we find ourselves at the edge of the battlefield, the roar of chaos overtaking everything. A wave of noise crashes over us—screams, metal clashing, and the deadly hum of fayte charging the air.

"I'm not leaving," the Bone-Wielder growls, his body shuddering with exertion. Fayte is finite, even for a Wielder. Breaking that many bones at once has drained him. And why? Why did he save my life? Why has he suddenly changed sides, leaving Draevena's army to join Tryx and me? He seems as unnerved as I am by this strange connection between us, borne from our Gifts. Perhaps that has changed everything for him.

"Then please, go back and save my mother and sister," I insist, my voice catching in my throat. I scan the battlefield—the aemortals, their fayte sparking through the air, the silicrites circling overhead, golems lumbering forward, weapons glinting in the sun. Blood stains the sand. "You can Wield in the courtroom. Please," I beg, my eyes locking onto his, sending something fizzing in my ribcage.

He hesitates, his blue gaze flashing with something I can't decipher, but then he nods once and turns back, breaking into a run as he retraces our steps.

Good. He'll die out here, without his fayte. Perhaps he'll die anyway, trying to rescue my mother and sister, but I suspect the courtroom aemortals are more distracted by their injuries than by inflicting pain.

"Your Highness," Tryx calls urgently. To me. "We're losing."

I can't process everything all at once. We stand slightly above the chaos, set back. The noise is deafening—the roar of combat, the clash of steel, the cries of the wounded. My mind latches onto the flashes of colour and light, the frenzied movements of the battle. Tryx leaps forward, disappearing into the chaos, a whirlwind of silver. He pulls enemies in with reckless abandon, spinning them into his storm before spitting out their ruined bodies.

And every inch of my body screams as I realise what this means.

My army has arrived. Kaelion has arrived. My stomach bottoms out, guilt turning physical. I've brought them here. They might all die, because of me.

They've brought real weapons—metal gleaming in the sunlight, fayte fizzing through the air. Longswords are hurled into the sky, crossbows fire in quick succession, axes and maces swing through thick aemortal skulls, leaving trails of destruction in their wake. Both sides are already clashing with weapon and fist, the chaos of battle unleashed. For the silicrites, it means nothing more than piercing their enemies before devouring them whole, or being destroyed in an explosion of black blood. The golems swing their fists from my right, their massive stone limbs scraping the ground with each lumbering step as they descend from the direction of the nearby mountains. Steel rattles against steel, the sound deafening as the battlefield comes alive with violence.

"Elira!" a voice screeches behind me. Draevena slams into me, her sharp nails digging into my skin, the gemstones in her hair clicking. She staggers, her ankle broken but already healing, no doubt aided by an army of healers brought to the courtroom. "Sign it!" she spits, the venom in her voice matching the fire in her eyes. She thrusts the deed into my chest, even as it's scrunched into oblivion.

But I can't look at her. Her nails pierce my flesh, but I force myself to scan the battlefield below, panic surging. *Where is he?*

My eyes fix on one army.

Coryns the colour of silver gleam through the chaos. I spot the familiar sight of Eryndal helmets and robes weaving through the fray, cutting down Draevena's forces. The Sable Legion. Silver-clad soldiers wreak havoc across the battlefield, hurling fayte and weapons, drawing blood with each blow. They tear through Kråkna's mountain people, the massive stone golems slaughtering the opposition with their crushing fists, the battle becoming a blur of blood and bodies, bloodthirsty screams and staggering golems. The Sable Legion is holding strong, a sea of shining silver against Draevena's forces. Aemortals from both sides are falling in the thick of it, blood flying through the air in arcs as I see Terragast raging through the bodies, his arms vast and destructive, tearing heads from bodies and gouging bones from flesh.

And then, through the madness, I see him.

The gold-amber eyes that I would recognise anywhere.

His eyes desperately rove across the chaos of the battlefield, darting over the screaming army of silicrites, even as he fights off three of the winged beasts at once. His gaze locks onto Draevena's fiery face, her mouth parted as though she's about to scream once more.

And then, finally, his eyes find me.

A surge of palpable, delicious relief floods his expression. His eyes, previously dark with storm, soften back to amber in an instant. But then, they linger on my bruises.

Rage. Unrestrained and powerful. It fills his gaze, burning bright and hot. With a roar, two massive beams of light explode from his hands—fayte-created swords, dripping with light and fury, cutting through the chaos around him.

"Kae!" I scream, pointlessly, as one of the blazing

swords hurtles toward Draevena. He throws it like a javelin, the air crackling with magic, a strike so powerful that the distance is meaningless.

"Fool," she shrieks, as it hurtles through the air. "If you kill me, there will be others! You have no idea what's in the mountains, I am but a *servant*." She wisps, disappearing in a crack that slaps the air around me. The sword bursts into nothingness just before it reaches me, dissipating into the air as if it had never existed.

"Protect yourself!" I scream again, but Kaelion cannot hear me over the deafening clash of battle cries, the shriek of metal on metal, the hissing sound of fayte cutting through aemortal bodies.

Kaelion doesn't wait. He uses the remaining sword, now burning with fury, to carve a path to me. He slashes through the enemy, decapitating mountain people with each swing, his jaw clenched, his face set in a mask of pure, thunderous rage. His presence on the battlefield is undeniable—he towers above everyone, his massive frame and powerful movements cutting through the fray like a force of nature. And then, finally, he's here in front of me. His hand snaps the burning javelin out of existence, the flame disappearing into the air. He doesn't wait. He pulls me close, his body enveloping me as he cradles the back of my skull in his hand, his breath sighing into my hair. His chest is warm against my head, and the pain in my bruises eases, just a little, beneath his touch. I can feel his strength, his heat, his anger.

"We only have a thousand soldiers," I shout, voice urgent as he lets me go. "They have so many more here. We can't survive this."

"We only have a thousand from Eryndal," he answers, his voice loud enough to cut over the hum of war, as his gaze sweeps back to the battlefield. The scene is endless, chaos stretching far and wide. His eyes fall upon a swathe of soldiers beyond the Eryndal forces —figures with coryns in deep maroons, pure gold, and royal navy.

"The Elemental Bastion decided to join us," he murmurs, yanking me into him so that he can press a kiss to my forehead, his relief that I'm alive spilling over everything. "We have troops from Solthera, Velispar, and Claran here. No one wants Draevena attending the quarterly Orynquorum, sitting at the table of Kings and Queens making major decisions. Too many aemortals remember the Thousand Cycle War—and they won't let history repeat itself."

Relief washes over me in a wave, mingling with a hope I hadn't allowed myself to feel. We have soldiers. They aren't just here to save my life – hello, sweet narcissism – but are here to swerve off a powerful potential enemy. We might even be able to win this. We might be able to yank Draevena from her position at the top, stop her destroying an entire land with her greed.

"I can't believe you came," I whisper, pulling back to look at him. His face is still devastatingly handsome, but there's weariness now, lines under his eyes that weren't there before. The stubble on his jaw seems darker, and his eyes—so vivid—hold a frightening intensity. Has this pushed him to his vice, drinking at The Howling Cask to drown his sorrows?

I think there is a weakness there, something I might need to look out for. But not right now. Right now, we have a battle to win.

"Of course I came," he replies gruffly, his gaze taking in every inch of me, like he's absorbing me back into himself. "You've consumed my soul, Elira. I'm half elation, half agony, and I want nothing but you for the rest of eternity. You're my Little Flame, burning me from the inside out, consuming me. So yes, I fucking came."

"But the quill," I gasp, my heart barely daring to hope that he feels the same as I do. "You said it wouldn't be needed."

"I was hurt," he growls, the admittance causing his eyes to flash. "I'm sorry. I wanted to protect myself. I didn't think you wanted… us."

Before I can respond, a sword flies from behind him, a flash of hurtling silver. Instinctively, I raise my hand, and my heart slams into my ribs, pain ricocheting through me, my forehead becoming ice and fire. I feel it. I have been freed. A burst of fayte leaves my palm. Golden light envelops the weapon, incinerating it midair in a shower of sparks and a loud hiss.

"Fuck," I gasp. "I have my fayte back."

Kaelion's expression shifts, confusion flickering across his face as he throws a protective fayte shield around us. "What happened?"

I take a shaky breath. "The potion must have worn off. Draevena gave me a potion to numb my fayte, in the gaol."

"Only your mind can break such poison, it cannot be broken any other way. Numbing potions are tricky like that, although I know the Isles are trying to solve-"

"You're telling me I could've broken it anytime?" I ask flatly, my eyes tracing the strong planes of his cheekbones, the immense depths of his amber eyes.

"Perhaps this is the first time you've had hope," he suggests, his voice thick. A vicious spell slams into the outside of his shield, making it spark with reds and crimsons.

"I'm sorry I said I regret everything," I mutter.

"I'm sorry I didn't break that fucking wall down and pull you from the forest," he growls, his jaw tight with frustration.

"But I survived," I point out, though it sounds weak even to my ears. "I didn't need you." He doesn't flinch, even though Seren's voice echoes through my mind, sighing with a mixture of resignation and hopelessness.

"You're more than capable of doing anything on your own, Elira." His eyes lock onto mine, unwavering, before he turns his focus back to the battle. With a sharp flick of his wrist, he sends a spear of fire from his shield toward a passing silicrite, decapitating the beast instantly. When he looks at me again, his amber eyes burn, his gaze searing through me like molten metal. "But I want to be there. I want us to be a team. In things together. There will be times when I'll need you to save my ass."

"Like right now?" I suggest, my pulse quickening as a golem swings its massive stone boulder arm toward the shield. Without thinking, I raise my own hand, summoning a golden wall of fayte that blasts the golem backward, ripping its arm from its body. The ground shakes beneath us, and before I can steady myself, Kaelion grabs me, pulling me against him with a fierceness that takes my breath away. His lips crash against mine, and for a heartbeat, everything around us fades. The sounds of the battle, the chaos of the fight, swirl up to meet the stormy sky.

We pull apart, and instinctively, as if our bodies are connected, I twist and glance upwards. My eyes lock onto a glimpse of movement from a window, near where the courtroom must have been.

The Bone-Wielder jerks back before I can register the emotion on his face.

"I am the Blood-Wielder of Orynthys," I tell Kaelion, my voice shaking slightly as I introduce myself with something I'm still struggling to understand.

He licks his bottom lip, then nods. "I'm truly honoured to learn of your Gift."

His complete lack of surprise forces my eyebrows up. "You knew, didn't you?"

"I saw that you were a Wielder. I didn't know what you could Wield, but I'm sorry I didn't tell you. I rather thought becoming aemortal might be enough of an adjustment to be getting on with. I'm sorry for not teaching you how to control your fayte, how to use it. I hoped... I hoped you wouldn't find yourself locked up in another bastion, honestly."

"It's a truly terrifying Gift," I admit, but his words light a spark inside me. I have this terrible Gift, one of the most fearsome Gifts in the entire empire. And yet, Kaelion doesn't recoil. He doesn't look horrified or disgusted by what I am. He doesn't see me as a monster, even though I've killed without understanding why or how. Looking at him now, bloodthirsty and furious, I realise just how deeply I love him. The intensity of it swallows me whole. From the moment he arrived, searching for me, looking at me, I knew he loved me too.

I have nothing left but love and hope. Draevena has stripped everything else from me, but the small flicker of hope that we might actually win this battle — that we might defeat the Cecedit Mountain army — burns brightly within me. Draevena had tricked everyone. She promised her people a better future in the empire, and she promised my father a love that was never real. My best chance lies in harnessing my abilities.

Now that I can feel my fayte returning, I might actually be able to help. The shrill cry of a silicrite cuts through my thoughts, and before I can react, something hard and heavy crashes into my body. I'm swept off my feet, thrown to the floor with bone-jarring force. Stunned, I feel the hot breath of the creature as it leers into my face, the leathery skin scraping across mine, the sickening crack of my rib breaking again.

I scream, even as I writhe and twist away, those rock-hard legs coming for me again and again, ready to puncture my skin, flay me. My nose is still injured, hot mucus running into my mouth, flying into the air as I fling myself further away, moving by whatever means necessary. And then another one is on me. As it lands upon my wrist, twisting my arm, sending my bones screaming in agony, I throw my hand up, blasting fayte and singing its wing.

Kaelion is there, ripping apart the silicrite on top of me, sending hot, black blood spurting across my face, as I create a ball of terrible fayte and hurl it at the other silicrite, tearing the skin from its body as all of the colour drains from its face. It falls, grey, to the ground, and then another five are upon us, legs ripping at my skin, tearing at my hair. As one gouges a deep line in my leg, my flesh tearing apart and sending sparks of pain through me, I lift both of my hands.

And I say words—words I have not planned, words I hadn't realised were there, waiting to be spoken.

"I am the Blood-Wielder of Orynthys," I mutter urgently, as Kaelion rips a silicrite's head from its body. It feels like something inside me is telling me what to say. An ancient voice, a voice of a Divinity. "I am developed from the blood-given Gift of the Divinity of Body. I give my soul to the empire of Orynthys, I accept the power that has been granted to me. I am Elira Corvannis, the Blood-Wielder of Orynthys."

And then I am rising. The silicrites closest to me stop to watch.

For aemortals cannot fly. And yet, fly I must be doing, as I rise above the crowds, tugged by invisible hands. I can spot Draevena in her red robes, fury rising in her eyes as she wrenches a head from a member of the Sable Legion's body, her hands sparking in bright blue flashes. I don't feel like I'm flying so much as being yanked up by the universe. No pressure touches me; rather, I feel as if I'm entirely weightless. I can taste an unusual tang of fayte on my tongue, something colder and more silky than the usual iron taste.

But I don't have time to wonder. And, fuck– literally everyone on the battlefield is staring at me. Better say something profound, I guess.

"I can't fly," I clarify, imposter syndrome eating at me. "I am a Blood-Wielder, but that is all. I suppose the Divinity of Sun or something must be helping me."

Well done, Elira. Terribly profound. I think people at the back are writing it down to remember later.

I clear my throat. Open my mouth to speak again, to offer everyone on the battlefield one last chance before I drain half of them of blood.

But everything starts to move rapidly. Below, a group of silicrites launch themselves onto Kaelion, while a member of our Sable Legion is sliced through, his body falling in two, his helmet cut apart, brain on show. I open my mouth, horrified—

And then Draevena sends a ball of fayte in my direction. Spiralling blue fayte hurtles towards me so quickly that I barely register it before it's too late.

As it hits me, I fall.

CHAPTER SIXTY-FOUR

"Elira," a soft voice speaks.

I open my eyes, though I am already standing. Around us, Thekla looks more vibrant than before. Fleshy green reeds poke through the purple mist, and the ground flows like a summer stream. There is still a faint smell of old leather and sweaty boots. In front of me, a maiden with translucent skin, blue veins, and a crown of wriggling orange hair smiles at me. Across her forehead, a silver shape shimmers, the rune looking like two arrows combined.

"You must use your Gift now," she trills, her voice the light gold of harp music. I blink. Have I died? I must have, to be in Thekla again. This time, I don't hear the echoing moans or the screams of dark souls passing the borders. I only hear giggling on a light breeze, the sound of violins playing from far away. The air is warm upon my lips.

"I am the Divinity of Body," the woman explains kindly. She touches the symbol on her forehead. "I have been waiting for you to use the Gift I gave you. To use it properly."

I can't seem to move my mouth. I look down— I am only a shadow of myself, my body barely visible.

"I have granted three Gifts, and the other two are busy using theirs." She laughs, and as I look up, I don't miss the shadow that passes across her eyes. "You must use yours now. You know what it is."

I nod, my head sluggish and slow. My body feels disassociated from my mind—probably because I'm actually lying broken on a battlefield, my brain hallucinating.

"Now, back to Fjaldorn you go," she sings, moving forward to stroke my face with her hand. Her touch is cold and soft, and fills me with something giddy. "Don't make me regret choosing you, Elira. You are a Wielder, and you will Wield."

Why is my Divinity trapped in death?

I don't have time to think on it. I'm leaving Thekla, yanked from behind by forces I can't control.

My head is so dizzy that I almost black out again, but I resist. I sit up and see Prince Kaelion right in front of me, the smell of cedarwood so overwhelming that I want to crawl forward and grab him right here. But making love in the middle of the battlefield is not useful right now.

"You're alive," he sighs. Pain instantly fades from his face, replaced by relief. Above him, the purple sky rages. He holds a shield of fayte, but it is struggling to resist the army pressing against it, every Kråknar aemortal now realising where I lie. "Thank fayte."

I struggle to stand, my mind reeling. The pain has lessened significantly. In fact, it's essentially gone. I look down. My newly twisted wrist has healed. My leg is no longer gashed open, the bone visible. My skin is shimmering with the soft glow of fayte.

Draevena has clearly given up her most precious weapon, thinking it fit to kill me. She has realised that I will not sign, and her only hope is to kill me and then battle for the position of Queen. But I will not let her.

"Elira," Kaelion cries, as I lift myself into the air again. It is easy. It shouldn't be this easy; I've never seen an aemortal fly of their own accord. I've met Wielders now—the Major General, and the Bone-Wielder—and Seers: Elrind, Kaelion, the dark-haired girl.

The Bone-Wielder was a ridiculously impressive Wielder.

But none of them, to my knowledge, can fly.

Prince Kaelion reveals his huge fayte-created javelins again, as silicrites take to the air to reach me. He throws one straight through a winged creature, capturing a golem at the same time, skewering them together until they burn in a flare of red.

"Since when can you fly?" he calls, his voice gruff as he pants, fighting off more creatures.

"Does it make you fancy me even more?" I ask, as my whole body flares with levity and power.

"As if that was possible," he grunts back, decapitating an enemy soldier. My heart soars and swells in my chest. I need to get Prince Kaelion and our entire army out of this land and back to the safety of Eryndal.

"Where's Draevena?" I scan the battlefield. Silicrites dart towards me, but I've created my own fayte shield, using powers I didn't know I had. It feels as though I once learned how to use fayte, how to create shields, and it's coming back to me as a distant memory. Like being reborn.

"Over here, Elira, darling," Draevena calls, her voice cutting through the sounds of the battle, as if I'm tuned to hear only her. I turn, and shock runs through me. I tumble down from the air, my stomach bottoming out as I land back on my feet, just in time for a golem to unintentionally stand on my foot, snapping a bone.

I shriek, stumbling forward.

Draevena has Tryx bound, the towering silver whirlwind wrapped in golden lashings of fayte. He rages next to her, swelling, struggling to break free of the binds. Anger surges inside me.

I summon that other kind of fayte. The one that feels born of anger, the one that represents a terrible Gift, one that is unkinder than fayte, more lethal than fayte. I send the shadow of this power—not golden, like its benevolent counterpart—towards Draevena, intending to drain her of blood.

But a guard jumps in front of her.

My fayte shadow envelops him, glowing redder and more furious in movement than the usual golden hue, before draining him of blood. I watch as it leeches from his face; he falls to his knees, his skin clinging to his bones, his flesh turning grey. His eyeballs shrink to raisins in their sockets. Just like the Sable Legion guards at the border. The forest creatures. The guards in my cell.

I drained them all of blood.

Draevena whips a fayte blade out of thin air, using it to slice through the centre of the towering monolith that is Tryx. The sound is unlike anything I've ever heard. Tryx shrieks as he is cleaved in half, the scream halting every single person on the battlefield, ringing out around the clouds, slapping against the sleek stone of the palace. Silicrites return to land from the sky, clouds seeming to freeze in their relay, everyone watches as towering silver whirlwinds become the maimed, bleeding body of a cat on the floor.

The cat turns to fire in an instant. I know it is Prince Kaelion who has done this, not wanting us to witness Tryx in that state. Dead. Killed by the kind of fayte we've underestimated—fayte that can kill a being of his ilk.

Tryx is dead. My mind feels numb. Everything slows down as time loses its meaning. The battlefield reeks of sulphur and ash.

"Do you not realise what I am?" Draevena hisses, her voice slow and terrible, laced with sparks. She grows, her whole face contorting into something truly horrific as her body literally grows. "I have bought Wields. I have slashed throats, collected long-forgotten prisoners, sought—"

She screams as every single bone in her body is broken.

I feel him before I see him. The Bone-Wielder,

standing at the top of the palace steps. I glance over, and relief floods through me as I see his amber coryns, his summer-sea eyes. My mother and Seren are behind him, arms wrapped around each other, and the sight of them sends a lump flying to my throat.

The Bone-Wielder looks frighteningly, terribly powerful, his dark hair whipping around his face as if in his own personal storm.

I turn back to the twisted Draevena, who has collapsed to the ground, her hair writhing of its own accord, rattlesnakes of treachery. Her arms and legs are broken, but her backbone seems intact, her skull complete, and I wonder at the powerful man's small mercy.

A hand grabs me, but I don't have time to be pulled into Prince Kaelion's chest. I stumble forward, a new pain in my side, knowing that if the Bone-Wielder can affect Draevena, so can I. It's my time. Sable Legion members have hurried to surround me, slaughtering silicrites and Kråknara as they form a protective barrier, their silver helmets a hazed horizon in my peripheral.

I raise my hands, close my eyes, and will the Divinity of Body through every part of me. She is not Lesser, only rarer, and this distinction seems unbelievably important as I will her into me, as I awaken the drop of Divinity that surges through my veins. My coryns burn as she seizes hold of me, merging with me, her power flooding from my skull to my shoulders, along my arms, into my hands. It tastes like summer mountain honey, like ancient stone, like metallic lemons, pricking every part of my senses until my whole body seems to hum.

I open my eyes, clenching my teeth. Crimson shadows envelop Draevena's body, lines like strings of metaphysical spit clawing between her body and my hands. My arms shake, as I slowly kill the woman that has threatened my kingdom. Pain roars through my palms, as if I am taking down more than just an aemortal woman, a woman of fayte and nightmares. I am destroying a force so mighty that pain splinters up my arms, dancing bright lights appearing in front of my eyes. Would I die to kill Draevena? I don't have time to consider it.

I swell, and push harder, power shuddering through me.

I will kill her if it's the last thing I do.

It's draining me. My power subsides, fayte shrivelling my mind, my skull, as if someone has placed a vice around my head.

I can't see. Can't feel my tongue, can't feel anything, apart from this raging consumption of energy that plucks every part of my body. I want to scream, but my throat is plucked raw, my mind spent. She is too powerful. She is more than just aemortal. I am becoming nothing, a vortex, a black hole—

An additional surge of power ploughs into me. I daren't turn, daren't see where it comes from, but it gives me that final push I need, blasting through my arms, shuddering through me. I siphon her of blood until every last drop is free of her flesh. A sudden understanding, a sudden vision, as if sent from Draevena herself, grips hold of my mind: winter howling outside a cabin window, peeling mould from indistinguishable foods, hard training and bleeding knuckles, abusive families with soulless, loveless eyes. A *need* for something more, a need for life to be *more*.

All of this passes through my mind in a flash.

And then her memories are gone. She lets out a blood-curdling shriek, as her last breath sears itself into all of our memories.

And then she is no more. Draevena is bloodless, shrunken, destroyed. The slash of red lipstick on her bloodless lips is the only mark above her shrunken robes, her flesh already the colour of decay. A resounding silence rings through the air, all armies stopped, battle ceased. I drop my hands, my vision returning, my head spinning as my arms feel like sodden wool yanking my shoulders from their sockets. Kae grabs my shaking body and pulls me into him, so I can hear the paced *badum-badum-badum* of his heart, his mouth murmuring words into my hair that are lost in the fog of my skull.

She is dead.

"Go through Thekla and beyond," commands a voice. I look towards the newly emerged figure stepping forward beside our Queen. The Queen of Eryndal, her face etched with grief, her demeanour shrunken and ruined. She clutches the arm of the palace Mancer to her right—the necromancer who brought the undead child back from death, who must have wisped them straight into the end chapter of this battle.

"You cannot be here," I whisper, though she does not hear. Every single member of the Sable Legion, along with the neighbouring realms of Solthera,

Velispar, and Claran, falls to their knee, genuflecting. They bow their heads to Her Majesty, as a new breeze brings a mournful song that rolls around my ankles.

The surrounding Fjaldorn army, their faces confused but their honour responding, also kneel, the thump of their armour splitting apart the ground. Only the mountain people, ruddy and fuming with a pain born in the darkest depths of the Cecedit Mountains, remain standing, looking at me with dark eyes. Because I killed Draevena. Because I am the reason that my torturer, my father's torturer, is finally dead. Because now, I am the heir to the throne of Fjaldorn. They will not have the power they were no doubt promised, and they have lost their leader.

"I appeared only to see her fall," the Queen murmurs, looking down at Draevena's desiccated corpse. The necromancer closes his eyes briefly, and I think we all sense the soul of Draevena leaving her body and entering Thekla. There's a strange, hollow noise, like the rasp of a wind instrument, as everyone on the battlefield stands still, surrounded by the bodies of their comrades.

Except for those staring at me, their eyes bleeding into my soul.

I blink. And blink again. The weight of everything that's just happened presses down on me. My lungs seem to turn to husks in my chest as I struggle to breathe, my mind spiralling. My forehead throbs, my coryns burning on top of my skull. What the hell happens now? Where do we go from here? I trip backwards and fall against something hard and warm. Prince Kaelion wraps his arms around me, cradling me.

He kisses the back of my head, then spins me around to face him.

"I love you," he says, looking deep into my eyes. He cups my face in his hands, his gaze staying fixed on mine. "I love you, Elira."

"Your Highness, she's shaking terribly," someone pants from beside us. "She might be going into shock. Should I send for a healer?"

"No," I say immediately, my eyes still locked on Kae's. Prince Kaelion. Prince Kaelion who loves me. "We aren't finished. I need to help, need to talk to the remaining Kråknara. We have a battle to end."

"Spoken like a true warrior." Kae releases my face. But not before I see the glimmer of hurt that sweeps through his eyes. I didn't say I loved him too. I can't. Not right now. I'm in shock, I can't think, my mind is filled with screaming and suffering. The blood spilled across the battleground sends my thoughts spiralling into a frenzy.

"Your Majesty, you need to go." I turn to see Major General Drystan, head of our Sable Legion, shouting towards the Queen. He stands, holding a decapitated silicrite head in one hand, swinging it idly. His helmet is the most severe of all—a towering silver crown that screams "big dick energy." The Earth-Wielder. The Earth-Wielder who is *still fucking alive* after locking me in a cellar to die. I'll deal with that one later.

It looks like he had been using the silicrite head as a weapon, but at least he's trying to protect Kaelion's mother. Yes, she needs to leave. We can't have both the King and Queen dying over my inheritance.

The Queen and the Mancer wisp away, her face briefly a picture of cold agony before they vanish. Prince Kaelion must know that his father is dead. That he died in front of me. I turn to him, to the beautiful man who stands waiting, but another figure captures my attention.

"Elira," a groggy voice calls. A handsome man with black hair staggers over, clutching his side where he's injured, the blood that dampens his tunic humming and calling to me.

"Elrind," I say, my mouth feeling like it's filled with chalk. Adrenaline still hums through me. I've drained much of my fayte taking Draevena's blood, making me appreciate just how difficult it must have been for the Bone-Wielder to break so many bones at once. I glance towards the castle steps, but he is gone.

Elrind lands in front of me, his feet planted, his legs bent to support his injured side. He looks completely different without the vast feathered band that usually mars his forehead. His eyebrows are thick, his eyes dark and unreadable, his forehead lined from where the band usually sits. "I'm allowed to take it off for battle," he says, smiling weakly. "It helps me to fight, knowing what the enemy is thinking."

"I bet." I feel my face peel into a genuine smile at the sight of one of my new favourite people still standing. He's injured, but standing. Kaelion steps up beside me, slipping his warm hand into the small of my back. Kråknara eye us, wondering what to do next. They still have weapons in hand, but it has become clear that they are leaderless. Some of them are humming, something low and deep.

Without Draevena, they are waiting to see what happens.

I must act. It is my time. I feel broken, rattled all the way through, but still, these people need hope. Hope, that most precious entity, the only thing that isn't traded in the shady backstreets of Grim Municipal. Hope is a beautiful thing; it keeps us fuelled when all else is lost, and for these fighters, their future is crumbling into nothingness on the ground.

I yank my shoulders back, and take a sharp breath in. I look at the surrounding troops, the spilled blood, the endless sky. This isn't so different from cheering people up in the sorting office. From commanding attention in The Dwarven Bombard. From striking up conversations as I meander through the alleyways of Grim Municipal, everyone glad to see their local postmistress.

And so I roar: "THE WAR IS OVER!" My spit hits the air, my lungs expand and flutter. My hair is picked up by the breeze and billows wildly down my back. Every single person listens, every head turned my way. "Draevena is dead. I am Elira Corvannis, the rightful heir to this throne, and I will take my position in this kingdom. The King of Fjaldorn will be saved. His Majesty will continue to rule Fjaldorn with the entire support of Orynthys. We will not let evil win. We will not let greed prevail. I call an end to this bloodshed, right now."

The cheering starts slowly. A rumble that grows and turns in the air, lifting faces, hands, hope. Silver helmets are thrown into the air, whirlwinds of coloured robes billow as wearers cheer, sunlight breaking through the sky, brilliant and blinding. In the midst of the celebration, ruddy-faced Kråknara continue with their humming. Their sorrowful dirge is interrupted by our own Major General, broken apart as he starts barking orders, ignorant to their soul-deep pain.

And so they turn and run towards freedom, towards the mountains that tower in the distance beyond the quaint-looking villages of my father's kingdom. No doubt these are the ones that cannot wisp, just like the majority of the Sable Legion, it seems. And still, the mountain people run. Some make it. Some don't. Blotches of blood streak the sand, like ink on wet paper.

Our Sable Legion falls into line, Major General Drystan throwing the silicrite head towards the palace before barking out orders. Everyone who surrenders and drops their weapons will be spared; anyone who resists will be killed. Troops are to reassemble, soldiers are to collect the dead and pile them up according to kingdom. These piles are to be burned and destroyed so that their souls may pass through Thekla; the Major General muttered something about necromancers bringing them back otherwise. The injured are carted away to the palace sickbay. I think I'm still shaking, but Kae's hand is steady on my lower back, and people are still looking to me for confidence.

Those with white coryns, the people of Fjaldorn, almost look proud, even though I was a stranger to them until today.

"Thank you, Elira," Elrind says, with a slight bow. "For everything. I'm sorry I thought you… the King…"

I look him in the eye and speak the words in my mind for Elrind to hear: "You're endlessly welcome." His face softens with relief as two voices cry my name. Their shapes are vague behind the new flames crowding over bodies on the battlefield, smoke burning strange colours in the air as souls pass through Thekla, unable to return.

And then they are here—my mother and Seren.

My mother and Seren.

My throat aches, my heart lurching, a choked sob leaving my lips. My body feels heavy from the weight of everything that's happened, and still, I yank them into me as they arrive in the centre of the battlefield next to us. The touch of their arms is the most beautiful thing I've ever felt as we hold onto each other, Seren's back shaking, Mother sobbing into my hair. These are not tears of sorrow, but relief, gratitude for our lives, gratitude for every single person on this battlefield.

Kaelion steps away and quietly instructs the Major General, making plans for our return journey.

The journey back to Eryndal. A place of inequality, social issues, of slums and hunger, dirty water and leaking sewers. But also, of hope. Of dancehalls and gold coins, eryndaisies and flower shops, taverns and elven wine, hot potato stalls and little girls who sit under the gallipot chute, saving soap shards for later. All things worth fighting over, all things worth protecting.

As Draevena's body festers on the ground, something nags at me. It's some of the things she said. She wasn't all wrong, and that's what's hardest to digest. Maybe she was wrong about all leaders being cruel, but she was right about the inequality in Grim Municipal. The lack of true leaders has led to army rule, and killed any semblance of democracy.

"Things in Eryndal need to change," I rasp to Kaelion, my throat raw. Ultimately, he is the ruler of our land. His parents are stuck inside, his brother is due to attend college. The responsibility starts and ends with him.

"I agree," he says, straight away, surprising me. "I've been thinking the same. Screw upsetting people by being around the mortal city more, I want to be around, to make change, to promote equality, make the city a better place to be."

I nod. It's ironic that it was Draevena of all people that lit that spark inside me. But I have the contacts, the skills, everything I need from working as a postmistress. I just need to expand out everything I've learned. To help the people with what they need, to make Eryndal fair. I need to do that while learning how to harness fayte, how not to suck the blood out of everyone I meet, and how to wisp so I can build a relationship with my father.

Easy.

"I'm so fucking glad they didn't kill you," Seren mutters, pulling back, the dirt on her face streaked with tears. Her eyes glitter as they hold onto mine, pride ripping straight from her soul and wrapping me in wonderful intensity. "But I'm not going to call you Your Highness or anything, alright?"

"That's just fine." I manage a weak grin, a flash of

amber flickering in the corner of my vision. "That's just fine."

CHAPTER SIXTY-FIVE

"A postal worker shall show due respect to the Divinities of Orynthys, ensuring that no bias or favouritism is shown toward any deity or their followers, and that both gods and royalty are honoured equally in their service."

Orynthys Postal Manual, Volume 2, Section 1.1

"I'm not sure royalty isn't just glorified titles, you know," I muse. "Surely my new Gift trumps a pithy prince title."

He's settled into the armchair opposite me, his lips curled into a messy smile, as if they can't decide between all-out happiness that I'm here and alive, and the grief that still overwhelms his body.

"I was so worried about you, you know," he growls. "You used to be the village postmistress, and to think that you were trapped there without your letter-openers…"

"I was a postmistress," I agree. "And now look at me." I cross my legs under my flowing silver gown. The exact silver of Prince Kaelion's coryns. "Killing enemies and shit. Wearing robes of silver."

"I like the silver robes."

"They make me stand out in Grim Municipal," I say ruefully.

"You always stood out."

His eyes glance down at my robes, thin and clinging to my legs. The whole palace has been in mourning for a week. The dead have been commemorated, their ashes sent into the Thealean Sea on mighty flamed pyres. The King's funeral is next week, and the Queen and her sons have spent days in their throne room mourning, discussing his life, accepting visitors from both the aemortal towns and Grim Municipal.

A surprising number of mortals have visited, including Nerissa, who came to pay her respects with a handful of dark flowers and a solemn curtsy for the royals. We spent a long time walking the grounds together, talking about my new position as heir, about how the King of Fjaldorn has made a speedy recovery now that the healers are allowed to fix him.

I have not heard from nor seen the Bone-Wielder since he broke Draevena's bones. His talent, much like mine, is coveted. He has likely taken off to nurture his skills in private, to recover from being Draevena's plaything for so long. Wielders are valuable assets to any land or army; Major General Drystan has already warned me that I'll need guards whenever I leave the palace. He told me that when he was apologising, for sending me to my death.

"You stabbed a soldier, Elira," he grunted at me, as I tried my best to control my hands. Don't drain him of blood. "That's always instant execution. You're lucky we let you live as long as we did." Oh, holy Divinities. I disagreed with the cruelty in which he doled out my punishment, but I almost understood. If someone had stabbed a member of my family, I would want them dead.

Nerissa and I discussed her pregnancy. "I didn't know... honestly, I didn't know how you'd react," she breathed. "With you being, you know..."

"Alone?" I challenged.

"Yes," she agreed. "You were so fiercely independent. I thought you might call me mad."

I smiled a sad smile, and listened to her stories about the boy at the butcher's shop whom she is seeing in a non-serious manner. She's asked me to attend her healer appointments. In fact, when she paid her respects to the Queen, I saw Dismal shoot her an interested look.

But I will not allow anything to happen there. Even if she wasn't pregnant and in need of rest and relaxation, she's mortal, and she's been hurt by aemortals before.

Which brings me to Prince Kaelion's bracelet. It was his best friend's bracelet, Riven Drystan's bracelet. Riven was the aemortal soldier who fell for Nerissa, who spent the night with her. When his father, Major General Drystan, found out about their passionate night, the Major General ordered the killing of Nerissa's parents. They were smothered by Terragast.

In retaliation, mortals murdered Riven the next time he was in Grim Municipal, trying to visit Nerissa at her adoptive parents' house. While silver might not work on aemortals, there are still ways of ripping us apart and burning the pieces. While I will never forgive the Major General for what he did to Nerissa's parents, I can see the grief on his face, the retaliation that will never heal his broken chest. An eye for an eye; he has tasted his own medicine, and he will never, ever recover.

Nerissa was understandably shaken when this came up during her visit to the palace. She and Kaelion discussed Riven at length, and I could tell that Kaelion felt he got something from the conversation, even if it opened up the old wells of grief that he's spent so long trying to heal, drinking away his pain. A best friend is a valuable type of love, and his was so cruelly obliterated. Now, his best friend and his father have been taken.

"Have I told you how beautiful you look in aemortal coryns? If not, then perhaps I should be sent to Thekla." Kaelion looks at me, no hint of embarrassment nor fear on his handsome face. I lace my fingers together, ignoring the flutter his gaze sends up my thighs. "You are too delicious for words."

A blush rises on my cheeks, and my stomach swoops and dives. "Thank you, Prince Kaelion."

"Please, call me Kae." He cocks his head to one side, eyes sparkling.

"I think we're beyond the point where you need

to flirt with me," I say, and we both breathe in, taking a moment, because we are not sure where this leads.

We have been through so much. So much bloodshed and heartache. His father has been killed, his mother has been rendered weak from breaking her deal with the Divinities, even if only for a single breath. We are in a place of tenderness and shock. But still, he looks at me like he wants to fuck me hard and forget everything else until tomorrow.

"I only thought about you." His words take me by surprise. He stretches out his long legs in front of him and looks at me, eyes blazing. "I have a whole fucking kingdom to run, and all I've been able to think about since I saw you that first time is you. When I was trying to obliterate the wall, I could barely think. I was so panicked about you striding into Xandryll without training, with only Tryx for company. When I saw the two healers, all I thought about was how I was going to steal azizova petal, so I could send a version of myself into Fjaldorn."

"All for a city postmistress." I smile, his words burning me.

He lets out a soft laugh. "I know I once… I once said that I have to run from my own mind, or else I feel like I destroy everything. But I'm starting to feel better, since you've been around. I feel like I don't need to run anymore."

I can't help myself from standing up and walking over to his armchair. I look down at him, as he mutters, "I have been a product of vices and escape." Fayte knows his eyes are beautiful. I've memorised every shade of amber, every fleck of blue, every emotion that seems to see right into my heart. "But not anymore. It's always been you. That very first time I saw you, when you were being arrested by the Legion, I thought: oh, there she is. That is a strong, beautiful woman. That is the woman that I will go to Thekla and beyond to save."

I lean forward and run my fingers through his hair. He closes his eyes and sighs, as my heart cracks again, and mends again. "I've never needed saving," I mutter, but I'm joking. I remember what Tryx had said: *It's not so bad to need people.* "I think it might be my turn to save you."

He opens his eyes again, and the look he gives me almost kills me in its intensity. I lift my robe slightly, so that I can move forward and better straddle his legs. His eyes darken, his gaze dropping to my mouth.

"You've had to control yourself for far too long." I lean down and touch his chin, pulling it up so that he's got a direct view of my face. And the space where my robe drapes down, revealing my naked breasts underneath. His eyes widen.

"But first," I say, dropping down to rest on his knees, my buttocks finding purchase, "I want to say sorry. I'm sorry that I got upset at you going to another woman's house, when you were at perfect liberty to do what you wanted. Sorry for thinking that I could control you. I guess I'm so used to being in control of everything in my life, that I've been freaked out by all of these feelings."

"These feelings," he murmurs, looking at my lips. "And what feelings might those be?"

"Oh, you know. Just the odd one or two, here and there."

He lifts his hand and traces my cheek with his fingers. "I wanted to fucking kill her for taking you." He trails his fingers up until they meet my coryns, and I purr as he strokes one and then the other. The sensation is so similar to being stroked on my most sensitive areas of flesh that I almost close my eyes. "Instead, I had to hear from Disryn and Elrind that you'd killed the king and taken off. I was already on the edge of my control, and then they told me that you'd gone. I almost killed both of them, right there."

"But you knew I wouldn't have killed the...?"

"Instantly," he says, his eyes growing sad as he brings his hand down to my collarbone.

"And you came as soon as you could."

"I did." The corner of his mouth quirks into a sexy smile, as he pushes his grief down. We'll deal with that later. I'm here for a long time, it seems.

"And you want me to stick around?" I ask, as he teases the fabric from my collarbone. I move further up his legs, working my thigh muscles around him as I shimmy. He gets tired of waiting and grabs me by the buttocks, pulling me fully on top of him. His hardness presses against his hunting clothes and weighs against my robes.

"I do," he growls, leaning in to kiss me on the nose. He pulls back. "I think you suit life with a prince."

"Are you suggesting I wed Dismal?" My cheeks burn as I call his bluff. I've used the word 'wed', and yet I want to see how he reacts.

"Absolutely fucking not," he snaps. Jealousy flares through his eyes before he grasps my hips and pins them with his hands. My joy at his answer is replaced by a wave of pure want.

"Oh, really?" I pant, as he devours my neck. "I didn't think you liked me."

"I more than fucking like you." He groans as I slip my hand into his leathers. I watch his amber eyes go wild with lust. They mirror my own. "Ever since you appeared in the street with your little tunic on, I've wanted you. Ever since I saw that bastard mortal trying to kiss you at the tavern, it drove me wild with jealousy. I wanted to rip him to pieces."

"Rhett is okay, really," I mumble, as he presses his hips into my hand, and I feel him fully as I squeeze and move.

"Rhett is fucking *not* okay," he growls. "But that's a matter for a different time. Right now, we're talking about me and you."

"And how hard I make you," I tease, gasping with pure lust at how solid he gets for me.

"I'm trying to be serious, Elira." He tugs at my robes as if they're an inconvenience. "What do you want? Do you want to stay here? Do you want to... be with me?" His huge arms momentarily pause in curling around my robes, our closeness pressing against one another. He looks into my eyes, his face a picture of nerves and vulnerability. I lean forward and brush my lips across his.

"I do want to be with you, yes," I murmur, firelight warming my back. "And you? How do you feel?"

"I feel," he replies, tilting my head back and cupping my jaw, his fingers hot and heavy, safe and strong, "that I am in love with you, Elira Corvannis. I have been from the moment I saw you, and I should have kept hold of you rather than leaving you to get kidnapped and nearly killed. I hate that that happened, but I will spend the rest of my life making it up to you, if you'll let me."

I crush my mouth against his, pressing my chest to his body, feeling our heartbeats merge as he lifts my robes. We pull back so that he can sweep them over my head, and he throws them onto the floor. I wear only a scrap of lace; knickers that the palace staff deemed suitable for an heir. They have started dressing me much more mightily since the empire news declared my position to every land.

His eyes devour my body, as my heart swells and my groin aches. He loves me. A prince loves me. I murmur, "The rest of your life," as he dips his head and pushes my breast into his mouth. "That's a long time."

He pulls back, his mouth wet, my nipple glistening.

"It is." An unsaid challenge flashes across his eyes, as he gently pushes me up to standing.

"If you will have me, I want you forever. Fucking forever and a day if that exists," he growls, standing up as well, and swooping down to deliver a deep kiss. He leans down and grabs me, twirling so that I end up seated in the armchair, my legs spread.

He groans and falls to his knees.

"If this is a proposal, I must say, it's very unusual," I comment, my voice breathless, my eyebrow raised. He leans forward and kisses each of my eyebrows in turn, forcing the raised one back down, as he cups my face again.

"I've never felt like this. Ever. You've fucking broken me, Elira. I've never felt so out of control in my life. I've never even *had* a life before you. And if you don't want to be my noblewoman, if you don't want to spend forever with me, then I understand. I completely understand. I have uprooted you from everything that you knew, I have forced your break-up with The Courier's Keep, I have changed your entire existence."

"Please don't mention The Courier's Keep at a time like this," I say, leaning forward and undoing his belt. It takes me less than an in-breath to undo his hunting trousers.

"I've never wanted anything as much as I want you," he says, his voice serious now, even as his length is revealed. His substantial length. I look up at him, at the ripples of muscles in his chest, his dazzling, tanned face. His lips, my favourite pink, and his eyes, those deep, amber pools that could suck me in forever.

"I love you, too. So fucking much." I hold the arms of the chair briefly, dealing with how to say everything that I feel without falling apart. "Every time I have to leave you, I feel as if someone has stolen a limb. Every time we're apart, I feel as if I've undergone some sort of chemical mutilation, losing part of my chest, or my heart, or whatever. And if you're asking me to be your mate, your partner, to be at your side when you need it, to help lead this kingdom, and to one day perhaps unite two kingdoms across the empire, then I am in."

I look up at him, truth juddering out of me. "I am really fucking all in. I love you, Kae."

He closes his eyes, falling to his knees in front of me, his face glorious as he accepts my love. And then he mutters, "Two kingdoms across an empire. *Two powers, one fate.*"

"Two powers, one fate," I reply, stunned. It was written on the walls before any of this happened. We are both heirs to thrones in Orynthys. The Map of the Monarchy is under lock and spell in my father's kingdom. Only a select few people know that Kaelion isn't on it, and my father has agreed to keep it that way.

We have one shared fate, and we both have Wields; his in Giftseeing and mine in blood. The Bone-Wielder saved my life. I cannot begin to think about that right now.

He's back on me in a heartbeat, his mouth crushing mine, his body pressing against my thighs, working them open. I stop thinking about the prophecy, the thrones, as I return the strokes of his tongue, the muscles of his arms pressing against me, his trousers somehow getting flung across the room in the frenzy. Air hits my body as he whisks my knickers off, and they meet a similar fate, flung against a far wall. He groans, his hands working their way up my back, into my hair, which he pulls over my shoulders, before moving his mouth to my neck.

"You're so fucking hot," he mutters.

"I think this might be the horniest proposal in the history of-" I start, but he grabs me by the sides and lifts, propelling me into the air to join him. I wrap my legs around him as he holds me, his muscled arms barely expending any energy to keep my whole body lifted against his.

"I'm not sure that you said yes," he growls, falling to his knees and laying me gently on the soft rug floor.

"Do you really need me to say 'yes'?" I tease, as he swoops down to devour my nipples.

"If you feel like it," he purrs against my skin. "It would be nice to know where we are." Except, I know exactly where he is, as he moves downwards and puts his head between my legs, forcing my knees to buckle over his shoulders. Oh, fayte. Oh, Divinities. Oh, everything that is destructive and beautiful in this empire.

I gasp in breath after sharp breath as his tongue works, waves of sheer pleasure throwing my head back against the rug. He shows no mercy, knows exactly what he's doing, and oh my fucking Divinities, it's good.

"Oh, fayte," I judder out, my hands above my head, my body open for him. I taste a tang of iron in the air, and know that I have successfully called my magic – for once in my life – at a time when I don't actually need it. I tell my hands to cut it out, and feel the glow subside, even as the prince pushes me close to the edge.

"Please don't kill me with your magic before you've even learned how fun it can be." He takes me again, firmly, his tongue circling that most sensitive part, and I cry out, wondering whether everyone in the palace can hear us. I don't care. Lust, waves of heat that devour my mind, crashes through me, and I'm lost in his mouth, as he pulls my hips up towards his face, all the better for tasting me. Sunlight seems to blast across my vision, my whole body shakes, and when his fingers join his tongue, working me apart, revealing everything for his pleasure, I climax.

Light shudders through my closed eyelids. My whole body trembles. He holds me close to him as wave after wave breaks over me, as I fall over the edge of eternity, lost in a world of feelings and oblivion.

He lets go of my limp body and moves upwards, his face finding mine, my eyes blinking open just enough to see the contours of his strong jaw, the pleasure that shines from his eyes.

"Beautiful," he murmurs, kissing my forehead. "Though I do hope the people of Orynthys were prepared for what they just heard, and don't think I'm murdering you." I shake out a laugh, as I reach down. My whole body is pounding with pleasure, still in the reverberation of eternity. He gasps as I grasp him, his teeth grazing my flesh as he presses his hips into me. Fayte, this man is huge. Every muscle in his body is built like a warrior, tanned and smooth and perfect, every line made for staring at.

Our mouths meet in a kiss, and I move my hand, guiding him towards me. Towards where he needs to be.

"Elira," he murmurs, and I can feel him pressing into me, as I move my hand away.

"Are you asking for permission?" I tease, breathless, my legs wrapping around him, waiting.

He bites my lower lip. "As ever, my lady."

I groan. He pulls back and locks eyes with me as he pushes forward and into me, eyes locked with mine, pleasure and anticipation reflecting back at me. He consumes every inch of me, until he can push no further, and I moan, feeling his girth, feeling the stretch as I get used to Prince Fucking Kaelion between my legs.

"There are no words for how this feels," he growls, followed by a sigh of pleasure. I gasp as he leans down and kisses me deeply, resting his elbow by the side of my head. "Fuck, I want you so badly. In every single way, in every single room of this palace." He starts to rock, finding a pace that is both sensual and deep, pinning my hands above my head again. He likes to have the power, I've noticed, but he isn't arrogant with it. Perhaps he knows that I need to relinquish control sometimes, to feel that anything could happen.

With every movement of his hips, I gasp, bracing against the rug beneath me, lifting my hips so that he can drive deeper. He grows in speed, as I tighten my legs around him, stars filling my vision, his elbow stopping him from crushing me to death. "You are everything I've ever needed," he says, his eyes locking onto mine.

It's all I wanted to hear. He senses my body tighten, he senses that I am reaching another edge, and he plunges deeper, satisfying himself, until we come together, bodies shaking, taking me further than I've ever gone before. I cannot be with this man. I will almost die every single day.

"I promise to do everything in my power to keep you alive," he whispers. Oops, I must have spoken out loud. He kisses me, as my whole body trembles and simmers. "I will never get enough of your body," he murmurs, swooping down to tug my lower lip with his teeth. I shudder and gasp, as he stops his hips moving, as he stays still.

Gently, he moves away and falls to the side of me.

"I fucking love every single thing about you," he says, trailing a finger down from my mouth to my collarbone. He trails it down my body until he's back between my legs, where he lazily circles, my whole body reacting and sparking, my arms and legs almost numb from pleasure. "I didn't want to. I tried not to. I felt sure it meant that I would die in a mere forty cycles, choosing to go when my mate eventually passed."

"I thought you said you loved seeing me that first time, in my tunic," I mutter, as his fingers still slowly play.

"Oh, I did. Trust me, it looked fucking hot on you. But I wasn't sure that my kingdom would ever forgive me, dying so soon when I have so much to do."

"You have such a filthy mouth, Prince Kaelion," I murmur. I've noticed that he really dials up saying 'fuck' when he's naked.

"It's not a great time to insult me," he mutters, slipping a finger inside me. I gasp, as he playfully watches my face. "You don't look like you have much energy left, and I'm feeling rather powerful."

"Bastard," I mutter, as any other thought falls away. He laughs, and I push him backwards so that he forced to lie down, facing up to the turret ceiling. Before he can protest, I straddle him, my body commanding all of his attention as I work my way down on top of him. He groans as I lean forward, my breasts above his face, and show him just how much energy I have left.

"By the way," I whisper, my lips moving right next to his ear, "it was a yes. I will be your mate."

He bucks and arches his hips, grabbing me with the kind of strength only an aemortal can exhibit. As he crushes his mouth against mine and takes me deeper, harder, I barely have a chance to ask him if he's happy about my acceptance.

CHAPTER SIXTY-SIX

Everything feels touched by sunlight as we waltz down the steps in the early evening light. Nerissa and her new apprentice are coming to join us. Nerissa's boyfriend refuses to join aemortals for a drink, and is strongly against *our kind*. I don't let it eat at me; there is time to work on him. To show him that we are just the same as mortals, really.

Mother and Seren are already in The Dwarven Bombard, saving us a table. They have warned the band playing that there is a future King who would very much like to play the lute tonight. Kaelion has no idea. But I never bought into the whole *Kings don't play lutes* thing. Let the man play.

Elrind is joining us later with his new partner in tow. Apparently, he is a soldier, and they met on the way back from the battle in Fjaldorn.

The funeral was a beautiful, meaningful event. The music, the readings, it was all... moving. Beyond moving. I have no words.

Prince Kaelion has his fingers slipped through mine, as we walk down Quiet Street, heading for Old King Alley. We haven't spoken since the pyre was set alight, the entire aemortal audience then travelling back to mourn privately at home.

The Queen went to bed early, asking only to be left alone. She is a strong woman; she will continue to rule Eryndal, but I am glad she is taking time out to heal. Dismal said he might join us later, depending on whether he can finish writing a paper he is prepping for his course. He has jumped into a frenzy of learning, studying, staying up late to read by candlelight, his eyes growing more bloodshot with each day that passes.

Kaelion said it is how Dismal handles grief. He throws himself into his studies so he doesn't have to think about anything else. And we will respect that. While Kae is finding it hard to open up, to fully grieve his father, both the Queen and Dismal are handling the King's death in their own ways.

Still, I don't want Dismal coming to The Dwarven Bombard and potentially chatting up Nerissa. That is an event I would happily miss.

Neither the prince nor I feel light, despite the dappled sunshine, the peace of the alleyways. The King died for me. Tryx died for me. Tryx. It hits me hard, right in the gut. Tryx was my segway into this world, the one who came to see me in my cell, the one who appeared when I was in the courtroom. He risked everything for me, and I miss him more than my bedraggled heart can handle.

The dark-haired girl is still recovering after

having her spine broken, but I have sent word to contact me when she is ready for company. I want to see her. The Bone-Wielder has disappeared, it seems, although I have left a tentative message for him as well.

I have caused nothing but chaos and death.

But Isolde is alive. Seren ran straight to the gallipot when we arrived back at the palace and spent the next two days curled up in her girlfriend's bed. Isolde is a bit shaken, a bit off, but that's to be expected. Their flower business has not suffered from their time away, and Seren, Mother, and I did the flowers for the King's funeral, Serenity Flowers back in action.

But still. There is something inside me now. Something that tastes of hard metal, that presses against my skull at night. A monster that lurks there, a Gift I did not ask for. No matter how much I try to be grateful, glad that I have a Gift that was able to defeat Draevena, it also feels like a curse. To be able to control blood – to drain it, Wield it, manipulate it – is surely the stuff of nightmares. I cannot even begin to think how the Bone- and Flesh-Wielders feel about their own Gifts. Perhaps they have had millennia to get used to them. But the Bone-Wielder had seemed around my age, albeit immortal. Perhaps he considers such pain-rendering a curse as well.

I'm sure that I will never know. Despite his amber coryns, so different from Fjaldorn's colouring, he is part of that kingdom or a neighbouring one no doubt, a kingdom that I might be set to inherit, but that – hopefully – I will not need to for a long, long time. My father is back in full health. He has been to visit us at Eryndal Palace, and I have free clemency to wisp into

Fjaldorn anytime I would like.

Once I learn how to wisp, that is.

I feel weird about having a *father* out there in the world. I feel a strange sense of grief for all of the years without him, as silly as it is, alongside a whole host of mad fucking feelings: betrayal, excitement, fear, heartache.

Now I'm engaged to a prince and the daughter of a king, people in Grim Municipal are treating me differently. I still help at The Courier's Keep, and people have been coming to the door to ogle me, making me beyond self-conscious. Life's got a bit weird, and my brain doesn't really like change, but I'm dealing with it.

And it has perks. Kaelion and I stayed in bed for a full forty-eight hours, making love and feasting on the strawberries and picnic items that the palace staff left outside my door. We are lost in a world of love and grief, the universe prodding us from various angles but always together, always a team in the middle of the madness.

But what now? How are the prince and I to truly deal with everything that has happened? How can anyone begin to shed the events of the last few weeks and start again?

"Are you alright?" Kaelion's voice breaks through my thoughts as we arrive at the crossing of Quiet Street and Old King Alley. He looks at me with a mixture of concern and tenderness, as if he can read the weight of my thoughts. His fingers are strong between mine.

I nod slowly, trying to shake off the heavy feeling that presses on my chest. "Just thinking."

Kaelion squeezes my hand. We've walked past the entrance to Old King Alley, where I first stabbed the silicrite. I'd tasted metal in the air, smelt fayte as the silicrites prowled, and it's only now that I realise it was my own magic I was always sensing; my own power. The wolfsbane might have stopped me from developing coryns, might have hidden my fayte from the world, but it was there. Suppressed, controlled underneath layers of my analytical personality, pushed to somewhere that my mind couldn't fully realise it. But it was always there.

I used to think that suffering was a result of allowing too much darkness, of letting evil prevail. But now I understand that I created my own suffering by obsessively pursuing perfection. I wanted to be free of any dark, any uncertainty, because I feared them both. Perfection was my attempt to tidy up a messy universe. But that wasn't sustainable. I needed to find balance, to accept that darkness is a part of me, that it's necessary.

"Look," the prince says, drawing my attention back to the present. He points toward The Courier's Keep. A new notice has been pinned to the shutters. I raise an eyebrow, curiosity replacing the heaviness in my chest. He knows I spent countless cycles in that little office. That place held me together when everything else seemed to fall apart.

We walk up to The Courier's Keep. The golden-framed paper catches my eye, and I approach it with a sense of quiet reverence. It feels like the past and future colliding in this small, humble place.

"'The Elfin Postal Service,'" I read aloud, "'would like to formally thank Her Royal Highness, Princess

Elira of Fjaldorn, for her cycles of dedication under the Orynthys Postal Network. While her duties are no doubt set to change, she holds the utmost respect from every postal elf, and our other sponsors.'"

I grin, light pulsing through me. I never imagined that my simple, quiet life as a postmistress would lead to something like this. I miss the elves, miss the gossip and the conversation of working in the sorting room, but we have elves at the palace, and more gossip than I can possibly handle. And besides, I've already started working on improving Grim Municipal, and relations with the aemortals. I'm in a unique position as the kind of heir who hasn't had my head up my own arse my whole life.

I have also been granted clemency to visit The Shattered Isles, where I'll take classes from a Wielding expert. There might be other Wielders there. We can learn together.

I read the elven notice again. "That's nice," I say, inhaling deeply. Scents of mead and cedarwood fill the air, mingling with the crackling warmth of the evening. It's a strange but comforting mix. As I prepare to walk away, another notice catches my eye. This one's hastily pinned, the paper crumpled and torn, the handwriting unfamiliar, no doubt that of the new apprentice that Nerissa hired.

My pulse quickens as I read it.

I swallow. My brain cannot take it in. The prince has not noticed, distracted by a man pushing an applecart down Quiet Street. I read the words again, feeling my insides rearrange themselves, feeling dread cut through the sunshine that filters through the early evening air.

Three of us were gifted by the Divinity of Body: The Bone-Wielder, the Flesh-Wielder, and I. One of us has been reported missing.

The words send a chill through me, as Kaelion's fingers brush my wrist.

"Shall we head to the tavern?" he asks, lifting my hand and kissing my palm, his voice warm but cautious. His father dying has been hard for him, and yet he has had to be a master of self-control, as always. He has only been once to The Howling Cask that I know of, returning in the early hours of sunlight smelling like mead and araq.

I cannot worry him with this. Cannot burden him any more than I already have.

The gentle motion of his lips against my skin reminds me of how far we've come. The world feels different now. He mourned for his father, alongside his entire kingdom. I nod, the news lingering in the back of my mind. There's still so much uncertainty, so much I cannot do. But for now, I'm here. I'm alive, and I'm with Kaelion. Together, we've survived everything that was thrown at us, and maybe, just maybe, we're on the edge of something new. Something better.

"To the tavern," I say, squeezing his hand as we head down the street, the candlelight of The Dwarven Bombard flickering ahead of us.

My bones ache as we walk, a trace of fayte lingering in the sweet dusk air.

THE NEXT INSTALLMENT

Fayte & Blood is the first in a new romantasy series, set within the empire of Orynthys.

Keep your eyes peeled for the second installment, Fayte & Bone, coming in 2025!

Follow the author on Instagram and TikTok to get the latest updates. @worldofvieve

Thanks for reading! <3

THE END

Printed in Great Britain
by Amazon

3ecb658a-a38a-46cd-a6dc-f48d11416ff6R01